Unleashing Mayhem

Unleashing Mayhem

Dakota Destruction Book 6

Millie Copper

Written by Millie Copper

Edited by Ameryn Tucker

Proofread by MDC Proofreading

Cover design by Dauntless Cover Design

Also by Millie Copper

The Havoc in Wyoming Series

When a series of coordinated attacks devastate the United States, the people of Bakerville, Wyoming, must come together to survive. Unfortunately, not everyone has the town's best interest at heart. Some are striving for personal gain during the apocalypse.

The Montana Mayhem Series

A group from Bakerville, Wyoming strikes out on their own while searching for the desires of their heart. Unfortunately, the road will not be easy, and sometimes the heart is hardened and deceitful.

The Dakota Destruction Series

After a series of coordinated attacks devastate the United States, Katie and Leo sacrifice everything to help their country. But some things aren't as they seem. Is it time to go home and start fresh, or can something good come out of this terrible situation?

Wyoming Fall Series (In The October Fall World)

In the blink of an eye, an EMP changed everything for Lauren and her family. Now they are in a fight for survival, trying to keep their loved ones alive as society collapses around them.

Nonfiction Books

Millie has penned seven nonfiction, traditional food focused books, sharing how, with a little creativity, anyone can transition to a real foods diet without overwhelming their food budget. Many of her books also include preparedness and food storage tips.

Find these titles at:
MillieCopper.com

Join My Reader's Club!

Receive a complimentary copy of *Looming Mayhem: A Dakota Destruction Prequel*. As part of my reader's club, you'll be the first to know about new releases and specials. I also share info on books I'm reading, preparedness tips, and more. Please sign up at:

MillieCopper.com/Join

Chapter 1

Merissa

The old diesel pickup growls beneath me, its vibrations a constant reminder of what might be fueling it. The engine's rumble seems to carry dark whispers of its origins, making my skin crawl despite the morning sun warming the covered truck bed.

Nestled in the makeshift bed of blankets and pillows that Deputy Shaw's people set up in the camper area, I still feel every jolt of the road ripple through me.

"Just a few miles," Mother Pearl reminded me when we'd left, her voice carrying a steady assurance I've come to rely on in recent months. "Opal's place is as safe as anywhere these days."

Each bump tightens the knot of worry in my chest, and my hand reflexively rests on my belly to shield the fragile life inside. The irony isn't lost on me—Merissa Weaver, a trained medic and medical student, is now a patient in hiding. My knowledge doesn't comfort me; it makes every twinge feel like a warning. Moving to the ranch is a risk.

Preterm labor has me on bed rest, and an attempt on my life—along with Katie Burnett's—has forced us into hiding. I've been staying with Mother Pearl, Alice Williams, and Katie's informally adopted children in a safe house near Deputy Shaw. Meanwhile, Katie, her husband Leo, and Captain Williams are sheltering in temporary housing at the med school.

"Look! Another deer!" Nico, sitting next to me, points toward a cluster of bare trees, his excitement momentarily distracting me from my dark thoughts. He presses his small hands against the side of the truck bed, bouncing slightly with enthusiasm as he looks out the window of the camper shell. "It was huge! Like the one in my picture book, 'Rissa!" Gerry, Katie's half-grown dog, catches onto Nico's excitement and is also looking out the window.

I follow Nico's gesture but see nothing beyond winter-stripped branches swaying in the South Dakota wind. The skeletal trees cast strange shadows across the snow-patched ground, their bare limbs scratching toward the steel-gray sky.

"I missed it," I tell him, managing a smile. "You have much better eyes than I do."

"That's 'cause I'm the lookout," Nico declares proudly, puffing out his chest. "I can spot anything suspicious. Captain Williams said so." The little boy beams at the compliment, and I'm struck by how resilient children can be. Here we are, fleeing from dangers I barely understand, and he's treating it like an adventure.

Our guard, a stoic young woman who's maybe twenty years old, keeps her gaze fixed on the horizon, scanning for threats without a hint of a smile. Her reserved demeanor is familiar by now—she's been with us since we went into hiding. It's only been three days, but it feels like a lifetime.

Through the back window of the cab, I catch glimpses of Pearl and Alice, each cradling one of the babies. Pearl's weathered hands move with a slight tremor as she adjusts the blanket around little Caleb's face when the baby stirs. Alice mirrors the gesture with Zach, but her movements are gentle and steady, absent Pearl's careful hesitation.

Alice has taken a liking to the orphan, treating him more like her own grandchild than anything. It's obvious she loves Nico and Caleb, too, but there's something special in her relationship with Zach. Both Pearl and Alice are being extra careful with the babies, just as our driver is being careful with me, slowing almost to a crawl when the road gets rough.

Pearl tries to hide it, but her exhaustion is clear. Moving to Opal's farm had been her idea—a necessary one. At the safe house, Deputy Shaw kept us supplied with water, firewood, rations, and guards, but it wasn't enough.

With me on bed rest, two infants, and young Nico, Pearl and Alice were overwhelmed. Pearl rarely voiced her struggles, yet the way her shoulders sagged or her hands shook in quiet moments gave her away. Even Alice, twenty years her junior, was feeling the weight. And with Pearl sick . . .

Another bump, gentler this time, but my muscles tense anyway. Captain Williams's warnings echo in my mind. "Stress could trigger labor again." I close my eyes and try to focus on my breathing, the way the labor exercises suggest. But instead of calm, my mind fills with images of hospital beds and homemade body bags. How many of the dead have been desecrated to keep these vehicles running? Did Rand Hendricks know? Is that why he—

"'Rissa?" Nico's small hand pats my arm. "Are you sleeping?"

"No, sweetheart." I open my eyes and force myself to stay in the present moment. "Just resting a little."

"Like the babies?"

I glance through the window again. Both infants appear to be sleeping soundly despite the truck's jostling. "Yes, like the babies." Their tiny faces are serene, untroubled by the gravity of our circumstances. Caleb's small fingers curl around the edge of his blanket, while Zach makes faint sucking motions in his sleep.

The children have already endured so much. Nico, only four years old, lost both of his parents. He, along with the infants' birth mothers, had been living as part of the Preacher's cult.

When we first met Zach, he was only a couple of months old and dangerously underweight. It was the night the National Guard stormed the Preacher's compound. Caleb's story began that same night. His mother, Kemeera, was in labor, and he was born just hours after the raid, with Katie assisting in his delivery.

A few weeks later, Mindy—Zach's birth mother—died of hemlock poisoning. Before she passed, she asked Katie to care for her son. Not long after, Kemeera disappeared, taking her young daughter Shawna with her but leaving behind baby Caleb and Nico, whom she'd been caring for.

Katie and her husband, Leo, didn't hesitate to step in, embracing the children as their own. The Williamses have been supporting this newly forged family, and together they've grown inseparable.

The road curves ahead, and I can see we're heading into more remote territory. The landscape opens up before us, a patchwork of winter-brown fields and scattered stands of trees.

An old windbreak of cottonwoods marks the next-door neighbor's land. It wasn't long ago when Gary Hayward's barn caught fire, and he lost his life in the blaze. There was talk the fire was deliberate, payback for some of the man's actions, but I don't know if anything ever came of the investigation. Last I heard, his wife Misty was doing her best to keep things running. They'd brought in more workers and now play a bigger role in supporting the community.

As Opal's ranch comes into view, part of me wonders if this is smart, being so far from medical help if something goes wrong with the pregnancy. But the other part knows we have little choice. A sharp kick from within reminds me at least one of us is feeling strong today.

Besides, Opal has some medical training, having worked at the small Canyon Lake District Medical Center when they've had emergencies. And I've successfully delivered three babies since I started working at the Guard District Hospital. I try not to think about the other two deliveries. One when we lost the mother and the other in which both mother and infant perished.

Of course, it's considerably different delivering someone else's baby compared to my own. I find myself once again wishing Katie was holed up with us. Not only because I'd feel better having her with me if I found myself in preterm labor again, but so she could be with her children.

The thought of Katie sends a pang of hurt through my heart. How hard must it be for her and Leo, separated from their children? Even if it's temporary, even if it's for everyone's safety, it feels wrong. Then again, everything about this situation feels wrong.

"Will there be chickens?" Nico asks, his face bright with hope. "Grandmother Pearl says farms have chickens."

"More than chickens. They have milk cows, beef cattle, and goats. And my horses live here. Remember me telling you this?"

"And your friend Mr. Cox takes care of them?"

"That's right. He does." Walt Cox is a friend of mine and of my late husband, Braedon. The three of us belonged to a mounted archery club, where we practiced shooting arrows on horseback, honing our aim while riding at a gallop. It was as much about skill as it was trust—trust in our horses and in each other.

Back then, it was just for fun, a hobby I thoroughly enjoyed. Now, in this apocalyptic world, archery has become a necessity, and the ability to loose an arrow from horseback can mean the difference between life and death.

Walt isn't just an expert archer, he's also a master bowyer, having crafted dozens of horse bows. With ammunition running low, his skills are more valuable than ever. Not only is he already teaching people how to shoot but also how to craft bows themselves. He plans to begin horseback archery lessons once the winter weather lets up.

"Can I ride your horse?" Nico's excitement draws a rare smile from our usually reserved guard.

"We'll see. My horses might be a bit much, but I think Opal has a nice slow one who may be perfect for you."

The truck slows, and I catch the scent of wood smoke in the wind. Ahead is Opal's ranch, and hopefully, safety. But as we draw closer to our destination, I can't shake the feeling we're not just running from something—we're running toward something too. I pray we're ready for whatever that might be.

The guard at Opal's gate recognizes our vehicle immediately. He lowers his rifle and waves to his partner to open up. As we pull through, I notice additional men positioned strategically around the perimeter. They're well hidden—I only spot them because I see movement.

Opal's place always has some security, but this is more than I remember from last time. The additional sentries are oddly comforting. The female guard, Abby, will stay behind to act as my personal protector. I'm not exactly sure why Deputy Shaw felt this was necessary, but he did.

Well, I guess I do know why. The threat to my life is real, and being on bed rest to prevent another bout of preterm labor means I'm far from my best. A few weeks ago, I might have believed I could fight back, relying on the self-defense moves I've not only learned but taught to others, along with always carrying a sidearm.

Even with Abby here, that hasn't changed. Pearl and Alice too—we all understand the need to stay vigilant in this new world, knowing our handguns might be needed. They've been necessary before.

Opal hurries down the front steps of her weathered farmhouse, her silver hair flowing freely. She moves with the same grace as Pearl, though there's more urgency in her stride. "Pearl! Merissa!" she calls out, the faint remnants of her childhood Oklahoma accent barely detectable, rushing toward the truck as we come to a stop. "Let's get you inside where it's warm."

She pauses a moment to greet Alice Williams. "I know we've met in passing," Opal says. "I'm looking forward to getting better acquainted. And these babies. My! They are just too adorable."

"Careful now," Mother Pearl tells me as our driver helps me navigate my way from the truck bed, Abby standing by with her rifle in case a bad guy magically appears. My legs are stiff from the drive, and the cold air bites at my cheeks. The world tilts slightly as I stand, and both Opal and our driver steady me. "I'm fine," I insist, though my legs feel like water. "Just need to get my land legs back."

"I've got everything ready." Opal takes my arm, her grip gentle but sure, steadying me as we navigate the worn wooden steps. The ancient boards creak beneath our feet, a familiar sound that somehow makes this place feel more like a shelter than a hiding place. "The woodstove's been burning steady all morning."

Inside, the familiar scent of Opal's home wraps around me—wood smoke and something baking. Bundles of dried herbs hang from the ceiling beams, their rustic shapes adding to the room's lived-in charm. The woodstove radiates welcome heat, its iron surface gleaming in the afternoon light that's filtering through lace curtains. She's arranged a bed in the corner of the main room, partially hidden behind an old decorative screen.

"I know it's not ideal," she says, gesturing toward the sleeping area, "but I didn't want you dealing with stairs in your condition. Besides, you'd be stuck up there all alone while we had all the fun down here." She wiggles her eyebrows at me.

I shake my head in response but truly appreciate her efforts to make sure I'm included.

"The screen should give you some privacy, and you'll stay plenty warm here by the stove."

"It's perfect, Opal. Thank you." And it is. The bed looks inviting, piled high with quilts, and the warmth from the woodstove has already started to bring feeling back to my cold fingers. She's positioned it so I can see out the west-facing window, and if I lean forward a bit, I can catch a glimpse through the window by the front door, which faces east.

"Now then," Opal says, helping me settle onto the bed while Pearl and Alice get the children situated. "I've got tea brewing and some fresh cornbread about ready to come out of the oven. Nico, would you like to help me check on it?"

The boy's eyes light up as he nods enthusiastically and follows Opal toward the old wood cookstove. I can hear her already explaining to him about the chickens in the coop out back, making good on Pearl's promise of farm animals.

As I listen to the gentle crackle of the woodstove and the comfortable sounds of family moving about the house, some of my tension eases. We may be in hiding, but at least we're together, and for now, we're safe.

Chapter 2

Katie

The constant flow of patients keeps my mind from drifting to my children. I lean against the cabinet behind the desk and close my eyes for a moment. Since morning rounds, we've dealt with three emergencies—one ending with the death of a little girl not much older than my Nico.

My hand aches from filling out charts, but the dull throb in my chest lingers longer. I haven't held the boys since Tuesday morning. At least they're safe with Alice and Merissa. Safer than they would be with Leo and me, or so I have to believe.

"You're going to hurt your neck sleeping like that, Mrs. Burnett." Leo's voice pulls me from my thoughts, his hand briefly brushing my back.

I smile at his loving tone. "Well, Mr. Burnett, for your information, I'm not sleeping." I straighten, rubbing my neck. "Just resting my eyes while trying to focus on this chart."

"The little girl?"

I drop my shoulders and nod. "I know we did everything we could, but it still hurts."

"Thinking of our boys? Gerry?"

I let out a breath as my eyes fill with tears. "Always."

My husband takes a step closer to me. The heat from his body brushes against my skin, grounding me in the moment. "Are you okay, Katie?"

I swallow hard. I'm not okay. He knows it, but I love that he's here to check on me. "I will be. It just never gets any easier."

"No."

"Will it? Will I ever not hurt so much when we lose someone?"

He moves his hand to my back and rests it there. The heat of it soaks into my skin. "I doubt it. Part of what makes you such a good nurse, and what will make you a good doctor, is how much you care for your patients. For everyone around you. Which reminds me . . ."

He lowers his voice to barely a whisper. "Deputy Shaw should be here shortly with an update. To let us know they got to the farm okay."

I give him a shrug and something I hope is a smile. "Moving to Opal's place was smart. I know Nico will love it. But what I'd really like from Shaw is for him to come by and say they've figured out who is behind these atrocities and they've put them into custody. Then we can go home. We're supposed to be a family."

"They're doing their best— "

I raise my hand. "I know all of that." My voice comes out with more of a snap than Leo deserves. He hates this just as much as I do. I drop my shoulders and roll my neck. "We could leave," I whisper.

"We've talked about this."

"Let's talk about it again."

"We will." He removes his hand from my back and adjusts the sling on his other arm. The badly broken arm is healing, but whether he'll ever have full use of it again is in question.

His hand moves to my cheek. "Let's wait and see what Shaw says when he stops by today. Maybe he'll have an update for us. Besides, this is better than— " The emergency entrance bursts open, cutting him off.

"Help! Someone help us!" a scream echoes through the corridor.

Two teenagers stumble through the entrance, supporting a woman between them. Blood mats her gray hair, staining her shirt dark. Her head lolls forward, chin against her chest.

Dr. Arnetta Wolff is there in an instant; I'm right behind her. "What happened?" Nettie asks as we guide the woman to the nearest treatment room. The woman's breathing is shallow and irregular.

"She fell," the girl says, her voice trembling. She's maybe fifteen, with dark circles under her eyes that speak of sleepless nights and poor nutrition—a common sight in the world we live in. Her brother looks about twelve, tears streaming down his dirty face. "Down the front steps. Slipped on a patch of ice."

She fell down the steps? The injuries tell a different story. As we transfer her to the bed, I catalog them quickly. Multiple broken ribs are evident from the way her chest moves. Extensive bruising across her torso suggests internal bleeding. Probable skull fracture.

The woman's body goes rigid.

"She's seizing," I call out. "Help me turn her on her side!"

The convulsions rack her body. Blood-tinged foam appears at her mouth, suggesting lung involvement. Then she goes still.

Too still.

"No pulse," Nettie announces, immediately starting chest compressions. "We need to maintain her airway."

I position myself at the head of the bed and tilt her head back to open her airway and prepare for bag ventilation. "Get them out of here." I motion to our medic, nodding toward the kids while checking for breathing.

"Mom!" The boy breaks free of medic Jesse Talbot's grip and lunges toward the bed.

"Maintaining airway," I announce, struggling to keep her head positioned correctly through the damage to her face. Blood makes everything slick and the Ambu bag slides away.

"You killed her!" The boy's accusation pierces the controlled chaos. He turns toward his sister, his face twisted in anger. "This is your fault! You— "

"No!" The girl's fist connects with his face before anyone can react.

"Switch," Nettie calls, ignoring the altercation happening around us. I take over chest compressions, knowing I'm probably breaking even more ribs, while Nettie provides rescue breaths. If we can get her heart beating on its own, we may have a chance to save her.

Behind us, the siblings crash into the supply cart. Glass shatters. The girl is screaming, clawing at her brother while he throws punches. Leo, with one arm in a sling, is doing his best to separate them, while Jesse reaches for the girl.

"Get them out of here now!" Leo shouts as fellow med student Matt bursts through the door.

"I've got him," Jesse announces, wrapping his arms around the boy's chest and pulling him back. The boy kicks and thrashes, trying to break free.

Matt grabs the girl's arms from behind and pins them to her sides. "Come on, miss. Let's give them room to work." She struggles against his grip, still trying to go at her brother, using words no one her age should know.

"Move!" Leo orders, using his good arm to help guide them toward the door. "You can't be in here."

Jesse practically carries the boy out while Matt manages to maneuver the still-fighting girl into the hallway. Leo pulls the door closed behind him.

"She's got a mouth on her," Nettie mutters. Louder, she says, "No way this is a simple slip and fall."

Through the window in the door, I see them pull the siblings apart, leading them to opposite ends of the corridor. Their shouts grow fainter with every step.

"Katie." Nettie's voice pulls my focus back. "We need to concentrate on their mother."

I nod, resuming compressions. But in my gut, I know we're already too late.

We work for another twenty minutes. "That's it," Nettie says quietly, her voice heavy with defeat. "Time of death, 1347."

My stomach churns as I catalog the injuries. Defensive wounds on the arms. The pattern of the bruising. The skull fracture.

Nettie catches my eye, her expression grim as she shakes her head.

"I'm going to check on her children." And find out what nightmare just walked into our hospital. Terrible things happen these days, but this . . . this is different. If what the brother said is true, then the girl is responsible for this.

"I'm taking a break," Nettie says, her eyes focused on the dead woman. "A long one."

I pause, studying the young doctor's expression. Like me, Nettie was thrown into this world unprepared. She had been a med student on a summer internship when the planes went down.

At first, like many, she thought the coordinated attacks on five planes at five different airports were isolated acts of terrorism. Even when the first responders at the crash sites were killed in massive explosions, she never imagined the violence would spiral into something bigger—nothing that would touch her life so directly.

But as the attacks escalated, each one more devastating than the last, Nettie found herself stranded in Rapid City. When nuclear devices detonated on both coasts and a high-altitude EMP wiped out most of the continental US, her internship abruptly became a full-fledged medical practice. When we first crossed paths, she seemed to manage her new reality with remarkable composure. Now, though . . . I'm not so sure.

"Are you okay?" I reach out to squeeze her shoulder. She stiffens at my touch, turning the gesture into something awkward.

"I'm fine. Just dandy. Always a pleasure to discover a child is willing to kill their parent . . . over what? What do you think could have happened to cause— " She motions toward the dead woman on the table. Her voice drops to a whisper. "How could she do this?"

"I don't know," I admit with a shake of my head. Like many teens, my relationship with my mom wasn't always sunshine and roses. But this is so far beyond what I can comprehend as okay or not okay that it's hard to grasp how anything could escalate to this.

Was the mom abusive, and the girl was defending herself? The damage to the body seems excessive for self-defense, but maybe that's what happened.

"I'll be back in a few minutes. I'll take care of cleaning her up and getting her ready for Hugo . . . um, Bowski. I suppose it'll be Bowski, right?"

Nettie shakes her head. "That's another thing I'm struggling to wrap my mind around. Hugo always seemed so nice. I watched him interact with a deceased family on more than one occasion. He was respectful and . . . and . . . I can't believe he was really part of the group desecrating bodies." Tears fill her eyes as she speaks. "At least the little girl from this morning won't be disturbed."

Nettie is one of the few who was briefed on the situation with Hugo—our undertaker, mortician, and coroner. The entire thing is deeply unsettling. As a respected and essential figure in the Guard District, we depended on him to care for our dead.

A few days ago, a man arrived at the hospital, speaking in disjointed fragments and hinting at a major conspiracy in the area. He asked Merissa and me for help, but his rambling made so little sense that we assumed he was having a psychotic break. When Dr. Murphy stepped out of the break room, the man fled.

The next day, he approached us again on the street as we were walking home. Before we could have much of a conversation, a sniper shot him, and Merissa and I were forced to run for our lives.

The incident put Merissa into preterm labor and had all of us looking over our shoulders. Leo and I were again attacked and barely escaped while the guard with us was injured. He'll be fine, but the continued incidents have required many safety measures. Among those were Merissa and her mother-in-law Pearl being taken to a safe house—and now Opal Maher's ranch—along with Alice Williams and our children.

I smile as I think about my instant family. Zach, the orphaned infant of Mindy, along with the even younger Caleb—abandoned by Kemeera—and four-year-old Nico are a delight. I miss them more than I could ever believe possible. If I close my eyes, I can see them. Hear them, even. Nico is probably playing with our puppy, Gerry, and laughing as they chase each other around.

I straighten my shoulders and shake away the thoughts of family. There's no time for daydreaming, not with everything happening around us.

Nettie knows the basics of Hugo's plan, but she doesn't know where my children and Merissa are being moved. That information is tightly guarded for their protection, as is what Hugo did. I can only imagine the uproar when the truth gets out—when people learn what was done to their loved ones' bodies.

Deputy Shaw knows the truth will have to come out eventually. He's hoping to dismantle the entire ring of corruption before making it public. But he's running out of time. The weather will break soon, and burials will need to begin. Once that happens, it'll be impossible to keep the secret any longer.

"Go take your break," I tell Nettie. "I'll find you if we need you."

The guard watching over the teen girl straightens as I approach her room. She's secured to the bed, dried blood on her knuckles, tears streaming down her face. I move past without entering. I need to check on her brother first.

I hear the boy's voice before I reach his treatment room. "She just went crazy. Started screaming about how Mom was trying to control her life, how she couldn't take it anymore."

Captain Williams and Leo work on cleaning the cuts on his face as he talks. Blood has dried beneath his nose, and his right eye is swelling shut.

"Has this happened before?" the captain asks as he applies antiseptic to a particularly nasty gash.

"Not like this, but yeah. She gets so mad sometimes. Like something inside her breaks." The boy's voice cracks. His eyes meet mine as I enter. "My mom? Is she—"

I look at Captain Williams. His expression changes as he reads the answer on my face.

"Son," he says quietly, setting down the gauze, "I'm sorry. They did everything they could, but your mother didn't make it."

The boy's face crumples. His shoulders begin to shake. "No! No, no, no!" The words come out in gasping sobs.

"I'm so sorry," I whisper, my throat tight.

"It's my fault. I should've stopped her. I tried to get between them, but— " His words dissolve into heart-wrenching cries.

Captain Williams places a gentle hand on the boy's shoulder. "This is not your fault. Do you understand me? None of this is your fault."

"Do you have any family you can stay with?" Leo asks after the boy's sobs begin to quiet.

He shakes his head. "Dad died when everything first happened. Got sick after the EMP. Mom said it was pneumonia, but I don't know. You didn't have the hospital then, and that was before the ration chips were set up. We barely had enough food most days, but Mom always made sure we ate something."

"Your sister," Captain Williams says carefully. "You mentioned she changed. When did you first notice the difference?"

"After Dad died. She started getting angry all the time. Mom said she was grieving, that we all grieve differently." He wipes his nose with his sleeve. "But it got worse. She'd throw things, break stuff. Sometimes she'd just stare at nothing for hours. Mom tried to help her, but . . ."

My heart aches for this family torn apart by the apocalypse. How many others are out there, struggling with grief and trauma until they snap?

"What's going to happen to her?" the boy asks in a small voice. "To my sister?"

"We'll have her examined," Captain Williams assures him. "Try to understand what happened and see if we can help her."

"And me?"

"There's a place you can stay. People who will look after you."

I think of the orphanage, already stretched thin with so many displaced children. Another casualty of our broken world. The boy is older than most of the children there. While kids his age are allowed, most tend to run away, deciding they can make it on their own.

Maybe Opal Maher would be willing to take him in? Jason Wheeler, another teenage orphan, stays with her. He, too, has been having a difficult time, but Opal is determined to improve his life. I'll suggest this to the captain when we're alone.

For a moment, my thoughts run wild as I toy with the idea of volunteering to escort the boy to Opal's. That would let me see my own children while I am there. But that's not happening. Like them, we're under protection, too, living at the med school with guards watching over the school and hospital. Whoever Hugo was working with wants us dead.

The reasoning behind it all still escapes me. They think we know more than we do, but it doesn't add up. Shaw and his team have already investigated the warehouse where the bodies were stored before burial. They've uncovered the truth—or most of it. The numbers don't align. The bodies found don't match the deaths we've recorded this winter, and the toll has been devastating.

Where the missing remains are is anyone's guess. Even Ritchie Kasubowski, who helped Hugo recover the bodies, but wasn't involved in the desecration, has no clue about other storage sites. Shaw has people searching, though he doubts they'll find much. He believes the bodies were discarded after the fat was harvested for biodiesel. It's a grim reality—too sad for words.

The captain continues cleaning the boy's wounds while I check his vitals. His pulse is still racing, but steady. The physical injuries will heal. The emotional ones . . . those will take much longer.

Deputy Shaw arrives as we're finishing up. He takes one look at the scene and his expression darkens. Another tragedy to add to his growing list of investigations.

"I'll need statements," he says quietly to me. "But they can wait. We'll see if we can get him settled."

I nod, grateful for his understanding. We've all seen too much death, too much suffering. Sometimes the best we can do is try to pick up the pieces and keep moving forward.

Chapter 3

Katie

As I watch the captain and Leo continue to care for the boy, my thoughts turn to my own children. Shaw quietly told me my family had left for the ranch, and my heart unclenches just a fraction, though worry still gnaws at the edges of my mind.

I want to ask more questions, get the details of the trip and find out when we'll know they arrived safely. But there's no time for such a conversation. Deputy Shaw has gone to check on the sister; her brother's brief description is enough for him to know she needs to be taken somewhere secure.

When they've finished examining the boy, we escort him to the chairs. "Can you wait here a few minutes?" I ask. "We're going to see what we can do about finding you a place to stay."

"My sister? Will she . . ." His voice fades away as a noise sounds down the hall. Deputy Shaw is escorting the sister out of the room. She is hanging her head and doesn't look up.

"Chloe?" the brother calls. "Did you hear? She's dead. You— "

Her head snaps up. "She deserved it! The way she is—the way she let Dad die! You know she deserved it."

"No." He shakes his head. "She's our mom. She didn't mean for Dad to die, she just— "

Chloe surges forward, almost slipping out of the guard's grasp. "Stop it! Stop it, you little brat."

Deputy Shaw steps in and brings her to an abrupt stop. "That's enough, young lady."

She continues to yell obscenities as the men frog march her down the hall.

"Where will they take her?" the boy asks.

We don't really have a jail in our district. The Guard District did use the brig that was at Camp Rapid, but an explosion on Christmas Day took out the jail and surrounding buildings, resulting in numerous deaths. They've put something new in its place, something supposedly more secure. That's where Hugo is being kept. Will they take the girl there too?

"They'll take her someplace safe," Captain Williams responds. "Where she won't hurt you or anyone else and maybe she can get some help."

"The main hospital?" I ask.

He tilts his head. "I called them on the radio. They have a secure psych ward where she can be evaluated."

I'd heard about this initiative coming together. Nearly twenty-one months into the apocalypse, cases of mental disorders and psychosis are becoming increasingly common.

That's why Merissa and I were so quick to dismiss the whistleblower—who we later learned was Hank Timbs, a reporter who had covered various crimes in Rapid City before the EMP. We suspect he was doing something similar when he uncovered the situation involving Hugo and the handling of the dead. Now we just need to uncover everyone Hugo is working with so they can be brought to justice, and Leo and I can finally return home to our family.

So far, it seems Hugo isn't talking. We rely on Shaw to keep us in the loop about not only Hugo but everything else outside of what's happening in our own little bubble at the hospital and med school. None of us have even left the grounds since the last attack on our lives.

With the boy sitting in a chair, watching as his sister is escorted out the door and toward the pickup truck, Captain Williams motions me toward the nurses' station.

"We'll get him set up at the orphanage for now. But I was thinking— "

"Opal would probably take him," I interrupt.

"I was hoping she might."

"I could . . ." I stop my sentence at the shake of his head.

"Until Shaw says otherwise, it's not safe for you to leave the security of the hospital. Believe me, I'd love to deliver the message myself. Get out and stretch my legs." He motions to his leg in a walking boot, thanks to an infection that resulted in the partial amputation of his foot.

"But for now. We stay here. We stay safe so we can see our loved ones again. At least Shaw let us know everything went fine with leaving for the ranch. That's a relief."

"Very much so." I nod my agreement while trying to tamp down my lingering concerns. I won't feel completely relieved until I know they arrived safely.

"I've called in the death," Williams adds. "Bowski will be here shortly."

"I'll get the mom ready for transport."

As I prepare the body, I take in the damage. I'm not sure exactly what the daughter did, but the broken bones are extensive. Perhaps she could have been saved if things were normal, if we had a regular hospital with all the bells and whistles. But that's not how it is. As Doctors of the Apocalypse, we do the best we can with what we have.

Once I have her ready, I take a break, waiting for either Bowski to arrive and retrieve her or for the next patient to show up. Maybe Nettie is feeling like talking now. When we first met, she was kind and helpful. I was a nurse, and Leo was a medic.

Leo and I had come to the Black Hills as part of the United Volunteers. But when an unfortunate event occurred, the governor ordered the Volunteers to leave. Leo and I felt at home at the hospital, so he petitioned Captain Williams to let us finish our one-year commitment under the South Dakota National Guard. I didn't find out until later that the Guard didn't offer a one-year option like the Volunteers. Joining the Guard meant an eight-year commitment.

Our petition was accepted, but joining the Guard was delayed due to Leo falling from a horse and breaking both arms. The right arm, broken at the humerus, healed well. But his left arm didn't heal properly. After a secondary injury, it was rebroken and required external fixation for repair.

Dr. Bollinger, an orthopedist, handled the procedure and recently removed the external hardware. The doctor will return in a few weeks to hopefully allow Leo to start using his arm again. His injury has been a challenge for him, both physically and emotionally. Our marriage suffered, but we're doing better now—better and ready to provide a loving home for Nico, Caleb, and Zach.

If only people would stop trying to kill us so we could live in peace.

Joining the National Guard is no longer something I'm interested in. I'm not even sure I want to continue with my studies to become a doctor. It's a lot to juggle while trying to care for the children. I'm not making any decisions yet, but deep down, I know what I want. Unfortunately, what I truly want just isn't possible in this world.

I push open the door to the break room, scanning the space for Doc Nettie. The room is empty. She must have finished her break and moved on to one of the other areas in the hospital. As the doctor on call today, she's likely busy.

Earlier, Captain Williams had been leading us med students on rounds when everything went sideways. Maybe she and the captain are catching up somewhere, reviewing the day's events and evaluating the students' performances.

Not long ago, those meetings would have taken place in Captain Williams's office. But after it came to light that Alice Williams had assisted her elderly neighbors in ending their lives—and that her husband had helped cover it up—Williams was stripped of his hospital oversight duties.

Major Stone took his place, immediately claiming the captain's office and forcing Williams to relocate to the break room. Even with the major away on some top-secret mission with his handpicked team, his belongings still occupy the space. But today, the captain isn't in his usual spot in the break room.

The empty break room increases my unease. Nettie had been deeply shaken earlier in the day when we lost the little girl. And then for the mom to come in, beaten so severely. The way Nettie stiffened when I touched her shoulder, her voice when she'd whispered, "How could she do this?"

Working where we do, living in the time we are, we see many terrible things. Each one seems to take a bigger toll on us. Nettie's personality has changed. Mine has, too, I'm sure. Some days I don't want to be here. To see yet another sickness or injury I can do nothing about. I know it's the same for Doc Nettie.

Something nags at me. The call room. Sometimes, when things get to be too much, that's where we go. The quiet helps. I'll heat up some water and take her a cup of tea. I move the kettle to the front of the woodstove and add a few pieces of wood to kick up the flames.

While the water heats, I prepare the mugs with an herbal tea mixture made by Stella Swensen. She was part of the med school but decided it wasn't for her. She now acts as our pharmacist, preparing plant-based medicines derived from seeds, berries, roots, leaves, bark, or flowers for healing purposes.

Stella's also teaching us how to make and prescribe these herbs. We have very few commercial medications remaining from before the collapse, and to my knowledge, there's nothing currently being produced on a large scale.

I choose a healing winter blend tea that has rose petals, rose hips, ginger, and other things I can't recall but Stella insists will help boost immunity during this never-ending winter.

Thankfully, this winter has been easier than the last. Leo and I were still living in Wyoming then with my family. Most of the community moved up to the ski lodge for the winter where there was plenty of firewood and the tighter space was easier to defend.

Some people suggested the excess cold and massive snowfall was due to nuclear winter, thanks to the bombs detonated on either coast, but others said it was just a regular Wyoming winter in the mountains.

While we've had plenty of cold and snow this season in South Dakota, it's probably a regular February. The last few days have even been pleasant, and the snow has started to melt.

As the kettle begins to whistle, I think about how many days until spring. Today's the nineteenth, so it's just over a month until the equinox.

With the hot mugs steeping, I add them to a tray and carefully make my way from the break room to the call room. The door is closed but unlocked. "Nettie?" I call softly as I push it open with one hand while balancing the tray in the other.

She's slumped in the chair, her head tilted at an odd angle. Something's wrong.

"Nettie?" My voice sharpens with concern.

No response.

The tray clatters onto the small table by the door, mugs sloshing but staying upright. I rush to her side, my fingers seeking her carotid pulse. Nothing. Her skin is still warm. "Help!" I shout, lowering her to the floor. "I need help in here!"

Another day in our apocalyptic world just got worse.

Chapter 4

Katie

Leo appears in the doorway first. "Help us in here!" His voice echoes through the building. "Captain!" The desperation in his tone carries down the empty corridor. Even with one arm in a sling, my husband is already moving to help, his boots squeaking against the worn linoleum as he rushes to my side.

"Please, God, please help us," I murmur, releasing a shaky breath. Focus on what needs to be done. Deal with emotions later.

Tilting her head back, I check her airway; it's clear, yet she's not breathing, and her heart isn't beating. Why? The question burns in my mind as I assess her condition. The call room suddenly feels smaller, more confining. What happened in the time since I last saw her? How long ago was it? Forty-five minutes? An hour?

I press the heel of my hand against her sternum and stack my other hand on top. The rhythm I've drilled into my head—hard and fast, like a drumbeat—keeps me going. "Come on, Nettie," I beg, pushing down with all the strength I can muster.

Sweat trickles down my temple despite the February chill seeping through the windows. The room smells of wood smoke from the stove down the hall, mixed with the familiar antiseptic hospital scent. Each thrust sends a jolt through my arms, already sore from the day's earlier efforts.

My hands pump against her chest as I try not to think about how this is the third time I've done this today—first on the little girl this morning, then the murdered mother, and now Nettie. My arms burn from the effort, but I can't stop. I won't stop. The little girl and the mom didn't make it, but Nettie . . . she must.

Images flash through my mind with each forceful push—the little girl's still face, the mother's broken body, now Nettie. Three deaths would be too many for one day. Too many for our small hospital that's already struggling to keep going. Too many for me.

"What happened?" Captain Williams appears in the doorway, hurrying to us despite his walking boot. His face, usually composed, shows genuine fear as he takes in the scene.

"Found her like this." My voice catches.

Leo meets my eyes, his face pale. We've both seen too much death lately, but this—this is personal. Nettie taught us, mentored us, and became our friend.

"I think we need Stella. These symptoms— "

"They're the same ones Landers had," Leo finishes my thought. He grabs the Ambu bag to provide rescue breaths. We added basic medical equipment to each room after the hostage crisis—when Melvin Cabal, Trooper Carter Schroeder, and Geoff Landers took over the hospital. The Ambu bag is part of that emergency kit, but I'm not sure respiratory support is going to be enough.

The memory of Landers hits me hard—how quickly he went down, with the same devastating symptoms. We barely saved him then, and that was with Stella right there. Now precious minutes have passed with Nettie on her own.

At least with Landers, we watched it happen. His words had slurred, his body swaying before he collapsed. But Nettie . . . what happened? My eyes catch on the papers scattered across the side table, the pen lying beside them. She was doing her charting.

"Should we intubate her?" I ask, knowing it would help secure her airway.

"We need to move her to a treatment room," the captain responds. He steps out of the room and calls for Jesse Talbot.

The captain's voice bounces off the walls, urgency evident in every syllable. From somewhere down the hall comes the sound of running feet and a gurney rattling. At least we're not alone anymore.

When Jesse appears, the captain tells him to use the radio and call for Stella. "We may need her," he adds.

"May need her?" Leo mutters under his breath. "We definitely need her." His good hand tightens on the Ambu bag. "She saved Landers. She can save Nettie too." The determination in his voice almost masks his fear. Almost.

While it's true Geoff Landers is still alive, he's in a nearly vegetative state. Whatever poison that crazy Addison used did a number on him. I'm not entirely sure his condition can really be referred to as saved.

Please, God, not Nettie. Please bring her back to us.

Med student Matt appears alongside Jesse. They quickly get Nettie onto the gurney while I pause compressions. "Should I continue?" I ask the captain, already preparing to climb onto the gurney and resume compressions while they move her.

"Let's get her to the room. Keep bagging." The captain's voice is steady, calm under pressure, like he's done this a thousand times, which he has.

I'm feeling anything but steady. Finding Doc Nettie like this . . . I'm not sure what happened. She was upset earlier, but she didn't seem sick, just exhausted like we all are. Nothing that would lead to this.

The image of her face from earlier flashes through my mind—the way she'd stiffened when I touched her shoulder, how her voice had dropped to a whisper when talking about Hugo. Had she known something? Discovered something? The thought sends a chill down my spine that has nothing to do with the cold of winter.

We get her to the treatment room. "I've got it." The captain takes over compressions, his movements strong and steady, honed by years of experience. "Katie, check her eyes."

I shift positions, lifting each eyelid carefully. Her pupils are dilated but responsive. Not fixed like our earlier patients. We still have a chance.

"Got a weak pulse," I announce, fingers pressed to her neck. "Hold compressions."

The thread of life beneath my fingertips is faint but unmistakable. Like a whisper in a storm, but it's there. We haven't lost her. Not yet.

The captain nods. "Keep bagging, Leo. Let's not lose this."

"We won't," Leo says firmly, his good arm steady as he maintains the rhythm with the Ambu bag. The determination in his voice matches what we're all feeling.

I'm watching her chest rise and fall with each breath. The pulse on my fingers is there, but it's faint. It's not enough, not yet. We need more. The supplies laid out on the metal cart mock us with their inadequacy—no cardiac monitors, no advanced medications, not even proper diagnostic equipment.

We're working with the basics, like battlefield medicine from another century. The apocalypse stripped away our technology, leaving us with nothing but our hands, our knowledge, and our determination.

"Stella's on the way," Jesse says, his voice tight with stress. His hands are shaking as he works the gurney into position.

The gurney locks into place with a metallic click that seems too loud in the tense room. Jesse's nervousness is understandable—we all feel it.

I look up at the captain, sweat trickling down the side of my face despite the season. "Should we start fluids?" I'm already moving to the cart with the IV supplies.

The reusable IV bags are treated like treasures in our resource-starved world. Each bag is painstakingly refilled with carefully prepared fluids, every drop as valuable as gold.

"Do it," the captain responds as he continues to monitor Doc Nettie.

"Is she . . . improving?"

The question hangs in the air, thick with desperation. The room constricts around us, as if the walls echo our unspoken dread. The soft whoosh of the Ambu bag marks each second passing, every breath a battle against time slipping away.

The captain looks at me, his face betraying nothing, but the gravity of the decision lingers in his eyes. "We'll keep doing what we can. And we don't stop until we've tried everything."

His words echo with memories of similar moments—how many times have we stood in this room, saying these same words? How many times have we lost despite our best efforts? But there's steel in his voice now, a determination that feeds my own resolve. We've lost too many. We won't lose Nettie.

The door bursts open, and Stella stumbles in, breathless and still clad in her winter garb. "What's her status?" she asks, her voice strained as she moves quickly to the side of the gurney.

Snow still clings to Stella's boots, melting onto the floor.

"Weak pulse, not breathing on her own," the captain reports. "Katie is going to start an IV."

Stella steps next to Nettie, checks her pupils, and assesses her condition quickly. "Let me work," she says softly, more to herself than anyone else. "Do we know what happened?"

"I found her like this," I say while tying the tourniquet.

"Was she sick?"

"No. She was fine. We had a rough morning, and she needed some space. I-I was taking her a mug of tea."

The mugs still sit in the call room, steam no longer rising from them. Would I have found her sooner if I hadn't stopped to make tea? Would it have mattered? The what-ifs threaten to overwhelm me, but I force them aside. Focus on the now, on what we can do.

"Tea? What kind?"

"She was already down. I didn't give her the tea."

"Did she eat anything?"

"I. Don't. Know." I say, enunciating each word. Frustration edges my voice. Questions without answers, just like everything else lately. Who killed the whistleblower? Who's working with Hugo? Did they get to Nettie? Why are they targeting us? The mysteries pile up while we struggle just to keep people alive.

Leo catches my eye. His look conveys so much, telling me to calm down and stay professional. I release a breath through my nose as I get the IV set up. He's right, of course. Losing control won't help Nettie. It won't help any of us. I focus on the IV insertion, finding a vein through sheer determination. The flash of blood in the catheter is a small victory.

"It reminds me of Landers," Leo says.

The words hang in the air like a physical presence. None of us want to say it, but we're all thinking the same thing. Addison. The name itself has become synonymous with fear in our community. First the hemlock poisonings, then Landers. Now this? Is Addison responsible for what is happening to Nettie? It only makes sense.

"You think she was poisoned?" Stella asks, as she moves to the medicine cart and pulls out a small vial, shaking it gently. "This might help revive her, but there's no guarantee."

Stella's tinctures and herbs have become our lifeline, a stark contrast to the modern medicine wiped out by the EMP. The irony is clear—survival now depends on remedies from centuries past. What was once cutting-edge is gone, leaving us to save lives with ancient methods.

IV in place, I step back. My entire body aches from the effort of the chest compressions. "Is it enough? Will it even work?"

Stella doesn't answer right away. I watch as she uncaps the first bottle—the cayenne tincture. The same thing that saved Geoff Landers. "I hope you're praying," she finally says.

I nod as I send another silent petition to God.

The pungent spicy aroma fills the air as she opens the bottle. My mind flashes back to that day . . . Landers on the floor, Trooper Schroeder dead beside him while Melvin Cabal snickered. He seemed to care little whether his nephew lived or died. But we saved him—to a point. We have to believe we can save Nettie—not just to keep her alive, but to help her truly live, breathe, and reclaim the life she deserves.

"Remove the bag," Stella instructs with a nod. Opening Nettie's mouth, she lets several drops fall under her tongue. Within moments, Nettie's eyes begin to water.

We all lean forward, watching for any sign of improvement. The watering eyes—just like Landers. The same progression. My heart races with a mixture of hope and fear. If this is the same poison, we know the treatment. But it also means someone got close enough to poison her. Someone got past our security. Just the thought of that brings a sinking sensation to my middle.

I take a breath, the gravity of everything settling in. "I don't want to lose her," I say, more to myself than anyone else.

The words catch in my throat. We've lost so many—friends, colleagues, patients. Each death chips away at our resilience, at our hope for rebuilding some semblance of a normal life. Nettie represents more than just another doctor—she's a link to the world before, to proper medical training, to everything we're trying to preserve.

The captain's gaze locks on mine, his face set in grim determination. "We'll do what we can, Katie. And we won't stop until we've tried everything."

His quiet confidence steadies me, as it has so many times before. Even with his own injury, even after being stripped of his administrative duties at the hospital and med school he's built, he remains our rock. The one who keeps us going when everything else falls apart.

"There we go," Stella murmurs, reaching for the osha root tincture next. The earthy scent fills the air. More drops under the tongue. "Come on, girl. Fight."

Nettie's body jerks suddenly. A rattling gasp escapes her lips.

"Roll her!" Stella orders. We turn Nettie onto her side just as she starts retching. Nothing comes up but bile, yet her breathing grows stronger with each heave.

"That's it." Stella rubs Nettie's back. "Get it all out."

I check her pulse again. Still weak but steadier. "Pulse is improving."

The thread of life under my fingers feels stronger now, more defined. Like a whisper becoming a voice, hope becoming reality. But she's not out of danger yet. We all know how quickly things can turn.

"She's breathing on her own," the captain adds.

Nettie's eyes flutter open, unfocused at first. She tries to speak but only manages a weak mumble. Her usually sharp gaze is clouded and confused. The strong, capable doctor who taught me so much now looks fragile, vulnerable. Another reminder of how quickly our world can change.

"Don't try to talk yet," Stella soothes. "Just breathe."

"How?" The captain voices the question we're all thinking. "If she was poisoned, how did anyone get in here? We've got guards at every entrance. Addison got to Landers, but how could she get inside the hospital?"

The implications send a chill through the room. Someone either slipped past our security or—worse—is already inside. I glance at the doorway, suddenly aware of how exposed we are. How many could be working against us?

I nod, remembering the trouble with Addison. Like Stella, she has some herbal training, but unlike Stella, who spent years perfecting her craft to become a master herbalist before the apocalypse, Addison knew little about herbs or medicine until everything changed.

She learned what she could from books, advertising herself as a midwife and doctor, trading her skills and selling potions. Many of her remedies were untested, and she lacked knowledge of proper dosages, leading to numerous issues we had to address when people she supposedly treated would arrive at the hospital.

The contrast between the two women couldn't be starker—Stella working to heal, Addison to harm. Both use nature's medicines, but for very different purposes.

Addison had delivered the poison—hemlock she likely harvested and turned into a tincture—to the Preacher's cell. Within hours, he and his followers were dead, their mass suicide preceded by a cryptic note filled with what seemed like religious ramblings at the time. Then she found the safe house where Mindy and Kemeera were hiding. Mindy consumed the poison too.

I think of baby Zach, Mindy's son, now part of our family. Did his mother take the hemlock willingly, or was she forced? He'll grow up with questions that have no answers, another innocent caught in this endless cycle of violence.

The Preacher's last words from his letter make more sense now, after what we've learned about Hugo's activities with the dead. A shudder runs through me. But none of this explains why Nettie is here, fighting for her life. The pieces of the puzzle are there, but they don't fit together. Not yet.

"Better question. Why Nettie?" Leo says grimly, echoing my thoughts. "Who would want her dead?"

I remember Nettie's distress earlier, her reaction to the murdered mother. "She was upset about the case. About Hugo." My mind races. "Could there be a connection?"

The captain's expression darkens. "We need to get her somewhere secure. And find out what she might know."

"The med school building," Leo suggests. "We're already sleeping there and have extra security in place."

"Agreed." The captain nods.

"Not yet," Stella replies. "She's not stable. Bring in extra security to the hospital for now."

"Of course," the captain agrees. "Talbot? Call the guards. Tell them we had a breach. Get Shaw back here now."

I study Nettie's face. Her color is improving but she still looks haunted. What did she discover that made her a target? And how many more people will be hurt before we uncover the truth?

Stella administers another dose of the herbal tinctures. "Someone tried real hard to make this look natural. Like she just collapsed from stress. If Katie hadn't found her so quickly . . ." She leaves the sentence unfinished.

"Why?" Nettie's voice is barely a whisper.

"Save your strength." I squeeze her hand. "You're safe now."

But none of us are truly safe. Not while Addison is out there. Not while Hugo's conspirators remain hidden. Not while someone is willing to kill to keep their secrets.

Chapter 5

Katie

Moving Nettie from the treatment room feels like a small victory. Her condition is stable enough for a regular bed, though watching her silent form as we transfer her makes my heart ache. The immediate crisis may be over, but something isn't right. The way she keeps her eyes closed, how she turns her face away from us—it's so unlike the strong, capable doctor I know.

"I'll stay with her," Stella offers, settling into the chair beside the bed. "You need to get back to your duties."

She's right. The apocalypse doesn't pause for personal crises. People still get hurt and still need care. The converted dental surgery center we call a hospital stays busy, especially considering we're the primary care facility for the Guard District.

I linger in the doorway and watch Nettie's chest rise and fall. The guard posted outside—I think his name is Anderson—gives me a reassuring nod. "I won't leave my post, ma'am."

"Um, yes. Thanks," I reply, wondering why he's referring to me as *ma'am*. I mean, he's young, no doubt about that. Maybe twenty. But I'm not that much older than he is. Certainly not old enough to be *ma'amed.*

Back in the treatment room, I find Leo cleaning up. Even with one arm in a sling, he manages to be useful. Sometimes I think he pushes himself too hard, but then, don't we all?

"Two more patients waiting," he tells me. "Chainsaw accident—already in exam two with Williams—and a case of severe stomach pain."

The day blurs into a familiar rhythm of treatments and charts. The chainsaw victim loses two fingers—there's no hope of reattachment without microsurgery capabilities. The best we can do is clean the wound and suture it closed. The stomach pain turns out to be appendicitis, something we might have confirmed with imaging before the EMP. Now we rely on physical exams and experience.

"We need to operate," I tell the captain when he comes to check on us. "The symptoms are clear."

He nods grimly. "I'll finish here. You'll assist."

It wasn't a question, but I'm still caught off guard by the assignment. Usually, I'm relegated to nursing duties during surgeries, still being a student in the Doctors of the Apocalypse program. But with Nettie down . . .

"Of course."

Deputy Shaw arrives as we're prepping for surgery. His face is drawn with concern as he pulls us aside. "My people have gone through everything," he says. "Every entrance was covered. No one suspicious entered the hospital today."

"Could someone have slipped past?" Williams asks.

He shakes his head. "I don't see how. We've compared the logs with patient records. Everything matches up. Every person who came through those doors was either staff or a patient, and we can account for all of them."

The implication sends a chill down my spine. If no one got in . . . "An inside job?"

"Maybe." His expression tells me he's thinking of something else, but before I can ask, the captain says we need to get into the OR.

"Thank you, Shaw," he says with a curt nod. "Can you leave the guard?"

"Absolutely. And we'll keep checking, see if anything new comes up. And the driver returned. Everything went fine. They're safe."

He doesn't use any names, but we know he's referring to Alice, Merissa, Pearl, and the children arriving at Opal Maher's ranch. I smile as tears of gratitude fill my eyes. "I have a note ready. When can it be delivered?"

"Couple of days. We want to let things ride for now."

"Okay. Sure." I try not to show my disappointment. Writing notes to Nico and the babies, which Alice or maybe Merissa or Pearl read to them, is the only way I have of staying in contact. Nico sends drawings in return while Alice and Merissa add short notes.

The appendectomy takes over an hour. Without modern anesthesia, we rely on nerve blocks and careful timing. Every cut must be precise—we can't waste supplies redoing anything. My arms ache from holding retractors, but the patient survives. One more victory in a day that desperately needs them.

When things finally slow down, I find Stella still sitting with Nettie. "Go get some rest," I tell her. "I'll take over."

She studies me for a moment before nodding, likely taking in my own disheveled appearance. "Call me if anything changes."

I sink into the chair she leaves behind, my eyes on Nettie's face as the daylight fades. Outside, Anderson hands off his post to Oscar Harrington—my old next-door neighbor. Through the window, snow drifts down steadily, blurring the view beyond.

"You should go home too."

The whisper startles me. Nettie's eyes are open, though she's staring at the ceiling rather than looking at me.

"Not much of a home right now," I remind her. "Just a cot in the med school building. Besides, I want to be here."

"Why?"

"Because you're my friend. My teacher." I lean forward. "Nettie, what happened? Who did this to you?"

She closes her eyes again. "I'm done."

The words don't register at first. Or maybe I don't want them to. "What do you mean, done?"

"Just done." Her voice cracks. "I can't . . . I can't keep watching people die because we don't have the right equipment or the right medicines. Can't keep telling parents their children are gone, or children their parents won't wake up. Or watching people lose their ever-loving minds and doing terrible things. I'm not strong enough."

Understanding hits like a physical blow. "You . . . you did this to yourself?"

She doesn't answer, but her silence says everything.

"I don't understand," I whisper. "You took something?"

"You think Stella is the only one who knows about different herbs?" she asks quietly. "There are things. Fast, relatively painless. Effective. At least, that's what the books say. Guess I should have gone with my first instinct and kept some of the hemlock. There'd be no coming back from that."

My chest feels too tight. "Why didn't you talk to someone? To me?"

"And say what?" Now she does look at me, her eyes bright with tears. "That I'm failing? That every day feels harder than the last? That I wake up dreading what new tragedy I'll face?"

She draws a shaky breath. "I had my life all planned out. I gave up so much to become a doctor. I was on track. Things were going to happen for me. Then I could—but no. The world fell apart. I made more terrible choices and ended up here. Now I'm just . . . guessing. Playing pretend while people die."

"You're not pretending," I argue. "You're saving lives."

"I'm losing more than I save. We all are. That mother today . . . if we had a proper trauma center, proper equipment . . . The little girl." Her voice catches.

"But we don't. This is our reality now. We do what we can with what we have."

"And it's not enough," she whispers. "It will never be enough."

I take her hand, remembering all the times she's done the same for me when I felt overwhelmed. "Maybe not. But we're not alone. We face it together."

She tries to pull away, but I hold on. "I can't do it anymore, Katie. I'm not as strong as you."

"Strong?" I almost laugh. "I'm terrified every day. Ask Leo—I wake up crying many nights. Remember what a mess I was when I got here? How deeply I was mourning the loss of my mom. You helped me through that. Helped me build my confidence."

"I was mean to you."

"Sometimes," I snicker. "But it was more of a tough love thing than mean. I know I was a mess. But you, Nettie, you're always so strong."

"Obviously not."

"You are. You keep going. We all keep going because people need us. Because every life we save matters."

"The little girl this morning— "

"Would have died twenty months ago too. Some things are beyond our control, with or without modern medicine." I squeeze her hand. "But some things we can control. Like being there for each other."

She's quiet for a long moment. Outside, the snow falls harder, muffling the world. Finally, she whispers, "I'm so tired."

"I know." I brush away my own tears. "So, we'll rest. And tomorrow, we'll try again. Together."

She doesn't answer, but she doesn't pull her hand away either. We sit in silence, my thoughts drifting to what we've lost, what we're fighting to save, and the price we pay to keep going in this broken world.

The sound of footsteps in the hall reminds me that life goes on. Somewhere in this hospital, someone needs help. Someone is fighting to live while my friend chose to die. The irony isn't lost on me.

"I want to go home," she says, her voice barely above a whisper.

I clear my throat, a nervous habit I've been trying to break. "Not yet. We need to make sure— "

"No. I mean *home* home. Back to where I'm from."

I pause as I consider this. Nettie lived in Kansas. She's received mail from home a few times, but she doesn't talk about it. I've tried, considering Leo is from Southern Kansas near the Oklahoma and Missouri state lines and we both attended Kansas State in Manhattan.

Before I can piece together a response, she says softly, "I have a little girl, you know."

My breath catches. "A little girl?" I repeat, the words landing heavier than I intend. "You have a child?"

"Yeah. My mom and dad are raising her. It was only supposed to be temporary, while I finished school. Once I was a doctor—a real one, not whatever it is I've become—then we'd be together again. My folks even talked about us all moving wherever I was able to find work. They love her, but it's a lot for them at their age."

"How old is she?"

"Seven."

"Seven," I repeat with a nod, attempting the math in my head.

"She was born the summer before my senior year of high school. When I got pregnant, I thought that was it. All my dreams were done. But my parents offered to help. We would have made it. Done all the things we planned, but all the stuff . . . the EMP. I should have gone home the day the planes hit. At least I'd be there with them. I'd know how they were doing."

"You've received letters."

"Not for months. I don't even know if they're still alive."

"It's just the weather," I say with confidence, motioning toward the window. "None of us are getting mail. It'll start up again."

I know I'm telling her something neither of us can be sure of. The mail system was fledgling at best with letters arriving at odd times. But the weather truly does seem to have things on hold for the time being. If we can just make it to spring, we should all be hearing from our loved ones. At least that's the hope. The truth is, none of us know what's happening anywhere but here. It's hard to keep up hope some days, especially when we're surrounded by death.

"The little girl today . . ."

"Around the same age as my daughter. As Alisa."

I nod slowly, my fingers still wrapped around Nettie's hand. Being away from family is hard enough, but from your own child? I can't even fathom it. I've only had Nico, Zach, and Caleb in my life for a short while, yet I hate being apart from them. At least they're nearby, and I get regular updates. Nettie's daughter is two states away, with communication barely reliable. "Maybe we could try the radio," I offer.

"You're the only one that knows."

"The captain— "

"No. Absolutely not. I don't even want to think about what he'd say. It's already humiliating enough that he knows about what happened with Bollinger. I'm still not over the shame of that."

I don't know the specifics of what went on with Nettie and Dr. Bollinger, but something definitely happened. It all came to light when Chastity Marrow was still alive. She and Bollinger had a thing, and so did he and Nettie. Those few days when Bollinger was acting as the rotating doctor were . . . awkward, to say the least.

Bollinger, though, seemed to revel in it and loved seeing the women go at each other and vying for his attention. He may be a good doctor, an excellent orthopedist and probably responsible for saving Leo's use of his arm, but he's a terrible human.

"We'll figure something out," I promise, not sure at the moment exactly what that will be. "But, Nettie, you can't do this again. You can't try and . . . and hurt yourself." My eyes fill with tears as my voice cracks.

"I suppose I'll have to tell the captain this part, at least. I know they're looking for an assailant. I hate that I wasted Shaw's time."

"Would you like me to go get him?"

She lets out a sigh. "Might as well."

I give her hand a squeeze before releasing it and sliding the chair back. "I need to leave the door open, okay?"

"Why not? I'll be a freak show soon enough."

"No." My voice is firm. "No one will think that. This is hard for everyone. We're going to help you. I promise."

She nods, and I hold her gaze for a few moments, reluctant to leave. But eventually, I step away.

"Katie?" Her voice stops me at the door. "I'm sorry."

"Don't be sorry. Just be here. We need you. I need you."

As I step into the hall, I realize I'm shaking.

"Everything okay?" Oscar asks.

I shake my head. "Keep the door open, okay? Stay right here."

He raises his eyebrows but responds only with a nod.

I nod back, then hurry past. How many others are struggling like this? How many of us are barely holding on?

The apocalypse didn't just take our technology, our medicines, our comfortable lives. It's slowly taking our hope, our strength, and our will to continue. But we can't let it. We have to keep fighting, keep trying, and keep living.

Because if we don't, who will be left to put this broken world back together?

Chapter 6

Katie

The door at the end of the corridor opens, the bell ringing to signal Deputy Shaw's return, bringing a brief stillness to the hectic hospital hallway. He gestures for the captain to join him, and Leo and I follow. Without a word, we all move toward the break room.

Once we're inside and the door is shut behind us, he whispers, "The children are fine. Alice, too, of course. I know I gave you a brief update earlier, but I wanted to give you better info. The driver said they had zero problems. As planned, I've left their main guard with them. She's been staying at the house since the first day. She knows what's at stake. Nico's been helping with the younger boys. Gerry too—that pup's turning into quite the protector."

I release a breath through my nose. Being separated from them, every day feels like an eternity.

"And Pearl? Merissa?" Leo asks.

"Managing." He shifts his gaze to the captain. "We'll continue having Poppy Gardner make house calls to monitor Merissa's pregnancy."

"Yes, that's the best plan," Captain Williams agrees. "Opal Maher has some medical training too. She'll be in good hands. I want Poppy to see her at least weekly. If she has any more preterm labor, we'll want to consider bringing Merissa back to town. She can stay in the med school with us."

"Sounds like a plan." Shaw's expression grows serious. "About what happened today. Captain, you said there wasn't actually a breach?"

Captain Williams shakes his head. "No. Nettie . . ." He pauses, choosing his words carefully. "She tried to take her own life."

Shaw's face shows no surprise, just a deep sadness. "I was afraid of that. We're seeing more of it lately. The winter's been hard, and with the flu epidemic, the reduction in rations . . ." He runs a hand over his face. "It's wearing people down. Some folks are giving up."

My mind flashes to Nettie's revelation about her daughter. How much harder must it be to keep going when you don't know if your child is even alive?

"I do have some good news," Shaw continues. "The boy from earlier—the one who lost his mother? We have him staying at Poppy's house. He seems to be doing okay, all things considered. Poppy suggested she take him with her to Opal's place when she goes there for Merissa's next exam. That's Tuesday, I think she said. We hope Opal will take him in."

"That's perfect," I say, remembering how the ranch has helped other troubled youth. "Jason Wheeler seems to be doing better out there. Opal has a way with people."

The captain nods thoughtfully. "Actually, that gives me an idea. Once Nettie's stable, maybe some time at the Maher ranch would do her good too. Better than sending her to the psych ward at the main hospital like her patient."

"Fresh air, good food, and Opal's particular brand of wisdom," Shaw agrees. "Could be exactly what she needs. Opal's going to have a full house. Think she'll mind?"

"She won't mind," I say quickly.

"We'll need to watch Nettie closely for a few days first," the captain adds. "And I've arranged for a psychiatrist from the main hospital to come assess her. She was more than willing to come over now that they have the inpatient system put in place."

"Will she want to take Nettie back with her?" I ask, thinking that wouldn't be nearly as good of a choice as Nettie going to Opal's ranch.

"She didn't say that. Just that she'd visit us. She suggested there may be others who need her help while she's here. She's working to find a driver and security for the trip."

The way the captain says it makes it sound like an almost impossible journey. It's five miles. The distance between us and the main hospital used to mean nothing. Now it might as well be five hundred. I remember our trip there just weeks ago, when Leo needed the hardware removed from his external fixation. We'd taken the hospital's biodiesel pickup, transporting Elliot Tillman for his physical therapy. His father Duncan went along, and our friend Josiah Talbot provided security.

The memory of that day still haunts me. The attack came out of nowhere. Josiah died protecting us. After Josiah's death, new protocols were put in place for official travel between districts. The fact that they're arranging for a psychiatrist to make the journey shows how seriously they're taking Nettie's situation.

"Will she stay in the hospital until then?" I ask.

"Maybe," Captain Williams responds. "But I think moving her to the med school makes more sense. She'd be more comfortable, but we'll see. I have a radio conference set up with the psychiatrist for 1800 hours. We'll decide what's best to do then and I'll have a better idea as to when she'll arrive."

"The med school might be better," Leo suggests. "More privacy, and we're all there anyway. Of course, we're working long hours, and it may be best for Nettie not to be alone."

I nod in agreement. The converted offices where we've been sleeping aren't luxurious, but at least they're secure. And Nettie won't have to face the constant stream of patients and staff who'd inevitably discover what happened. But what will we do with her while we're on shift? Being down a doctor now, we'll have to figure out how to make this work.

The other med students—Matt, Jeff, and Kerry—have gone home to get some rest. Dr. Murphy, the only real doctor left alongside Captain Williams, came in as soon as Williams sent for him. He'll stay on the overnight shift, and Jeff will return as backup. Murphy and Jeff work well together, so it's no surprise Jeff offered to help out.

I'm supposed to be off by now, back at the med school apartment, sleeping until I'm due back at midnight for a nursing shift. We've already been rotating shifts to provide more coverage, even before Nettie's incident.

Poppy Gardner, who runs the newly formed nursing school, has assigned some of her better-trained students to cover partial shifts, which has helped. That's how I can take just a half shift tonight before resuming my med school duties tomorrow. Still . . . it's a lot.

The last few days have taken a toll on all of us. In some ways, I can see how Nettie became so worn down that she considered giving up. Depression is difficult, especially if you don't have a light at the end of the tunnel. For me, that light is Jesus. Learning to rely on Him to carry me through the darkest moments has been life-changing.

It's not always easy, and I still struggle, but knowing He's there gives me strength and hope when I feel like I can't go on. Trusting in His plan reminds me that, even in the hardest times, I'm never truly alone.

Nettie doesn't have that comfort. She's made it clear she's not interested in God or anything He has to offer.

"We'll need to keep this quiet." The captain's voice is low and guarded. "The last thing we need is for people to lose faith in their doctors."

"Or for others to get similar ideas," Shaw adds grimly. "We're already seeing it. She's the fifth this week. We've been doing wellness checks and asking supervisors to let us know if they notice anything among their staff, but we can't be everywhere. People are scared, hungry, and losing hope. It's a bad combination."

I'm well aware that self-harm has increased in recent days. There had been a wave of it in the early days of the apocalypse, when people first realized that our world had changed for good. During the first winter, there were still many deaths, but things seemed to lessen over the summer. Of course, Leo and I had only arrived in Rapid City then, and we hadn't heard all the rumors of what was happening, but the summer days did seem to bring people hope.

Then in the fall, we had new troubles with the Preacher and his followers wreaking havoc on the town and causing so much death and destruction. Now, with the long, dark days of winter taking a toll, it seems the suicide rate has increased along with illness and violent deaths.

I think about the little girl we lost this morning and the mother murdered by her own daughter. So much loss in one day. How do we keep going when everything seems to be falling apart?

But then I remember Nico helping with his baby brothers, and Gerry protecting them all. Even in our darkest moments, there are glimmers of light. We just have to be strong enough to see them.

"What's the situation with the remains?" Leo asks. "I know you said you would have a team protecting them."

Shaw sighs and shakes his head. "We do. Around the clock. What Hugo and his cohorts did to our dead is . . . disturbing."

Disturbing is an understatement. I can think of many more words to use, including disgusting and immoral. Not to mention we believe they weren't only using the fat off the bodies of the recently deceased, but they also killed to keep their secret.

Kerry Hendrick's husband, Rand, disappeared a few weeks ago. Bowski believes Rand somehow stumbled upon the biodiesel operation and was killed to keep it quiet. I've heard rumors of others who've disappeared in recent weeks. Did they also become casualties of Hugo's operation?

What I really don't understand is why they did it. Making biodiesel is a fairly simple process, but it doesn't explain their actions. South Dakota and the surrounding states are known for oil production. While Pennington County, where we live, doesn't have as many wells as some other areas, there are still several. Extracting crude oil from the ground doesn't require electricity, which has always been common in remote areas, even before the EMP.

The reciprocating pump, often called a nodding donkey, thirsty bird, or pumpjack, is a common sight at onshore oil wells. It's usually powered by a combustion engine running on natural gas, often tapped directly from the well. At least that's how Leo explained it when we first heard about Hugo's operation. I'll admit, I don't completely grasp how crude oil is refined, but I've heard of small, makeshift refineries being set up.

Winter has made everything harder, but it's still appalling that Hugo and the others did what they did. Another concern is figuring out exactly who these "others" are. To my knowledge, only a handful of people connected to Hugo have been identified and apprehended, but the operation is believed to be much larger. At least now the remains of the dead are being protected, though I suddenly feel an overwhelming need to avoid adding to their numbers.

"Do you think we could have the therapist meet with others while she's here?" I ask. "Maybe spread the word and have some group sessions?"

"It's a good idea," Williams agrees. "With Nettie and the teenager from this morning, along with what Shaw is discovering, it's obvious people need mental health treatment. It's always been something we've known was needed, but we're just stretched so thin."

"Maybe you can suggest it when you talk with her on the radio? See if she can adjust her schedule to allow for group sessions?"

"I'll propose it."

"What time is it now?" I ask.

The captain checks his watch. "Just past 1600. We've got some time before the radio call. Katie, why don't you go sit with Nettie? Let her know what we're thinking about the Maher ranch. See how she feels about it. I'll wake Stella so she can relieve you in about half an hour. Sound good?"

I nod, grateful for something concrete to do. Something that might actually help. Bringing in a psychiatrist, even if only for a short while, may be just what our district needs.

I find Nettie awake, staring out the window at the falling snow. Oscar gives me a nod as I approach—he's been vigilant at his post, though I notice he's positioned himself to give Nettie privacy while maintaining security.

"How are you feeling?" I ask, settling into the chair beside her bed.

"Tired. Embarrassed." She turns from the window to face me. "I heard voices in the hall. Shaw?"

"Yes. He's been checking on things." I pause, choosing my words carefully. "We've been talking about what happens next. The captain's arranging for someone to come from the main hospital—one of the psychiatrists."

"I suppose that's necessary." Her voice is quiet but not resistant.

"There's something else. Once you're stronger, they're thinking about having you stay at the Maher ranch for a while. Get some fresh air, good food. If Opal agrees, the boy who lost his mother today will be there too."

Something flickers in her eyes—interest, maybe even hope. "Opal Maher's place? I've heard good things about what she's doing out there."

"She has a way of helping people heal." I lean forward and take her hand. "And you're not alone, Nettie. Shaw says there are others struggling too. The doctor might do some group sessions while she's here."

"Others feeling lost?" A tear slides down her cheek. "I guess I'm not the only one missing family."

"No, you're not. And maybe we can find a way to get word from Kansas. About Alisa."

Her fingers tighten around mine. "The captain said he'd talk to the radio folks at Camp Rapid. Do you know if he's done that? If they'll let us call?"

"I don't know. But if he said he would, he will. You know the captain. Sometimes just having a goal, something to work toward . . ." I trail off, remembering my own dark days after Mom died, how faith and purpose helped pull me through, but it was still difficult. Even now, I miss her. Some days are harder than others.

"Thank you, Katie." Her voice is stronger now. "For finding me. For understanding."

Outside, the snow continues to fall, but somehow the room feels warmer. Sometimes hope, like healing, comes in small steps.

And sometimes that's enough to keep going.

Chapter 7

Merissa

Evening falls on Opal's ranch, quiet and cold under a blanket of fresh snow. I watch from my bed near the woodstove as fat flakes drift past the window, each one catching the golden light from inside. The steady warmth wraps around me, but it can't quite touch the chill that's settled in my heart since about half an hour ago when I caught Mother Pearl massaging her side, her face pinched with pain she thought no one could see.

The babies are asleep in the playpens we brought for them, and Gerry is on the floor nearby. Nico's upstairs in what used to be Opal's sewing room, now turned into a bedroom for the three young boys, probably dreaming of the chickens he helped feed earlier. His excitement over collecting eggs was infectious, momentarily making us all forget why we're really here.

"More tea?" Opal's voice draws my attention to where she, Pearl, and Alice sit at the kitchen table. The ceramic teapot, painted with faded blue flowers, steams between them.

"Please," Pearl says, holding out her cup. She catches my eye and smiles, but there's something in her expression that makes my chest tighten.

"This blend is wonderful," Alice comments, warming her hands around her cup. "I taste lemon balm, but there's something else . . ."

"Ginger and a touch of mint," Opal explains. "I grow the ginger in the greenhouse and the mint's taken over a section of the garden. I dried as much of it as possible." She motions to the herbs hanging from above. "Pearl, remember when Mama used to make something similar?"

"For every ailment." Pearl nods. "Though she'd add whatever herbs she thought would help. Sometimes made for some interesting flavors."

The sisters share a laugh, and I'm struck by how alike they look in this moment—their silver hair glowing in the lamplight, their faces etched with years of wisdom and weathered by hard times. But where Opal's expression is open and easy, Pearl's holds something back.

"Speaking of Mama's remedies," Pearl begins, and my heart races. This is it. She's going to tell them. "I've been thinking a lot about how she always said the truth was the best medicine."

Opal sets down the teapot, her movements deliberate. "Pearl?"

"I saw Captain Williams at the clinic a few weeks ago." Pearl's voice is steady, matter-of-fact. "Found some bumps. Here." She touches her side. "And under my arm."

The silence that follows feels infinite. I want to close my eyes and pretend I'm not hearing this again, but I force myself to watch. To be present. To be strong for Pearl.

"Oh, Pearl." Opal reaches for her sister's hand. "What did the captain say?"

"What you'd expect. Could do a biopsy, but without proper treatment options . . ." Pearl shrugs. "I've made my peace with it." She glances at me, giving me a sad smile.

"Made your— " Opal starts, then stops. Her face works through several emotions before settling on something between determination and grief. "No. There must be something." She stares at the ceiling as if the perfect remedy for treating cancer would fall out of the drying herbs. Opal sits up straight. "Mistletoe."

"Mistletoe?" Alice echoes, a crease in her brow as she nods. "I remember Chris saying something about that a few years back. It was in one of his medical journals."

Opal smiles. "Maybe we can get a message to him."

"I'm not sure if the journal with the information was moved to the hospital or lost in the fire." Alice shakes her head. Only days before the sniper shot the whistleblower, the Williamses' home was destroyed by fire—suspected arson. Katie and Leo, along with the three children and Gerry, were staying with the Williamses when the fire happened, displacing all of them to the small guest house at the back of the property.

"Then we'll ask Stella Swensen. Surely, she's aware of these studies? She may even have an extract already. We have trappers going out tomorrow. I'll have them search for it in the woods. Maybe— "

"Opal." Pearl's voice is gentle but firm. "We both know those treatments were to ease suffering, not cure cancer."

"You don't know it's cancer," I find myself saying, the words escaping before I can stop them. All three women turn to look at me, and I feel my cheeks flush. "I mean, the captain said it might not be."

Pearl's smile is tender. "Perhaps. But either way, I'm not going to spend what time I have left chasing maybes. I want to be here, present, especially with the baby coming." Her hand gestures toward my swollen belly. "God has His plan, and I trust in that."

"But how can you just accept it?" The question bursts from me, full of all the fear and anger I've been holding back. "How can you trust in a plan that might take you away from us? From your grandchild?"

The room goes quiet again, save for the crackling of the woodstove and the soft whisper of snow against the windows. Pearl studies me for a long moment, then slowly rises from her chair. She comes to sit on the edge of my bed and takes my hand in hers.

"Faith isn't about understanding the plan, dear heart. It's about trusting the Planner." Her fingers are warm from the teacup, strong despite everything. "When Braedon and Tomas died, I couldn't understand why. Still don't, some days. But I know God didn't cause it—He grieved with us. And He's with us now, in this room, in this moment."

"I want to believe that," I whisper, tears spilling down my cheeks. "I do. But it's so hard."

Alice speaks up from the table, her voice soft. "When Chris was deployed, I struggled with the same questions. Why would God send him into danger? Why should we have to be apart? But then I realized something. My fear came from trying to control everything. The moment I surrendered that control, gave it to God . . . that's when I found peace."

"Doesn't mean it's easy," Opal adds, coming to join us by the bed. She perches on the old trunk that serves as both a seat and storage. "Pearl, I'm angry. I'm scared. I want to fight this with everything we have. Let me see what I can find out about the mistletoe, okay?"

"I know you want to help." Pearl squeezes her sister's hand. "And I love you for it. But right now, what I need most is to be surrounded by my family. To watch these little ones grow." She looks at the sleeping babies, then at me. "To meet my grandchild. To share whatever wisdom I can while there's time."

A kick from within punctuates her words, strong enough to make me gasp. Pearl places her hand on my belly, and another kick follows, as if the baby knows—as if it's trying to reach out to its grandmother.

"See?" Pearl's eyes shine with tears and joy. "God gives us these moments. These precious gifts. That's what I want to focus on."

"Will you at least let me explore options?" Opal asks, her voice thick with emotion. "I'll check my herb books. Maybe Stella Swensen can help too? Have you consulted her?"

"Not yet," I say. "The captain planned to check her again. He did say there was a chance it was just inflammation." It's obvious to me that the tone of my voice implies I don't believe that. Neither does Pearl.

Outside, the snow continues to fall, building drifts against the windows. Inside, we hold each other close, sharing tears and memories and love. The babies sleep on, peaceful in their ignorance of adult sorrows. Somewhere upstairs, Nico might be dreaming of gathering eggs, of simple joys in a complicated world.

I feel another kick, gentler this time, like a reminder. A reminder that life goes on, that even in the midst of grief and fear, new life grows. New hope emerges. Pearl's right—we don't have to understand the plan. Maybe faith is just this. Sitting together in the growing darkness, holding onto each other, trusting that even when we can't see the path ahead, we're not walking it alone.

A sound from upstairs breaks the moment—Nico's footsteps, followed by his small voice. "Nana Alice?"

"Yes, sweetheart?" Alice wipes her eyes quickly before turning toward the stairs.

"I can't sleep. The wind's making scary noises."

"Would you like some warm milk?" Opal offers, already moving toward her cookstove.

Pearl starts to rise, but I notice her wince slightly. I reach out and take her hand. "They've got it. That's why we came here."

"Yes, I s'pose so. It was nice of Kevin and Shawn, along with all the others, to stay in the bunkhouse tonight. Give us a good old-fashioned hen party."

I chuckle at the term. "Isn't a hen party a bachelorette party?"

"Is it? I thought it was just a gathering of women. But my guess is, we'll be having a bachelorette party soon enough." She squeezes my hand. "That is if you allow Ritchie Kasubowski to have his way."

I shake my head. "Bowski knows I'm not ready for marriage. Braedon's only been gone since October— "

"There's no requirement you have to mourn a certain amount of time."

"I understand that, Mother Pearl, but it's still unseemly. Besides, I'm not in any condition to be getting married. Not only am I as big as a house, but I'm confined to bed . . . and hiding out."

"I'm sure he'd be more than happy to marry you from your perch on the pillows."

"Wouldn't that make for some lovely memories? And what about the hiding out? He doesn't even know where we are."

She waves her hand. "Deputy Shaw said they're getting to the bottom of the atrocity. Once they do, you'll be safe. I'm surprised they didn't put Ritchie under protective custody too. Isn't he in danger?"

I shrug and shake my head. "I asked Shaw. He said he suggested it, but Bowski insists he's protected. He's the one who blew the case wide open but did it in a way that didn't point to him. Hugo's now in protective custody but isn't talking."

"And Hugo is the mortician, right?"

"Mortician, coroner, and undertaker all in one," I remind her. Hugo's been in charge of retrieving and cataloging the dead since the early days of the EMP. With winter here, burying isn't an option, so he was storing the remains until summer. The explosions and the flu have taken many lives. Now, to learn they've been filleting what little fat remains on the bodies—after nearly two years of food rations—and rendering it into oil is horrifying.

Bowski argues it's a pointless effort. It takes about eight pounds of fat to produce a single gallon of biodiesel. Before the apocalypse, excess body fat was abundant; now, it's scarce. Hugo and his still-unknown partners were growing desperate. Even with the rising death toll, it wasn't enough. Soon, people in long-term care centers started dying unexpectedly, and strange deaths occurred in the hospital—cases no one could explain.

The situation became so dire that Bowski hid a pair of elderly sisters, close friends of his. One was recovering from sepsis in a long-term care center when rumors began swirling about an Angel of Death killing patients. Those rumors pointed at Alice Williams.

In the early days of the disaster, Alice had helped her neighbors end their lives, even though it was their wish. Her involvement in this, however, led to blackmail, which sparked a series of events that eventually put her and Captain Williams in the crosshairs of former sheriff Melvin Cabal.

Knowing Cabal as we do, Alice and I have often speculated that he's likely involved in the situation with Hugo. If that's true, he shouldn't pose a threat to us—he and his nephew, Geoff Landers, are in custody.

We don't even know where they're being held. The last we heard, Landers was in a semi-vegetative state after barely surviving a mysterious poisoning. We suspect Addison, a self-trained herbalist and midwife who was also Landers's girlfriend, was behind it. Not your typical love story, but nothing too shocking given the strange events that seem to happen in the Black Hills.

Sometimes I wonder if Mother Pearl and I made a mistake leaving Montana for South Dakota. But Pearl's need to be with Opal was the main reason we came. And now, if Pearl is truly sick, which is becoming harder to deny with each passing day, being with Opal may turn out to be a blessing.

The sound of spoons clinking against mugs drifts from the kitchen as Opal and Alice prepare Nico's warm milk. I rest my hand on my belly, feeling the baby shift. Pearl may be right about not chasing maybes, but I'm not ready to give up hope—not for her, not for any of us. The world might have changed, but we're still here, still fighting. And tomorrow will bring what it brings.

Chapter 8

Merissa

The lantern casts a warm glow over the paper as I search for the right words. This is my second attempt at this letter. I scratched out the first in my journal, just like the other two I've written to Bowski since I started hiding out—a practice run to try and get the words right, along with a way to get all my feelings on paper.

Letters are our only way to communicate, and journaling has been my lifeline, keeping me steady since Braedon died. Even though I've already reworked this letter once, it still doesn't feel right. Bowski's notes have been so heartfelt, and compared to them, my replies seem flat. Tepid, at best. I can admit there's something wonderful between us, but the guilt of it being too soon after Braedon's death holds me back.

The woodstove crackles, its warmth seeping into the room. Kevin just stoked it before heading out on guard duty, and now I catch the faint sound of boots crunching through snow. Peering out the window, I spot the men moving toward the barn, their shadows long in the early light.

Dear Bowski,

That's all I write before I pause. Should I call him Ritchie? No, he's always been Bowski to me, even now, when we're . . . whatever we are. I glance at his latest letter, brought back from town by Shawn. He's been making a point of staying in touch with Deputy Shaw, trading news and supplies between us and town. The paper's already soft at the creases from how many times I've read it.

I'm safe. I know that's what you want to hear first. The baby's doing well too, kicking and punching like a cage fighter. Being on bed rest is driving me crazy. Mother Pearl keeps reminding me it's only temporary, but it feels like it's been forever.

I pause, tapping the pencil against the paper. There's so much I want to say, but the words feel trapped somewhere between my heart and the page. In the original version of the letter, I mentioned Opal. I must avoid that. Even Bowski isn't supposed to know where we are.

I read his letter again: *I miss seeing you at the hospital. Everything feels off-balance without you here. Even Jacquie Haley mentioned how things seemed wrong without you. She's not even gossiping much about you being gone, just said she hoped you and your baby would be okay.*

The baby kicks, as if sensing my emotional turmoil. Nearly eight months pregnant with my late husband's child, and here I am, writing what amounts to a love letter to another man. Braedon has only been gone a few months, but it seems like much longer. Our life together—in Livingston—has taken on the haze of a distant dream, a memory from another time.

Being married to Braedon had been wonderful. Our meeting felt like fate—or as he liked to say, ordained by God. I loved my work as an engine captain with the Forest Service, even though my days and weeks were often unpredictable and exhausting, especially during wildfire season. The few years before the EMP were especially intense, with blazes erupting not just in Montana but across the West. It kept me busy, but I didn't mind. Braedon understood it was more than a job to me. It was part of who I was.

Before joining the Forest Service, I spent eight years in the Coast Guard as a Damage Controlman—or DC, as we called it. I loved the variety. On a cutter, we did everything from firefighting to welding, and engine work to plumbing. Every day brought something new. After my time in the Coast Guard, I traded ocean waves for smoke-filled skies and found my next calling in firefighting.

Braedon had his own remarkable career, serving twenty years in the Army before retiring and starting his own security firm. Somehow, amid all of that, we both became interested in mounted archery, which is how we met. It was one of those moments that felt too perfect to be coincidence, the kind of meeting that changed everything.

Our life together had been good. Until it wasn't. After Braedon's dad passed, my husband started talking about wanting children—something that was never part of my plan. We were separated but hadn't divorced when the attacks on our country began. When the EMP hit, we ended up sheltering together, joined by Mother Pearl, Braedon's brother Tomas, and Tomas's wife.

It didn't take long for our separation to fade into the background. We found ourselves living as husband and wife again, doing whatever was necessary to get through each day and helping Pearl do the same. That first winter was brutal. The food rations left us all too thin and too tired. By spring, things started to improve, giving us a sliver of hope.

Then the guerrilla attacks began. Bands of transients swept through, putting everyone in danger. In the final showdown with those trying to take over Livingston, both Braedon and Tomas were killed. Leaving Tomas's wife, Courtney, and me as widows and Pearl—at age seventy-two—having outlived her husband and children.

I continue writing, deciding to stay on safer topics: *The new snow is beautiful. Nico longs to go outside and make snowballs and snow angels.*

I don't tell him he's now able to do that since we've moved to the ranch. I didn't even tell him in my last letter that we were relocating. I consider if there's some way I can drop hints that he'd understand so he'd realize where we are, but I don't want to risk it. I can't imagine the letter would fall into the wrong hands, but if it did then I'd be putting everyone in danger.

I pause again, reading Bowski's words: *I know you're struggling with how you feel. I understand. Take all the time you need. I'm not going anywhere.*

His understanding only makes it harder somehow. If he'd pushed, demanded, maybe I could justify pulling away. But his patience, his gentleness—it draws me in even as it terrifies me.

The sound of movement upstairs pulls me from my thoughts. Pearl and Opal will be up soon, preparing for the morning. Today's Sunday, and Shawn Maher will be leading the service. Another thing I'll miss because of this bed rest. I've heard him preach before—his way of explaining scripture makes it all feel so accessible, so real. Growing up, church was something we did on holidays—just a tradition without meaning.

Even in the early years of my marriage to Braedon, we rarely attended. But after his father died, everything changed. His church attendance became more frequent, much like his sudden desire for children. I know they were connected, but I never understood why. I couldn't grasp why he said God was calling him to something greater, to be more. But lately, I'm beginning to understand.

I set aside Bowski's letter and continue with mine: *I wish I could tell you everything that's in my heart, but I'm not sure I understand it myself. Sometimes I feel like I'm betraying Braedon's memory just by missing you. Other times, I think maybe this is part of God's plan, though I'm still learning to trust in that. Mother Pearl says God doesn't expect us to understand everything, just to have faith. I'm trying.*

More sounds come from above—footsteps, quiet voices. The house is waking up. Through the window, I can see the sky beginning to lighten. Kevin, Shawn, and Jason moved back into the house last night, spending a few days living in one of the bunk houses to give us time to settle in and make sure Nico and Alice were comfortable. The shuffling of sleeping arrangements reminds me of how many lives have been disrupted by this situation.

My friend Walt Cox lives in one of the bunkhouses, back at the main ranch for now after spending time in one of the shacks along the property line. Most of the outbuildings have been converted to housing. It takes a large group of people to keep the ranch running smoothly.

Shaw's guard Abby spends her days either in the house or patrolling outside while sleeping in one of the women's dorms. Sometimes, I wonder if the others who work and live here know why we're here. Do they know we're hiding out? Opal said not to worry about that. Most of the people here never go into town, plus she trusts them. They wouldn't be here if she didn't.

Stay safe, I write, then hesitate over how to end the letter. Love feels too strong, too soon. Yours isn't quite right either. Finally, I simply sign my name, folding the paper carefully and sliding it into an envelope. Someone will collect it later, along with any other messages that need to be delivered to town. Or maybe it'll wait until Poppy Gardner arrives to check on me and the baby.

It was decided she'd be the least likely person to be expected to be monitoring me. As a nurse, she'll know what to look for should things start going wrong again. As a physician in training, I should know these things myself. And I do, but somehow when it's my own body— my own child—my professionalism is a little murky.

"Good morning, dear." Pearl's voice startles me. She's standing at the bottom of the stairs, wrapped in her robe. Gerry pads down the stairs behind her. "Writing to Bowski?" Does she look pale? It's hard to tell in the dim light.

I feel my cheeks warm. "Just updating him on things. Don't worry. I didn't mention moving to Opal's place."

She smiles knowingly but doesn't comment. Instead, she heads for the kitchen where Opal is already moving around. The smell of mint tea fills the air.

"Morning, Merissa," Opal calls out. "Did you sleep well?"

"Well enough," I answer, though truthfully, I've been awake for hours. The baby seems most active at night lately, and my mind won't quiet down enough for proper rest.

The men return from morning chores just as breakfast preparations are underway. Kevin stomps the snow from his boots at the door, his beard frosted white. "Cold enough to freeze the horns off a bull out there," he announces, heading for the coffee. "Just a few days ago, I thought spring was on the horizon. Now it seems winter is trying to make another stand."

Shawn follows, carrying an armload of firewood. He carefully sets it by the woodstove, adding a few pieces to the blaze. "Morning, Merissa. Shame you'll miss the service today. I'm sharing some passages about faith in difficult times."

"I'm sorry to miss it too," I say sincerely. "Maybe you could stop by later? I'd love to read the passages."

He nods, warming his hands by the stove. "Happy to. Keeping your baby safe is the most important thing. Maybe we could move a bed out there? Figure out a way for you to join us?"

"Only a few weeks and I'll be able to start getting up more. Then I'll be more than happy to move around and get the labor started."

The next hour passes in a blur of activity as everyone prepares for the day. Pearl helps me change into fresh loungewear and makes sure I'm comfortable before she goes to dress. The others move around the house with practiced efficiency, knowing exactly what needs to be done.

"We'll bring you back a plate from the potluck," Opal promises as they prepare to leave. "And I'm leaving a thermos of tea right here by your bed, along with the pitcher of water." She also motions to the commode sitting next to the bed. I hate using it, and knowing others have to empty it, but it's necessary.

"Thank you." I try to keep the disappointment from my voice. It's not just missing church—it's missing the community, the sense of belonging that's become so important in this post-EMP world. But keeping the baby where he belongs is what's important right now.

I don't know my exact due date, but I can guess based on how I'm measuring. We estimate I was thirty-four weeks when the preterm labor started. Before the EMP, thirty-seven was considered full term. Now Williams prefers thirty-eight weeks, if at all possible. Without NICUs, every extra day inside counts.

Williams says it's a balancing act—keeping the baby in long enough to grow stronger but not so long that complications arise. I can tell he's worried, even if he hides it well. The hospital's resources are stretched thin, and a premature baby would need more than we can provide.

Still, I remind myself that every kick I feel is a small victory, proof that he's still holding on.

"Try to rest," Pearl advises, tucking the blankets around me. "The baby needs it. C'mon, Gerry. You can come and hear all about the Lord too."

Gerry's ears perk up and his tail wags as he follows Pearl. Soon they're gone, and the house falls into silence. I pick up Bowski's letter again, but the words blur before my eyes. Maybe Pearl's right about needing rest. I close my eyes, listening to the pops and cracks of the fire.

I don't mean to fall asleep, but the next thing I know, I'm startled awake by a sound that makes my blood run cold—the urgent clanging of cowbells. Not the gentle sound of cattle grazing or the bell that rings to call folks in for a meal, but the sharp, deliberate ringing that serves as the ranch's warning system.

My heart pounds as I struggle to sit up. The house is still empty—everyone's at church. Through the window, I can see people running, but I can't tell if they're running toward something or away from it. The bells continue their frantic warning.

I grab the extra blanket from the foot of my bed and wrap it around my shoulders as I swing my legs over the side. Captain Williams was clear about bed rest, but if there's danger . . .

The baby kicks hard, as if protesting my movement. The bells ring louder, more urgent. Someone outside shouts, but the words are lost in the wind. I push myself to my feet, one hand bracing against the wall, the other cradling my belly. If I can just make it to the window, maybe I can see what's happening.

The floor creaks beneath my feet as I take one careful step, then another. The bells keep ringing, and now I can hear more shouting. My legs feel weak; I haven't walked more than the couple of steps to the bedside toilet since arriving at Opal's place. But fear drives me forward. Whatever's happening out there, I need to know.

I'm halfway to the window when the front door bursts open.

Chapter 9

Merissa

The door swings open as Walt Cox storms in, my guard Abby right behind him. Both faces are grim. "Get down," Walt orders, already moving toward me with purpose. The cowbells continue their frantic warning. Abby takes a position by the front door and peers out the window.

"What's happening?" I ask, my legs trembling as I try to maintain my balance.

"Raiders. At least a dozen of them." Walt's strong hands grasp my shoulders, guiding me back toward the bed. His calloused fingers are gentle despite his urgency, careful with my pregnant form. "They're all around the perimeter." His voice is steady, but I can hear the tension underneath. "They're better equipped than the usual riffraff we get out here. Military-style formations. The safe room's too far for you."

My heart pounds. Mother Pearl is out there. Everyone is out there. "But— "

"No." Walt pulls pillows and blankets off the bed and piles them onto the floor. "There," he says, his usual slow southern drawl clipped and worried. "Get yourself down there and I'll move the bed to conceal you."

He offers me an arm and helps me onto the pile of bedding. Once I'm in place, he spins the bed to offer me some protection. The metal frame scrapes against the wooden floor, leaving fresh marks on the well-worn boards. "If there's a breach, we'll flip it. The walls will support the mattress and give you cover." He positions himself between me and the window, rifle at the ready. "Pearl would never forgive me if anything happened to you or that baby. We'll do what we must."

Gunfire erupts outside. I flinch at the sharp cracks, trying to identify the weapons. The different reports tell their own story. Some sound like hunting rifles, others semiautomatics.

I reach for my own pistol. My hands wrap around the familiar grip. Even with my heart racing, muscle memory takes over as I check the magazine and chamber. The weight of the weapon is reassuring, though I don't want to fire it unless I have to. I know from experience the noise shocks my baby. Even what is happening now has him moving and jerking.

The gunfire intensifies. Footsteps pound on gravel, and commands ring out, blending with the shots. I recognize Kevin's voice but can't make out the words over the chaos. The cowbells have stopped, but their warning has been replaced by something worse. The rumbling growl of engines. Vehicles are approaching fast.

"They've got trucks," Walt mutters, adjusting his position to better provide me protection while still scanning out the window. "That's new. Most raiders around here have been on foot. A few on horseback."

"They won't get through," Abby says from her position by the door. "Shawn and the others will stop them."

Glass explodes inward as a bullet smashes through the window near Walt, sending glass spraying across the floor. The morning sunlight catches in the shards, casting dancing rainbows across the walls. Walt barely flinches as he tightens his jaw. "Stay down," he reminds me as I move closer against the wall.

The baby kicks hard, responding to my fear and adrenaline. I force myself to take deep breaths, one hand on my belly, the other keeping the pistol ready. Captain Williams's warnings about stress and preterm labor echo in my mind, but there's nothing I can do about that now.

There's another explosion of gunfire, followed by a scream. Someone's hit. A female from the pitch of the voice. Was it Pearl? Alice? I hate being stuck here, helpless, while people I love are in danger. More shots ring out, followed by shouts and the sound of breaking glass. Someone else screams, a man's voice this time.

Walt shifts position slightly, keeping his rifle trained on the door while maintaining cover. "They're trying to circle around back," he says quietly. "Kevin already has people there. They'll know what to do, how to stop them."

As if to confirm his words, I hear shots from the ridge behind the house. The raiders' engines rev in response—they're moving, but whether they are retreating or repositioning, I can't tell.

"How many live here?" I ask, trying to calculate the odds in my head. "Those who know how to fight?"

"Enough." Walt's voice holds a certainty I want to believe. "Kevin's been preparing for something like this. Most of the ranches around here have been hit in the past month. It was just a matter of time. We know to band together. Hayward's men will help if they heard the call."

A sharp pain grips my abdomen. *Not now*, I plead silently. *Not now.* I focus on my breathing, trying to stay calm, trying to will my body to cooperate. The baby moves restlessly, responding to my tension.

More gunfire, but it sounds farther away now. The raiders must be pulling back. Walt doesn't relax his vigilance, though. He knows as well as I do that this could be a ruse, trying to draw us out.

"Looks like they're retreating," Walt confirms, but he doesn't lower his rifle. "Still, we wait for the all-clear."

Minutes crawl by like hours. Finally, we hear Shawn's voice calling out the code word they've established. "Sunrise!"

"Dawn's promise," Walt calls back, completing the exchange. Only then does he lower his weapon slightly. "Stay here. I'll check— "

The door opens before he can finish. Kevin stands there, blood running down one arm but his eyes alert. "We're clear. Got four of them. The rest ran."

"Casualties?" Walt asks the question I can't voice.

"Nothing fatal on our side. Opal and Mrs. Williams are working on them. Once they've finished triage, we'll take those who need it to the district hospital."

The relief makes me dizzy. Or maybe it's the aftereffects of the contraction—I'm not sure which. "Do they need me?" I ask, trying to focus.

Kevin shakes his head. "They're fine. Pearl— "

"Merissa?" Pearl's voice carries as she strides into the house, Gerry trotting at her heels, his nails clicking softly against the floor. He looks up at me, tail wagging, then nudges his nose against my hand like he knows something's wrong.

"Merissa, are you all right?" Pearl sounds strained but looks okay.

"I'm fine." My voice shakes. "The baby's fine too." I think. I hope.

Pearl appears before me, her eyes scanning the changes in my sleeping area. Gerry circles once before sitting neatly at her feet, glancing between us like he's keeping watch. Shaking her head, she tells Walt to put things back to right. "I thought we'd be safe here."

"Now, Miss Pearl," Walt drawls. "This here's just a minor setback. Like a fox in the henhouse—makes a ruckus but ain't nothing we can't handle."

"Minor setback?" Pearl's voice rises slightly as she helps me to the chair. "Those raiders had vehicles, Walt. Vehicles! This isn't some random group of desperados."

"Ain't nothing but troublemakers getting above their raising," Walt insists. "We showed 'em what for, didn't we?"

"Above their raising?" Pearl shakes her head as she starts organizing the bedding. "Sometimes I wonder about your expressions, Walt Cox."

"Been using them longer than you've known me, Miss Pearl," he says, helping her straighten the mattress. "And I ain't been wrong yet."

"That's debatable," Pearl mutters, but there's a fondness in her tone that takes any sting out of the words.

I watch them as they work, shaking my head at their familiar back-and-forth. I've seen this dance between them countless times since Livingston. The contraction catches me mid-smile, mild but definitely there, and I try to keep my face neutral. But Pearl's sharp eyes miss nothing.

"You're having pains, aren't you? I can see it in your face."

I nod reluctantly. "Two so far."

"Let's get you back into bed." Pearl turns to Walt. "Thank you for keeping her safe. Help me get her back to bed, then you go tell Opal and Alice what's happening with Merissa."

He meets her eyes and something unspoken passes between them. "Of course," he says simply, the teasing gone as Walt understands the need for seriousness.

The next hour passes in a blur of activity. The seriously injured are transported to the district hospital while Opal and Alice treat the rest. Somehow, Alice managed to get the babies to sleep and they, along with Nico, are in their bedroom upstairs.

Guards are posted, weapons are reloaded, and windows are boarded up. Abby maintains her watch near the front door and Walt at the window. Through it all, I'm forced to remain still while Pearl watches me for signs of labor. She has me drink a glass of water and lie on my left side, per Opal's orders. It's the same orders I'd give to a patient of mine.

There have been no additional contractions. False labor, brought on by stress. But it's a sharp reminder of how precarious my situation is. *A few more weeks*, I think, resting my hand on my belly. *Just stay put a little longer.*

"Try to rest," Pearl says, settling into a chair beside my bed. Gerry takes a spot on the floor next to her.

"Was it . . ." I hesitate, not sure I want to know. "Was it because of me? Do they know we're here?"

"No," Walt answers from his position by the window. "This is the fourth ranch hit this week. They're getting desperate, looking for food and supplies before winter's last push."

"But they had vehicles," I point out. "You said that was new."

"And concerning," he agrees. "We'll need to strengthen our defenses. This won't be the last attack."

Pearl reaches over with her good arm and takes my hand. "We'll be ready next time. We protect our own."

I squeeze her hand, thinking of how close we came to losing everything today. The baby kicks, as if in agreement, and I feel the fierce surge of maternal protection that's become so familiar these past months.

Outside, the sun continues its arc across the sky, indifferent to the violence that marked the morning. Inside, we begin the process of putting our world back together, knowing it could all fall apart again tomorrow. But for now, we're alive. We're together. And sometimes, in this broken world, that has to be enough.

Chapter 10

Katie

After two days of planning and countless radio calls, the biodiesel pickup finally pulls into view, arriving from the main hospital. From a treatment room window, I watch Dr. Elizabeth Powell step out of the passenger side, her coat pulled tight against the cold. Even from here, her sharp gaze sweeps the area, cataloging every guard stationed along the perimeter.

The past forty-eight hours have been a whirlwind. Nettie's condition is stable, but she remains withdrawn, spending most of her time in the converted office spaces of the med school building that we've made her temporary quarters. A steady stream of visitors—Stella, Kerry, Poppy Gardner, nursing students, and me—rotate in and out to sit with her. It helps, a little. But we all know she needs something more. Something beyond what any of us, or even a therapist, can give.

Through our conversations, it's become clear that Nettie needs to know God Himself—there is no substitute. When we talk, she describes feeling overwhelmed by darkness, using words like "depressing," "stifling," "helpless," "hopeless," and "defeated."

I understand these emotions deeply. My own experience has shown me how knowing God and Jesus can transform such darkness into light, offering hope and strength in life's bleakest moments.

I wish I could help Nettie understand that she doesn't have to bear this burden alone. God's grace knows no bounds, and His presence brings a peace that surpasses any earthly comfort. While faith isn't an instant solution, it offers a lifeline—one that can gradually transform despair into hope and defeat into victory. I pray she'll reach for it.

"Katie?" Dr. Reggie Murphy's voice startles me. He's standing in the doorway, fidgeting with his stethoscope. "The captain wants us in the conference room to meet Dr. Powell."

Something in his tone catches my attention. Tension? Uncertainty? Before I can analyze it further, he's gone, his footsteps quick against the linoleum.

Leo joins me in the hallway, his good arm brushing against mine. "You okay?"

"Just tired." It's true enough. Between regular shifts, watching Nettie, and worrying about our children, sleep has been elusive. "Did you see Murphy just now? He seemed . . ."

"Off?" Leo nods. "He's been jumpy since the captain announced Powell was coming. He worked with her at the main hospital before transferring here, so I'm not sure what that's about. Maybe he's just worried about how she'll assess Nettie."

"Maybe he likes her? Powell, I mean. He said they worked together, right? Maybe . . ."

Leo bops my nose. "Don't be playing matchmaker, Katie Burnett."

I widen my eyes in mock innocence. "Who, me? I'd never— "

"*Riiiight.* Merissa and Bowski?"

"I didn't put them together."

"But you have gone out of your way to make sure they find ways to spend time with each other."

"Yeah. Except that's on hold now. Even Bowski isn't risking leading anyone to Merissa and our kids. I'm not even sure he knows they've moved to Opal's place."

"Shaw's keeping Bowski apprised of things, just like he does us," Leo assures me. "But you're right. I think Bowski believes they're still at the safe house."

The break room is already crowded when we arrive. Even though Major Stone has yet to return from whatever mission he was sent off on, he's still claiming the office that used to belong to the captain, making the break room a pseudo-office.

Captain Williams stands near the window, deep in conversation with Dr. Powell. Up close, she's shorter than she appeared, probably not much over five feet, with steel-gray hair pulled back in a severe bun, but her eyes are kind when they meet mine. In many ways, she reminds me of my mom, though I can't pinpoint exactly why. Maybe it's the quiet authority she carries or the way her gaze seems to see more than what's on the surface.

The realization hits me like a wave—unexpected and bittersweet. It's comforting, but at the same time, it stirs an ache I thought I had buried. I suddenly miss Mom's voice, her warmth, and the way she always seemed to know what to say, no matter how impossible things felt.

This woman isn't her, of course, but for a fleeting moment, it feels like a small piece of my mom is standing here in the room with me. It's enough to make my throat tighten, and I have to look away before the emotion becomes too much to hide.

"Ah, Sergeant Burnett." The captain waves us over. "Dr. Powell, this is Katie Burnett, a nurse and one of our medical students. She's been instrumental in Dr. Wolff's care."

I swallow hard as I attempt to pull myself together. "Hello, Doctor. It's a pleasure to meet you."

"Please, call me Elizabeth." Her handshake is firm and confident. "I understand you found her?"

I nod, the memory still fresh. "She's doing better. More alert, though still . . ."

"Withdrawn?" Elizabeth suggests. "That's to be expected. I'd like to observe her interactions today before beginning formal sessions tomorrow." Her eyes sweep the room, lingering briefly on Murphy before continuing. "I understand you've arranged group sessions as well?"

"Yes," Captain Williams confirms. "We've had several people express interest." He quickly introduces Leo as Dr. Murphy shifts near the door. "Perhaps I should check on my patients— "

I tilt my head as I take Murphy in. I'd thought maybe it was a romance thing, but Murphy is probably in his midthirties, and Elizabeth is closer to sixty. I mean, it's possible, but . . .

"Actually," Elizabeth interrupts smoothly, "I'd value your input on Dr. Wolff's condition. You worked with her directly, correct?"

"Of course." Murphy's smile doesn't reach his eyes. "Although the captain has more experience with her. I've only been here a few weeks."

Something about the exchange feels off, but before I can process it, Captain Williams gathers the group's attention.

"You've all had a chance to meet Elizabeth Powell? We're fortunate to be able to have her with us for the next two weeks." He turns to her. "Dr. Powell?"

"Yes. Thank you. As some of you may know, your projects here, with the medical and nursing schools, are highly anticipated. We're hopeful that your model will be something we can duplicate. Higher education, as we once knew it, is unlikely to return anytime soon. Doctors and nurses—and therapists—will continue to be in high need." She pauses as she glances around the room, making eye contact with as many of us as possible.

"While I'm here, we'll treat this as something like clinical clerkship. It'll be brief and not nearly as in-depth as necessary, but I hope to give you some useful knowledge to help your community. And not to worry. While I'm here, I'll also do what I can as a medical doctor. Even though psychiatry is my specialty, I did go to medical school and had all the rotations." She gives a smile that is brimming with confidence.

"We look forward to learning from you," the captain says. "That's not all. Depending on how things go, we're discussing sending you out one or two at a time to train with Dr. Powell and the other therapists at the main hospital. This will take some organization and planning and is unlikely to happen before the weather improves, but the more mental health knowledge each of us has, the better."

"Indeed," Elizabeth agrees. "Some of you will be more likely to embrace this than others. For those, we may even wish you to have more comprehensive training. Dr. Williams—um, excuse me, *Captain* Williams, has made a schedule to allow everyone to sit in on several of the sessions. You'll be there to observe. There will also be a special one-on-one session with each of you where you'll be the client. We want to ensure all of you are feeling heard and getting the support you need."

The discussion about the doctor's visit and the accompanying plans lasts around twenty minutes. As it concludes, Williams instructs us to check the schedule for our assigned times for both the community sessions and the separate meeting for medical staff. All therapy sessions are set to take place in the med school's conference room.

As the group files out, Williams has me stay behind. "Dr. Powell wants you there for her initial meeting with Nettie."

"Okay," I agree, not sure how I can help.

Elizabeth gathers her bag. "I'd like Dr. Murphy to join us as well. That is if you think the three of you can be spared for a bit."

Dr. Murphy is shaking his head, but the captain quickly says, "That'll be fine. We're just across the parking lot and can easily be retrieved if needed."

The walk from the hospital to Nettie's room in the medical school gives me time to study our visitor more carefully. She moves with purpose, asking precise questions about Nettie's treatment. When Williams answers, she listens intently, her head tilted slightly as if cataloging each response.

Dr. Murphy seems to be dragging his feet, walking behind the rest of us and not participating in the conversation.

Nettie's sitting up when we enter, a book open in her lap. She smiles but her eyes widen slightly. Stella is sitting with her, reading her own book.

"Dr. Wolff." Elizabeth steps forward. "I'm Elizabeth Powell."

"You can call me Nettie."

"Thank you. And please, call me Elizabeth." Her smile is warm and inviting.

Nettie visibly relaxes as she gives a nod. Her gaze travels to the rest of us. "Is it going to be a group session?"

Dr. Powell laughs. "No. Not exactly. I did want to go over the treatment you've been receiving and thought it would be wise to have doctors Williams and Murphy here. I've reviewed the chart notes, but sometimes it's better to talk about it." She glances around the room. "Can we bring some chairs in?"

"We can," the captain agrees. "Or we could move to the conference room. We have a fire going in there."

"Nettie? Do you have a preference?" Elizabeth asks.

"Either is fine." Nettie's voice is stronger than it's been, though still quiet. "A fire probably would feel nice."

"Will you need me?" Stella asks.

"For the first few minutes, while we review everything. Then you and the others will be able to leave." She turns toward me. "Dr. Burnett, I'd like you to stay and chat with us." She turns back toward Nettie. "Are you okay with that?"

With a shrug, Nettie agrees that it's fine.

"Um . . . okay," I say. "I can stay, but I'm not a doctor. You can just call me Katie. Or Sergeant."

Her eyebrows shoot up. "Oh, yes. I should have noticed your uniform. You and your husband are the remains of the United Volunteers, correct?"

"Right."

Stella and the male doctors are only with us for about fifteen minutes before Elizabeth tells them she has enough info. To be honest, I'm not entirely sure what she gained from the meeting. We already discussed everything on the walk over. I did notice she watched Nettie during the question-and-answer session. Maybe there was a hidden reason I'm not aware of.

Before the others leave, Elizabeth asks Murphy to stoke the fire for us. Her posture remains composed, but her focus is sharp, eyes locked on Murphy as he works. She sits at the table, one hand resting on her notebook, the other lightly gripping her pen, though she isn't writing. Her stillness is deliberate, almost calculated, as if she's quietly dissecting his every move.

When he's finished, she seems to relax slightly. "Thank you, Reggie. I'll have Sergeant Burnett walk me back shortly. Perhaps you and I can spend some time catching up?"

"Uh, yep. Sure," he mutters before scurrying out of the room.

Nettie and I exchange a look that includes her lifting a shoulder. I'm glad to know I'm not the only one who is finding Dr. Murphy's behavior odd.

The next hour reveals Elizabeth's skill. She guides the conversation naturally, letting Nettie set the pace. When Nettie mentions Alisa, Elizabeth doesn't push, just offers quiet support. By the end, some of the tension has left Nettie's shoulders.

"I'll see you tomorrow morning," Elizabeth promises. "Perhaps we could walk a bit if you feel up to it?"

After Nettie agrees, we walk her back to her room, where Stella is waiting. Following a brief goodbye, I trail Elizabeth into the hall. She pauses, her attention lingering on the schedule pinned near the nurses' station, as if studying it.

"Tell me," she says quietly, "how long has Dr. Murphy been handling complex cases here?"

The question catches me off guard. "He's only been here about a month. Didn't he come directly from the main hospital?"

"Mm." She makes a note in her small notebook. "He was at the main hospital, but also took a rotating spot. Did he work here as a rotating doctor before coming on permanently?"

I shake my head.

"And he's fully involved in the medical training program?"

"Do you mean with training the doctors and nurses?"

"Yes, is he one of the instructors?"

"He assists, yes. We do rounds with him, but he doesn't teach in the classrooms. Is something wrong?"

She closes her notebook with a snap. "Not necessarily. I'm simply gathering information." Her eyes meet mine. "Sometimes people aren't exactly who they claim to be. Especially since the apocalypse changed everything."

Before I can ask what she means, Kerry Hendricks appears at the end of the hall. "Dr. Powell? The captain wants to discuss the group session schedule. He sent me over to ask if you'd meet with him."

"Of course." She touches my arm briefly. "We'll talk more later. Will you walk back to the hospital with us?"

"I'll be there shortly. I need to stop by my apartment."

I watch them walk away, Elizabeth's posture relaxed but alert. Something about the conversation about Murphy niggles at my mind, like a puzzle piece that doesn't quite fit.

"Everything okay?" Nettie asks as she and Stella appear at my side. Both are dressed to go outside.

Surprise registers on my face. Nettie responds with a shrug. "Dr. Powell's suggestion of a walk sounded good. Stella thought so too."

Stella's smile includes a slight raise of her eyebrows.

"Good," I agree. "It's warmed up a little bit, so it should be nice."

As the women walk away, I head to my room. The whole thing about Murphy is weird, and Dr. Powell's questions remind me of when Leo and I were at the main hospital and spoke with the orthopedist, Bollinger. That doctor mentioned reminding Captain Williams to send him evaluation reports. Could there be a connection?

"Oh! Of course," I say aloud, shaking my head. Bollinger must've told Dr. Powell to check on Murphy. Make sure things are going okay with our latest drama. No doubt everyone's heard about Captain Williams losing control of the hospital—a bizarre twist.

He still oversees medical operations, but Major Stone, a National Guard officer with no medical background, has the final word. Rumor is it's to teach Williams a lesson after he protected his wife from Melvin Cabal. Williams doesn't regret it, though, and insists he'd do it all again.

For a time, we feared he and Alice might actually face charges, but the military cleared him, and civilian law has their hands full of current worries. Our relief was short-lived when Stone took over the hospital, vowing to implement changes. Thankfully, whatever pulled Stone away from Rapid City has kept him out of the picture for now. But does he know about Nettie? That she tried to end her own life?

If he does, I can't shake the feeling he'd twist it into another strike against Captain Williams—for reasons no one can figure out. We're not even sure why Stone was called away. The details are sketchy.

Lieutenant David Paul says he doesn't even know. He does know he took a small team with him, including a captain he's worked with for years and several of the enlisted men he personally chose. Paul wasn't even told exactly where they'd gone. He insists that isn't uncommon. His rank doesn't warrant knowing what those above him are doing.

If Stone wanted us to know, we would. The fact that we don't means only one thing. Whatever he's doing, it's not meant for our eyes—or our questions.

Chapter 11

Merissa

Two days after the attempted raid, I'm dozing in the afternoon sun when the sound of approaching horses pulls me from my half-sleep. Shifting position, I peer through the front window.

It's Poppy Gardner. Tall and willowy, she still carries a trace of elegance from her modeling days. Her loosely tied auburn hair gleams in the sunlight, coppery highlights catching the eye. She's driving one of the hospital wagons—and she's not alone. Beside her sits a woman, while between them a young boy huddles, his shoulders drawn tight against the cold.

Pearl appears in the doorway connecting to the kitchen. "Poppy's early for your check-up."

"And she's brought company," I say, unable to keep the worry from my voice. We've been so careful about keeping my location secret. Each new person who knows increases the risk.

Pearl moves to the window with Gerry by her side, watching as the trio climbs out of the wagon. Walt and Shawn are also there, helping them down. "That'll be the psychiatrist the captain mentioned in his note. The one who's been helping at the hospital." She pauses, studying my face. "You're worried."

"Aren't you? We don't know her."

"We know the captain. He wouldn't send anyone here he didn't trust completely."

"And who else is with them?"

Before Pearl can respond, the front door opens. Poppy enters first, her cheeks red from the cold. "Merissa! Pearl! Beautiful day for a ride, though I think winter's got at least a few more storms brewing."

The boy follows her in, his eyes darting around the room before fixating on the floor. His coat is too big for him, probably borrowed, and his dark hair needs to be cut. Behind him comes the psychiatrist, a woman much shorter than Poppy, dressed practically for the cold. As she removes her stocking cap, she sends a smile in my direction.

Standing at the doorway is Abby, ever present to keep me safe, and shaking her head. She's not at all happy about the appearance of extra people. Gerry, too, seems to be shaking his head as he sniffs the air.

"Pearl, Merissa, this is Dr. Powell," Poppy says, helping the boy out of his coat. "And this young man is looking for a place to stay. His mother passed at the hospital two days ago."

The boy's shoulders tense at the mention of his mother, but he doesn't look up. Dr. Powell places a gentle hand on his shoulder.

"You must be Robert," Opal says, coming down from upstairs. "I'm so pleased to meet you."

The boy nods but keeps his eyes on his shoes. "I was just finishing getting your room ready. You'll share with another boy. He's a few years older than you at sixteen. I heard you're twelve, is that right?"

"I'll be thirteen in a few weeks," he mutters.

"Perfect. You and Jason will share. Nico and the babies also sleep upstairs."

He lifts his gaze quickly before dropping it again. "Babies?"

"They're asleep right now, but you'll meet them soon. They're only a few months old."

I watch his face and see a small smile, along with a nod. "I heard you have horses?"

"That's right. Horses, cattle, chickens, and goats. Have you had animals before?"

"We had a dog. He died a few years ago."

"We have dogs too. Have you already met Gerry?" She motions to the pup, who wags his tail, thumping it against the floor. "And barn cats. Would you like to go upstairs and see your bedroom?"

He quickly looks at Dr. Powell, who gives a nod. "If you're ready, go on with Mrs. Maher."

"You can call me Opal. Everyone does."

His nod of agreement is followed by him slowly walking behind her toward the staircase. I half expect him to look back at the doctor before he takes the first step, but he doesn't. It probably helps that Opal is talking to him the entire way, telling him more about the barn cats and how one of the mothers is expecting a litter.

Once Robert and Opal have reached the top of the stairs, Dr. Powell turns toward me. "Thank you for allowing me to visit. I've heard much about you from Katie Burnett."

"Have you?" I try to keep my tone neutral, but Pearl shoots me a warning look.

"Nothing scandalous," Dr. Powell assures me with a mischievous smile. "Just that you're someone she trusts completely. When Poppy mentioned she was bringing Robert here, I asked to accompany her. I've been trying to visit as many of our scattered community members as possible. These times take their toll on everyone's mental health. Plus, I heard you have a boy here that could use some extra attention."

She's referring to Jason Wheeler. Jason came to live with Opal a few months ago after an unfortunate incident. He and the men he was traveling with were crossing the neighbor's land. Hayward, who we later found out was having his own mental health issues, sicced his dogs on the trio. The mauling left Jason injured and the other two dead.

Opal has done her best to help Jason through things, but he's recently taken to various forms of self-harm, such as cutting. This is often referred to as nonsuicidal self-injury or NSSI. Having a psychiatrist visit with him will hopefully help. And, if nothing else, I should be grateful the doctor is here for that.

But I also realize Jason could have gone to her. Shawn makes regular trips into town to deliver meat and other items to the ration centers. He could have taken Jason in for a visit instead of compromising our security by bringing a stranger here.

Pearl gestures to a chair. "Please, sit. Would you like some tea?"

"That would be lovely, thank you."

"Poppy?" Pearl asks as she steps toward the kitchen.

I catch Poppy's eyes following Pearl, her expression attentive as she observes each motion.

"None for me, thanks. I heard you had some injuries from the attack the other day." She motions toward the plastic-covered window. "Thought I'd check on them while I'm here. Make sure they're healing fine."

"Do you know where the infirmary is?" Pearl asks.

Poppy nods as she rebuttons her coat. Meeting my gaze, she says, "I'll be back soon." She pauses. "Where's my mind? I almost forgot about the notes I brought." She reaches into an inside pocket and pulls out several folded pieces of paper. "Something for everyone." She smiles as she hands them to Pearl.

My heart skips a beat. What I'd like more than anything is to be able to go to a private spot and devour the note Bowski sent me. Instead, I thank Poppy as she walks toward the door.

As Pearl puts my letter on my nightstand, I take the chance to study Dr. Powell. Her demeanor is poised yet approachable, every movement measured and intentional. She doesn't glance around the room or pry into why I'm here. Instead, she remains still, waiting patiently for Pearl to return with the tea.

"How are things in town?" I ask, unable to help myself. "At the hospital?"

"Things seem fine," she answers carefully. "I understand there's been some changes lately with the National Guard taking over. We've had similar struggles at the main hospital, though not to the same extent."

"People are accepting the change to the Guard running things?"

"It's different is all. We didn't have someone like Captain Williams at the helm. And while an officer has been assigned to oversee things, she's more of a figurehead only. Though I will say, she's been very supportive of getting our mental health ward into place."

"That's good. Definitely helpful," I reply, biting back any comment about how unhelpful Major Stone has been throughout this transition. At least his absence on his top-secret mission has given the staff a much-needed break.

Alice mentioned more about it in a letter from the captain, though the reason for Stone being called away remains a mystery. Word has it he's taken a small team with him to handle . . . something. Whatever it is, one thing's certain. Once Stone gets back, he'll waste no time making life miserable for everyone in the Guard District Hospital. "And Katie? The others?"

Dr. Powell's expression softens. "They're well. Worried about you, of course, but managing. Katie's thrown herself into her work, which helps. She misses the children terribly. I promised her I'd bring back all the news I could. Mrs. Maher said the babies are sleeping. And the older boy? Nico?"

"Also napping, much to his dismay. He insists he's much too old but always falls asleep anyway. The boy—Robert," I say. "We've heard little about him. Shawn was only given a note that he needed a place to stay."

The whistle of the kettle pauses her response. When the quiet returns, she smiles. "He needs stability and routine. A chance to grieve in a safe place. Much like you need rest and peace to bring your child safely into this world."

I tense slightly. "What exactly have you heard about my situation?"

"Only that you're on bed rest and need to avoid stress." She leans forward in her chair. "Would you like to talk about how you're handling that? It can't be easy, being confined when your instincts surely tell you to be up and doing things."

The offer is gentle and professional, but I hesitate. "I appreciate the offer, but . . ."

"But you don't know me," she finishes. "And in your situation, that's wise. Let me be clear. I understand you're here for your safety. I've been told the barest of details, and that is enough. My role is simply to offer support to those who need it."

Pearl, carrying a tray with tea, moves carefully toward us. "Merissa's not just worried for herself."

Dr. Powell nods. "Of course. You're protecting your child. Not just yours but the ones upstairs. Katie told me how fond you've grown of them. And Alice? Dr. Williams's wife. I've heard about her. Is she here?"

Something in her tone, the way she speaks of Katie and the children, eases some of my tension. Still, I look at Pearl, who's always been excellent at reading people.

"Alice is out in the barn," Pearl responds. "She's been helping with the chores while the babies nap."

"That's good. I'm sure it helps her to stay busy."

"Perhaps you could tell us more about your work with those you've been seeing?" Pearl asks. "The ones struggling with our new reality?"

For the next few minutes, Dr. Powell talks about her work and her observations of how different people cope with trauma and loss. She's insightful but never pushes too hard, never pries too deep. When we hear sounds on the stairs, she pauses.

"I should visit with Robert," she says. "Make sure he's feeling good about this. But I'd like to return if you're willing. Sometimes it helps just to have someone to talk to who isn't directly involved in your situation."

Smiling, I shrug. "I'm not sure that's necessary. But some of the others here— "

"Oh, yes. Captain Williams asked me to visit with young Mr. Wheeler. I'll make sure I do that." She smoothly gets to her feet as Robert and Opal appear at the base of the stairs. "Well, Robert, should we take a look around the ranch?"

"Okay," he agrees, still avoiding eye contact.

"I'll send Poppy in to do your exam," Dr. Powell says as she and Robert get into their winter gear. Opal also dresses to go outside.

After they're gone, I glance out the window, catching a glimpse of Dr. Powell as she walks with Robert toward the barn, her measured steps matching his hesitant ones. There's something reassuring about how she moves through our world, calm and purposeful, as if mental healing is just as important as physical survival.

Chapter 12

Merissa

After they're gone, Pearl lifts her eyebrows at me. "She seems nice enough." She reaches down to pet Gerry's head. "For a shrink."

I can't help but laugh—Pearl has a way about her. The kind that used to drive me crazy but, over the past few months, I've learned to accept. She says exactly what's on her mind, often with a sharp edge, but if she loves you, she'll move mountains for you.

For years, during my marriage to Braedon, I felt her disapproval. Disappointed in her son's choice of a wife? Absolutely. We clashed often, and I was sure I'd never measure up in her eyes. But over time, something shifted. After the EMP, as we all fought to survive, the tension between us eased. Maybe she mellowed. Maybe I did.

When Braedon and Tomas died, Courtney—my sister-in-law—decided to head west to find the remnants of her family. I knew I couldn't leave Pearl behind. I didn't just need to stay with her; I wanted to. Moving to South Dakota, where her sister Opal lived, felt like the right decision.

Pearl and I make small talk for the few minutes it takes for Poppy to return. "Everyone looks like they're healing well." She smiles as she removes her coat. "I'm just glad it wasn't worse. When we heard about the trouble, it took everything Captain Williams had not to rush out here himself. The Burnetts too."

"Seems there's always some kind of threat, no matter where we are these days." The disgust in Pearl's voice is evident.

"I suppose that's the truth," Poppy agrees. "Now, let's get you checked. Are you okay with your mother-in-law staying?"

"Sure."

We're quiet as she works. "Blood pressure's good. Any more contractions since Sunday?"

"No. Just the two during the raid."

"You were here?" She motions to the broken window.

"Sort of." As I describe Walt's setup for protecting me, her face grows serious. "That was smart of him to have you secured, but still . . ." She sighs. "Did you speak with Elizabeth?"

"Dr. Powell? Some."

"She's here to help. I've worked with her enough to trust her completely. She's helped Katie tremendously with her separation from the children and has been a lifeline for Dr. Wolff."

"Nettie Wolff?"

Poppy meets my gaze. "You haven't heard?"

"Is something wrong with her?"

Swallowing, she gives a slow nod. "She tried to take her life. Katie found her in time, and she's doing better, but Elizabeth plans to stay a few weeks to work with Dr. Wolff and do community sessions. There have been many similar incidents. We're entering what could be considered a mental health crisis."

"Why'd Nettie do it?"

She shrugs. "I'm not certain. I'm just glad she's getting the help she needs. And that others are too. There's even talk that Elizabeth might remain past the planned time to help train the doctors. Maybe give them more ways to recognize problems. Like the boy . . . the one living here— "

"Jason."

"Yes. Captain Williams was already speaking with her about his situation. Then, when Dr. Wolff . . . well, it just made sense for her to visit. To help. Too bad she's here at the same time that creepy Bollinger's on rotation. He's supposed to arrive on the first of March. At least Major Stone is still gone. That man . . ." She shakes her head.

"Rumor is, he's taken several people from the Guard to use on whatever it is he's doing. I'm not even sure General Truss knows what the major is up to. He took a captain too. Rangler—do you know him?"

I shake my head.

Poppy scoffs. "You're not missing anything. I knew him before the EMP—he's as bad as Stone, maybe worse. Neither of them are an officer or a gentleman. In my opinion, they both lack basic human decency. Two peas in a pod, neither worth the trouble. And now, they've taken others with them. Some I don't know, but at least one was a menace even before the EMP. The only reason he got into the

Guard was because Rangler vouched for him. What does that tell you?"

I shrug. "I don't know any of them except Stone, so . . ."

"Humph. If you know Stone, you know them." She takes a breath, as if composing herself. "I'm going to measure you."

As she takes my fundal measurement, I sift through the mountain of information she's unloaded on me. Poppy's like a walking newspaper—happy to share the latest gossip under the guise of news.

My thoughts drift to Bollinger being here. He and Dr. Wolff had some kind of relationship back when she worked at the main hospital. From what I've heard, it didn't end well. Did his looming arrival as a rotating doc push her toward that suicide attempt?

Nettie's a good doctor—quiet, reserved, but skilled. Especially considering the circumstances she's been thrust into. She was just a med student doing an internship when everything fell apart.

"You've grown." Poppy smiles. "Must be the fresh farm air."

"And the increased food," Pearl adds. "The ranch isn't under the same ration system as those living in town."

"That's a plus, for sure. Did you get a chance to visit with Elizabeth? Anything you wish to discuss with her? You can trust her, you know."

"It's not that I don't want to trust her," I say, wincing as the baby delivers a particularly strong kick. "But every person who knows where I am— "

"Increases the risk." Poppy takes my hand. "But sometimes we need to balance physical safety with emotional well-being. You're isolated here, dealing with so much. It might help to have someone to talk to who understands trauma and grief."

"I have Pearl," I protest. "And I'm not exactly isolated. Have you seen how many people live on this ranch? It's almost a small town in itself."

"That's true." Poppy's voice softens. "And how much do you tell all these people about your fears? I'll be back to check you next week. Hopefully, that awful Major Stone will still be gone. He insists on us reporting to him every minute of every day."

"If he's back, will you be able to get here?"

"I'll figure something out. I promise." Poppy smiles. "I can bring Elizabeth with me."

I glance at Pearl, not wanting to admit that one of my biggest fears is losing her.

Pearl meets my gaze, and her weathered face shifts into a small smile. "Poppy, would you mind examining me while you're here?"

"Have you been ill?" Her eyes go wide. "Were you injured in the attack?"

Pearl waves her hand. "Nothing like that. I was in the safe room, sound and secure. Though if something like that happens again, I'll make sure I'm with Merissa." She sends me a smile before turning her attention back to Poppy. "I have a couple of bumps. Spoke with the captain about them before things went crazy."

As Pearl details what the captain told her, I watch her mannerisms. She moves carefully as she points out where the bumps—which are really lumps—were found.

I look away, blinking back sudden tears.

The exam takes many minutes. Poppy takes copious notes so she can report back to the captain. As they wrap up, she says, "Since I haven't examined you previously, it's hard for me to say if things have advanced. But clinically . . ." Her voice fades away as she shrugs.

"I understand." Pearl nods. "My main goal right now is to be here for Merissa. To make sure she's safe and the baby is safe. What I want more than anything is to see him born."

Later, after Poppy and Dr. Powell have left with promises to return next week, I watch from my window as Opal shows Robert around the yard. His shoulders aren't quite as hunched now, and I even see him smile at something she says.

"He'll do well here," Pearl says, joining me at the window. "Opal has a way with lost souls."

"Like she did with you?" I tease, trying to lighten my own mood.

"Like she did with all of us." Pearl sits in her chair beside my bed. "Even if she is my baby sister, she's always had a way about her. A way that made people feel safe. What did you think of Dr. Powell?"

I consider the question carefully. "She seems genuine. But can we trust her?"

"I think we can. More importantly, I think we might need to." Pearl's hand drifts to her side, where the lumps are. "None of us knows what's coming, Merissa. We all need someone to talk to sometimes."

Through the window, I watch as Opal leads the boy back toward the house. Another soul seeking shelter in this broken world. Another life changed forever by circumstances beyond their control. Maybe Pearl and Poppy are right. Maybe sometimes the bigger risk is in not trusting, but in trying to carry everything alone.

The baby shifts within me, and I rest my hand on my belly, feeling the strong movements that have become so familiar. In just a few weeks, this child will join our family, never knowing the world that came before. Never knowing his father or the life we might have had. But he will know love, safety, and the strength that comes from learning to trust again.

My gaze drifts to the note on the nightstand. I'm eager to read it but am holding off until later when the house is quiet and I can have some privacy. A part of me feels like everything I need is already here, along with Bowski's notes. Writing in my journal—and writing back to him—feels like all the therapy I could ever ask for.

"I'll think about it," I tell Pearl, and she smiles, understanding all I'm not saying.

Outside, the winter sun begins its early descent, casting long shadows across the snow. Another day ends, bringing us closer to whatever changes tomorrow will bring. For now, we have this moment of peace, this small victory of another life saved, another soul finding refuge. In this new world, sometimes that has to be enough.

Chapter 13

Katie

A week into Dr. Powell's visit, the changes with Nettie are noticeable. She's eating better, participating in group sessions, and even helped with inventory yesterday. But this morning, her anxiety is back, evident in the way she keeps glancing at the calendar on the wall and checking her watch.

"Dr. Bollinger arrives tomorrow," she says quietly as I suggest we take a break. "Elizabeth thinks maybe I should stay in my room while he's here."

The suggestion surprises me. Bollinger is scheduled to stay for two weeks. "Because of what happened between you?"

She nods, her fingers plucking at a loose thread on her sleeve. "It wasn't just the relationship. I mean, it was the relationship, but mostly it's because of the way I am when I'm around him. Then the whole thing with Chastity. That's still embarrassing, and— " The sound of footsteps in the hall cuts her off.

Dr. Murphy appears in the doorway, his usual nervous energy even more pronounced today. "Sergeant Burnett, the captain needs you."

I give Nettie a look. She responds with a nod. "I'll finish up here and then head to the break room." I must give her a look of concern because she reaches her hand out and touches my arm. "Don't worry. I'm fine."

"Now," Murphy insists. "He said it's urgent."

The edge in his voice makes me look up sharply. His face is pale, almost sickly, and he won't meet my eyes. Before I can question him further, he's gone.

"He's been acting strange," Nettie observes. "Ever since Elizabeth arrived."

"You're sure you're okay on your own?"

"I'm fine. Glad to be able to do something around here. Maybe I'll be able to see patients soon. Just simple cases."

I give her a smile. That has been discussed, but I'm not sure Elizabeth believes she's ready, and now with Bollinger arriving . . . "I'll meet you in the break room."

Leo intercepts me in the hallway, excitement evident in his features despite the early hour. "Bollinger's coming tomorrow."

"I heard." I touch his good arm, sharing his anticipation. Nearly six months of limited mobility has been hard on him. "Maybe you'll finally get cleared for full duty."

"That's the hope." He falls into step beside me. "But if I do, we'll need to make a decision about the National Guard."

My stomach tightens at his words. We haven't discussed it much lately, but I think that's still his goal. Once upon a time, it was mine too. Now, after everything that's happened, I'm not sure what I want to do.

The captain's voice drifts from an empty patient room. ". . . and Poppy says Pearl's condition is concerning."

We enter to find Williams deep in conversation with Shaw and Dr. Powell. Poppy stands near the woodstove, warming her hands.

"Katie, Leo." Poppy's smile is genuine but tired. "We were just discussing the plans for Tuesday's visit to check on Merissa."

"I have a letter for Nico," I say. "It's in my room. I can run and grab it."

"Poppy will stop by on Tuesday morning," Captain Williams assures me. "You can give it to her then. Let's discuss the treatment plan."

Poppy turns to face us. "Merissa is still on strict bed rest. She had a few contractions during the attempted raid on the ranch."

My lips press into a tight line. The news of the raid had been concerning. Both Poppy and Elizabeth said they were assured it was easily stopped. Upon hearing about it, Shaw sent a team out to the farm. His guard that is there told him they believe it to be similar to the attacks that have been happening on other farms and ranches in the area and not because of Hugo's operation.

We all discussed moving them back to town but, in the end, decided they were probably still safer on the Maher ranch than here. Plus, Nico is having a wonderful time. At the safe house in town, he wasn't even able to go outside for fear of being discovered. But there, he loves the outdoors and farm life.

"Even with that scare," Poppy continues, "I'm optimistic she'll carry to term." She pauses before glancing at the captain. "Pearl, though . . ."

Williams shakes his head. "We'll discuss that privately."

The exchange of looks between them sends a chill down my spine. Before I can ask, Murphy bursts in.

"Captain, we need you in treatment room two. The chainsaw victim from last week, his wound's infected."

As Williams hurries out, Dr. Powell's eyes follow Murphy. There's something calculating in her gaze that reminds me of her earlier questions about his experience.

"Speaking of infections," Shaw says, "we may have one in our investigation. I think we've identified another member of Hugo's operation."

That gets everyone's attention. "Who?" Leo asks.

"Can't say yet. But we're close. Very close." Shaw adjusts his gun belt. "Once we round them all up, once we know you're safe, we'll bring your kids home."

Home. The word echoes in my mind. But where is home now? Here in Rapid City, where danger lurks around every corner? Or back in Bakerville, where our medical training could help our old community?

"Katie?" Dr. Powell's voice pulls me from my thoughts. "A moment?"

She leads me down the hall to one of our storage rooms. "I need to know everything about Dr. Murphy's involvement in patient care. Particularly any unusual outcomes or questionable decisions."

"Why?"

"Because I'm increasingly convinced he's not who he claims to be." She glances toward the door. "And in our line of work, false credentials can be deadly."

"I don't understand. He worked with you at the main hospital. He was sent to us after you all vetted him, right?"

She lifts a shoulder. "Sometimes we see only what people want us to see. Then, later, new information comes to light."

"Look, if there's a problem, tell the captain." My words have more snap than I intend. I clear my throat. "Did you tell the captain?"

Her mouth goes into a tight line. "Chris Williams is aware of my concerns. But with the situation concerning him, he's understandably hesitant to move forward with anything that may— "

A crash from the treatment room interrupts us. Then shouting and running feet.

"I need some help in here!" Murphy's voice rings out. "The patient's crashing!"

We rush toward the commotion, but Dr. Powell grabs my arm. "Watch Murphy," she whispers. "Watch how he handles this."

As we enter treatment room two, I see the captain starting chest compressions. Murphy stands back, hands shaking, face ashen.

"Dr. Murphy," Williams calls, "we need you to— "

Murphy's already backing toward the door. "I'll get . . . I'll get Stella."

"No time! Get over here."

Murphy pales further and shakes his head. "Of course. I— "

"Now!"

"He's crashing," I note, taking in the patient's pale, clammy skin. His hands shake as he tries to sit up, only to fall back against the pillows. "Murphy, what did you give him for the infection?"

"Pokeroot tincture." Murphy grabs the treatment chart.

"Pokeroot?" I repeat, shaking my head. That isn't what I'd reach for to treat an infection.

"How much?" Captain Williams's voice is sharp.

Murphy checks his notes. "Um . . . I'm not sure."

The patient retches suddenly, violently. His eyes are growing glassy, and lethargy is setting in, even as his body tries to purge itself.

"Is it a reaction to the medication?" I ask.

"Looks more like an overdose," the captain replies. "Burnett, help me get him on his side. We need to clear his stomach—now!"

I grab the necessary supplies while Captain Williams explains the procedure to our increasingly drowsy patient. Dr. Powell assists in positioning him while Murphy stands back, his face a mask of concern.

"Could the tincture have been more concentrated than usual?" Powell asks, her tone carefully neutral.

"I followed the standard preparation," Murphy responds. "Unless . . ."

"Questions later," Williams cuts in. "Let's focus on saving him first."

Working quickly, we perform a gastric lavage, using a tube to empty the contents of his stomach. It's not a pleasant procedure, but gradually his symptoms begin to ease. His color improves and the lethargy lifts.

"That could have been fatal," Powell observes quietly.

"Indeed," the captain agrees. "Pokeroot is powerful medicine—the line between therapeutic and toxic is razor thin." He meets Murphy's gaze. "And not what we'd usually use for an infection like this."

"But it treats infections," Murphy says quickly. "The tincture must have been stronger than I realized."

"Must have been," Powell agrees, but her eyes never leave Murphy's face. "We should check the bottle's concentration. Where is it?"

"Why did you use pokeroot?" I ask, retrieving the bottle from the medicine bin.

Murphy frowns. "For his infection. I already said that."

"Did you check the treatment manual?"

Before Murphy can respond, Shaw appears in the doorway. "Captain, a moment? It's urgent."

"Keep monitoring him," Williams tells me, gesturing to our recovering patient. "Dr. Murphy, stay with Katie. Log his vitals every fifteen minutes."

As they step into the hall, I check our patient's pulse. Steady now, stronger. The gastric lavage did its job. But something nags at me.

Stella's organizational system for the tinctures is meticulous, with careful labels showing concentrations. We've all been trained repeatedly on proper dosing. And we've been trained on what to use. If there's a question, we have a medical treatment book in each room. I glance at the book, sitting where it should be but still closed. Normally, we'd open it to the correct page and leave it there during the treatment. Did he try to treat by guessing?

"I'll check his vitals," I say to Murphy. He's not even paying attention. Instead, he's looking out to the hallway where the captain and Shaw are huddled close together.

"Can I help?" Elizabeth asks, her eyes on Murphy.

"I'll finish his vitals and then do a wound check. Dr. Murphy?"

"Yeah?"

"Were you able to clean his wound?"

"Um, no. I was going to have one of the nurses do that."

"Okay. Well, I'll take care of that."

"Great, thanks. I'm taking a break." Murphy is already out the door.

Elizabeth and I watch him go. She makes a clucking noise with her tongue before saying, "Well, then. Good thing I've been helping out so much this week. You and I can get Murphy's patient sorted out."

I finish checking vitals before we move on to assessing the wound. The patient has stirred a few times but seems to be resting easily. His pulse is steady, his BP is normal, and he's breathing without difficulty. This was a close call.

Is Murphy right? Was it a mistake anyone could make? Did he try to treat from memory instead of checking the dose? Even though Elizabeth seems to have her suspicions about Murphy, this doesn't mean anything regarding his abilities as a doctor. It may show he was careless or in a hurry, but I'm not sure it's at all conclusive.

As we're completing the wound check, we hear the squawk of the CB on the nurses' desk. With the door closed, we can't hear what is said.

A sharp knock at the door startles both of us. Leo pokes his head in. "We're under lockdown."

"Lockdown?" Elizabeth asks, more curious than concerned.

"Why?" I ask, my voice cracking as I consider what this means.

"Unknown. The CB and walkie-talkies are both going off. Something's happening at Camp Rapid. Shaw isn't too happy about being stuck in here with us." He raises his eyebrows while he gives a nod. "Lock the door and secure the shutters."

"Where will you be?" I ask as I move toward him.

"Patient room. I'll see you soon." He gives me a quick kiss, a rarity in public, before reminding me to lock the door.

My hands are shaking as I engage the locks.

Elizabeth is standing near the window, peering out. "I don't see anything amiss."

"We can't see Camp Rapid from here. Let's get the shutters closed." The internal shutters, made of slabs of hardwood, slide shut on a track system. The hope is if bullets start flying, we'll be protected, but we'll do other things too.

"Let's move the gurney." We take our patient's gurney to the corner, out of the path of projectiles, and then I move the metal medicine cart, the same kind used for storing tools, into place in front of the bed.

"Pull a couple of chairs over," I say as I take my sidearm from its holster. If the room is breached, I want to be ready to protect our patient and us. I already know Elizabeth doesn't carry a gun. The captain asked her on the day she arrived. She made a point of saying she knows it's common now, but she just can't wrap her head around actually doing it.

When we're in place and as secure as we can be, Elizabeth leans back in her chair. She doesn't seem very bothered by the situation. I've been in lockdowns before, and my heart rate is responding as it usually does. It's elevated and I'm nervous. My eyes keep darting toward the door.

"Shall I check our patient's vitals?" she asks.

"Um, yes. That's a good idea."

"You keep watch." There's a note of teasing in her voice. "I'll handle it."

"You think I'm being silly?"

"No, dear. Of course not. I understand there are protocols in place. I'm just unsure how an emergency at Camp Rapid, which is what . . . several blocks away? How will that affect us?"

"The last time there was an emergency at Camp Rapid, we were overrun with injured."

"Did you have a lockdown first?"

"No, I wasn't working that day, but there was no warning. The explosion just happened."

"That explosion wasn't contributed to the Preacher, right?"

I shake my head. "He denied it."

"Vehemently." She nods.

I tilt my head. "You met him?"

"I was brought in to interview him and his followers. I had some previous experience with cults, so it made sense."

I want to ask more, but she's starts checking our patient's vitals. Her focus shifts entirely to him.

Elizabeth finishes recording the vitals and returns to her chair. From somewhere outside comes the sound of running feet and then shouting—too muffled by the shutters to make out the words. I tighten my grip on my sidearm, but Elizabeth continues as if we weren't interrupted.

"The Preacher said something interesting during those interviews," she says quietly. "About having friends in unexpected places. People who could access anywhere, even secure facilities. At the time, I thought he was just rambling, trying to seem more important than he was. But now . . ."

The footsteps pause at the door. Then comes the unmistakable sound of metal against metal—someone trying keys in the lock.

"Is the lockdown over?" Elizabeth asks in a low voice.

"If it is, they'd be knocking. Not trying to get in here." I move between the door and our patient, my sidearm against my thigh. Whoever's out there, they're not following protocol.

Chapter 14

Katie

There's a pause with the key in the door, followed by a knock. "Katie?"

Relief floods through me at Leo's voice. "Everything okay?" I call through the closed door.

"Yeah, they're dropping the lockdown."

I undo the lock, frowning as he steps in. "Why'd you use the key first?"

"What? Oh." He runs his hand through his hair. "Sorry, distracted. Wasn't thinking."

"You look pale," I say, studying his face. With dark circles and lines on his face, the exhaustion is evident. The past week has taken its toll on all of us.

"Just worried," he admits. "I should have sheltered with you. But the captain asked me to make sure the patients in room two were okay. All I could think about was getting to you."

"Do we know what happened?"

"Not yet. Shaw went to find out." His eyes scan the room, taking in how we've positioned everything. "Smart move with the medicine cart as cover, though I hate that you've had enough practice to know exactly where to put it."

"Just like always." I give him a strained smile.

"You're okay? Your patient?"

"He's stable. We're okay. See you later?"

He hesitates, his good hand flexing at his side. "I'll be in room two if you need me. I'm going to start checking vitals."

"Okay. See you soon."

He nods, already heading back to his duties. The sound of his boots echoes down the hall, mixing with the general murmur of the hospital returning to normal operations. I watch as he leaves, thinking about how worn out he looks.

"Your husband looks concerned," Elizabeth says.

"He's tired. We all are."

"Yes, I suppose that's true."

Elizabeth helps me return the room to its normal setup, then we check our patient's vitals. He's resting comfortably now, the pokeweed incident seemingly behind us.

Captain Williams arrives as we're finishing up; Nettie is at his side. He examines the patient thoroughly before turning to us. "Your shift has ended, right, Burnett?"

"Yes, sir. Back on at 2100 hours as a nurse." We used to always have twelve-hour shifts, but the med school and rounds have made that difficult for me, so I'm taking shorter shifts while the other nurses pick up the slack. They're not always happy about it, but they know in the end it'll be better. We'll have more trained doctors, and with Poppy Gardner's nursing school, we'll be adding additional nurses.

"Would you and Dr. Powell mind walking Nettie back to the med school apartments? I'll have one of the guards escort you."

"Is it dangerous?" Elizabeth asks.

"Probably not," the captain replies. "But until I hear from Shaw about the reason for the lockdown, we're not taking any chances."

"Do you have any idea what happened?" Elizabeth presses.

"Not for certain, but it may involve Hugo."

"Hugo?" The name sends a chill through me. "What happened?"

"I'm not sure, but since he is jailed at Camp Rapid . . ." He leaves the sentence hanging with a shrug.

The walk to the med school is quiet, save for the wind that rustles through the bare branches, a soft, whistling hum in the air. Our guard scans our surroundings as we cross the parking lot. Nettie and Elizabeth are speaking quietly. Nettie doesn't seem overly disturbed by the lockdown, but Elizabeth wants to ensure she's okay. We're nearly halfway when Bowski pulls up in the morgue truck.

I wave and he stops, rolling down his window. "Do you know what happened?" I ask.

"Not for certain. I know they don't need me, so that's something."

"No deaths. That is good," I agree. "The captain thought it might involve Hugo."

"It might. Maybe we can get to the bottom of this situation. You and Leo can go home. Be with your kids."

"And you can see Merissa," I add.

"Yup. That too. Writing letters back and forth is nice, but not enough. Seriously, though, Katie. I know how hard this must be for you. You all just barely became a family and now this."

Tears fill my eyes as I nod. "It helps that Shaw and Poppy bring us updates. It's not the same, of course, but it helps. Part of me wonders if they'll even remember me."

"They will," Elizabeth pipes up.

"Oh, please forgive me. Have you two met?" I step back from the truck to allow Bowski to view Elizabeth.

Before I can do a proper introduction, she sticks her hand through the window. Her professional demeanor doesn't falter even as the cold wind catches her scarf. "I'm Elizabeth. I've heard a lot about you. I don't envy the job you have."

"And I've heard about you." Bowski's gaze shifts to Nettie. "Dr. Wolff." He gives her a nod.

The tension in the air thickens. Nettie pulls her jacket tighter around herself but meets his gaze steadily. "I suppose you've heard," Nettie says, her voice strong as she meets his eyes.

Bowski shrugs. "David Paul asked me to tell you hello if I saw you." His voice carries a gentleness that catches me off guard. It's the same tone he uses when speaking about Merissa.

"Thanks." Nettie turns toward the med school. "See you later, Bowski," she calls over her shoulder. Elizabeth offers a quick goodbye and falls into step beside her.

"See you later," I say.

"Sure," Bowski replies. His hands tighten on the steering wheel. "By the way, I saw Opal. She rode with Shawn to bring in rations. She said to tell you everyone is doing well. You all sent a new boy there?"

I open my mouth to ask what she said about Nico but stop myself just in time. Bowski doesn't know they all moved to Opal's place. When he saw her, she would have been cautious. She'd use caring for Robert—the boy whose sister killed their mother—as a way to convey things are fine with my children.

"Yes. A boy who was having some trouble. We thought he'd fit in. Opal is trying to help Jason Wheeler, and it just made sense to have Robert go there too."

"Well, from what she said, he's doing okay. They both are."

"Great. Thank you. I'm glad to know that." The news warms me despite the biting wind. I give a wave, very happy about this update, and scurry to catch up. When I do, Elizabeth asks Nettie about David Paul.

"He's the gentleman you were dating last fall?"

"Dating? Not exactly. We were friends, sure, but it wasn't going to go anywhere."

"Why's that?"

She glances in my direction. "We wanted different things. He wanted someone who would be his . . . his helper. What's the word, Katie?"

"Uh . . . wife?"

Nettie rolls her eyes. "Yeah, that too, but there's some churchy word he used."

"Helpmeet?" Elizabeth suggests.

"That's it," Nettie agrees.

"I'm not sure that's a bad thing," Elizabeth says. "It is good that he was looking for a suitable mate. Someone who would complement his strengths and weaknesses."

"Yeah, well. That's not me. David is a wonderful man." Nettie's voice takes on an almost sing-song quality. "Better than wonderful, but I'm not suited for him."

"Because you have a child?"

"That's one reason." Nettie sighs as I open the door to the building. The guard tells us he'll see us later and that he's on roving patrol. His presence is both reassuring and a reminder of why we need him here.

The warmth inside hits me like a wall, bringing feeling back to my frozen cheeks. Nursing school classes are in session, and they've kept the woodstoves going nicely. We remove our winter gear, hanging jackets on hooks.

Nettie sits on the bench to remove her boots as Elizabeth asks, "There're other reasons?"

"You know about me," Nettie says, without looking up. Her fingers fumble with the laces, betraying her emotion. "How can someone like me be the wife—the helpmeet—to someone like David? He's so . . . so perfect."

Sitting next to her on the bench, I snort out a laugh. The wooden slats creak beneath us, the sound echoing in the empty foyer. "David?

Perfect? No. He's kind and has many great qualities, but he's not perfect. He'd be the first to tell you."

I stop talking, realizing that saying anything more could betray his confidence. Not that I know that much, but Lieutenant David Paul is a good friend of Leo's, and we've spent time together.

He's mentioned many times how God, and the National Guard to a lesser degree, have helped him turn his life around. Before that, he'd been adrift, unsure of his purpose and carrying the weight of past mistakes. "He doesn't pretend to have it all figured out," I add, my voice softening. "But that's what makes him real, you know? He tries. Every day."

"Beautifully stated." Elizabeth smiles. "That's pretty much what we all need to do. Try every day. Even before our world fell apart, people had troubles. Challenges. Some were just better at hiding them. But trying—really trying—is what makes the difference. It's what keeps us moving forward, even when it feels impossible."

"That's easy for you to say," Nettie mutters as she slips on her inside shoes. "You're not separated from your child. Wondering if they're even alive. Wondering how your parents are doing."

Elizabeth's smile remains in place. "But I am."

My head snaps in the psychiatrist's direction. She's been here a week, but we haven't spoken much about her personal life. Other than her working in the newly set up psych ward at the main hospital, I know little about her.

Nettie pulls her lips into a tight line before muttering, "Sorry."

"You didn't know." Elizabeth deftly undoes her boots while standing and slides into her house shoes. "Shall we have a cup of tea? Do you have time, Katie?"

"Sure." I'm tired and ready for bed, but I want to hear more of Elizabeth's story.

"Where are they?" Nettie asks as she refills the teakettle.

"Florida."

I draw in a sharp breath, the single word hitting hard. "Florida?"

"Yes. They're in the Wasteland. As far as I know, there weren't any nuclear detonations where they were. My parents retired to St. Pete Beach. My daughter was visiting them. She's about the same age as you, Katie. She'd just finished her junior year of college."

"Me too." I nod.

Nettie grips the kettle tighter, her face softening. "I'm sorry. I didn't know."

"How could you?" Elizabeth replies, her tone calm but firm. "It's not something I lead with."

Teatime turns into a counseling session, with Elizabeth's confession seemingly helping Nettie find a place of understanding. Steam rises from our cups, carrying the sharp scent of Stella's herbal blend— something with mint and chamomile that seems to ease the tension in the room.

I'm caught off guard when Nettie brings up David Paul again, wistfully mentioning how she wished things had turned out differently with him. "Of all the men I've known . . ." She pauses and cracks a smile. "And I've known a lot. He was the only one who seemed interested in me. The real me. Not just . . ." She clears her throat and gives us a knowing look. "In high school, college, and med school, I flitted from guy to guy just passing the time."

She traces the rim of her cup with one finger, her voice growing softer. "With David, it was different. He saw past all my defenses, my carefully constructed walls. Maybe that's why I ran."

I keep a slight smile on my face as she speaks, but inside, I'm puzzled. The Nettie I thought I knew would never admit such vulnerability. She's always been one to keep to herself. I had no idea she carried such regrets, especially where David Paul was concerned.

Nettie has always seemed so self-assured, the kind of person who could brush off the past like crumbs from a table. Hearing her wistfulness about him reveals a vulnerability I never expected. I understand, to some extent, why she didn't tell him about her daughter or her past. But it saddens me that she didn't realize she could trust him.

It's heartbreaking for David too. He genuinely cared for Nettie and wanted their relationship to work. Even now, he's come by the hospital just to ask about her after hearing what happened. The last time I saw him, his concern was written in every line of his face. He didn't want to see her—he said that wouldn't help anyone—but he needed to know she was okay.

Elizabeth and Nettie are still chatting—more like old friends than therapist and patient—when I excuse myself. The setting sun casts long shadows through the windows, reminding me of my upcoming shift.

Since moving into the med school, my shifts at the hospital have become nothing short of erratic. Being next door to the hospital and without other obligations, Leo, the captain, and I often pick up extra shifts.

With Nettie currently on leave, we're always shorthanded, which makes the extra help valuable to the hospital. But it's also exhausting. I'm not sure I really mind, though. At least when I'm working, I'm not thinking about the children or Gerry.

Dr. Bollinger's arrival tomorrow should be something to look forward to. And I am, but only to a point. The thought of Leo finally getting cleared for full duty brings mixed emotions. I want it for Leo, of course, but it means things may change . . . again.

As the rotating doctor, Bollinger gives the regular physicians some relief, but I'm not sure how much, considering we're shorthanded to begin with. Elizabeth has been a help in the week she's been here, but she's the first to admit her clinical skills are rusty.

Captain Williams, like Leo and me, is forcibly separated from his wife. Sometimes I catch him staring at the photo he keeps in his pocket, his thumb brushing over Alice's face. He and Alice have been married for nearly thirty years. They've endured other times apart during his National Guard obligations or medical conferences, and this separation isn't any easier for them. Like Bowski and Merissa, they're exchanging notes and letters via Deputy Shaw.

The letters arrive on scraps of paper—old receipts, margins torn from books, anything that can hold words. But each one is precious. Shaw and Poppy have been incredible, doing what they can to keep us connected with our loved ones while we're in exile. Maybe *exile* isn't the right word, but in many ways, that's exactly what it feels like. Only a few miles separate us, but it might as well be light years. I don't feel physically any closer to my children here than I do to my family in Wyoming.

My fingers brush against Nico's latest drawing, folded carefully in my pocket. How much longer will this be necessary? I know it's the best thing—the only thing—we can do to keep them safe. With the attempts on Leo's and my life, the shooting of the whistleblower, and Merissa and me running for our lives, I can't take any chances. I refuse to put the children in danger. But even knowing that, it still hurts to be apart.

Chapter 15

Katie

After changing into my sleeping clothes, I open the drawer of my nightstand. My Bible is there, its dog-eared pages and underlined verses bearing witness to how often I've sought comfort in its words these past months—just as my mom did before me.

Beside it is my growing collection of drawings from Nico. I add the newest one to the pile, smoothing the crayon-creased page with a quiet smile. These small tokens, scrawled with love and misspelled words, feel like a lifeline, connecting me to a world that seems so far away. Nico scrawled my name on it in uneven, oversized letters, with the "K" backward. The crayon marks are pressed so deeply they've left indentations in the paper, his determination evident in every stroke.

"Found another one under his pillow yesterday," Alice wrote in her last note, sent in with Shawn on one of his visits to deliver food to the ration center. "He draws them before bed, says it helps him remember your face." They're Nico's little reminder that he hasn't forgotten me. Alice has been working with him, helping him learn to form the letters. He made a separate drawing for Leo with his name on it.

I decide to pull out the stack of pictures. The first one is a swirl of bright colors—red, green, and blue crayon strokes tumbling over each other in joyful chaos. At the center, there's a stick figure with spiky hair holding hands with a much taller figure with long, wild hair; I assume it's supposed to be me. He's used almost every crayon in the box, creating a rainbow world where everything is possible. There's a big yellow sun in the corner of the page, its rays zigzagging across the top.

The second drawing is simpler. A square house with a triangle roof, a crooked chimney puffing out looping smoke, and three stick figures standing in front. Two—Leo and me—are holding stick-figure babies. Each figure has a broad smile, the kind only children draw, stretching almost beyond their faces. It makes my chest tighten and ache at the same time.

I run my finger over the paper, the blank side of what had once been an invoice for a car repair, imagining his small hand gripping the crayon, pressing too hard like he always does. The wax has built up in places where he went over and over the lines, making sure they were just right. These little pieces of him make the distance feel both harder and easier to bear.

I pull out my latest note and add a few lines to it. I address it to Nico but mention Caleb and Zach in it too, knowing Alice, or maybe even Pearl or Merissa, will read it to him. My note is written on an old envelope, already used and torn open sometime in the past—a past that included electricity and regular mail service.

Paper, like everything in our broken world, is a limited commodity. People are beginning to make paper, but it's not the smooth, highly processed paper of before. I've seen samples of the new paper—thick and uneven, with bits of plant fiber still visible throughout. It's rough and lovely but also very limited.

The wind howls outside my window, rattling the panes in their frames, as I wonder how much longer we can continue on with our limited resources. Will we ever have the conveniences we were so used to? Is the new wave of suicides partly due to people who are realizing things will never go back to the way they were?

Have they, like Nettie, just had enough? Tired of missing and worrying about their loved ones. Of seeing death and misery every day. Of not having enough food, even with community rations. The thought of food makes my stomach growl. I've eaten today, but it's never enough.

The memory of home comes unbidden, bringing with it the scent of freshly baked bread. When we lived in Wyoming with my family, we rationed food, but we never really went hungry. While portions were controlled, it always seemed to be enough. It helped that there were fewer people and an abundance of wildlife in their location over the mountains from Yellowstone National Park. It also helped that they were very intentional and organized with the food storage.

There were several ranches and farms in the area that added to the coffers. One of the farmers grew commercial sugar beets. While not my favorite food—not by a longshot—the mild, earthy flavor isn't unpleasant. Raw, they're a bit too bland for my taste, with just a hint of sweetness that doesn't compare to fruits or even other root vegetables. But when cooked, they soften and become sweeter, though still not overpowering, with a subtle, almost nutty undertone. They're the kind of food you don't crave, but when you have them, you don't mind.

Sugar beets, field corn, and barley were our main carbs. Greenhouses supplied limited fresh vegetables. Dairy cattle and goats gave us fresh milk, and chickens gave the occasional egg—depending on how well they were laying. Culled cattle, goats, and chickens, along with elk, deer, and bighorn sheep kept us in protein. Sometimes I wonder why we ever left.

The population of Rapid City and the Black Hills is considerably higher than our little area of Bakerville, Wyoming. And people continue to arrive in this area specifically because of the rumors of rebuilding. It appealed to us too.

When Leo and I first joined the United Volunteers, we expected to be sent to the Western Wastelands to help clear that area. When our unit was sent to Rapid City, it was a pleasant surprise. We'd heard about the rebuilding efforts in South Dakota and how they were leading the way in getting the nation back on its feet.

Other places were also touted as having things together. Billings, Montana, only about an hour or so from Bakerville, was considered a hub of progress. It was the kind of place that gave people hope, a beacon in the midst of so much despair. But hope, it seems, isn't invincible. Something went wrong. Drastically wrong.

We learned about an attempted insurrection during the Christmas meal at Camp Rapid. Information was coming in through coded radio messages, and there were concerns that, since the military had been infiltrated, something similar could happen at the bases in South Dakota.

Later that day, the explosion at the Camp jail occurred. We still don't know who was behind it. The Preacher was suspected but denied any involvement, and to my knowledge, nothing has come to light that points to the perpetrators.

The explosion at Camp Rapid, followed by a devastating flu outbreak that swept through the region, marked the beginning of stricter rations. Since Leo, the captain, and I moved to the med school and went into hiding, we're no longer able to go out to collect our own ration chips and food. Shaw has made arrangements to bring us our allotment, but this week's allocation wasn't nearly enough for three people for a full week.

At least we have plenty of tea, homemade by Stella. It helps keep the hunger at bay. It's not exactly filling, but the warmth offers a small reprieve, a momentary illusion of comfort.

After finishing my note for Nico, I settle in under the covers. I've dillydallied so long that my nap will only be a few hours before I'm back on shift at the hospital. I curl up and pull the covers tighter around me as the chill of the room contrasts with the warmth of sleep slowly creeping in.

At some point, I feel a light touch on my shoulder, warm and steady. Leo's voice cuts through the haze, quiet but clear. "Time to get up," he says, his hand lingering on my shoulder.

"Already?" I mutter, burrowing further into the covers.

"I made you some dinner."

My stomach, ever the realist, growls its approval, pulling me fully from sleep. I sigh. "Okay. Feels like I just fell asleep." I stretch and slowly make my way from the bed. Leo is sitting in the chair by the window, his profile outlined by the faint light of the moon filtering through the curtains. His eyes follow me as I shuffle toward him, curiosity and affection mingling in his gaze.

"What?"

"Sometimes I can't get over how beautiful you are."

I laugh as I run a hand through my hair. "I'm sure I'm quite the sight."

He doesn't laugh, just watches me with a quiet intensity that makes my breath catch. His hand reaches out, brushing a stray strand of hair from my face. "You are," he says softly, his voice steady and warm.

Before I can respond, his hand lingers against my cheek, and I find myself leaning into the touch. He lets out a quiet breath, almost like he's trying to memorize the moment.

"I don't say it enough. But I mean it every time."

I sink to the edge of the bed so we're face-to-face. His hand drops to mine, his fingers curling around mine in a way that grounds me. For a moment, we just sit there, connected in the stillness, the chaos of the world outside held at bay.

After a long moment, the spell is broken, and I clear my throat. "I need to get ready to go. Are you excited about Bollinger?"

He shrugs. "Trying not to get my hopes up. This arm's been nothing but trouble with how it hasn't healed right."

I can see him in the mirror as I work my hair into a bun. The bandage is no longer on my ear; the frostbite sustained several weeks ago is mostly healed. Even my finger looks okay. We thought I might lose the tip of it, but the color has improved enough that the captain thinks it may heal properly. "Bollinger said it looked good when we saw him last. The external fixation corrected the malunion."

"Rebreaking it corrected the malunion, but yes. He did sound hopeful."

"And you haven't been having any trouble. Not even much pain, right?"

"Very little."

"Well, I'm praying everything will be fine. He'll examine it and say it's as good as new—or will be soon."

"And then what, Katie?"

I close my eyes as I consider my response. "And then we will know what our options are."

"The more I think about it, the less I want to join the National Guard. I'm leaning toward the same thoughts as you've expressed. Finish our commitment to the Volunteers and then see if we can continue med school as civilians. I'm confident Captain Williams will be fine with that. He's said as much."

There's more I want to say. To convince him that not joining the Guard is the best choice for us. For our family. I want to lay out every reason and list every risk until there's no room for doubt. But in recent months, I've learned not to push.

That's not always easy for me. I'd prefer to drive my point home until he bends to my will. But Leo's not the type to be convinced— he's the type to dig in his heels. And I love him for that, even when it frustrates me. Changing the subject seems the wiser move.

"Did you ever find out what happened at Camp Rapid?"

"Someone tried to kill Hugo."

I stop midmotion to look at him. "Really? He's okay?"

"They got away. And it's assumed they were there to kill Hugo, but— "

"How'd they get near him? With all the security there?"

"Unknown. That's being investigated. General Truss is fit to be tied. Following the Christmas Day explosion, they'd tightened their security even more. How they even got close is a mystery. Captain Williams says it has to be someone on the inside. I'm sure they'll figure out who."

"Someone who was working with Hugo?"

"Probably."

"And if they find them, we can go home?" My voice is filled with hope.

"Hopefully. But for now, we're here and Shaw is going to try to increase security. He's concerned if they went after Hugo, they might come after you."

"But I don't know anything."

"They are worried you do. That Hank Timbs told you what he knew before— "

"Before they killed him. What about Merissa?"

"Nothing has changed at the ranch. They still have plenty of security. She's fine. Alice is fine. Our children are fine."

The way he says "our children" warms me from the inside. We never planned on having kids—never even talked about it, not with everything happening in the world—but the boys are ours. I don't know if I could love them more if I'd given birth to them.

"Come eat," Leo says, pulling me from my thoughts. "I made venison steaks from that small roast. And there might be a surprise for dessert."

"Surprise?" I eye him suspiciously. Leo's definition of surprise once included dandelion coffee, which was as terrible as it sounds. But his grin is genuine, playful even.

"Bowski stopped by." He reaches into his pocket and pulls out a small cloth-wrapped package. "Remember how Merissa and he went to that secret restaurant? Apparently, he visited there again and brought something back for you. Honey candy. He left some for Poppy to take when she visits Merissa too." He unwraps one piece, holding it out to me.

"Do I have to wait for dessert to eat it?"

"Of course not."

The honey candy melts on my tongue. For a moment, the weight of everything—the fear, the hunger, the uncertainty—fades away. I imagine Nico having a taste, his eyes going wide with wonder. *Soon*, I tell myself. Soon we'll all be together again, sharing simple joys like honey candies and bedtime stories.

For now, though, I have this moment with Leo, this tiny taste of sweetness in our bitter world, and somehow that's enough to keep hope alive.

Chapter 16

Katie

After too many hours on my feet, I'm still moving. Barely. An emergency kept me past my shift ending at 0600—a happy emergency for a change. The birth of a healthy baby boy. Mom and son are both resting comfortably, and we're now preparing to start morning rounds. My brain feels fuzzy around the edges, but it was worth it.

"Katie?" Leo touches my arm. "You're swaying."

"Tired." I straighten my posture, forcing alertness. "Dr. Bollinger will be here soon?"

"Should be." His good hand flexes at his side—a nervous tell I've come to recognize. "I'm hoping we can get through rounds first."

Captain Williams leads us through each patient's case. Murphy's accidental overdose from yesterday is stable. His wound looks better, and there are no signs of residual issues from the pokeweed. We'll discharge him.

Our delivery mother is resting, her newborn strong and healthy—one of the healthiest babies I've seen born since I've been in Rapid City. Of course, the baby reminds me of Caleb and Zach, along with my sisters' children. Sarah had a little boy about six months after the EMP. My sister Calley had a little girl a few weeks after we lost our mom. Their babies were both born fat and healthy thanks to adequate rations.

I attended Caleb's birth, and he was heartbreakingly frail. Unlike Sarah's and Calley's plump, rosy babies, Caleb looked like he had already been through a battle just to be born. Yet, even then, there was a spark of fight in him—a stubbornness that told me he wasn't going to give up easily. And he hasn't.

Both he and Zach have been steadily putting on weight since we removed them from the Preacher's compound and even more so since the boys started living with us. I can only imagine how much they are thriving at the Maher ranch with fresh goat milk in abundance.

We continue checking patients and discharge another person to the long-term care facilities run by Poppy Gardner. Another patient, whose been having trouble with their blood pressure dropping, will remain in the hospital.

The sound of an engine in the parking lot draws everyone's attention.

"Right on time," the captain says. I notice Murphy tense slightly at Bollinger's arrival, his hand unconsciously moving to adjust his stethoscope. He positions himself slightly behind our group, as if trying to become invisible.

Bollinger seems to be on the grumpy side, mentioning how things seem a little rough now in the Guard District.

"Oh?" Captain Williams asks. "Did you have trouble?"

"Not directly. But I'm glad I have my escort." He gestures toward the soldier who arrived with him, Bollinger driving and the additional man riding shotgun in the old pickup truck. I can't help but wonder what kind of fuel the truck is using. Is it powered by the human-based biodiesel? The thought of it gives me a sick feeling.

"And it's not just here," Bollinger continues. "Things are dicey all over. This round of my traveling doc gig has been less than pleasant. I've been doing this because I know there's a need. A way for me to assist my comrades in arms, so to speak. Help those of you operating on such a thin line. I know you're all overworked, and if my spending a few days giving you a break can help, I'm happy to do it. But not at my peril."

"Well, look who's here." Elizabeth Powell strides toward us, her heels clicking against the cracked linoleum.

"Oh, Elizabeth. I didn't expect to— " Bollinger's voice falters as he adjusts his glasses.

"I've been working on a theory," she interrupts smoothly. "Winter's taken its toll on everyone. Longer days should ease the strain."

"Hmm. Not sure I'd pin it on daylight. But hey, you're the shrink, not me." His shrug is almost smug.

"That's correct," Elizabeth replies, her tone snapping like frostbite.

Bollinger chuckles awkwardly. "Well, maybe you can run a study on that theory of yours. When you're not too busy, of course."

Elizabeth's eyes narrow, her smile razor-sharp. "Funny. I didn't realize *you* were the one handing out research assignments now."

He bristles but recovers quickly, raising his chin. "I'm just saying, it's good to see you're keeping busy. Not everyone thrives under pressure."

"Pressure reveals character." Elizabeth's eyes briefly cut to Murphy.

He shifts uncomfortably, his gaze bouncing between Elizabeth and Bollinger. The color drains from his face as he takes a hesitant step back.

Elizabeth's attention lingers on him for a beat before returning to Bollinger. "Speaking of which, I trust you'll figure out a way to settle in? Hopefully, the hospital's . . . challenges aren't too overwhelming."

A faint flush creeps up Bollinger's neck. "I'll manage just fine, thank you."

"I'm sure you will." Elizabeth's tone drips with mock reassurance. "After all, we're all in this together, aren't we?"

She turns on her heel and walks away, leaving him standing there, his forced smile fading.

"Uh, well . . ." Captain Williams clears his throat, his tone carefully measured. "Dr. Bollinger, we're just wrapping up rounds. Care to join us?"

Bollinger nods curtly. "I didn't realize Elizabeth was here. Is there a reason?"

Our small group shifts uneasily, the other med students exchanging glances. I catch Leo's eye and give a slight shake of my head. Has Bollinger not heard about Nettie?

The captain squares his shoulders, his chin rising just a fraction as he responds. "Dr. Powell is here to provide training to my med students. We've set up community therapy sessions, along with some individual appointments. It's not only helpful for the students to learn how psychiatry works and how to better help their patients, but also for our district. You said yourself, things are tense."

"Ah, yes. Well, I'm sure Elizabeth is happy to share her special brand of insight—useful, I'm sure, in its own limited scope."

His condescending tone is not lost on me. Not that I'm surprised. I've seen Dr. Bollinger a few times now and have discovered he is mostly a chauvinistic pig. He's managed to talk down to me in each exchange, and the way he treats the nurses and staff he works with is nothing short of appalling. He speaks to them as if they're barely competent, dismissing their input with a wave of his hand or an exaggerated sigh. And then there's the whole thing with Nettie and the late Chastity Morrow.

When he visited back in December, he seemed to enjoy fanning the flames of their rivalry, always with just the right comment or sly glance to keep them at odds. I remember watching Nettie grow quieter with each passing day, her usual confidence dimming, while Chastity grew sharper and bolder, as if trying to outpace whatever game he was playing. Nettie finally snapped, and the two women ended up in a heated shouting match right in the hallway.

Bollinger wasn't just unprofessional, he was cruel. And now, with Chastity gone, I can't help but wonder how much of their tension was his doing. Nettie insists Bollinger didn't contribute to her suicide attempt. Mostly, she is just embarrassed about their tryst and the way she acts when around him—like a love-sick teenager. In my opinion, the man is toxic, plain and simple, and yet somehow, he keeps landing on his feet.

I guess I can't deny his skill as a doctor—especially as a surgeon. That is no easy task in our apocalyptic world. He's been willing to hone his craft to adapt to current conditions. And I'll always appreciate what he's done for Leo.

My gaze drifts toward my husband. He's nervous about today's appointment. It's easy for us to see the bone has healed well this time. There are no lumps to indicate a second malunion. But I know Leo still has pain and weakness. Partly due to being instructed to not use it, but he worries—and I do too, if I'm being honest—there's more to it than just not having used the arm for nearly six months. It won't be long now. We'll finish the rounds and then Leo will have his exam.

There's little drama as we wrap things up. Elizabeth has made herself scarce, and Dr. Murphy has disappeared entirely, mumbling something about patient charts that need his attention. The captain's brow furrows at this excuse—we all know morning charts are already complete.

Williams turns to our team of med students—Kerry, Matt, and Jeff, along with Leo and me. Merissa is still officially on the roster, but with her forced bed rest and the need to keep her hidden for her own safety, there's no doubt she'll be far behind when she's able to return. The captain makes sure to keep her updated on the required reading via notes, but missing out on things like rounds and patient care is an issue.

Originally, the captain's goal was to have all of the med students fully trained within two to three years. Trained well enough to move to a different hospital and be competent. Of the original eight, only Kerry, Jeff, and Matt remain here today. Others, like Stella, determined being a doctor of the apocalypse wasn't the right fit for them.

Stella is focused on our natural medicines, and another previous med student is now taking Poppy Gardner's nursing classes with the goal of focusing on the patients in the long-term care facilities.

I know Merissa will return after her baby is born and the whole thing with Hugo is wrapped up. She's excited to be a doctor and feels she can do it—with Pearl's help—even with having an infant. I wish I had her confidence. I'm not sure I can do it, not with my new instant family. But that's a problem for another day. For a day when I can be reunited with my children. Today, the focus is on Leo's arm and how it has healed.

"Katie?" Leo touches my arm. "Did you want to come with me? Dr. Bollinger is going to wash up and then he'll be ready to examine me." He gives me a thoughtful look, as if waiting for me to catch up. "The other students are taking a break, and we'll meet them in the classroom."

"Oh. Okay."

"You all right?"

"I'm fine. I was just— "

"Woolgathering?" He gives me a smile. "You definitely seemed lost in thought."

"I guess I was."

"The boys?"

"In a roundabout way, yes. They're always there, always on my mind. No matter if I'm thinking of something else, it always seems to go back to them."

He gives me an understanding nod. "Same. It's like a piece of me is just out of reach—four pieces, counting Gerry. No matter what I do, no matter where I go, I can't stop thinking about them, wondering if they're okay. It's like part of me is always missing."

I feel the ache in his words, hear the longing in his voice. It's as difficult for Leo as it is for me. They're not just absent—they're a constant presence in my mind, whether I'm awake, asleep, or lost in thought.

Dr. Bollinger emerges from the lavatory, his earlier tension with Elizabeth now gone, his self-assurance back in full force. "Burnetts! How're my favorite sergeants?"

"Ready to use my arm again," Leo admits with a forced smile.

"Right, right." He looks toward me. "Do you have an exam room ready for us?"

"Um, yes. Exam room three is empty."

"And you'll be assisting us, nurse?"

"Nurse Haley will be assisting," Leo says, resting his hand on my shoulder. "Katie will be in the room as my wife."

"Good enough."

Within two minutes, the four of us are in the exam room. Leo has removed his shirt and Jacquie Haley is looking less than pleased with her assignment. She's mentioned before how Bollinger is a condescending womanizer—only the words she used were much more colorful.

"Well, let's see this arm of yours, Sergeant." He gestures for Leo to lift his arm. "Any pain?"

"Very little. Some stiffness in the mornings."

Bollinger's examination is thorough, his usual arrogant manner toned down by focused professionalism. He tests range of motion, strength, and nerve response. Occasionally, he makes notes, but his face gives nothing away.

"Well?" Leo finally asks.

"It's healed about as I expected."

"Is that good?" The tension in Leo's voice is painful to hear.

"Good? Yes, compared to how it was the first time I saw you. I'd say my expertise gave you an arm that you'll find to be quite useful."

"Quite useful?" Leo repeats. "What do you mean by that?"

"Well, you'll still have some limitations, but for the most part, it'll be fine."

"What kind of limitations?"

Bollinger sets down his clipboard. "We'll know more as you regain some of your strength. I'm going to give you some exercises that I had the PT department put together for you. You'll still be limited on weight and movement for a month or so. I brought a brace along with me, something a little less cumbersome than what you've worn the last few weeks. You can take it off when you sleep and bathe, but keep it on for . . . oh, six or eight weeks while you regain your strength. I want you to remain in the sling during that time too."

"And then?"

"You'll continue to improve over the next several months to a year. We'll know then what your full capabilities are."

The room goes quiet. I can almost hear Leo's hopes crumbling. "This doesn't sound very promising."

Bollinger meets Leo's gaze directly. "Your arm will never be what it was. But we saved it, and you'll have most of the use of it. I know you thought I'd be signing off for you to join the National Guard. That's not happening."

He holds up a hand as Leo starts to protest. "Maybe when I see you again, say in June, then you'll be ready. But to be honest with you, I wouldn't get my hopes up on that. I see no reason why you can't continue your physician studies. You should be able to be a fine doctor. Not sure how surgery will work out—of course, the meatball surgery we do these days might be fine. But I don't see you being a soldier."

Leo's face goes blank, the way it does when he's trying to process something painful. I reach for his hand, but he pulls away and abruptly stands.

"So that's it?" His voice is tight. "Six months of healing, the external fixation, all the therapy, and I still can't— "

"You can do plenty," Bollinger interrupts. "But military service requires full range of motion, full strength. The break was complex, Leo. The fact that you have as much function as you do is remarkable."

I watch Leo's shoulders tense as the future he'd envisioned unravels. Right out of high school, he joined the Marines. We met after his service, during his college years at K-State. He was juggling college, construction work, EMT training, and debating a career as a paramedic.

When the rebuilding efforts started, he wanted to rejoin the Marines. But with the way things were, they weren't taking people who couldn't prove they'd been honorably discharged. Leo had left all his important paperwork in a safety deposit box back in Manhattan, Kansas. Joining the United Volunteers was the closest he could get to serving his country. Being strong, being capable—it's part of who he is.

"The medical training," Bollinger continues, his voice gentler now, "that's where you can make a real difference. We need doctors more than we need soldiers right now."

"He's right," I say softly. When Leo turns to look at me, I see the struggle in his eyes—anger, disappointment, maybe a touch of relief? At least that's what I'd like to think.

"Why don't you go ahead and get dressed," Bollinger says, gathering his notes. "We'll go over the exercises in a bit. And I'll be here for two weeks. I want to check you again before I go to see if your mobility is increasing."

Both Bollinger and Jacquie leave. She gives a soft pat on my arm and sends Leo a sad smile on her way out.

"Leo . . ."

"Don't." His voice is rough. "Don't try to make this okay."

"I wasn't going to." I move to stand beside him. "I was going to say I love you. That this doesn't change anything about who you are."

Leo's hand finds mine. Through the door, we can hear the bustle of the hospital continuing—patients being treated, lives being saved. Not by soldiers, but by healers. Maybe that's what we both need to remember.

We came to Rapid City to help rebuild, to make a difference. The uniform doesn't matter as much as the work. And now, with our boys waiting for us, maybe this is God's way of pointing us toward the path we're meant to take—not as soldiers, but as a family of healers.

Chapter 17

Merissa

"He's really taken to ranch life," Alice says, gently rocking Zach as she watches through the window. Robert follows Opal across the yard, carrying a pair of five-gallon buckets that look almost too heavy for him. "Amazing what a difference just a week can make."

Pearl nods, shifting Caleb to her other shoulder. "Opal says he's up before dawn, eager to help with chores. Jason's been showing him the ropes."

"That's good for Jason to have someone to mentor," I say, thinking of the troubles the boy was having when Opal brought him to the hospital a few weeks prior—before the attempt on my life and my preterm labor.

The morning sun streams through the window, warming the room despite the lingering winter chill. From my position in bed, I can just see Nico trailing behind the older boy, trying to match his longer strides. His constant chatter carries faintly through the newly installed window salvaged from an abandoned house.

"The babies are thriving too," Alice comments, smoothing Zach's wispy hair. "Katie will be amazed at how much they've grown."

A shadow crosses Pearl's face at the mention of growth. She reaches up to rub her temple, a gesture I've noticed more frequently these past few days. "Pearl?"

"Just a headache," she says, but her voice sounds strange, distant. Caleb stirs against her shoulder, his small, fussy noises breaking the quiet. Gerry rises abruptly, his ears flicking forward as he moves to Pearl's knee. A low whine escapes him—soft, urgent, and entirely unlike his usual sounds.

"Are you sure you're okay?" Alice asks.

"Fine. Just fine. I'll take another dose of willow bark when Opal comes back in."

Alice nods. "Speaking of Katie, did you see the notes she sent with Shawn? Nico's had me read the one she sent him so many times the paper is beginning to wear out."

"It's not easy for the boy," Pearl says, patting Caleb's back. "He was just getting used to having a family, and then to have things change so drastically. I hope they're getting the troubles wrapped up so they can all be back together soon." She meets Alice's gaze. "So you can be back with your husband."

"Yes. Me too," Alice agrees. "At least I get to be with the babies and Nico. I feel like we've all become family. Leo and Katie are like the children I never had. These are the grandchildren. I always wanted kids, but the Lord never blessed us in that way. Now we've been given a second chance—Chris and I—an opportunity to help Katie and Leo with the boys. I know the timing was rough. With Leo's arm injury and joining the National Guard hanging over their heads, along with the med school."

"Do you think they'll join the Guard?" Pearl asks, one hand holding Caleb securely against her while the other rests on Gerry's neck. The dog leans into her knee, silent now but alert, his posture almost protective.

I shake my head and stay quiet. Katie doesn't want the military. She only joined the United Volunteers to cope after her mom's death, figuring a year-long commitment was manageable. The National Guard would demand more than she's willing or able to give, especially now, with the boys in her life.

Katie wants to be a mom, not a soldier. I'm not even sure she wants to be a doctor. Nursing suits her well enough. She's good at it and seems to find some satisfaction in the work, even if it wasn't her original plan. She went to college to be an artist, but there's not a lot of call for art in the apocalypse.

I'm pretty sure Captain Williams put both Katie and Leo in the med school program to help them if they did join the Guard. He knows how the system works, having spent years in it himself. As doctors, they'd have a much easier time than in other roles.

"I can't imagine she will," Alice says, pulling Zach closer to her. "Chris agrees with me. We'll see about Leo. A lot will depend on the results of his arm healing. I believe Poppy said Bollinger is expected today. Surely, he'll see Leo first thing, right?"

"Maybe?" I say. "It's hard telling. I guess we'll learn more tomorrow. Poppy said she'd be here by late morning."

Pearl nods. "Times like these, you realize how much we took for granted. Having ambulances, emergency rooms . . ." She bounces Caleb gently as he starts to fuss. "Now we're back to house calls and hoping someone nearby knows what they're doing."

"At least we have the small hospitals in the various districts," Alice adds. "Plus, Chris's med school and Poppy's nursing school. Really, it could be a lot worse. Pretty soon Merissa will be back on her feet— "

"If I'm ever back on my feet," I grumble, though I know the bed rest is necessary.

"Won't be much longer now," Pearl says softly. "To think, in just a few weeks, he'll be born. Healthy and happy. Then you'll go back to doing what you need to do. Braedon would be proud of how you've handled everything."

The mention of Braedon brings the usual mixture of emotions—grief, love, and gratitude for the child he left me. But lately, there's been something else too. Something that feels almost like peace.

"Robert asked about the archery equipment in the barn," Alice mentions, clearly trying to shift to a lighter topic. "Walt said he might teach him the basics. Jason's already learning, and of course, Nico is sure he's old enough to join them."

"Really?" I lean forward slightly, interested. "Archery would be good for all of them. Not from the horses yet, especially not Nico. But Walt's an expert. He'll be a great teacher." I sigh, wishing I could join them. I haven't ridden my horse since before I discovered I was pregnant. He was brought to South Dakota by Walt and a few others who traveled east with us before continuing on. That's one thing I'm certainly looking forward to. There's something freeing about being on a horse.

"Nico loves being part of the group," Pearl says with a small smile, nodding toward the window where Nico's voice carries clearly as he chatters away to Jason. Her smile falters as she presses a hand to her head again. Gerry leans into her knee, his small frame trembling slightly as he makes a low chuffing sound, his unease clear.

"Let me take Caleb," Alice offers, but before she can move, Pearl's eyes roll back.

The seizure starts subtly—a slight tremor in her hands, a tightening of her jaw. Gerry lets out a sharp bark and circles nervously at her feet. When Pearl's body goes rigid, he jumps back, ears pinned, but doesn't stray far. Caleb begins to slip from her grasp.

"Pearl!" I try to push myself up, but Alice is already moving. She practically throws Zach onto my bed—he lands safely but starts wailing—and lunges for Caleb just as Pearl's arms begin to jerk violently.

"Help!" Alice shouts toward the window as she cradles Caleb against her chest. She manages to guide Pearl's convulsing form away from the chair, lowering her to the floor. "Someone help us!"

I gather Zach close, holding him tightly as he trembles against me, while my eyes stay fixed on Pearl. Her body thrashes against the floorboards, her movements uncontrolled and terrifying as horrible choking sounds escape her throat. Gerry paces in frantic circles around her, his claws clicking against the wood as he whines, his nose darting toward her face before he skitters back, unsure of what to do.

"Turn her on her side!" I direct, my medical training kicking in despite my panic. "Keep her airway clear!"

Alice manages to roll Pearl onto her left side, still clutching Caleb, who screams in unison with Zach. Both babies' cries pierce the air, but I barely register them over the sound of Pearl's labored breathing and the dull thud of her limbs against the floor, mixed with Gerry's low, distressed whines.

"Gerry, stop!" I command. He drops to the floor instantly, his head resting on his paws, watching Pearl with wide, uncertain eyes.

"What do we do?" Alice's voice shakes. "How do we get help?"

"The bell. The one hanging by the front door. Three short rings, then three long—that's the medical emergency signal!"

Alice hesitates, looking between Pearl and the babies. Gerry lifts his head slightly, then drops it again as if nodding his approval.

"Give me Caleb," I say, already shifting to make room. "I can handle them both. Go!"

She hands Caleb to me and runs for the door. Seconds later, I hear the frantic clanging of the bell, its urgent pattern cutting through the morning air.

Pearl's seizure continues. I count the seconds in my head, fighting every instinct that screams at me to go to her. The babies wail. Zach is in my arms and the younger Caleb is on the bed, my hand rubbing his belly as I try to soothe them while keeping watch.

Gerry creeps closer to Pearl, his belly low to the floor. He nudges her arm with his nose before retreating, his tail tucked tight against his body. He circles back again, whining softly as if urging her to respond.

Finally, the convulsions begin to slow. Pearl's breathing remains ragged, but her limbs stop their violent jerking. Outside, shouting cuts through the air, followed by the hurried sound of running footsteps.

Opal bursts through the door first, her face white with fear. "Pearl!"

"Seizure," I say quickly. "Started over a minute ago, closer to two. She's coming out of it now."

"Zach and Caleb?" Opal asks, dropping to her knees beside her sister. Gerry scoots back, as if he understands that Opal needs space to tend to her.

"They're fine. I've got them." I look toward the door where Jason and Robert hover uncertainly, Nico trying to peer around them. "Jason, take Nico upstairs."

Pearl's eyes flutter open, unfocused and confused. She tries to speak but only manages a weak moan. Gerry whines in response.

"Don't try to talk," Opal soothes. "You're okay. We'll send for help."

Alice returns, breathless from running. "Kevin's getting the wagon ready. Walt's saddling his horse. Do we want to take her to the med center? Or see if the doctor can come here?"

Opal meets my gaze. "I think we should see if he'll come here. Would you agree?"

"Probably. He may want to take her in, but it'd be best to let her rest. Have him come to her." I clear my throat and lower my voice. "The seizure . . . it may be a sign the cancer's spread."

"To her brain?" Opal's voice breaks on the question.

I nod, unable to say the words. We all know what this means. The timeline we thought we had—months, maybe longer—has just shortened dramatically.

"Please ask Walt to go," Opal directs Alice. "Have Kevin and Shawn come inside. I'm going to need their help."

Within minutes, Kevin and Shawn arrive, and Walt leaves to fetch the doctor. Opal directs the men to bring in a cot for Pearl, setting it up beside my bed. "We can move her bed down later if needed," Opal says. "For now, she'll rest here until the doctor has a look at her."

Pearl has regained consciousness but remains visibly exhausted, her eyes staying shut. She murmurs a few slurred words—not unusual, given the circumstances. Alice is there, checking over both babies before taking Zach from me. "Are you okay holding Caleb while I put this one in a fresh diaper?"

"I'm fine. Caleb needs to be changed too."

"Yep. He's next." She nods before taking Zach away.

"The headaches," Opal whispers, her voice cracking. "She's been having them for days, but she was downplaying them. Said the willow bark was stopping them. Promised she'd mention them to Poppy. She didn't want to worry anyone. Stubborn. That's what she is. Plain stubborn."

I wish I could go to her, hold her, but the baby in my arms and my own restricted movement keep me in place. "Help will be here soon. That's what matters."

"But for how long?" Opal wipes her eyes. "What do we do now? The first crew of trappers didn't find the mistletoe. The second crew will be back in a day or two, but I hold out little hope. I asked them to look for it anyway—showed them photos from one of my books— but it'll take weeks to make the tincture. I'm not sure . . ." Her voice fades away as she shakes her head.

This time, Gerry pads over to Opal and gently nudges her arm with his nose. He lingers close, his presence a quiet comfort as he watches her with soft, understanding eyes.

What Opal doesn't say is she's not sure Pearl has weeks. Not if it's spread to her brain. Will she even survive long enough to be here for the birth of her grandchild?

The baby kicks, strong and insistent, as if reminding me of Pearl's determination to meet them. I rest my hand on my belly, sending up a silent prayer. Just a few more weeks. Please, just give us a few more weeks.

Chapter 18

Merissa

"Looks like a dormitory in here," Pearl murmurs from her twin bed, her voice still slightly slurred but carrying a hint of her usual dry humor. The bed, moved down from the guest room upstairs, sits only a short distance from mine, a skinny nightstand separating us.

"At least we're in good company," I reply, watching her face for any signs of another seizure. She's been sleeping most of the time since yesterday's episode, waking only for brief periods. The doctor from Canyon Lake District confirmed our fears—the cancer has likely spread to her brain.

The thought of the doctor's visit sends a chill through me. The Canyon Lake District doctor seemed trustworthy enough, carefully examining Pearl while explaining everything he was doing. Abby stood by, watching his every move, ready to pounce should he do anything she deemed unacceptable.

His genuine concern showed in the way he'd taken extensive notes and promised to research treatment options. But in these times, even good people could inadvertently cause harm. One casual mention of seeing me here to the wrong person could bring disaster.

The thought of armed men storming the ranch makes my heart race. In my panic over Pearl's condition, I hadn't considered the risk of having another outsider know our location. The biodiesel conspiracy has already cost lives—what's one more to them? Keeping me quiet because of what they think I know could be deadly to not just me and my unborn baby but to everyone living at Opal's ranch.

Pearl shifts in her bed, grimacing slightly. "Stop fretting, dear. I can hear your thoughts from here."

"I'm not fretting," I lie, adjusting my position against the headboard. My journal lies open beside me, pages filled with things I want to tell Bowski but can't bring myself to put in an actual letter. How do you tell someone you're falling in love with them while hiding from people who might want you dead? How do you explain that you're terrified of losing your mother-in-law before your baby arrives?

A noise from outside draws my attention. Looking out the window, I spot Robert and Jason splitting wood, working in companionable silence. The boy who arrived only a week ago already seems like he's been here forever. Inside, the house is unusually quiet—Nico and the babies are down for a nap, a minor miracle in itself. Poppy is due to arrive after lunch. I suspect she'll bring Elizabeth Powell with her so she can check on Robert's progress and visit with Jason again.

"I think we might actually manage that Bible study today," Opal says, appearing from the kitchen with Alice behind her, both carrying two steaming cups of tea. "If we're quick, before the little ones wake up."

"The work never ends," Alice adds, setting a cup within my reach. "But we need this too."

Pearl struggles to sit up straighter, and Opal quickly moves to help her, adjusting pillows with practiced ease. The sisters exchange a look brimming with unspoken words. In the time since we've arrived in South Dakota, their bond has deepened. Now, with Pearl's condition worsening, every moment seems precious.

I close my journal, sealing away the thoughts meant for no one. The pages hold all my fears, my guilt, my hopes—things too raw to share even with Bowski. The journal has been my confidant since Braedon died, helping me maintain my sanity in a world gone mad.

Opal settles into a chair between our beds, her well-worn Bible in her lap. Alice takes the rocker near the window, positioned to keep an eye on both us and the yard beyond. The afternoon sun catches in her silver-streaked hair, reminding me suddenly of Katie. Does she know about Pearl's seizure yet? If not now, she will soon, once Poppy visits. I never even told Katie about the lumps Pearl found. More because Pearl asked me to keep it quiet than for any other reason.

"I've been reading Psalm 147," Opal begins, her voice soft but clear. "It seemed . . . appropriate." She clears her throat and begins to read. "He heals the brokenhearted and binds up their wounds. He determines the number of the stars and calls them each by name. Great is our Lord and mighty in power; His understanding has no limit."

The words wash over me, catching in my throat unexpectedly. He calls the stars by name. Each one, in all that vast expanse of sky. I think of the nights in Livingston, standing watch with Braedon, learning the constellations as we guarded against raiders. He knew them all, could trace their patterns in the dark. "God's nightlights," he called them, half-joking but completely serious.

If God knows each star, calls them by name . . . He knows my name too. Knows this baby's name, even before I do. Knows Pearl's name, and exactly how many days are written in her book.

A tear slips down my cheek, then another. Pearl's hand finds mine across the gap between our beds, her grip weak but present. When I look at her, I see my own tears mirrored in her eyes.

"Sing to the Lord with grateful praise," Opal continues reading. "Make music to our God on the harp."

Pearl's fingers tighten around mine. It's hard to want to give praise to God when things seem so dire, but the scriptures tell us to give thanks in all circumstances. It's not easy when someone you love is dying.

My greatest comfort is the peace that Pearl seems to have. She knows Jesus and knows she'll be with Him along with her husband and sons. Other than hoping to live long enough to meet her grandchild, she seems to have fully accepted what will happen. It's the rest of us who are having challenges.

"Those verses about the stars," Alice says softly, "they remind me of what Chris always says—that even when everything seems chaotic, there's order in God's creation. The stars follow their paths. The seasons change. Life goes on."

"Life changes," Pearl corrects gently. "But God remains constant."

I think about all the changes in my own life—from Coast Guard to Forest Service, from wife to widow, from fighting fires to healing people. Now here I am, carrying new life while hiding from those who have no respect for it. Through it all, something—someone—has been constant, even when I didn't recognize it.

"Merissa?" Opal's voice pulls me from my thoughts. "Would you like to read the next verses?"

I hesitate, then nod. She passes me the Bible, its pages worn smooth with use. The words blur slightly through my tears, but I manage. "The Lord delights in those who fear Him, who put their hope in His unfailing love."

Hope. Such a small word for such a powerful thing. I think of Braedon's hope for a child, a hope I didn't share until after he was gone. I think of Pearl's hope to see this baby, even as cancer eats away at her. I think of Bowski's patient hope, waiting for me to be ready.

"His unfailing love," I repeat softly, one hand straying to my belly as the baby shifts. "Even when everything else fails . . ."

"Even then," Pearl agrees. Her voice is tired but sure. "That's what carried me through losing Tomas and Braedon. What carries me still."

A sound from upstairs—Nico stirring from his nap—breaks the moment. Alice rises smoothly and heads up to check on him and the babies before they can fully wake and disturb our peace.

"We should do this every day," Opal says, taking the Bible back as I pass it to her. "Even if it's just for a few minutes. We all need this anchor."

I nod, surprised to find I mean it. There's something here I've been missing, something Braedon tried to share with me but I wasn't ready to receive. Something about faith being more than rules and rituals— being about relationships, about trust, about hope that doesn't depend on circumstances.

Pearl's eyes are growing heavy again, the effort of staying awake taxing her limited strength. But her hand remains in mine, warm and present, as Opal continues the verse. "He spreads the snow like wool and scatters the frost like ashes."

Through the window, I watch the last traces of the recent snow melting in the afternoon sun. Another storm is coming—we can feel it in the air—but for now, there's this moment of clarity. Of understanding that perhaps all these changes, all these trials, have been leading me here. Not just to this ranch, this physical sanctuary, but to this place of finally being ready to trust in something bigger than myself.

Opal finishes the chapter and puts the Bible aside, moving to her sister's bed. "Rest now," she tells Pearl, adjusting her blankets as her sister drifts off to sleep. But I remain awake, watching the sun paint patterns on the wall, thinking about stars with names and unfailing love and the God who somehow knows and cares about it all.

My journal lies closed beside me, but for once, I don't feel the need to write. Some moments, some revelations, are too profound for words. They can only be lived, experienced, and accepted like the gift they are.

Outside, life on the ranch continues—wood being chopped, animals being tended, children beginning to stir. But in here, in this moment, something has shifted. Something has changed. God has called me to Him. Called me to be one of His children. I'm ready. Ready to believe. Ready to acknowledge that Jesus died for me and lives again, offering me grace and a new life.

Chapter 19

Katie

It's been three days since Leo got the news about his arm. Three days of watching him wrestle with what it means for our future. The exercises Bollinger prescribed are helping his mobility, but this morning during rounds, I noticed him rubbing his wrist, his jaw set tight.

When I asked if he was okay, he shook his head. "Don't worry about it, Katie," he said, his tone sharper than I expected. A beat passed before he sighed, guilt softening his expression. "Sorry I snapped. This is just . . . hard."

That was hours ago, but his words still echo in my thoughts as I leave the treatment room.

"Ready for a break?" Elizabeth falls into step beside me. "I've been going over some interesting documents."

Something in her tone makes me pause. "What kind of documents?"

"Well . . ." She glances around the empty hallway. "Would you join us at the med school? Dr. Bollinger and Captain Williams will be meeting us there."

My stomach tightens. "Is this about Nettie?"

"No." She starts walking, clearly expecting me to follow. "This is about Reggie Murphy."

I furrow my brow, wondering why I'm being included in anything to do with Dr. Murphy.

We take a moment to put on our outerwear. The weather is almost springlike compared to recent weeks, though a chill still lingers in the air. Crossing the parking lot in silence, we head to one of the small offices the captain decided to take over since Major Stone laid claim to his original office in the hospital.

Stone's been delayed again, his top-secret assignment keeping him away from the hospital. We heard yesterday, not directly from him but through Lieutenant David Paul, that he should be back in a few days.

No one seems disappointed by the delay. During his brief time here as the hospital's lead, Stone left an impression, but not a good one. Even Dr. Bollinger, not one to critique leadership openly, said it's been the same story at the other hospitals.

Since mid-February, all Rapid City medical facilities—hospitals, clinics, and care centers—have been under the authority of the South Dakota National Guard, by order of the governor. For most places, that oversight has been minimal, leaving medical doctors to run things as usual.

Stone set out from the beginning to make it clear he was the one in charge and, while not a medical doctor, knew what was best for the hospital, med school, and nursing school. It'd be comical if it wasn't a life-and-death situation. Having someone who knows nothing about medicine running a medical facility makes zero sense.

At least the main hospital is still running smoothly. The addition of the mental health and physical therapy wards has been invaluable.

One of our patients, Elliot Tillman, is staying in the PT ward. Bollinger brought back an update on his progress, and it's encouraging. The paralysis was only temporary, and he's even walking now. He still has a long way to go, but it's believed he'll recover fully in time. Whether he'll recover enough to return to his position with the Guard is still unknown, but considering we expected him to die from his injuries, it's a huge victory.

Captain Williams and Bollinger are already in the office, heads bent over a stack of papers. Williams looks up when he hears us. "Elizabeth, Burnett—thanks for joining us."

"Of course, sir," I respond, still wondering why I'm here.

"Close the door," the captain says. "Burnett, I'd like you to take notes." He slides a pile of paper in my direction. "What we're about to discuss needs to be recorded and stay contained. At least for now."

"Here's the file," Bolinger says, shifting a stack of papers toward Elizabeth. "My driver returned with it about an hour ago."

"Have you gone through it?" Elizabeth asks, sorting through the papers.

"I've glanced at it." Bollinger adjusts his glasses. "The irregularities started showing up at the main hospital. Small things at first— terminology that seemed slightly off, procedures done in unconventional ways."

"And yet you sent him to our hospital." The clip of Captain Williams's words is unmistakable.

"He got results." Bollinger shrugs. "His patients did well. Besides, he volunteered, and you are a teaching hospital."

"Most of his patients did well." Elizabeth's voice is careful. "Even while I've been here, there seems to be . . . gaps in his knowledge. Things a trained physician should know instinctively, but he has to stop and think about."

"Like the pokeweed incident," the captain adds. "Herbs are new for us, since the lights went out and pharmaceutical manufacturers have closed down. Mistakes happen, no doubt, especially when we're learning something new, but the entire incident could have been avoided had he taken the time needed instead of rushing in blindly."

While I'm there only to take notes, my head bobs automatically. Dr. Murphy didn't even have the med book Stella made open to use as a reference. It was almost like he was trying to do it from memory. I'm not sure that means much, other than he was careless, but it's obvious the mistake still concerns Captain Williams.

The implications start to sink in. "What are you saying?"

"We're beginning to believe the man we know as Dr. Reginald Murphy is an impostor," Elizabeth says, spreading out several papers.

My throat goes dry. "And?"

Bollinger cuts in, "And we used some of the information he gave us. Made inquiries via the ham radio and suspect the real Dr. Murphy died during the riots that followed the bridge bombings."

"We suspect this," Elizabeth adds. "But we don't know for certain. There could be more than one Reginald Murphy out there."

"Humph. Doubtful," Bollinger scoffs.

The captain leans forward. "Our Murphy arrived at the main hospital last summer with paperwork that looked legitimate. Given the chaos after the EMP, no one questioned too deeply. He knew enough medical terminology, had enough basic skills . . ."

"But he's been treating patients!" The words burst out before I can stop them. "Prescribing medications, performing procedures— "

"Successfully, for the most part," Elizabeth acknowledges. "Which is why this is complicated. He obviously had some sort of medical training. He certainly knows enough to be able to care for patients."

A knock at the door makes us all jump. Through the frosted glass, we can see Murphy's silhouette.

The captain makes eye contact with each of us. Elizabeth stacks the papers and flips them over. I cover the notebook with a few lines of info on it. "Come in," Captain calls, his voice steady.

Murphy enters, his expression shifting as he takes in the scene. For a moment, there's complete silence. Then Murphy's shoulders slump, just slightly. "How long have you known?"

"Known? Only recently," Bollinger snaps, his tone clipped. "Suspected? Since your rotation through the main hospital. Your grasp of emergency medicine was . . . impressive at first glance. But there were gaps—glaring ones. Things any *board-certified emergency physician* would know without hesitation."

"I saved lives." Murphy's voice has an edge of desperation. "When everything fell apart, when people were dying in the streets, I helped. I made a difference."

"You had medical training?" the captain asks.

"I was a volunteer firefighter and EMT in the small town I grew up in."

"That was honorable work. This . . ." Williams gestures to the file. "This is fraud."

"Is it?" Murphy's laugh has a bitter edge. "What makes this any different from what you're doing, Captain? Training people to be doctors in two years instead of ten? Giving them responsibilities beyond their training?" His gaze falls on me as he lifts his eyebrows.

I feel my cheeks warm. He's not wrong.

"That's different," Captain Williams says, his voice hard. "We're honest about who we are and what we're doing. We don't pretend to be something we're not."

"The world changed," Murphy insists. "The old rules don't apply anymore. I had skills, knowledge. People needed help."

"Tell us what happened," Elizabeth says softly. "The truth."

Murphy sinks into an empty chair. "It was chaos. After the bridges . . . people were panicking. The hospital was overwhelmed. I was in Kansas City visiting a friend. I thought I could help. I jumped in, doing what I could to help the paramedics. Dr. Murphy—the real one—he was trying to help everyone. But things were going downhill fast."

He swallows hard. "Someone brought in a gun. Started demanding treatment. The doctor stepped between them and a patient. He died protecting her."

"And you took his credentials," Bollinger states flatly.

"Not right away. I picked up his badge. His identification. Thought I'd make sure his family knew. We looked alike—close enough, anyway. I kept working, doing what I could. But more doctors were dying or leaving. People needed help. I'd been an EMT for five years. I knew more than most people still around. It was crazy. You had to know what it was like. Things went from bad to worse to unbelievable. When the EMP happened, I figured . . ." His voice faded away as he gave a shrug.

"You became him," I say, the pieces falling into place. His nervousness around other doctors, his hesitation with certain procedures, the way he defers to others when things get complicated.

"I studied every medical text I could find. I learned. And I helped people. Murphy and I were about the same age. Same skin tone. My hair was longer, but I cropped it close like his and messed up the ID badge just enough to make it blurry. The driver's license . . . that didn't look enough like me, so I dropped it along the way. I heard about the stuff that was happening in Rapid City. How the town was coming together. The different district hospitals. The food supplies. I was starving in KC. Everyone was. Starving or being murdered."

"Until you made mistakes," Elizabeth points out. "Like with the pokeweed."

Murphy flinches. "Anyone could have made that mistake."

A commotion in the hallway interrupts us. Shaw's voice carries through the door. "Captain! We need you. Now."

Williams opens the door to find Shaw, face grim. "We found another storage facility. Like the one Hugo was using. There are records. Names. People we know."

The Hugo investigation and Murphy's deception crash together in this moment, each important but demanding our full attention in completely different ways.

The captain turns back to Murphy. "Don't leave this room." To Shaw, he says, "Can you get a guard in here?"

"I can," he agrees, looking only slightly confused.

"I'll explain as we go," the captain assures him.

Seemingly satisfied, he uses his radio to have someone come to the med school.

When Shaw's finished, the captain asks, "How bad?"

"You need to see this yourself. You'll be protected. Don't worry." He glances at me. "Katie should come too."

"Stay with him until the guard arrives," Williams tells Elizabeth and Bollinger. "We'll determine our next actions after I'm finished. Burnett, with me. Shaw, can you grab the other Sergeant Burnett?"

"He's waiting by the truck." Shaw gives me a quick glance. "It'll all make sense soon enough."

Leo meets us in the parking lot, his surprise at seeing me evident. I lift my hands in a shrug, palms up, as if to say, *Don't ask me—I don't know either.* Without a word, we climb into the bed of Shaw's truck.

In a low voice, I ask, "Why is the captain having me come along?"

"Not sure. As soon as Shaw showed up and told me what was happening, I suspected I'd be coming along." He leans closer to me. "How'd it go with Murphy?"

"You knew about that?"

"Mm-hmm. The captain thought about having me join you, but decided Murphy might feel threatened. He asked me what I thought about you documenting the meeting. You did okay?"

"It was surprisingly calm. Murphy caught on almost immediately to what was happening." I recount what Murphy—or whatever his name is—told us.

"I hate to admit it," Leo says, "but until the captain said something to me a few weeks ago, I never suspected anything. He's a good guy. A good doctor. I guess he makes mistakes, but everyone does at times." Leo rubs his wrist. I know he wonders if the doctor who set it originally, the late Eugene Newsome, made a mistake.

I reach for his hand and wrap our fingers together. "Remember how Bollinger asked about him when we were there for your exam?"

"Not really. That visit's a bit of a blur. We'd just lost Josiah."

Closing my eyes, I think of our friend Josiah Talbot. That was a terrible day, and I'm not sure why Bollinger's words stuck with me, but they did. Especially after Elizabeth arrived at our hospital and asked about Murphy and his training.

As Shaw pulls out of the parking lot, I notice the stalled cars lining the streets. They've been here since the collapse began. Some were left behind when they ran out of fuel, while others died in place when the EMP hit. Nearly every road and street in Pennington County is cluttered with these unmoving vehicles. I've heard they're setting up a work crew this summer to start clearing them out and moving them to parking lots as part of a cleanup effort.

The storage facility is only a couple of blocks away, hidden behind what used to be an auto repair shop. I consider asking the captain why I'm here but figure he'll tell me soon enough.

"We found ledgers," Shaw says, leading us through the building. "Detailed records of every process. And supplies delivered to specific locations. Including the hospital."

My stomach lurches. "Our hospital?"

"The main hospital and several of the other district hospitals. Look at this." He hands the captain a notebook, its pages filled with neat handwriting. "Deliveries of 'fuel' to multiple locations. But it's the names that matter. The people who were involved."

Williams flips through the pages, his face growing darker. "Some of these people . . . they're still in positions of authority."

Finding this new information, I wonder how much longer this can be kept quiet. I glance around at the people helping. All have been handpicked by Shaw, but it's still a considerable number.

It reminds me of a phrase I heard somewhere: Three may keep a secret, if two of them are dead. I have no memory of who said that, but it sticks with me now. The more people who know, the closer we are to the truth spilling out—whether we're ready or not.

My stomach tightens as I glance at the faces around me. They're focused and determined, but how many truly understand the storm that will follow when this comes to light?

For now, everyone moves with purpose, each task carefully assigned. But the weight of what we're hiding feels like it's pressing down on all of us. Secrets like this don't stay buried forever. And when people find out what was done to their loved ones, there's going to be so much hurt and anger. That anger could spill over into something none of us are prepared to handle.

"Sir," one of Shaw's officers, part of the Citizen Patrol under his command, calls from a back room. "We found more."

Shaw sends a team to secure the area while we continue poring over the records. Familiar names leap off the pages, each one tightening the captain's grim expression. It's no shock to find former sheriff Melvin Cabal among them.

"We'll need to move carefully," Shaw says. "Some of these people are powerful. Connected."

"They desecrated our dead," Williams responds, his voice hard. "Used them for profit. No one's above answering for that. The question is, who do we trust to help us do it?"

Shaw closes the ledger with a decisive snap. "We start with the names we know are clean. Build our case carefully. And we make sure justice is served—for everyone they've wronged. I know a few people who can help us, but we'll be careful."

He turns to Leo and me. "This is good news. It'll help us go public—and it'll protect you. We're almost there."

"It's almost over?" I ask, my chest tightening. "Does that mean we can go home? Be with our boys?"

"I'd say we're getting close. Close to this whole mess being wrapped up and able to get back to your normal lives."

Tears well in my eyes as I whisper a quiet prayer, thanking God for who He is and all He does. I ask, if it's not too much to ask, to please let me see my boys soon. A wave of peace washes over me, and I feel a quiet certainty—somewhere in all of this, God's plan is at work, even if we can't see it clearly yet.

Chapter 20

Katie

Bowski and his team arrive before we've made much progress cataloging the dead. The easygoing charm he's known for is gone, replaced by a grim determination. His gaze sweeps the scene, and his posture stiffens, as though bracing for the enormity of what lies ahead.

"I'm glad we found it," Shaw tells him quietly. "I was beginning to wonder if we would before this whole debacle became public."

"How many?"

"We're still counting. Could use your help with that." Shaw glances toward Leo and me. "The Burnetts are going to assist with identification. It's good we found the bodies now. A few more days of this warm weather and they could start decomposing, making identification difficult. As it is, it's not going to be pleasant storing the bodies until the ground thaws enough for burial."

Bowski nods, then moves closer to us. "This might be wrapping up soon."

"Shaw thinks so," I confirm. "The ledgers name names. Once this goes public . . ."

"We can all go home," Leo finishes.

"About time." Bowski's voice softens. "Merissa's letters talk about how much she misses everyone. Pearl too. And your boys . . ." He trails off, seeing the emotion on my face. He gives me a smile. "They'll be happy to have you back."

A smile crosses my face as I think of the boys, but it quickly fades when I recall the note Poppy brought back from her house call. Merissa wrote to tell me that Pearl was sick—something they'd suspected for weeks, praying it wasn't what they feared. But a seizure a few days ago confirmed their worst fear. They believe Pearl has cancer that's metastasized. Merissa has asked that we include Pearl in our prayers.

Reading about Pearl brought a flood of memories rushing back. Cancer played a part in my mom's death. By the time it was discovered, there were no tests to confirm it, and with the EMP having wiped out modern medicine, there was little that could be done.

When she was injured during the battle for the town of Prospect, it felt like a blessing. She fell and severed her spinal column, leaving her with little sensation below her shoulders. Watching her die was still agonizing, but at least her pain was minimal. I can only hope they can do something for Pearl, to ease whatever pain she may have.

"Let's get to work," I say, forcing myself to focus on the task at hand. "The sooner we document everything, the sooner this nightmare ends."

The work is grim. Each home-sewn body bag, stacked like cord wood, reveals another horror, another family member someone's been missing. Some have identification, carefully logged in Hugo's meticulous records. Others are listed only as "John Doe" or "Jane Doe" with dates of "acquisition."

"Katie." Leo's voice catches as he examines one of the unnamed bags. "It's Rand Hendricks."

My heart sinks as I move to help him. Kerry's husband disappeared weeks ago, leaving her devastated and confused. Many whispered that he'd abandoned her, seeking better opportunities elsewhere. But Kerry never believed it.

Rand's face is peaceful, as if sleeping, but the marks on his body tell a different story.

"Document everything," Bowski instructs from somewhere behind us. "Every detail matters now."

In another part of the building, Captain Williams and Shaw discuss plans to expose everything. Names drift through the air—former sheriff Melvin Cabal, prominent citizens, military personnel. Some are already deceased, like former Trooper Carter Schroeder, Cabal's brother-in-law. Geoff Landers is also on the list. He's being kept somewhere in a military hold but is in a near-vegetative state.

"Cabal being involved makes sense," I say to Leo as we continue our grim task. "After everything with the Ploy operation . . ."

"I can't say I'm surprised," Leo agrees. "That man was wrapped up in all sorts of bad things—the drug Ploy, blackmailing Captain Williams, the black market. The thing is, he was already locked up when the whistleblower was killed and when we were ambushed."

"So, he didn't order it? Someone else did, right? But who?"

"That is the question, along with how deep it goes." Leo pauses in his documentation. "Remember what the Preacher wrote in his final note? About corruption in the hospitals?"

The thought stops me. The Preacher, for all his faults, had been adamant about returning to simpler ways. His belief that the EMP was God's judgment, his insistence on horses and walking rather than finding fuel alternatives. "He knew," I realize. "Maybe not everything, but he knew something was wrong."

"Oh, he knew all right."

My mind drifts to Kemeera's descriptions of the Preacher's teachings about an agrarian future. It seems unlikely he'd have been part of Hugo's operation. But how many others were? How many people that we see every day are involved in this horror?

"Think about it," Leo says as we move to the next body. "The Preacher's whole thing about God's vengeance—about how we needed to accept this new world instead of trying to recreate the old one. What if this is what he meant?"

"Using the dead to power vehicles?" I shudder. "It's certainly not accepting God's plan."

Bowski joins us, his face grim. "Found a dozen more in the back room. Records show they were brought in last month. They've already been, uh, processed." He hesitates. "One of them . . . it's Mary Foster's husband. The one everyone thought left with that trading group."

I shake my head. "I haven't heard about him."

Leo tilts his head toward his ear. "It was around the time you were recovering from frostbite."

"Oh." I drop my shoulders as the memories of that ordeal flash back. Not memories exactly. More like flashes. I took Gerry out into the backyard, and the next thing I knew, I was on the ground, being kicked and hit. Poor Gerry was also beaten, and we were left for dead. With temps below zero, we wouldn't have made it through the night. Somehow, Leo woke up and came looking for us.

I guess it's no wonder I missed someone else missing. That and I'm not familiar with the woman, but now that I hear her name, maybe I do remember someone saying Rand's disappearance was just like so and so's. Maybe so-and-so was Mary Foster's husband.

The names keep coming. People we knew, people we'd wondered about. Each discovery feels like another weight added to my shoulders, but also like pieces of a puzzle finally fitting together.

Leo moves onto another body bag and lets out a gasp. "Katie, can you, um . . . can you come over here?"

My pen halts midstroke as Leo's voice cuts through my focus. "What is it?" From his tone, I know it can't be good. Nothing in this building is good.

"Kemeera."

I take in a sharp breath. My baby Caleb's mom. The one who abandoned him and disappeared with—my eyes go wide. "Where's Shawna?"

"Her daughter?" Leo asks, glancing at the body bags stacked in a grim, orderly fashion. "Maybe in one of the remaining bags." His voice is flat and hollow.

So far, we've only found adults. I hate to think that could change. It's bad enough the adults were being used for fuel, the fat on their bodies filleted off and melted down. After nearly two years of rations, I can't imagine there was much fat left on some of them.

I'll be honest, when I first heard about this travesty, I didn't fully grasp the process of making biodiesel. I knew it was how we were powering our vehicles. Nearly two years into the apocalypse, the "Big Oil" fuels left from before everything fell apart were running low and, in the case of gasoline, had gone bad. I've heard there's still some diesel available in certain areas, but it's in short supply.

Biodiesel is made through biological processes instead of geological ones like those that create fossil fuels. Unlike traditional diesel, it's produced by converting oils, usually vegetable oil.

Bowski said there was a man, prior to the EMP, who used to drive around to the various restaurants in Rapid City and take their used cooking oils to turn into biodiesel. Restaurants are no more, and vegetable oils aren't mass produced.

Apparently, animal fats like lard or tallow can also be used, but we need those for human consumption to help with our weight and health. The idea of using human fat isn't much different from animal fats—yet it's a world apart. It's certainly a moral and ethical issue to think it's okay to run trucks on dead bodies.

There might be an argument for those who died of natural causes—such as the flu that went through our region, claiming hundreds of lives—but all of the mysterious deaths and disappearances? Those are certainly not okay.

"None of the body bags looks small, right?" I ask as I scan the area. The homemade body bags are stitched together from surplus fabrics. Some look more like crazy quilts than a shroud. They're made by those who aren't able to handle the physical labor crews, and different sizes are available. Once filled, Hugo or one of his team would then do a simple holding stitch to seal them.

"I don't think so. We'll just have to keep working and see what we find."

The captain and Shaw work methodically through the ledgers while we handle the bodies. Their voices drift over occasionally—mentions of government officials, military personnel, civilians in positions of power. The web of corruption seems endless.

"Hey, guys." Shaw approaches as we finish documenting another victim. "We found something you should see. Bowski? Will you join us?"

When we're gathered around, he holds out a notebook, different from the ledgers. The handwriting is familiar—Hugo's precise script. But these aren't just records of his victims. These are observations, details about the operation's scope.

"He was keeping insurance," Shaw explains. "Names, dates, their barter system. Evidence against those involved, probably in case he ever needed leverage."

"Smart," Leo comments. "Dangerous, but smart."

"This is why they tried to kill him in jail," I realize. "They knew he had this somewhere."

"And why they might have come after you and Merissa," Shaw adds. "If the whistleblower told you anything . . ."

I think of Hank Timbs, dying in the street before he could reveal what he knew. Of Merissa and me running for our lives. Of being separated from my children because someone thought we might know too much. I shake my head. "He didn't tell us anything. He died before he could."

"We'll need to move quickly once we go public," the captain says, joining our group. "These people won't go down without a fight."

"But we have proof now," Shaw responds. "Real proof. It isn't just Hugo's word against theirs."

Working through the afternoon, we document everything. Every body, every record, every piece of evidence that will help bring justice. It's exhausting and emotionally draining work, but knowing the end is in sight keeps us going.

When we open the last body bag, Kemeera's daughter, Shawna, is nowhere to be found. I'm glad about this, truly, but also wonder where the little girl might be. Is she with Addison, who disappeared at the same time as Kemeera and Shawna? Or has death claimed her, too, but she was spared the indignity of being added to Hugo's biodiesel plans?

I think about Addison and the last we knew of her. She used hemlock to poison the Preacher's flock. Kemeera and Shawna disappeared, and people thought they were with Addison. A little girl from the Preacher's cult told us there was unfinished business—that Kemeera had gone to finish the job. Now Kemeera's dead. Was the job finished? Maybe we'll never know.

"Can you talk to Hugo about Shawna?" I ask Shaw. "Find out if he knows where she is?"

"Oh, I'll be talking to Hugo all right. He's going to know everything we've found. Maybe that will get him talking."

"Good. Okay. But Shawna? I'd like to know where she is. Maybe . . . maybe she needs our help?"

The smile Shaw gives me is patient and tinged with doubt. If Kemeera's remains are here, it doesn't bode well for her little girl. "We'll do what we can."

I let out a sigh. While I'd love to get something more from him, a commitment that ensures he'll find Shawna one way or another, I understand it's not an easy task. "Thank you. And Kerry? You'll let her know about Rand?"

"I'll tell her," the captain says. "She's one of my staff. My student. My responsibility."

Bowski's team will secure the remains, holding them in a safe location until the weather breaks and they can be buried. A real burial, with dignity and respect. No more secret facilities, no more hidden horrors.

As we leave the building, the setting sun paints the sky in shades of orange and pink. I feel both drained and hopeful. If they can bust this whole conspiracy wide open, we'll be safe. We'll be able to go home to Nico, Gerry, and the babies without endangering them.

Merissa, Pearl, and Alice won't have to remain holed up in the house, not able to leave. Maybe Pearl's last days can be ones of peace, surrounded by the people who love her, instead of fear. Soon, justice will be served. Soon, this chapter of our lives will close.

But first, we have to survive making it public.

"Ready?" Leo asks, giving my hand a quick squeeze.

"Ready." I give a determined nod. "Let's finish this."

The drive back to the hospital is quiet, each of us lost in our own thoughts. Tomorrow, we'll begin the process of exposing everything. Tomorrow, the real fight begins.

But tonight, I'll write another letter to our children, telling them how much we love them and how we're working to make their world safer. And I'll pray—pray for justice, pray for safety, and pray for the strength to see this through to the end.

Because sometimes the hardest part isn't discovering the truth, it's surviving long enough to tell it.

Chapter 21

Merissa

The lantern casts a soft glow across my journal pages, barely enough to write by, but it's all I can risk this late at night. Pearl sleeps beside me, her breathing shallow but steady. Gerry is on the floor at the foot of her bed. Since the seizure, Gerry stays close, as if guarding her, watching for any sign that it might happen again.

The house has settled into its nighttime stillness, broken only by the occasional creak of old wood shifting in the cold. Today was almost springlike, with the sun offering a warmth we've missed. We even managed to open a couple of windows to let fresh air into the house. If these mild days keep up, I'll find a way to spend some time outside. Maybe I'll move a cot to the porch. The thought of it feels like a small luxury.

My letter to Bowski sits sealed on the nightstand, ready for Shawn to take into town tomorrow. It took three attempts—scratched out in my journal—to get the words right, to find the balance between what I wanted to say and what I could safely put on paper.

Today was another busy day. Not for me, of course; I spent it in this bed. And not for Pearl either. She's so drained from the lingering effects of the seizure that all she has the energy for is rest.

Kevin is on guard duty tonight and just left for his shift. Opal came down with him while he was getting ready. She checked on Pearl and gave her something to ease the pain. The headache had been bothering her so much that she was moaning in her restless sleep. In these quiet hours, when sleep won't come, I turn to my journal. Here, I can write what I can't say aloud, the fears I can't share—even with Pearl.

Especially not with Pearl.

I begin writing, the pencil scratching softly against the notebook:

Thursday night.

Poppy's visit on Tuesday gave confirmation of what we suspected. The baby is doing well—strong heartbeat, good position, growing as it should. But Pearl . . .

My hand trembles slightly, and I have to pause. Pearl shifts in her sleep, murmuring something I can't quite catch. The pain medicines Stella sent are helping her rest, but I can see how much effort it takes for her to stay present during her waking hours. No wonder it's easier to sleep. I continue writing.

The palliative care plan Stella sent is good. But watching the medicines work tells its own story. Pearl needed the stronger dose today, just like Stella warned we might see. The hope is after a little time on the treatment, she'll even out and will begin to have some good days. Time. Sadly, it's slipping away faster than any of us wanted to believe.

The baby kicks, a strong movement that makes me smile despite everything. Pearl had been so happy on Tuesday when Poppy suggested she feel the baby's movements during the exam. "Strong, just like its mama," she'd said, her eyes bright with joy despite her obvious fatigue.

Katie's note came with Shawn. She's worried, of course. Wants to help but can't leave the medical school, not with everything still unsettled. The Hugo situation has everyone on edge. But she promised to be here for me and the baby once it's safe. Said we'd raise our babies together. Alice will help too—she's already so good with Zach and Caleb. Nico, too, of course. They're family.

A tear splashes onto the page, smearing the ink. I brush it away carefully, not wanting to wake Pearl with my crying. But the tears come anyway, silent but persistent. She's so exhausted, spending much of her day sleeping. It's frightening just how fast she is fading.

I pray that Stella is right. That the remedies she sent will start working in Pearl's body. That she'll rally and have more time. Is that selfish of me? Maybe. But I know how important it is to Pearl to see this baby born. To hold him and love him. I also don't want her to be in pain. I guess I'm pinning most of my hopes on the herbs Stella concocted.

I wish I could do something. Anything. The second crew of trappers returned today. No mistletoe. Opal tried to hide her disappointment, but I saw her face when they reported back. We're running out of options. Running out of time.

Opal sent a note to Stella asking about mistletoe, but it's not something Stella had before the EMP. She doesn't have any now, nor does she know where to find it growing wild.

Pearl stirs again, and I pause my writing to watch her. Even if they'd found the mistletoe, it's too late. I know this. Opal knows this too. But there is still hope. In the lantern light, Pearl's face looks peaceful, younger somehow. The lines of pain that mark her waking hours are smoothed away by sleep and Stella's medicines. How many more nights will we have like this? How many more quiet moments?

The baby moves so much now. Especially at night, like it knows these quiet hours are precious. Pearl says it's practicing for keeping me up at night once it's born. She tells me all the things she remembers about when Braedon was a baby—how he never slept more than two hours at a time, how he always wanted to be held. I try to memorize every story, every detail. They're not just about Braedon anymore. They're pieces of Pearl I need to keep, to share with this child who might never know her except through our memories.

Sometimes, I catch Pearl watching me when she thinks I'm not looking. There's so much love in her eyes, but something else too. Not fear—she's past that—but worry. Not for herself, but for me. For the baby. For all of us she'll leave behind. I want to tell her we'll be okay, but the words stick in my throat. How can we be okay without her?

The baby shifts again, and I pause to rub my side where a tiny foot or elbow presses outward. Pearl said earlier today that she could see the movement from her bed. Her joy at such a simple thing broke my heart a little more.

Bowski's letter spoke about hope, about how sometimes the darkest times show us what really matters. When the EMP hit, his ex-wife and daughter were in California. He hasn't heard from them since. He hopes they were able to get out of the Wasteland and are living in one of the camps—or, even better, have found housing somewhere. But he doesn't know.

He's using all of his contacts to find out via the ham radio and, when mail was somewhat working, sending letters to people he knew in various places. I know he won't give up, but I also understand he may never know what happened to them. Bowski's found purpose in helping others, in being part of rebuilding something new from the ashes of what was lost. I want to believe that—that something good can come even from this pain. That's what Pearl would say. That's what she tries to show us every day.

A board creaks upstairs. It's probably just the house settling, but I pause to listen anyway. After a moment, silence returns. Pearl's breathing remains steady, peaceful in her medicinal sleep.

I continue writing, the words barely visible through my fresh tears. *Poppy says we need to be prepared. The seizure was just the beginning. There could be more, or other symptoms. If the cancer is in her brain now, it could spread through the tissue that holds her memories, her personality, everything that makes her Pearl. Stella's medicines will help with pain, anxiety, and keeping her comfortable, and might buy her more time, but they can't stop what's coming. Nothing can.*

I have to stop writing for a moment, overwhelmed by grief and the unfairness of it all. Pearl deserves to meet this baby, to hold her grandchild and see the family she helped create continue growing. She deserves so much more time than we have left.

Katie's right about one thing. We are family now, all of us. Not by blood, but by choice and circumstance and love. Pearl taught me that—how to open my heart, even when it hurts, how to find joy in small moments, and how to trust in God's plan, even when we don't understand it. Even now, she's teaching me. Even now, she's showing me how to face whatever comes with grace and faith.

The lantern flame flickers, reminding me how late it's gotten. I should try to sleep—tomorrow will bring its own challenges, its own grief, its own moments to cherish.

I don't know how to say goodbye. I don't know how to be ready for this. Pearl would say we don't have to be ready, we just have to be faithful. She'd say—

The sharp clang of cowbells cuts through the night, their urgent rhythm shattering the peace. Three quick rings, then two long—not the medical emergency signal, but something else. Something's wrong.

Pearl stirs at the sound, her eyes fluttering open. "Merissa?"

Before I can answer, boots thunder across the porch. Walt bursts through the door, his rifle ready. "Raiders," he says grimly. "Big group. Kevin spotted them coming up from the dry creek bed."

Footsteps pound overhead as the bells wake the household. Pearl struggles to sit up, but her movements are sluggish from the medicine. I close my journal and reach for my pistol, kept loaded on the nightstand.

"How many?" I ask, swallowing my fear.

"Too many. Hard to tell in the dark." Walt positions himself near the window, scanning the darkness. "Kevin's organizing the defense."

The stairs creak as the family descends—Opal carrying Caleb, Alice with Zach, and Jason guiding a frightened Nico. Robert follows close behind, his face pale but determined. Shawn appears last, already checking his weapon.

"Get them to the safe room," Walt orders, his eyes never leaving the window. "Jason, you know what to do."

The older boy nods while muttering, "Yes, sir. I'll take care of it." He's already moving to help the group prepare to leave the warm house. He's been trained for this since he first started living at the ranch.

"I'll help defend," Shawn says, checking his ammunition as Abby enters the house.

"Your dad wants you on the south side," she says to Shawn. "They're trying to come up from the creek."

Shawn holds Abby's gaze for a moment before saying, "You'll stay inside? Protect Merissa and Pearl? Yourself?"

Abby reaches for his hand. "We'll be fine. Take care of yourself."

I tuck their interaction away to consider later as Shawn hustles out the door. The sound of gunfire erupts from the direction of the barn. Pearl flinches at the noise, but her voice remains steady. "Opal, get those babies somewhere safe."

"Not without you," Opal protests. "Get your slippers on. I'll grab your jacket."

More shots ring out, closer now. The bell continues its frantic warning, but other sounds join it—shouts, engines, the crack of rifles. My hands tighten around the pistol as I scan what I can see of the yard through the window. Movement catches my eye—shadows darting between buildings.

"Walt!" The warning leaves my lips as muzzle flashes appear from the darkness.

The sound of gunfire erupts from the direction of the barn.

"Opal!" Pearl says. "You need to get everyone to the safe room."

"No time," Walt says. "They're too close. We defend here." His expression softens slightly as he looks at Pearl. "I won't let anything happen to any of you."

"Let's get everyone into the pantry," Opal says, helping Pearl to her feet. "Merissa, let's take you too."

I nod my agreement. The way Walt moved the bed last time worked, but the pantry is a better option, and walking that far won't be an issue . . . hopefully. As if responding to my tension, the baby kicks hard. Pearl reaches for my hand in the darkness, her grip weak but present.

Abby is at my side, asking if I need anything. "I'm fine. Just help Walt." I pass my pistol to her. "Use it if you need to."

"You should take it."

"I'm sure Opal is armed."

"You better believe it," Opal says. "Alice and Jason are too."

"Yes, ma'am." Jason nods.

"Always," Alice adds.

"Now let's get to the pantry." Opal motions to get us moving. "C'mon, Gerry," she adds, encouraging the dog to join us.

As we pass through the kitchen, she asks Jason and Robert to grab a couple of chairs. The windowless room is fully dark. More gunfire erupts from multiple directions. Through the chaos, Kevin shouts orders, followed by answering fire from our defenders.

"'Rissa?" Nico asks, reaching for my hand. "Can we turn on a light?"

"We'd better not," Jason responds.

"Not yet," Opal agrees. "Merissa, Pearl—sit down. Everyone else, find a way to get comfortable."

Robert shifts, bumping into something in the dark. "There's not much space in here." Gerry whines his agreement.

"We'll make do," Opal replies sharply, her tone leaving no room for argument. "We stay put until we know it's safe."

The gunfire intensifies outside, seeming to come from all directions. From this room, it's impossible to tell how close the raiders are, but the varying volume of shots gives some indication of their movement. Voices carry above the chaos, barking orders that are too muffled to make out clearly.

Pearl's ragged breathing beside me betrays her pain—the quick move to the pantry and uncomfortable chair are taking its toll. I'll admit, I'm hurting too. No contractions, but my back doesn't like this hard chair or close quarters. In the darkness, Nico presses closer to my leg, his small body trembling. Zach begins to fuss, but Alice quickly soothes him.

The sound of breaking glass—probably more windows—is followed by return fire from our defenders. The raiders must be trying to breach the house.

"Get lower," Opal whispers as shots sound closer. A hand reaches for mine—Jason, maybe, helping me from the chair to the floor. The same must be happening to Pearl since she mutters, "Hope someone plans on helping me up from here." I murmur my agreement.

Through the pantry door, Walt's voice rings out. There are fewer shots now, but they're more organized. The defending fire grows more strategic—short bursts rather than constant exchange.

The sudden increase in gunfire from the south suggests Shawn and his team are engaging.

Caleb starts to whimper, and Opal murmurs gentle shushing sounds. The baby in my womb kicks hard, responding to the tension in the room. Pearl's hand finds mine in the darkness, her grip weak but reassuring.

There's a crash somewhere in the house, close enough to make us all jump. More glass breaks, though from which room is impossible to tell. The gunfire seems closer now, or maybe it's just echoing differently through the house.

The muffled sound of hoofbeats reaches us, but there's no way to know if they're friend or foe. In the darkness, with these thick walls between us and the fight, we can only wait and pray our defenders hold.

"Abby! Watch the barn side!" Walt yells. His rifle cracks twice in quick succession.

The sound of approaching horses grows louder—many of them moving fast. But these are coming from a different direction. More raiders?

"That might be Hayward's people," Opal breathes, barely audible.

"Or maybe more bad guys," Pearl responds. "We're sitting ducks in here."

"Alice, hand the baby to Pearl. Merissa, you take Caleb. I want you two, Nico, and Robert at the very back. We're going to get in front of you in case there's a breach."

"How will we know?" Jason asks with a quiver in his voice. "If they get inside the house, how will we know?"

"We'll know," Opal responds as we all move in the tight space. Pearl and I are awkward as we shift on the floor, but somehow, we manage to scoot to the back of the pantry. Gerry positions himself by Pearl. I suddenly regret leaving my pistol with Abby. What was I thinking?

The intensity of gunfire changes, with shots becoming more sporadic. Their horses' hoofbeats retreat, moving away from the house rather than toward it. But we stay put in the darkness, listening as the sounds of battle fade into scattered shots, then just voices—familiar ones now, calling out to each other.

Still, we wait.

The minutes stretch like hours until, finally, Walt's familiar drawl reaches us through the pantry door. "All clear, folks. They're gone."

As Opal opens the door, letting in the lantern light from the main room, we begin the process of untangling ourselves from our cramped positions. Pearl's face is drawn with pain from sitting so long on the hard floor, and Nico's eyes are wide as he keeps his grip on my hand.

Even as Opal and the others help Pearl and me get to our feet, I can't stop thinking about how vulnerable we are. The raiders are gone for now, but they'll be back—or others will come. They're getting bolder each time. Plus, something about this attack felt different. More organized. More purposeful.

As we make our way out of the pantry, with Pearl leaning heavily on Opal while I rub my aching back, I realize this is our new reality. No matter how safe we try to make ourselves, danger is always waiting. But looking at the faces around me—at Pearl's quiet strength, at Opal's fierce protectiveness, at our family pulling together—I know we'll face whatever comes. We have to.

Chapter 22

Katie

The fallout from the Murphy situation stirs tension among the med students. Word of the fake doctor spreads fast, despite our late-night finish at the body holding facility. By morning, opinions are sharply divided.

Jeff is quick to defend Murphy, arguing that a lack of a license doesn't erase his usefulness. Kerry seems to side with him, but before rounds begin, the captain pulls her into the break room, asking Elizabeth to get us started on rounds.

She agrees with a nod before saying, "Don't forget, I'm here if you need me."

Something in Elizabeth's tone indicates she knows what the conversation with Kerry is about. And from the look on Kerry's face, I think maybe she knows too.

Murphy is still detained, held in one of the med school offices turned apartment, under guard, while the captain decides what to do with him. The way things are going, the med school is becoming more of an apartment complex than anything else.

After we wrapped up last night, we went over our next steps with Shaw. For now, Leo, the captain, and I are still waiting, biding our time until Hugo's biodiesel ring is exposed.

Shaw's confident that what we uncovered yesterday is the key to ending this danger and the key to being reunited with our children. They found several names of people involved, individuals Hugo was reporting to, but Shaw believes that's just the tip of the iceberg.

In multiple instances, Hugo hinted at someone else, someone behind it all. Shaw doesn't think it's one of the names we have, but someone else entirely. Another secret that still needs to be uncovered before things can return to normal. Before our children can come home.

We start our rounds with the woman who had the baby yesterday.

"Your vital signs are good," I tell the new mom. "We'll probably discharge you this afternoon."

"Good. My husband is working this morning but asked to get off after lunch. I'm not sure I'm up to walking alone."

"We'll have our medic drive you home. We always do that for new mothers."

She gives me a wide smile as she strokes her baby's cheek. "He's perfect, isn't he?"

"He's amazing. You are truly blessed."

"Thank you for your help. It was . . . difficult, but you were great with the way you reminded me to breathe. You're an excellent nurse."

I consider telling her I'm in training to be a doctor but realize the label doesn't matter at the moment. "You've got everything you need to be a great mom," I say instead.

Her smile softens, and she cradles her baby closer. "I hope so. It's just . . . a lot to take in, you know?"

"I do," I reply gently. "But you're not alone. Lean on your husband, and if you have questions or need anything, you can always reach out to us. That's what we're here for. Make sure you register him so your rations can be adjusted."

She nods, her confidence growing. The baby stirs, letting out a soft whimper, and she instinctively soothes him, her hands moving with the natural grace of a mother already finding her rhythm, as she helps him to nurse.

She's our only patient to check in the hospital. Elizabeth says the captain wants to have a quick meeting before we head off to the care centers for those rounds. "I'll check with him, but it'll probably be only a few minutes until he's ready to begin."

I spend a couple more minutes with the new mom and her baby, ensuring the baby has latched on well and is eating. Satisfied all is well, I tell her I'll be back later to discharge them.

As I turn to leave, I glance back and see her humming quietly to the baby, her earlier worries melting into a tender moment of connection.

In the hallway, I nearly collide with Kerry. Her face is drawn, eyes red from crying.

"Kerry, I— "

"At least now I know," she says quietly. "I always knew he wouldn't just leave. Rand wasn't like that. He loved me. We had our troubles, like all marriages do, but we loved each other and were determined to make it work."

Before I can respond, Captain Williams appears. "Burnett, will you join us in the break room?"

I glance at Kerry. She shakes her head and whispers, "He told me I can have the day off. But I do know what the meeting's about. Murphy."

Of course it is. I let out a sigh before wrapping Kerry in a hug. "I'm praying for you."

The room is crowded when I arrive. The other two med students, Matt and Jeff, are there. Elizabeth sits near the captain, while Bollinger leans against the wall with his arms crossed. I take a seat next to Leo. Lieutenant David Paul is sitting on the other side of Leo.

"Where's Murphy?" Jeff asks.

"Being brought over," Shaw replies. "Under guard."

"You think he's dangerous?" Jeff shakes his head, continuing his defense of the man he's come to call a friend.

Shaw shrugs. "Unknown. Things aren't always what they seem around here."

The captain clears his throat. "We need to decide how to handle both immediate and long-term situations. Dr. Murphy's deception, while serious, isn't our only concern right now."

"Well, it might not be the only concern," Bollinger says, "but it is serious. He practiced medicine without proper credentials."

"And saved lives," Elizabeth counters. "While I don't condone his deception, his skills are real."

Murphy arrives, escorted by two guards. Yesterday's nervousness is gone, replaced by quiet resignation.

"I'd like to make a suggestion," he says after the captain waves him to a seat. "Let me continue my training, properly this time. As a student in the program."

"I agree," Jeff says quickly.

"That's not— " Bollinger starts, but Williams raises a hand.

"You've proven you have basic medical knowledge," the captain says. "But how do we explain this to everyone? To our patients?"

"Tell them the truth," Murphy responds. "That I was an EMT who stepped up during a crisis, who made a bad decision but wanted to help. That I'm willing to learn properly now."

"The truth isn't always enough," Bollinger argues. "What about liability? Trust? Every patient he treated could claim malpractice."

"In the apocalypse?" Jeff scoffs. "We're all learning as we go. Even you, Dr. Bollinger, have had to adapt your surgical techniques."

"Not at the cost of my patients!" the man booms.

"No." Jeff levels his gaze. "Just at the female doctors and nurses you work with. If you'd keep it in your— "

"Enough, Thacker." The captain raises his hand, urging Jeff to be quiet.

Bollinger grumbles a few more times, making it clear he either doesn't understand what Jeff is referring to or is choosing to ignore it.

I watch Murphy's face. He seems calmer than he has in the days since Elizabeth and Bollinger arrived. The nervous mannerisms are seemingly gone, and the confident doctor we thought we knew is back in place. Was that all an act? A way to appear less competent, less threatening? It makes me question every interaction we've had.

"The issue isn't his current competence," Elizabeth says, her voice cutting through the growing tension. "It's the precedent we set. If we allow someone who falsified credentials to simply join the program, what message does that send?"

"That we value skills and dedication," Jeff counters. "Murphy's treated dozens of patients successfully. He's helped train us. I know you are all using the pokeweed incident as proof he's incompetent, but that could have happened to anyone. Captain Williams is an excellent doctor, and he still relies on Stella for difficult things. Look at Dr. Wolff. The first thing he did was call for Stella."

"But Murphy didn't call for Stella," I say, avoiding the fake doctor's gaze. "He didn't even open the dosage and treatment book she made for us to use."

"That was a mistake," Murphy agrees. "I'd been studying the information, and I thought I knew what I was doing. I had my herbs confused."

My mind drifts to all the patients Murphy has treated. How many lives has he actually saved? Many, no doubt. How many has he potentially endangered? Truthfully, no more than any of us. The captain's face suggests he's wrestling with the same questions.

I glance at Shaw. He remains in the meeting, but the guards that escorted Murphy from his med school room have left. Shaw's here more as a representative of our fractured government than anything.

With the hospital officially under the control of the National Guard, Lieutenant David Paul is here as that liaison. Major Stone was notified about the situation but was unable to return from whatever assignment he's on, so Paul and Captain Williams are the Guard's representatives and will report back to Major Stone and General Truss.

"There's also the matter of trust among colleagues," Bollinger presses. "How can any of us work alongside someone who maintained such a fundamental deception?"

"You don't even work here," Jeff says, the anger in his voice barely controlled. "I don't know why you even get a say in this."

"I have as much of a stake in it as any of you," Bollinger huffs. "When I'm on rotation or receiving patients from here, I need to know they've been properly treated. It's hard enough with— " Bollinger slams his lips shut.

"With what?" The captain leans forward in his chair. "What was it you wanted to say, Doctor?"

Bollinger waves his hand. "Never mind that."

"You sure?" Captain Williams presses. "Is there something additional on your mind regarding my hospital?"

"Your hospital? Pretty sure it's Major Stone's hospital." Bollinger shuffles his feet. "Look. My beef isn't with you, Chris. But I will argue that I have a say in the doctors you are producing here. Same as Elizabeth does and every other pre-EMP trained physician. We need to be confident you're producing quality doctors."

Murphy's shoulders have crept up toward his ears, but his voice remains steady. "I understand your concerns. I do. But I'm not asking to continue as a doctor. I'm asking to start over—properly this time. To learn the right way. As part of Captain Williams's program."

"And in the meantime?" Matt asks. "We're already short-staffed. We need a full-fledged doctor."

I close my eyes and shake my head. Nettie should be here. She had asked to join, but Elizabeth decided she wasn't ready for a discussion that would almost certainly turn into a debate.

Even though Nettie is no longer considered a danger to herself—the immediate crisis has passed—Stella is sitting with her. Elizabeth thought it was better to keep her occupied than to have her worrying about this meeting.

Like the rest of us, Nettie feels betrayed by Murphy and his actions. At Elizabeth's suggestion, she wrote a note outlining her position on Murphy and what she believes should be done.

The captain leans forward. "That's actually my primary concern. Not just staffing, but stability. Our patients, our community—they need to believe in this hospital, in what we're building here."

I find myself nodding. After everything with Hugo, after all the revelations about corruption and darkness in our new world, people need something to trust. But can we trust Murphy?

"Perhaps we're looking at this wrong," Elizabeth suggests. "Instead of seeing it as rewarding deception, we could frame it as redemption. A chance to set things right."

"Redemption?" Bollinger snorts. "That's a bit dramatic, don't you think?"

"Not at all," Elizabeth responds. "We're not just rebuilding a medical system. We're rebuilding trust, community, and hope. How we handle this situation matters."

I glance at Leo, seeing my own uncertainty reflected in his face. Yesterday, discovering Murphy's deception felt like a betrayal. Today, watching him face the consequences with quiet dignity, I'm not so sure.

"Let's be practical," the captain says. "Murphy has skills we need. Real, demonstrable skills. And he's willing to learn, to do things properly this time."

"He also has experience none of us wanted," Jeff adds. "Working through the collapse, the riots. That's valuable."

"I won't run," Murphy says quietly. "Whatever you decide, I'll accept it. But I'd rather stay, learn properly, and make up for my deception."

Bollinger pushes away from the wall. "This is insanity. You're actually considering— "

"I understand both sides," Captain Williams says, cutting through Bollinger's protests. "We're dealing with extraordinary circumstances. Our goal is to train people to provide medical care in this new world."

"Which is exactly why we need standards," Bollinger insists. "Structure. Rules."

Elizabeth leans forward. "Perhaps we could propose a probationary period? Murphy would start as any other student, but with additional oversight. Regular evaluations, documentation of his progress."

I watch Murphy's face carefully as they discuss his future. There's something almost peaceful about his acceptance of whatever they decide. It's so different from his previous nervous energy that I wonder how I never noticed the act before.

"I suggest we put it to a vote," the captain says, looking around the room. "Those directly involved in the medical program—at any hospital—should have a say."

"In Major Stone's absence, the general will have final authority," Lieutenant Paul, who up to now has been quietly taking notes, reminds them. "But he values the medical staff's opinion. He's made it clear that while the Guard oversees operations, the actual practice of medicine should be guided by those with expertise."

Bollinger crosses his arms. "And if we vote to allow this farce?"

"Then we document our reasoning and recommendations," Elizabeth replies. "Present a clear plan for Murphy's integration into the program, including oversight and evaluation protocols."

The captain nods. "All in favor of allowing Murphy to join the medical training program on a probationary basis?"

I raise my hand, surprising myself. Leo does, too, along with Jeff. Matt hesitates, shaking his head, before raising his hand only partway. Elizabeth's hand goes up after a moment's consideration.

The captain adds his affirmative vote. "I also have notes of support and yes votes from medical student Kerry Hendricks and Dr. Arnetta Wolff." The captain motions at papers on the table next to him.

Bollinger's face darkens. "I want my objection noted for the record."

"It will be," David Paul assures him. "I'll include both the majority opinion and your concerns in my report to General Truss."

"You should have included more actual doctors in the vote." Bollinger motions toward us med students.

Captain Williams pierces him with a look. "We should have included only personnel permanently assigned to this hospital. They are the ones who have and will continue to work side by side with Murphy.”

“I’ve stated my concerns about this,” Bollinger booms.

“You sent Murphy to us,” Captain Williams counters, his voice tinged with anger. “You knew there was something off and yet you recommended him to me directly.”

“I-I thought he was just young and that he’d benefit from your expert tutelage.”

Before anyone can respond, running footsteps echo down the hall. Medic Jesse Talbot appears in the doorway, slightly out of breath. “Captain, we need you. Building collapse. They were salvaging materials, and the whole thing came down.”

Chapter 23

Katie

The captain's already moving. "How many incoming?"

"Four so far," Jesse replies, his hand running over the back of his neck. "Two critical on their way. More coming once they dig the others out. It was a crew of over two dozen. The whole east side came down like a house of cards."

"Murphy," Williams turns to face him, his expression stern but reassuring. "Consider this your first test as a student. Help triage, nothing more. Talbot, get all the nurses and medics in here. Even Poppy's students. We're going to need everyone. Let's move, people."

The captain reaches out an arm, stopping Elizabeth. "I need Dr. Wolff."

She nods. "Minor injuries only. I'm not sure she's ready for full trauma."

"Whatever she can do. You and Bollinger too."

"Of course. I'll do what I can."

The controlled chaos of emergency response fills the hallway—prep teams gathering supplies and nurses clearing beds. Stella rushes in to check the medicine carts and then goes to the supply room. Even Bollinger sets aside his objections, rolling up his sleeves as he heads for the treatment room.

"What were they salvaging?" I ask as we hurry toward the incoming casualties.

"Taking a warehouse apart," Jesse explains. "They thought the structure was sound enough, but . . ." He shakes his head. "The whole thing just collapsed inward."

The first patients arrive in the back of a pickup truck, covered in dust and blood. Post-apocalyptic medicine isn't pretty, but it's what we have. And today, it's all that stands between life and death for our salvage crew.

"Treatment one and two," the captain orders as they bring in the first victims. "Katie Burnett, you're with me. Leo Burnett, assist Bollinger."

The time blurs into a stream of injuries—crushed limbs, puncture wounds, and respiratory distress from inhaled debris. Four treatment rooms are filled, and there's word of more coming. Additional volunteers are being rounded up to send to the collapse site and help with rescue efforts.

The treatment rooms' organized chaos reminds me of old war documentaries—minus the modern equipment we desperately need. Our IV stands are repurposed coat racks, and most of the stretchers are homemade. Triage is happening outside, with the seriously wounded brought into the hospital and those less wounded taken to the med school overflow ward.

My patient has a compound fracture in his left leg, the bone piercing through the skin. The sight twists my stomach, but I manage to say, "You're going to be okay. We'll take care of you."

He mutters something I don't catch.

"Captain," I call as he wraps up with someone else.

He joins me and shakes his head, a silent acknowledgment of what I already fear. Without x-rays, we're left with hands and hard-earned knowledge.

The man's face is gray from pain and blood loss. Sweat beads on his forehead, mixing with the concrete dust to form muddy rivulets down his temples. His breathing comes in sharp, irregular gasps.

Even with my limited experience, I can tell the leg is beyond saving. With the supplies we've got, it'll have to come off. The captain works quickly, cleaning the wound while I assist. Blood seeps between my fingers as I hold pressure on the wound, warm and sticky against the thin surgical gloves—one of our most precious resources.

"Steven," he gasps. His fingers clutch at my sleeve, leaving bloody prints on the fabric. "My son . . . he was right behind me when it fell."

"Try to stay still. They're still bringing people in," I tell him, trying to keep my voice steady. I gently disengage his grip, placing his hand back on the bed. "Everyone will work together to help with the rescue."

"He's just a boy. Only sixteen."

"Calm down," Captain Williams interrupts, his tone gentle but firm. "I need you to focus on staying calm right now. Your son needs you to stay strong."

"I'll let them know," I promise. "I'll make sure they know exactly where he was standing. Now try to relax so the doctor can finish his exam. Each breath, nice and slow."

Shoes squeak against the linoleum, sharp enough to pull my attention. Stella leans into the doorway of our treatment room. "I'm heading to my workshop to restock meds. We're already running low."

"Go," the captain says, focused on his work.

From outside, a truck rumbles closer, its brakes screeching before shouts break out. Another wave of victims. Another round of impossible choices—who to treat first, and what we can manage with what little we have left.

If we use all of Stella's precious tonics and tinctures, what will we do? The concentrates take weeks to make, and many of the herbs are only harvested at specific times of the year. She grows a good variety in her yard and greenhouse, but other items she wildcrafts, saying it's the better choice than cultivating them.

I glance out the window as Shaw's men unload more victims from the trucks. They move with practiced efficiency, their faces streaked with sweat and grime. Heavy gloves and debris-caked boots hint at salvage missions, while others carry the injured on homemade stretchers. Dust clings to everything, muting their features and making them look like ghosts in the harsh light of the late morning sun.

"Who do we have lined up to donate blood?" the captain asks.

"The usual people," I respond. "The ones we know are universal donors."

"Good enough. Get someone on the radio. See if some of the injured can be sent to a neighboring district hospital. This is going to be a long day."

A long day indeed. And beneath the rubble of a collapsed building, a teenage boy waits, clinging to the hope that rescue will come in time.

"I need more light," Captain Williams says as he examines the mangled leg. "And someone let me know when Stella's back. I want an update on our stock of painkillers. The stronger the better. We're going through things quickly."

Murphy appears with additional lanterns—our precious supply usually reserved for night emergencies. The small solar system, salvaged after the EMP, gives basic overhead lighting, but it's not always enough. The captain doesn't question it, just nods his thanks. We all know what's coming. What has to be done.

"Sir," I say quietly, stepping closer so the patient won't hear. "Did anyone go after Kerry?"

Williams sighs. "We'll send one of the new nursing students. Have Poppy pick someone. And get Talbot in here. We may need him to help with this leg." His eyes meet mine. "And Katie?" His use of my first name gives me pause.

"Sir?"

"Send word about his son. Make sure they know to look for him."

I step out of the room and nearly collide with Elizabeth as she works on someone in the hall. Her usually immaculate appearance is disheveled, hair escaping its neat bun, but she seems calm and confident. She's rolled up her sleeves, all trace of the refined psychiatrist gone.

"I may not be a surgeon," she says, adjusting the blood pressure cuff on her current patient, "but I can help with shock and trauma. Dr. Wolff is here too. She's in the parking lot, helping with triage. I'm checking on her regularly. She's doing better than expected with the pressure."

The barely organized chaos continues as more victims arrive. The hallway has become a river of motion—nurses weaving between patients on improvised stretchers, volunteers carrying supplies, family members pressed against walls trying to stay out of the way while searching desperate faces for their loved ones. I find Jesse assisting Bollinger with another crush injury. Matt and Jeff are both working triage. Medic Austin Chambers will have to do.

"The captain needs you," I tell him. "Amputation. I'll be right back to help."

His face pales slightly but he nods. As he heads to treatment room one, I make my way to the nurses' station where Jacquie Haley is coordinating rescue information. The desk has become a command center, covered with handwritten notes.

"My patient's son," I say. "Sixteen years old. He called him Steven. He was right behind his father when it collapsed."

Jacquie makes a note. "I'll tell 'em. But it sounds like it's bad. Finding him might be . . ."

A crash from treatment room two draws my attention. Leo appears in the doorway. "Need help in here!"

I rush in to find their patient convulsing. "What happened?"

"Brain injury," Bollinger says through gritted teeth. "Nothing we can do but keep him comfortable."

The next hours blur into a haze of blood and desperate measures. Every decision becomes a calculation—resources against needs, who can wait and who can't. My muscles ache from standing, holding pressure on wounds, and moving patients. The amputation is a success, if saving a life at the cost of a limb can be called that. At least the man might live to see his son again—if they find the boy in time.

As afternoon gives way to evening, the rescue efforts press on, relentless but slow. According to the foreman's count, Steven and two others are still unaccounted for, trapped somewhere in the wreckage of the collapsed building.

Nettie proves invaluable with triage and then treating the walking wounded, her calm demeanor keeping panic from taking hold. Murphy rises to the occasion, sticking to his duties and anticipating needs before anyone can voice them, proving his worth not only as a physician but in his willingness to work with us without holding a grudge.

"Katie." Elizabeth catches me between patients. "Take a break. You've been going nonstop."

"I can't. There's too much— "

"Ten minutes," she insists. "Get some tea and a snack. The kitchen brought food over. Catch your breath. You'll do no one any good if you collapse."

She's right, of course. My hands are shaking from exhaustion and hunger. In the break room, I find Stella.

"Any word about the boy?" she asks.

"Not yet. They've got three sections cleared, but— "

The door bursts open. "They found him!" Chambers announces. "He's alive. Trapped, but alive. They can hear him talking."

Relief floods through me, but it's short-lived. "How long until they can get him out?"

"Unknown. The whole structure's unstable. One wrong move . . ." Chambers runs a hand through his hair, leaving it standing on end. "Shaw just wanted me to let you know. Said it might help your patient."

"It will. He was coming around and asking if his son had been found."

"May take them some time. They're trying to shore up the surrounding walls first. Found someone from the original construction crew—a guy who helped build the place before everything went down. He's helping."

I close my eyes, offering a silent prayer. The words come automatically, a mixture of gratitude for finding Steven alive and pleading for his safe rescue. So many lives have changed today. So many families are affected. And there are still more patients to treat.

"I should get back," I say, but Stella catches my arm.

"Finish your break. Trust me, we'll need every bit of strength before this day is done."

She's right. Because even after they rescue Steven, even after we treat everyone we can save, we'll still have to face tomorrow. We'll need to replenish supplies, repair equipment, and document everything with our dwindling paper resources. We'll need to check on recovering patients, change bandages, and monitor for infection. The work never really ends, it just changes form.

But for now, we do what we can. We save who we can. And we pray that it's enough.

Chapter 24

Merissa

The sound of hymns drift through my window, carrying on the morning breeze. I can't make out the words, but the melody is familiar. "Amazing Grace," I think. The shop door must be open to let in the fresh air. Spring feels closer today. The sun is already warming the room despite the early hour.

I strain to hear the voices, to see if I can make out Pearl's. Yesterday was a turning point. She woke up alert and full of energy. The new medicines from Stella seem to be working better than we dared to hope.

Yesterday she spent hours in the kitchen, directing traffic from a chair while Opal and Alice prepared meals. She even helped with the mending, her fingers nimble enough for simple repairs, along with holding the babies as long as Opal or Alice were nearby. Gerry, her constant companion since the seizure, was never far from her side.

My thoughts drift to Mary Beth Jensen, probably sitting in that service with her children, trying to hold herself together. Just three days ago we lost Adam, her husband, in the raid. My heart aches as I remember her fear that she'd have to leave the ranch, that losing Adam meant losing their home too. Opal had been quick to reassure her that she was family, and the ranch was her home for as long as she wanted it.

Mary Beth is a mom to two young children, one around the same age as Nico and an occasional playmate for him. The other is a toddler still in diapers. While Mary Beth does what she can around the ranch, she has become the babysitter of the children while the parents are tending to their chores.

Opal has said more than once how she has a way with the youngest ones. "We've even thought about having her teach them. Something like a preschool. School is sorely missing. Maybe next winter we'll be able to do something more."

School is a conversation they've had more than once during my visits to the ranch and now that I'm living here. Opal makes a point of working with Jason, and now Robert, each evening to help them with their reading and math. Jason is smart—there's no doubt about that—but the books Opal has probably aren't advanced enough for him. I've written a note to Captain Williams, asking if he can find more suitable texts for the boy.

The baby kicks hard, drawing my attention back to the present. I rub my belly, feeling the strong movements beneath my hand. "Settling down would be nice," I tell him. "We still have ten days of this bed rest ahead of us."

Even with the excitement of the attack from a few nights ago, I haven't had any new contractions. The baby seems content to stay put, growing stronger every day. Still, after coming so close to losing him, I'm not taking any chances.

I smile, realizing I've been thinking of my baby as a boy lately. Not that I wouldn't welcome a little girl. For months, he wasn't a boy or a girl to me—just a baby that needed protecting. That came after I got over the shock and denial of being pregnant at all. At least I was able to tell Braedon we were having a baby before he died.

Sometimes, I let myself wonder how different life might be if he'd lived. Pearl and I would still be in Livingston; there'd have been no reason to leave with Braedon and Tomas still alive. I can almost picture Braedon's excitement about the baby on the way.

And I wouldn't be on bed rest since there'd be no biodiesel conspiracy to cover up. Maybe even Pearl would be okay. If things weren't so chaotic, would we have found the lumps sooner? Could Montana have treatments for Pearl that we don't have here?

The questions and thoughts threaten to overwhelm me, but none of them really matter. Braedon did die, and our life is here now. I'll do what I can to help Pearl as her illness takes over, hoping Stella's herbs will at least offer some comfort and enough time for her to meet her grandchild. I know Opal prays for a miracle—not just for relief from the pain, but for healing.

Walt has been coming into the house several times a day, asking Pearl what he can do for her. Each time, she tells him she's fine and to stop bothering her, her tone light but firm.

Sometimes I wonder, if they had more time, if she would have stayed living at the ranch instead of in town with me, if they might have moved from a simple friendship to something deeper. They've always had a playful, teasing relationship, the kind where there's a constant back-and-forth of light jabs and sarcastic comments, but underneath it, there's always been something more. I can't deny the way Walt's gaze lingers on Pearl, the quiet way he watches over her when he thinks no one's paying attention.

They've spent almost two years giving each other a hard time, but I know there's a connection between them that runs deeper than words. If things had been different—if Pearl wasn't sick—they might have had a chance to figure that out. But now, it's too late.

The morning passes slowly. I work on another letter to Bowski, trying to find the right words to describe everything that's happened without giving away where we are or worrying him unnecessarily. I can't mention the raid. No doubt the news of it has made its way back to town and he'd know where we are. To my knowledge, he still thinks we're in the house near Shaw and his Citizen Patrol folks.

Keeping this secret from him hasn't been easy, especially considering how many people know where we are. Strangers such as the doctor from Canyon Lake Hospital know, but I can't tell my boyfriend.

Boyfriend. The term makes me laugh. We're both well past the age of boy and girl, yet there's nothing else that fits. Maybe just friend, but it is more than that. Much more. Yet not so much more that I can call him some big word like fiancé. We haven't discussed marriage, not in so many words anyway. We've never even said we love each other, though I know it's there.

Soon the sounds from outside change. I close my eyes, imagining the group rearranging the chairs from church service to meal service. Abby arrives shortly after with a pair of bowls, balancing them carefully as she nudges the door closed with her hip.

"Mind if I join you? Thought you may not want to eat alone."

"That'd be great. Thanks. What is it?"

"Turkey soup," Abby replies, setting my bowl on the nightstand. "And fresh bread."

The wild turkey soup is rich with root vegetables, the meat tender. Even the bread is still warm, testimony to Opal's skill with the wood cookstove. We eat in comfortable silence. I catch something in Abby's expression—worry maybe, or sadness. She's been with us long enough to care, to understand what we're facing. "How's the cleanup going?" I ask, motioning out the window.

"Almost done. Walt and Shawn replaced the last of the broken windows in the bunkhouse this morning before service." She straightens her shoulders, and her professional mask slides back into place. "I wrote that note to Shaw, like we discussed. Asked for more support out here. These raids have to stop."

"You think he'll send help?"

"He has to. We can't keep losing good people like Adam." She pauses, then adds, "I made it clear in the note that I don't think these raids are connected to your situation. This feels different—more organized, yes, but also more random. They're hitting every ranch in the area, not targeting specific places."

"Or specific people," I agree. The raiders hadn't seemed to be looking for anyone in particular, just taking what they could get. "Still, I hate that my being here puts everyone at risk. I know Opal said she wanted us here. She understood, and Kevin agreed, but— "

"Don't," Abby says firmly. "Shawn said they were more than happy to have you here. I'm impressed by how they've kept it quiet. He says he doesn't hear anything in town about you being here or even the Hugo situation."

"The Hugo situation? People don't know?" I furrow my brow, wondering how it is that the community hasn't heard the remains of the dead were being harvested to use for biofuel.

"I guess not. I mean, some people, sure. Shaw told me and a few other patrollers, the ones who are spending extra time protecting the hospital. But they really wanted to keep it quiet."

"Hugo was taken into custody. Aren't people questioning where he is?"

"Not when they're around Shawn. Of course, he's there for a specific reason . . . to deliver food and supplies. Still, you'd think there'd be some talk about it. You know how the gossip flies around Rapid."

"Indeed. Who needs telephones and social media when you have the Rapid City Grapevine Express."

She snickers before taking another bite of her soup.

I hesitate a moment, before asking, "So . . . you and Shawn?"

"It's not . . . we're not . . ." Abby struggles for words. "It's complicated."

"In what way?" I ask gently. "He's a great guy."

She smiles as her cheeks take on a pink hue. "He's a wonderful man. A hard worker and so kind. The way he loves the Lord . . ." She sighs. "He's amazing."

"So, what's the issue?"

"I'm here for you."

Tilting my head, I furrow my brow. "And?"

"And when things are settled, I'll be going back into town. Back to regular patrol and that life. Besides, with the world we live in now, it seems selfish to think about something like romance when we're all just trying to survive."

Memories of Bowski and me at the dessert speakeasy several weeks ago rush over me. We were on a date, a romantic date, as were several others in the secret restaurant. "Love isn't selfish," I say softly. "It's what makes survival worthwhile."

Abby's quiet for a moment, absorbing that. "He asked me to go riding with him this afternoon. Do you think I should?"

"Do you want to go riding? If yes, then absolutely."

"Will you be okay?"

"Are you kidding me? You think Walt or Opal would let anything happen to me?"

"No, I don't figure they would." Abby gathers our empty bowls, her movements betraying a hint of nervous energy. "I should get back out there. If you're sure you don't mind, I'll go with him. I'll need to check the perimeter first. Make sure things seem okay. I'll tell Walt, but, uh, we're kind of keeping things quiet, you know."

"Sure," I reply, not mentioning that everyone in the house already knows about the budding romance. It was the topic of conversation yesterday while Opal, Pearl, and Alice were chopping vegetables.

"Okay, well, I'll see you later."

"Have fun riding," I call after her as she heads for the door. She doesn't respond, but her smile widens just a bit.

After she's gone, I shake my head. "Young love," I murmur. "Good to see some joy coming out of all this chaos."

I think about my own complicated feelings for Bowski, about finding love again in this broken world. It's not easy, but it's worth it.

The afternoon sun paints patterns on the floor through the newly replaced window. Somewhere in the distance, children's laughter mingles with the everyday sounds of ranch life—horses in the paddock, chickens in the yard, people going about their work. Life continues, despite everything.

The baby shifts again, gentler now, like he's finally settling down for a nap. I rest my hand on my belly, feeling the movement beneath. Nothing worth having comes easy. But here we are, making a family out of broken pieces, finding love in unexpected places, holding onto hope, even when it seems impossible.

Chapter 25

Katie

"Let us pray," Captain Williams says as he closes his Bible. Our small gathering shuffles as we reposition. Taking an hour to have a Bible study was Leo's suggestion, one which the rest of us readily agreed to.

The past few days have tested us all. After Wednesday's building collapse, we worked around the clock, losing too many patients despite our best efforts. But today's Bible study offers a moment of peace, a reminder that, even in our broken world, God's presence remains constant.

I squeeze Leo's hand as the captain leads us in prayer. Across the circle, Nettie sits close to Elizabeth, their heads bowed. It's good to see Nettie here—an unexpected surprise and one I can only believe came at Elizabeth's suggestion. Even Murphy came, though he sits quietly near the door.

"Amen," we echo together.

"Before we go," Lieutenant Paul says, "I'd like to read something." He opens his Bible. "I've been thinking about this one lately. 'God is our refuge and strength, an ever-present help in trouble.'"

The verse resonates deeply. These past months have tested our faith repeatedly, yet somehow, we keep finding the strength to continue.

"Anyone else?" the captain asks. "Does anyone have a verse they would like to share? Something for us to consider as we go about our day? Our week?"

Jesse Talbot clears his throat. "Something from James has been on my mind. 'Consider it pure joy, my brothers and sisters, whenever you face trials of many kinds, because you know that the testing of your faith produces perseverance.'"

"Appropriate," Elizabeth murmurs. "Especially now."

As we gather our things to head for rounds, one of Shaw's guards appears in the doorway. "Lieutenant Paul, you're needed at Camp Rapid immediately."

David's expression tightens slightly, but he nods. "Tell them I'm on my way." To us, he adds, "I'll catch up later if I can. This has been great. Very much appreciated." He pauses a moment as he meets Nettie's gaze. "And needed."

She dips her chin slightly, and a small smile flickers across her face. Earlier, before the study began, she and David had shared a few quiet moments in conversation. Elizabeth had tactfully stepped away, seeming to approve of their interaction.

Nettie is doing remarkably well. Following the disaster, where she resembled the old Doc Nettie I knew when I first arrived in Rapid, she and Elizabeth had a private session. Afterward, Nettie attended a community group session where the collapse was the central topic. Nearly everyone knew someone who had been in the building when it went down. It had been a significant project, requiring workers be brought in from other crews.

The cause of the collapse remains unknown, though under current circumstances, it's sadly not surprising. Accidents were common even before the EMP; now, with minimal equipment, they're even more frequent.

At the group session, there was lively discussion about the need to reassemble a salvage crew as soon as possible. The building shouldn't be left in its current state, and the steel beams and wood are desperately needed. In our post-apocalyptic world, nothing can be wasted.

Not everyone is in favor of returning to work on the building. Some believe it should be memorialized. Even though all the dead were recovered, it is still a place of profound loss. The collapse took lives and left scars on the community, both visible and unseen.

Those advocating for a memorial argue that the building's remains stand as a reminder of the fragility of life and the cost of rebuilding in such harsh conditions. They worry that salvaging the materials will erase this moment of collective grief, leaving nothing to honor those who were lost.

Others, however, are more pragmatic. Resources are scarce, and the steel and wood from the wreckage could mean the difference between survival and further hardship. For them, rebuilding isn't just practical—it's symbolic. Turning the remnants into something useful could be seen as an act of resilience, a way to honor the dead by helping the living move forward.

The debate remains unresolved, but one thing is clear. The building, whether as rubble or reborn, has become a focal point for the community's struggles and hopes. Not that it matters what the therapy group believes. Those in charge have the final say.

Rounds always start with our most critical patients. The father who lost his leg has developed a fever—a troubling, though not unexpected, complication given the circumstances. Stella has prepared a range of antibacterial remedies.

For him and others with early signs of infection, we're administering a mix of oral and topical treatments. Stella also reminds us to lean on prayer, calling it the most potent medicine of all, a sentiment that resonates in a world where hope is as vital as the scarce supplies we depend on.

The amputee's son, Steven, lies in the next bed, still healing from his own injuries. Despite the ordeal they've endured, Steven shows steady progress each day. The bond between father and son is undeniable; even in pain, they draw strength from each other.

Steven lost his mom and younger sister shortly after the EMP, leaving only his dad. We want more than anything to save his dad so that he doesn't lose the only family he has left. Both of them are fighting their own battles; Steven's injuries may be healing, but he's far from fully recovered.

"How's the pain?" I ask the father as I check his bandages.

"Manageable. More worried about him." He gestures toward Steven, who's finally sleeping peacefully.

"He's doing well," I assure him. "The fact that he's sleeping normally is a good sign."

Nettie is back to doctoring on a part-time basis. She's overseeing the less critical cases, those that are set up in the med school. After we finish rounds in the main hospital, we walk over there and she leads us through her patients.

The first is a woman not much older than me with multiple lacerations who's showing good signs of healing. She lives in one of the shared housing units in her own room, and Nettie suggests keeping her for a few days is the better choice. Elizabeth hovers nearby, monitoring how Nettie handles the interaction.

"The stitches are healing nicely," Nettie tells her patient. "Another few days and we can probably remove them. You'll need to keep them clean and apply the ointment."

"The ones on my face? Will they— " Tears fill her eyes as she shakes her head. "I'm going to look hideous." Her words come out in a whisper.

"We talked about this," Nettie says, her voice warm with compassion. "The cuts will heal and become much less noticeable, but it will take time. Scarring is natural, and with proper care, it can fade significantly. We're already doing the right things—keeping the wounds clean and following the regimen." Her tone is steady, reassuring without sounding dismissive.

The woman nods, though tears continue to streak her face. "I just . . . I don't know if I can face people like this." Her hand hovers over her cheek but doesn't quite touch the stitched laceration.

Nettie places a hand on her shoulder. "You've been through something traumatic, and these feelings are normal. But you're stronger than you think. Healing isn't just about the outside, it's about how you let yourself grow through this. We'll be here to help you, every step of the way."

Elizabeth watches quietly, her expression unreadable but her posture attentive. It's clear she's evaluating not just Nettie's medical competence but her ability to handle the emotional weight of her patients.

As we step back, Nettie gives an encouraging nod to the woman before leading us to the next patient. "She's doing well, all things considered," Nettie says under her breath. "But this is what worries me more than the stitches—the scars you can't see."

Her words hang in the air, an unspoken truth that none of us can ignore. Healing in this world is never just physical. Nettie knows that more than anyone.

The morning moves on steadily as we transfer several patients to Poppy's long-term care facilities. We visit each building to assess the residents. Poppy's care centers have been a valuable addition to our hospital, offering basic rehab and nursing-home-style services.

Many people who need just a bit more care than they can manage on their own move into one of the apartments, creating something similar to an assisted living center. Other buildings provide higher-level nursing care.

The nursing school will offer additional training to support this. After the EMP, many elderly patients died due to a lack of medication and proper care. Over time, this left only the hardier seniors. But with recent injuries, the need grows for long-term care.

As we visit the patients, something is said that reminds me of the Ebright sisters. One of the sisters was staying in the care center, recovering from a bout of sepsis brought on by a skin infection. When the rumor about the Angel of Death went through the buildings, the sisters disappeared. Poppy could hardly contain her frustration, unable to grasp how Elaine, ill as she was, could just leave, or why Marilyn allowed it.

A few hours after Poppy voiced her concerns about the missing sisters to the captain, Bowski arrived at the hospital. He told the captain he was responsible for their disappearance, explaining that he'd moved them without notifying anyone and that they were in a safe place. This came just as the whole situation with Hugo was coming to light.

Bowski assured us that he'd relocated the women for their protection, not wanting them to share the same fate as so many others—dead under mysterious circumstances. We still don't know where the sisters are, but Bowski insists they're fine, and that Elaine is recovering. I suspect Stella knows more about their whereabouts and may be providing the medications to help Elaine heal, but she isn't saying a word.

On his way from one patient to another, Leo touches my arm and asks, "Did you hear about the mail?"

"What?" My heart skips. "From where?"

"Not sure yet. But when Poppy called the captain into her office, she told him she'd just got a call from David Paul. He's going to be heading to the hospital soon with the mailbag and asked if she could get our ETA for returning there."

Hope stirs in my chest. It's been months since we heard from my family in Wyoming. The last letter came at Christmas, and since then, nothing. I had a brief radio conversation while we were scrambling to find a home for Kemeera and the children, hoping to send them to my family.

That plan fell apart when Kemeera disappeared with her daughter, likely because she was working with Addison. There were rumors of a final plan for the Preacher's vengeance. But now, Kemeera is dead, and Shawna remains missing, with the rumors leading nowhere.

"Maybe there'll be something for us?" I don't bother hiding the excitement in my voice. It's a fragile kind of hope, but right now, I'll take it.

"We'll know soon enough."

Back at the hospital, the news of mail spreads quickly. Staff and patients alike buzz with anticipation at the prospect of letters from afar. Information about what's happening beyond our immediate area is rare and precious. The occasional radio address from the so-called president offers little clarity and borders on the absurd. No one is even sure if it's the actual president speaking—or if there's even a United States left to govern.

His voice shifts from one public address to the next, sometimes noticeably different. He's offered excuses before—blaming a cold or other vague reasons—but the inconsistencies fuel more questions than answers. We don't even know where he is. He's in hiding, that much is clear, but the location remains a mystery. Even more uncertain is whether he holds the same authority he once did.

There's talk of states splintering off to form something new. South Dakota appears to be part of that movement, though nothing official has been declared. The rumors stem from cryptic announcements by South Dakota's governor and similar murmurings in other states. A key indicator of something brewing? The state military now controls South Dakota's hospitals, a move many believe signals plans quietly taking shape.

At least for now, Major Stone remains on whatever assignment was deemed more pressing. We spoke with the captain about it last night, and he shared his theory. Stone overseeing the hospital might have been a test, a way for him to prove he could handle the responsibility. A form of punishment, perhaps, for allowing Cabal to blackmail Williams and for concealing the situation with Alice.

The captain suggested that Stone's reassignment could be the general's way of phasing him out. "Maybe this is the first step," he said, shrugging. "Stranger things have happened." He even hinted that he might officially regain command of the hospital before long—a possibility that felt both hopeful and uncertain.

Williams being back in charge would be best for everyone. It's still beyond me why they'd ever put someone without medical experience in command of a hospital, and even more confusing how he could run the medical and nursing schools. Stone has no idea what we do here, and he doesn't appear at all interested in learning.

"Your temperature is up slightly," I tell the amputation patient as I check his vitals. The infection worries me, but we're doing everything possible with our limited supplies. "Are you having any trouble breathing?"

He shrugs. "Not much. Some, maybe. Steven said there might be mail," he says, his voice weak. "From other places?"

"Yes, though we don't know from where yet." I adjust his IV as I listen to his breaths. They don't sound terrible but maybe a little labored. "Try to rest. Fighting infection takes energy."

The afternoon rounds continue—more bandage changes and more monitoring of fevers and wounds. In the med school dormitory, those with less severe injuries show steady improvement. But my mind keeps drifting to that bag of letters. Could there be news from home?

"Burnett." The captain's voice pulls me from my thoughts. "Take a break. Get something to eat."

"I should check on— "

"That's an order." His smile softens the words. "Your husband's on break too. Spend a few minutes with him. Shouldn't be long until Lieutenant Paul arrives."

I nod, grateful for the break, though my mind lingers on the possibility of mail. I head to the break room, hoping food and company will help clear my head.

As I push through the door, Leo looks up from his meal, his tired eyes brightening when he sees me. We don't need words to share the relief of a few moments of normalcy. For a moment, everything feels lighter. The worries can wait.

Chapter 26

Katie

It's almost an hour later when Lieutenant Paul arrives with the mailbag. I've checked on my amputee patient twice since then. His fever is going up, and his breathing is becoming more labored. There's not much that can be done except to continue doing what we're doing and praying harder.

In the break room, several people gather around David as he sorts through letters. He started with the patients in the med school and hospital, moving from bed to bed, asking each person's name and carefully searching his bag for their letter. There were precious few, but David assured us there was more sorting to do and he would check with others for anything else. With people here instead of at home, things have gotten a bit muddled.

In theory, what's left in his bag should belong to the hospital or care center staff. Leo told me Nettie received mail, and Elizabeth went with her to open it. I can only hope the information inside doesn't set Nettie back.

"Chambers. Jacquie Haley. Kerry Hendricks." David continues sorting. "Ah, here's one for Alice Williams."

The captain perks up at that, stepping forward and saying he'll take it. He and Alice have been writing letters back and forth while she's been at the Maher ranch, but he hasn't seen her since everything started with Hugo, just as we haven't seen our children.

"From her cousin," the captain says, smiling as he puts the letter in his pocket.

David Paul knows the situation with Alice and how she's at the safe house. I'm surprised he mentioned her name, though maybe he did it to help maintain the cover of the safe house. Despite the Hugo situation dragging on for weeks now, it still seems mostly under wraps. I haven't heard any chatter among the patients about the dead being desecrated, nor have I heard anyone mention that Hugo hasn't been around.

Maybe people are growing numb to the disappearances, assuming Hugo's off chasing something better instead of being under arrest for crimes against the dead and a massive conspiracy to turn fat into biofuel. If the information were public, I'm sure tongues would be wagging. I'm honestly impressed they've managed to keep it quiet for so long, especially with all those involved being under investigation.

Jacquie Haley did ask about Alice, but the captain told her she was helping with Merissa while she's on bed rest. Weirdly, Jacquie doesn't seem concerned that the captain, Leo, and I are living in the med school or that we never leave the security of the area without guards. She does, of course, know about the attempt on my life, so perhaps she understands what's going on and realizes it's not something to be discussed. An oddity for Jacquie, but much appreciated.

So far, nothing new has come our way since the discovery of additional bodies at the second storage facility. Shaw told the captain he's hit a dead end, unable to find the ringleader behind the whole thing—the one Hugo didn't name in his notes and refuses to divulge during interrogation. Many more people have been detained and are being questioned, but Shaw says he's being careful. This involves more people than he ever imagined, and he's not sure who to trust anymore.

David Paul is one of the few from the Guard who was brought into the loop with the understanding that he, too, needs to keep it quiet. He was even asked not to tell his superiors, not even General Truss, something he had a hard time agreeing to at first but seemed to understand the necessity of. He's brought in a few people he trusts to help with the investigation and reports only to Shaw and the captain on their findings.

Not involving General Truss was a risk, one that the captain says could come back and bite them both. But keeping Alice, Merissa, and the children safe is more important at the moment.

"Burnett." David holds up an envelope. My breath catches, but he's already saying, "For Leo."

Leo takes it, his good hand trembling slightly. "It's from Evan Snyder."

My heart rate immediately increases. "Evan Snyder? Why would he be writing?"

"We'll find out soon enough. Let's see if there's anything else."

I nod, torn between the worry that our family's neighbor is writing to us while my family isn't, and the hope that there might be something more.

More names are called. Some people cry when they receive their letters, others clutch them close without opening them, as if savoring the moment. Some look disappointed when their names aren't called.

I try not to feel disappointed and try to remember that any mail getting through is a miracle.

"Last batch." David reaches into the bag. "Katie Burnett." He holds out two envelopes. "Looks like they're from Wyoming."

The paper feels fragile in my hands, precious as gold. I recognize my sister Sarah's handwriting on one and my mentor Belinda Bosco on the other. Tears blur my vision.

"Let's take a few minutes," Leo says, ushering me out of the break room and toward the wood storage room—a room that is not my favorite place in the building after having found a mouse in there once, but it'll give us some privacy.

With the door closed behind us, I ask him which we should open first. "Evan's?" I suggest.

"Sure. If that'll help relieve some of your worry. Or we could open Sarah's. It looks thick, like there are notes from everyone."

"Let's see what Evan has to say. I hope Doris is okay." Doris is Evan's wife and was one of my mom's friends. Early in the troubles, even before the EMP hit, Doris and my sister Angela were attacked while collecting supplies. Back then, people were still using money or trade goods, but things were starting to get volatile.

Doris and Angela were waiting by the truck while Jake, Evan, and the others were inside a building. The shots came out of nowhere. Doris's leg was shattered, and Angela's backside was peppered with buckshot.

When one of the men tried to drag Angela away after injuring her, she had no choice but to defend herself with her own handgun. Angela fully recovered from the assault, but Doris's leg was broken and badly damaged, leaving it weak and never quite the same.

Leo quickly scans the letter, the concern on his face shifting to a light smile. "Everything's fine. He wrote this months ago, when Jake told him about my arm not healing right and us trying to get enough info so we could enter the Guard as officers. He reminded me that if things don't work out, there's always a need for us in Bakerville." His gaze locks with mine. "That doesn't sound like a terrible idea."

We haven't had much time to discuss our plans, not with the building collapse and the daily chaos. Bollinger is one week into his two-week rotation. He's promised to examine Leo again before he leaves and once more in a few months when he returns, but we know not to get our hopes up for any significant change.

Although Leo won't be able to join the National Guard—unless some miracle happens with his healing—we still have med school here and a life we're building. Soon, we'll be reunited with our children, and things will regain some sense of normalcy.

Leo and I both know it'd be incredibly difficult to go home, no matter how much we miss our family. Travel is always a gamble, and I'd hate to take the children away from Alice. Over the past few weeks, as they've been in hiding, I have no doubt she's grown even more attached to them—and they to her. No, leaving South Dakota isn't an option right now.

"What did Sarah say?" He gestures to my envelope.

As expected, there are several pages, each folded separately. The first one I pull out is a collection of short greetings. My younger brother, Malcolm, scrawls a quick note, hoping Leo's arm is healing and that we had a good Christmas.

My adopted nephew, Marc—Sarah's oldest—scribbles something similar. His younger sister, Sissy, and brother, Andy, draw tiny pictures and write their names, though it's clear Sarah helped Andy with his. My nephew, Gavin, Angela's son, added his name and a drawing that could be either a pony or a dog; it's hard to tell.

There's also a note from Tony, Sarah's stepson, with a rainbow drawn by his sister, Lily. On the other side is a note from Tim Carpenter, Angela's husband, dated January 15—almost two months ago. Not terrible, considering the weather. It's no worse than the postal service we had before the EMP.

I snicker aloud, causing Leo to glance at me. "Sorry. I was just thinking about the time I mailed a birthday card to someone. Her birthday was in the middle of June. I sent it about a week before. She didn't get it until August. And that was years ago, well before all this." I gesture around the room. "Volunteer mail in the apocalypse isn't much worse, even with the weather."

Tim's letter is brief and to the point. Things are fine, but the winter seems to drag on. They're all looking forward to spring when they can leave the mountain and return to the main house. He adds that Mike, my sister Calley's husband, says hello.

Next, I pull out a letter from Angela. The words are tiny and close together as she tries to fit as much on the page as possible. Gavin is doing good. She and Tim are discussing having another child but neither of them is quite ready yet. There's so much risk in pregnancy and childbirth with the way things are.

One of the women living on the mountain with them, a lady I don't know who arrived with her husband last summer, died from what is believed to be an ectopic pregnancy. That was enough to scare her into waiting. She didn't want to risk leaving Gavin alone.

The other side of the paper is a letter from Calley. True to form, the letter is full of updates about people in the community, some light gossip, and a few observations about daily life. My mom used to say that if you needed to know anything, just ask Calley. She's always in the loop, but we never worried much about her sharing our personal concerns. Calley's got a way of knowing exactly what's worth keeping to herself and what's safe to pass on.

My eyes are blurry by the time I finish with Calley's letter. I take a deep breath, trying to compose myself before opening the next sheet of paper.

"Sarah?" Leo asks.

"Yes." Her words bring our family's world to life—stories about her baby, now walking; about Calley's little girl, crawling and standing, though still unsteady. She details how all the older children help with the babies. She tells us about her new husband, Jason, and their efforts to blend their families.

It's truly a motley crew. Jason brought Tony and Lily into the fold, while Sarah brought her adopted children—Marc, Sissy, and Andy— along with baby Tate, the son of her first husband who died while elk hunting. She finishes the letter by saying Jason and she are talking about having a child together. It sounds crazy, but right at the same time.

"Sarah's got her hands full," Leo says.

"No worse than a four-year-old and two babies. They don't even know about them. I have letters put together for my family, telling them all about Nico and how adorable Zach and Caleb are. How they came to live with us. If the mail's moving again, maybe I should give them to David and have him send them."

"Probably," Leo agrees. "What does Jake say?"

Jake's letter is shorter but no less precious. They're all safe. They miss us. They pray for us daily.

"So just Belinda's letter remains." Leo motions to the still-sealed envelope. "Ready to read it?"

Before I can answer, Chambers appears in the doorway. "Katie, the captain needs you. Your fever patient isn't looking good."

Reality crashes back. Letters from family will have to wait. Right now, we have patients who need us.

But as I hurry toward his room, I feel lighter somehow. Knowing our families are out there, surviving, hoping, praying—it makes everything else easier to bear.

Because in this broken world, hope arrives in unexpected ways. Sometimes in the form of letters, carrying love across the miles. Sometimes in the form of answered prayers and healing wounds. And sometimes, just sometimes, it comes in knowing we're not alone.

Chapter 27

Merissa

The late morning sun streams through the new window, warming my blankets as I work on another letter to Bowski. It's another nice day, giving me hope that spring will soon arrive. Pearl sleeps in the bed beside me, her breathing steady but shallow. Her energy has improved in the last few days, with her being up more than down.

Upstairs, the muffled sounds of Alice getting the children down for their morning nap reach me, while Nico protests that he's too old for one. Their familiar routine brings a smile to my face. Even in hiding, even with all the uncertainty, we've managed to create something normal.

The baby shifts, pressing against my ribs in a way that's become all too familiar. I adjust my position, grateful for the stack of pillows Opal insists on keeping nearby.

My journal lies open beside me, filled with things I wish I could tell Bowski but can't risk including in a real letter. I switch between writing in it and drafting words I can actually send.

At the top of the journal page is the date I'm counting down toward. March 17—nine days away. That's the day the captain and Poppy have determined will mark the end of my bed rest, assuming everything continues to check out at my regular exams.

My estimated due date is April 1, though it's really just a guess, given that the rations we had in Livingston dropped my body fat and caused amenorrhea. I suspect I'll have the baby shortly after being taken off bed rest. As long as he's healthy, I'm fine with that. I want Pearl to have as much time with him as possible. Poppy will be back tomorrow to reassess me. Maybe my end-of-bed-rest date will change, but for now, it stands.

The baby moves again, this time sending a lump jutting from my stomach. I place my hand on it, guessing it's his rump.

"More kicking?" Pearl's voice, thick with sleep, draws my attention. She blinks slowly, fighting the fog of medication.

"Kicking, moving, full-on gymnastics," I reply softly. "Your grandchild seems determined to become an athlete."

"Mmm." Her smile is tired but genuine. "Just like Braedon. He was always moving too. Never could sit still, even as a baby. Tomas, too, but not like Braedon. He could entertain himself easily. Braedon, though, was go, go, go."

The mention of Braedon brings the usual mixture of emotions—grief, love, and gratitude for this child he left me, along with the newfound peace I've been experiencing.

Walt appears in the doorway, his expression carefully neutral. "Just checking in. Need anything?"

"We're fine," Pearl answers, her voice stronger. "Though I wouldn't say no to a cup of tea."

He nods, lingering a moment longer than necessary. I pretend not to notice the way his gaze stays on Pearl, or how her fingers smooth her blanket self-consciously. Some things are better left unspoken. "Opal's out with the chickens, but I s'pose I can put the kettle on."

"I should hope so," Pearl says, shifting in the bed to a sitting position as Walt moves to the wood cookstove. Pearl's movement brings Gerry to his feet, and he moves closer to her. She reaches out and rubs him behind the ears.

"When do you expect Shawn and Abby back?" I ask, moving slightly to peer out the window. After yesterday's ride, Abby came in and asked if I thought it'd be okay for her to go into town with Shawn for deliveries today. She wanted to deliver the letter asking for additional security and patrols directly to Shaw. While I certainly do appreciate Shaw sending Abby as my personal bodyguard, she isn't really needed. Not with Walt hovering and watching my every move, as well as Pearl's.

"Sometime after lunch, I expect. That's when he usually gets back. 'Course, with Miss Abby riding along, wouldn't surprise me if they took the scenic route and stretched out the trip. No doubt he'll be back before chore time, though."

He refills the kettle from a hand pump in the kitchen. Kevin and Opal have made many changes to their previously modern home to accommodate the lack of electricity. "Do you need a snack to go with your tea, Miss Pearl? Looks like there're some biscuits left over."

"That'd be fine," Pearl replies, her voice taking on a note of surprise.

Walt busies himself with the tea preparations, his movements unhurried and practiced. The kettle begins to sing just as Opal returns from the chicken coop, carrying a basket of fresh eggs.

"Well, what's this?" she asks, setting the basket on the counter. "Walt Cox making tea? Has the world turned upside down again?"

"Your sister asked for tea," he replies simply, as if that explains everything. And perhaps it does.

Opal and Walt pull up chairs near our beds and we share soft conversation over tea and biscuits, chatting about the ranch's daily routines—how many eggs were gathered, which hens are laying best, and whether the new dairy calf born last week is thriving. These simple topics feel precious, like treasures salvaged from our old world. Pearl manages to eat half a biscuit, a small triumph that brings a glimmer of hope to Opal's eyes.

Pearl sets the rest of the biscuit down, her fingers trembling slightly. "I think that's enough for now," she murmurs, her voice barely above a whisper. Opal reaches over and gives her hand a gentle squeeze, a wordless acknowledgment of the effort it took.

The comfortable conversation ends with the sharp crack of gunfire. Single shots at first, then a burst of weapons. The cowbells start their frantic warning, the pattern fast and desperate.

Walt jumps to his feet and grabs his rifle that's leaning against the wall. Gerry also moves to attention. Seconds later, Kevin bursts through the front door. "They've breached the perimeter. Three trucks came up through the dry creek bed. They were inside before we even saw them."

"Inside the perimeter?" Opal asks, her voice hollow, as she retrieves her own rifle. Noises upstairs indicate Alice is rousing the children.

"They're here for me," I whisper, the realization hitting hard. Our secret is out, and they discovered where I'm hiding.

"Now don't be jumpin' to conclusions." Walt peers out the window. "Probably just some determined raiders. Get yourself to that pantry and stay there."

"I'll help Alice with the children," Pearl says, rising from her bed.

"No, you'll get to the pantry," Opal corrects, her voice surprisingly calm. "I'll help Alice and bring them in shortly."

"Hurry up," Walt orders, but even as he speaks, more shots ring out. "No, no time. Under the bed. Now!"

Pearl's already moving, her illness forgotten in the surge of adrenaline. Walt helps her to the floor while I struggle to maneuver my pregnant body down. The baby kicks frantically, responding to my fear as Pearl and I scurry under my bed. Gerry positions himself nearby, his throaty growl making his concerns clear.

Opal bounds up the stairs, her feet pounding on the treads. She hollers as she goes, "We'll stay up here. In the hall bathroom. That should be safe."

Kevin, stationed near the front door, tells her to put the children in the bathtub. "Grab the crib mattress. That'll help protect them," he adds.

"They're organized," Walt mutters from somewhere near the window. "Moving in formation like— "

Glass shatters. Walt's sharp gasp of pain pierces the air, followed by the heavy thud of his body against the wall and the clatter of his rifle hitting the floor.

"Walt!" Pearl's fingers dig into my arm as I realize my pistol is still in the nightstand by the bed. Why didn't I grab it?

"I'm fine." His voice comes from much closer now, tight with pain and barely above a whisper. "Just caught me off guard. Kevin— "

Boots scrape across the wooden floor—Kevin's, judging by the weight of the footsteps. More glass breaks. The sharp tang of gunpowder mingles with the blood smell. Walt's breathing grows more ragged, each inhale a struggle.

"They've got us surrounded," Kevin's voice comes from near the door. "Must have come— " His words are cut off as another volley of shots sprays the house. Something heavy thuds against the outer wall.

Above us, one of the babies is crying—impossible to tell which one through the chaos. Pearl's hand finds mine, her grip weaker than usual but still there. My heart pounds so hard that I wonder if the attackers can hear it. The baby moves again, as if sensing my terror.

"Here they come," Kevin says grimly, his voice barely audible over the shooting.

Then the back porch creaks—that distinctive third board that always protests under weight. Multiple sets of footsteps. Heavy ones. Deliberate.

"We know she's in there." The unfamiliar voice carries clearly through what must be our broken windows. "No one else needs to die today."

Gerry growls. "Shush, now," Pearl says. "You be a good boy and stay put."

The man's words send chills down my spine. How many have already died? Where are Jason and Robert? They were outside. Are they safe in the panic room that's attached to the shop?

Through my narrow view from under the bed, Kevin's boots shift position. More glass crunches under his feet as he moves. Walt's labored breathing seems louder now, though he hasn't made a sound beyond that.

"One woman," the voice outside continues. "That's all we want. Give her to us, and everyone else walks away."

My whole body trembles. The baby kicks again, hard enough to make me gasp. Pearl's fingers squeeze mine, but even that small comfort feels distant through my rising panic. The wood floor presses against my side, hard and unyielding.

A new sound catches my attention—the scrape of a boot on the front steps. Different from Kevin's measured tread or Walt's familiar stride. These steps are heavier and more purposeful. More than one set.

"Last chance," the voice calls out. "We don't want to hurt the kids."

The words hit like a physical blow. Opal, Alice, and the children are in the bathtub, just like Kevin suggested. Would a crib mattress really protect them? From flying glass yes, from a bullet at close range . . .

My throat tightens around a sob.

Suddenly, the house erupts into chaos. The front door splinters. Gunfire explodes from multiple directions. Through it all, I hear Walt's pained grunt as he tries to move, and Kevin's sharp orders—though the words blur together in the mayhem.

Pearl's raspy whisper reaches my ear. "The Lord is my shepherd . . ."

More footsteps pour into the room. The gunfire is deafening now. Something—someone—falls heavily near the bed. The thud is followed by a groan I recognize as Kevin's, followed by a whine from Gerry.

Smoke fills the air—tear gas, maybe, from the way it burns my throat and eyes. Or is it from gunfire? Pearl's prayer continues beside me, barely audible through her own coughing. "I shall not want . . ."

"Under the bed," someone barks. My heart nearly stops.

Boots approach—different from Walt's or Kevin's. These are polished, military-grade. They pause near my head. I squeeze my eyes shut, as if that could somehow make me invisible. The baby goes still, as if he also senses the danger.

"Here!" The shout comes from right above us. Rough hands reach under the bed. I try to pull away, but there's nowhere to go. Pearl's grip on my hand is torn away as she's dragged out first. Her prayer cuts off in a cry of pain.

"Don't hurt her!" I manage to get out between coughs. "She's sick. Please!"

They're already reaching for me, pulling me from my hiding place. The floor scrapes against my belly as they drag me out. I catch glimpses through my tears—Walt slumped against the wall, blood soaking his shirt. Kevin face-down near the door, not moving. Pearl struggling weakly in a masked stranger's grip.

"Please," I try again, one hand protectively covering my stomach. "I'm pregnant—due soon, but . . ."

"Just the pregnant one," a voice commands. "Leave the old woman."

Pearl crumples to the floor as they release her. The hands gripping my arms are relentless as they haul me toward the door. I try to dig in my heels, to resist, but my awkward pregnant body betrays me. Everything hurts—my back, my belly, my throat from the smoke.

Through my tears, I glimpse Walt trying to raise his rifle with his good arm. "No . . ." The word comes out as barely a whisper before someone kicks the weapon away.

They drag me onto the porch, the bright sunlight blinding after the smoky darkness inside. My bare feet catch on the wooden steps. The gravel of the driveway cuts into my soles as they force me toward a waiting vehicle.

Then a new sound cuts through the chaos—horses approaching at full gallop. Many of them. Shouts of alarm go up from my captors.

The hands gripping me tighten as someone yells, "Get her in the truck! Now!"

Rough hands shove me toward the back door of the quad cab truck. Pearl's voice carries from the house—no longer in prayer but in a desperate cry of my name. The baby gives a fierce kick, as if fighting against our fate just as hard as I am.

As they force me into the truck, my last glimpse is of Walt, somehow on his feet in the doorway despite his wound, his face twisted in helpless anguish. Then the truck door slams shut, and the engine revs as the truck peels out.

Chapter 28

Katie

The rich aroma of peppermint tea lingers in the hospital hallway as I make my way between patients. Today, I'm pulling double duty—starting with rounds alongside the med students, followed by a full nursing shift, and more rounds later. I don't mind the busyness.

Yesterday's mail delivery lifted everyone's spirits, mine included. Even those who didn't receive anything are hopeful, clinging to David's promise that more might arrive once everything is sorted. That glimmer of expectation has brightened the mood all around.

I pause outside room three, where my amputee patient rests. He gave us quite a scare yesterday when his fever spiked to dangerous levels. I spent most of the afternoon trying to bring it down, alternating between cool compresses and the herbal fever reducers. The infection in what remains of his leg had been aggressive, but this morning his color looks better.

"Good morning," I say, stepping into the dim room where the sunlight filters through frost-covered windows. The antiseptic smell mingles with the lingering scent of the herb poultices we've been using. "How are you feeling?"

"He's better," Steven says, uncurling from his cramped position in the worn leather chair beside the bed. His dark circles betray a night of worried vigilance. Steven has improved enough we could release him, but we've decided to keep him here with his dad.

With his mom gone, he'd be alone in the house, and even though sixteen is basically considered an adult in this new world, it doesn't seem right to send him home alone. "I think he was having a weird dream. Mumbling about horses."

His dad manages a weak smile. "No. I said I feel like I got stepped on by a horse, and I do, but I'm better than yesterday."

I check his vitals, noting with relief that his temperature has dropped to 100.2. Still elevated, but nowhere near yesterday's frightening 104. The stumped remains of his leg, while still angry looking, shows promising signs. The infection seems to be retreating.

"The medicines are doing their job," I say as I carefully examine the sutures. "And your body is fighting back."

"That's good," he says. "I was worried there for a bit. Thought maybe . . ." He trails off, but I know what he means. We've lost too many patients to the collapse. Even with the knowledge Captain Williams and Bollinger have, it's an uphill battle with our limited supplies.

"You're going to be fine," I assure him, praying it's the truth. "Just keep fighting."

I make notes in his chart, detailing the improvement in his condition. Captain Williams has been adamant about maintaining detailed records. "We're not just treating patients," he often says. "We're creating a blueprint for future medical care in our new reality."

At this morning's rounds, we moved a few more patients to either the med school with the least injured or to long-term care, where they're likely to remain for some time. We know some of them will never leave there, but Poppy and her people will care for them, making them as comfortable as possible. The ones who remain in the hospital are mostly stable now, though recovery will be long.

In the hallway, I hear Nettie's voice, cheerful in a way that is unusual. She's in the adjacent room, visiting a new patient. Not someone from the collapse but an elderly woman who slipped on a patch of ice. Nettie joined us on rounds this morning and recognized the injured woman as a former patient, chatting with her for several minutes.

"My daughter drew this," Nettie is saying. "She's quite the artist."

I peek in, not wanting to interrupt but curious about this new side of Nettie. She's holding a piece of paper, showing it to her patient. The change in her is remarkable. Just weeks ago, we nearly lost her, and prior to that, we had no knowledge she even had a daughter. Now, thanks to Elizabeth's intervention and ongoing support, she seems to have found her footing again in a new and improved way.

"Katie!" Nettie calls out, her voice carrying a warmth I haven't heard in months. She's perched on the edge of her patient's bed. The room smells of lavender—a sachet we often provide for our more anxious patients, though Stella has suggested we should supply it to everyone. "Come see what Alisa drew."

The drawing shows what I assume is meant to be their family home, complete with a garden and what might be chickens. It's dated mid-January, attached to a letter that arrived yesterday.

"She says they've started planning the spring planting," Nettie says, her eyes bright. "Can you believe it? In all this chaos, life goes on. They're planning gardens."

"That's wonderful," I say, genuinely happy for her. Elizabeth's visit has been wonderful. The way she's helped Nettie highlights why psychiatric support is so vital. After Elizabeth returns to the main hospital with Bollinger, I hope she'll continue working with Nettie on the suggestion of psychiatric training. In our new world, mental health care is just as crucial as physical healing.

"I'll visit with you later, Miss Martha," Nettie assures the patient as we leave the room.

"How's your patient doing?" Nettie asks, switching smoothly into doctor mode as we reach the hallway.

"Better. Fever's down, infection seems to be retreating."

She nods approvingly. "Good. We need a win."

"How are you?" I ask, raising an eyebrow.

"I'm okay. Really better than I expected. Elizabeth reminds me not to push. To do only what I am comfortable with and to watch for warning signs. Speaking of, I need to get back across the driveway. See you later?"

"No doubt," I reply with a laugh. Other than the day Leo, the captain, and I helped with the warehouse Hugo was using, I haven't left the hospital and med school compound. Still no updates from Shaw on the progress being made with wrapping the whole situation up. I'm hopeful it'll end soon and we can return to some sort of normalcy. At the very least, we'll be back with our children.

I continue my nursing rounds and pass by the nurses' station, where Dr. Murphy is deep into what Captain Williams likes to call an "accelerated reassessment of medical knowledge."

It's still strange seeing him, knowing he was practicing medicine without proper credentials. His EMT background and over a year of experience working under the guise of Dr. Murphy mean he's not starting from scratch, though. The captain believes he can be fully trained within six months, a far cry from the two to three years the rest of us face.

What's even stranger is his refusal to give his real name. He insists he's become Reginald Murphy and plans to keep going by that name, as if shedding his old identity altogether. The whole situation feels off, but no one seems willing to press him about it—at least not yet. My guess is, Captain Williams will get it out of him one way or another.

Murphy catches my eye and gives me a small smile. Despite everything, I can't help but admire his dedication. He could have run when he was exposed, but instead, he chose to stay and do things the right way this time.

Time passes quickly. Between patient rounds, chart updates, and study sessions, there's barely time to think about the letters Leo and I received yesterday. I finally got a chance to read Belinda's last night in the quiet of our apartment. As usual, it contained details of illnesses and injuries she'd encountered in their neighborhood clinic, along with questions about how I'd treat them. It's a game we play, a mix of chatting and learning.

After the captain and Murphy finish their lesson, I move to the nurses' station to update charts and try to make sense of our medical supply inventory.

Jacquie Haley is also on duty today. She did an inventory of things earlier and brought it to me for a second opinion while she takes a break. We're running low on several critical items following the mass casualty event, and I want to have a clear list for the captain.

The front doorbell's gentle chime echoes through the corridor. Lieutenant David Paul appears, his boots leaving wet marks on the floor from the melting snow outside. He's slightly out of breath, as if he rushed here. He's carrying his mailbag and a large box that seems unwieldy in his arms.

"Wow, someone got something nice," I say, eyeing the package.

David adjusts his grip. "Big at least. It's for the captain."

"Really?" I can't help my curiosity. "Hmm. More letters too?"

"A few." He shifts the box again. "For some of the folks at the hospital and other places. We got everything sorted. Sorry, I don't have anything additional for you or Leo."

"I understand." I shrug, but still have a twinge of disappointment.

"Where's the captain?"

I point to one of the patient rooms. "Just finishing up, I think."

"Good enough. I'll put it in the break room. Will you let him know?" David asks, as he heads in that direction, the box awkward in his arms. I turn back to my paperwork, trying to focus on inventory numbers instead of wondering about the package. How exciting to get something like that.

The quiet afternoon routine continues around me. Someone laughs in one of the rooms. A visiting family member steps out of a doorway. The captain steps out of the patient room, the door still ajar while he continues what he is saying.

I'm noting our dwindling supply of bandages when a scream sounds and the break room door flies open. Jacquie bursts out with David right on her heels, sprinting toward me. David's face is etched with alarm, unlike anything I've seen from him before.

"Get dow— " he starts to shout.

The world erupts in a catastrophic instant. The blast hits like a physical wave, shattering windows and sending papers swirling through the air like deadly confetti. The force lifts me off my feet, and time seems to slow as I'm thrown backward. The last thing I register is the stinging smell of smoke and the horrifying sound of splintering wood before darkness claims me.

Chapter 29

Merissa

The truck lurches forward, throwing me against the door. Every bump sends pain through my body. The baby kicks wildly, as if sensing my fear and the jarring movement. I try to brace myself with my hands, but they're trembling too badly to be much help.

"Easy on the bumps!" one of the guards beside me barks. "Captain wants her alive. He has questions for her."

"Shut it, Jenkins," the other guard snaps.

Captain? My thoughts churn. It couldn't be Captain Williams; he'd never be involved in this. But there aren't many others with that rank nearby. Most of the National Guard consists of enlisted personnel who signed up after the EMP. Unless . . . Poppy Gardner mentioned Major Stone's mission—what little she knew of it—and how he had a captain he handpicked for it. Could it be . . .

The truck skids around the turn, gravel spraying. Tires grind over loose stone, each bump jarring my teeth. Behind us, the ranch truck follows, its engine steady and determined.

Shouting cuts through the noise, sharp and purposeful, followed by gunfire—calculated, like they're firing back. It's not random anymore. The horses are following, too, likely Shawn and Abby, with whoever Deputy Shaw could send. But how many could he have spared? The Guard District is already stretched thin.

"They're cutting us off!" the driver yells. "Where'd they come from?"

"Don't be such a coward," the passenger growls. The seat creaks as he shifts position. "They're just ranch hands with hunting rifles— "

"Just get us to the creek bed," comes the reply. "We've got backup waiting."

The world explodes into chaos as something hits the truck hard. Metal screams against metal. I'm thrown sideways, then forward as the vehicle skids. My shoulder hits the wall and pain shoots through my arm. The baby kicks, as if sharing my fear.

The truck rocks with another impact.

Gunfire erupts closer now—precise shots picking at the truck's tires, maybe? I curl around my belly as best I can, trying to protect us both from the jolting impacts and flying bullets. "Please, Lord," I whisper. "Keep us safe."

The truck shudders to a stop. The two men in back with me lurch forward, one of them losing his grip on his rifle. It clatters across the floor. I kick it away before he can recover it. He lunges for me but another impact rocks the vehicle, sending him sprawling and knocking his face mask off. I don't recognize him. His partner scrambles to maintain his position, shouting something to the front cab that's lost in the chaos of gunfire and squealing brakes.

The driver curses as the engine stalls. Gunfire cracks and one of the men in front cries out in pain.

The back doors fly open, flooding the space with light. Both men in the back whirl toward the threat. "Contact!" one shouts, fumbling with his tactical vest. The other reaches for something at his belt—a radio? A grenade? The first man drops, clutching his shoulder. Blood seeps between his fingers, dark against his camouflage sleeve.

His partner raises his weapon, but someone appears at the other door. The rifle butt connects with a sickening thud, and the man crumples.

"Clear!" the voice calls out. "We need to move fast. Their backup could be here any minute."

"You idiots," the unmasked man gasps through clenched teeth. "You have no idea what you're interfering with."

"Secure these two and bring them with us," Abby orders, already moving toward me. "Shawn, get that driver!"

The driver's door opens as he tries to run, but Shawn's waiting. One quick struggle and it's over.

"Let's go, Merissa," Abby says, urging me out of the truck. "We need to move." Her voice is steady, despite everything happening around us. "Hold on to my arm." Her fingers are warm and strong against my skin, keeping me grounded.

She reaches for me, but a burst of gunfire forces her to duck. "Stay down!" she snaps, firing around the edge of the door.

"They're circling back!" someone shouts—one of the ranch hands, maybe? "Coming up from the creek!"

"Two teams!" another voice calls out. "Moving in from the east!"

"Get her out of there!" Shawn's voice carries over the chaos. "We've got you covered!"

Abby lunges forward, helping me scramble toward the door. My legs are weak, my bare feet struggling to find purchase. The baby moves again, strong and anxious.

"Almost there," Abby encourages. "Just keep moving. Don't look back, focus on my voice. Just a few more— "

Everything happens at once. Gunfire erupts from all sides. Abby shoves me down, shielding me as bullets hit the truck, each one ringing through the metal. Return fire cracks from the left—hunting rifles mixed with newer weapons. The ranch's defenders.

"Now!" Shawn's voice cuts through the chaos. "While they're pinned!"

Abby adjusts her grip on me. She half-carries me from the truck toward a ranch pickup. Gravel bites at my bare feet, but I barely register it. The wind whips dust around us, carrying shouts and the thunder of hoofbeats. The baby shifts again, pressing against my ribs as if trying to get away from the danger.

"Get her back to the ranch," Shawn orders. He's on horseback, rifle ready, covering our retreat. Four other riders in Citizens Patrol armbands provide additional cover. How did Deputy Shaw manage to spare that many?

"Watch your head," Abby warns as she helps me into the ranch truck. The metal is sun-warm against my palms. "Lie flat if you can. Make yourself small."

"Small?" I comment as I get as low as I can on the passenger's side of the single-cab truck.

"They're falling back!" Kevin's voice carries over the sound of the engine.

"Kevin's okay?" I manage to ask as we start moving. The truck's engine roars as we accelerate, the suspension creaking. "Walt? Pearl? The children?"

"Don't worry about that right now," she answers. "Let's just get you out of here."

The truck takes a turn too fast, and I grip the seat. "They knew where to find me. How did they— "

"Later," she cuts me off gently. "Right now, we need to focus on getting you back."

"What do you know about Walt?"

"Nothing. I didn't stick around to chat. As soon as we realized what was happening, when we saw you being tossed into that other pickup, we came after you."

The baby moves, gentler now, as if sensing we're safer. I rest my hand on my belly, feeling the strong movements beneath. "Thank you," I whisper—to God, to our rescuers, to everyone who risked their lives to save us. I send up a silent prayer that Walt, Pearl, and everyone in the house is okay.

"You know," Abby says conversationally, though her eyes stay sharp, scanning for threats, "you do have a knack for drama."

A laugh bubbles up despite everything. "Pretty sure it's not just me. This whole town—the entire region—seems to have its own flair for drama."

"At least we're never bored," she replies, checking the rear-view mirror. "Although I wouldn't mind a few quiet days. You'll have quite a story to tell your kid someday."

If we survive this, I think but don't say. Instead, I focus on the steady motion of the pickup and on my breathing. We're not safe yet—won't be until we're back behind the ranch's defenses—and maybe not even then, but we're alive.

The ranch buildings come into view. The truck is recognized by those on guard. The gates swing open.

"Almost there," Abby soothes.

I close my eyes, one hand presses to my belly where my baby is calm. No contractions. I send up another prayer of thankfulness.

Through the gate, I catch a glimpse of the house. Glass glitters on the porch where windows have been shot out. Shell casings litter the ground like brass confetti. Residual tear gas drifts from the broken windows. My heart pounds—I need to know if everyone made it. If Pearl and Walt are okay. If the children are safe.

"Let's get you inside and have Opal check you," Abby says, helping me down from the truck. "Then we can sort everything else out."

I nod, too exhausted to argue. The adrenaline begins to fade, leaving me shaky and weak. Whatever happens next, at least I'm back.

And maybe, just maybe, we can figure out who's behind all this before they try again.

Chapter 30

Katie

Consciousness returns in fragments. Pain. The taste of copper. Something wet and sticky on my face. The metallic tang of blood mingles with smoke, making me gag. Dust settles on my lips, gritty and bitter. A high-pitched ringing drowns out everything else.

I try to move. My body feels distant, disconnected. My fingers twitch against the tile, scraping against something sharp—glass maybe, or splintered wood. Somewhere beyond the ringing, I hear screaming. Or maybe that's just in my head.

"Katie!" The voice sounds distant, warped. It echoes oddly, weaving through the shattered spaces left by the blast. "Katie, can you hear me?"

I try to respond but only manage a groan. The effort sends daggers of pain through my chest. Each breath feels like swallowing broken glass, the simple act of inhaling becoming an exercise in agony— broken ribs, my medical training supplies helpfully. Possibly a punctured lung. The clinical assessment feels separate from my body's agony.

"Don't move," Elizabeth says. She materializes through the haze like a ghost, her white coat now gray with dust and smeared with something darker. When did she get here? She was across the driveway at the med school. "We need to assess your injuries first."

The ringing begins to fade, replaced by a cacophony of sounds. Shouting, crying, the crackle of flames. Wood groans overhead, threatening to give way. Somewhere nearby, glass continues to shatter, falling like deadly rain. Smoke burns my nostrils.

"The captain," I try to say, but it comes out garbled. My tongue feels thick and uncooperative, like I'm trying to speak through cotton. "David?"

"They're being helped." Elizabeth's tone is professional, but I catch the undertone of worry. Her hands move with practiced efficiency, though I notice they tremble slightly as she checks my pulse. "Right now, I need you to focus on staying still while we check you over."

My vision starts to clear. I'm on my back, staring at what's left of the ceiling. There's a hole where it shouldn't be. Jagged edges of concrete and twisted rebar reach toward the sky like grasping fingers. Sunlight streams through the gap, catching dust motes and smoke in its beams. The sight is somehow beautiful and horrifying at once.

"Multiple lacerations," Elizabeth says to someone I can't see. Her voice shifts into the clipped, professional tone we all adopt when trying to distance ourselves from horror. "Probable concussion. Definite broken ribs. Burns on her left arm and shoulder."

Now that she mentions it, my arm feels like it's on fire. The pain radiates in waves, each pulse matching my heartbeat, the skin pulling tight and hot. The pain had gotten lost in the general chorus of agony, but now it demands attention.

"Katie?" Another voice. Leo. His boots crunch through debris as he rushes to my side, nearly sliding on the dust-covered floor. The relief in hearing him nearly undoes me. "I'm here. Elizabeth, how bad?"

"Bad enough, but she'll live." Her hands keep moving, gentle but thorough, each touch telling her something about my injuries. She doesn't say it, but I can almost hear the rest of her words. "She'll live . . . for now." If they can keep the infection at bay.

"My patients?" I croak. The words scrape against my raw throat. "Steven? His dad?"

"Shh. Shh. Everyone is being tended to," Elizabeth soothes, though her eyes dart briefly to something beyond my field of vision, something she doesn't want me to see.

A shadow falls across my face as Leo kneels beside me. His eyes are red from smoke, and there's blood above his right eye. "Hey there," he says softly. "Sorry I wasn't here faster. We came running when we heard the explosion."

The explosion. The memory slams back with physical force. David with the box, me teasing him about someone getting a great gift, him taking it to the break room to leave it for the captain, his face as they ran, Jacquie . . .

"Jacquie," I gasp. Her name tastes like ash in my mouth. "Is she okay?"

Leo's hand tightens on mine, his calloused fingers trembling slightly. Elizabeth's methodical movements pause for just a heartbeat. The look that passes between Leo and Elizabeth tells me everything. A moment of shared grief, quickly buried beneath professional necessity. My eyes burn with tears that have nothing to do with the smoke.

"The captain?" I manage to ask.

"We need to get her out of here," Elizabeth says. She glances up at the creaking ceiling, where more debris shifts ominously. "The building is unstable."

"I've got a board," Jesse's voice calls out, followed by the scrape of equipment being dragged across the rubble. His usually cheerful face is streaked with soot and grim determination.

"Hey, Katie," Jesse says, his face appearing. He positions himself at my feet, his movements careful but confident. "Let's get you out of here."

"Hold on, Katie," Elizabeth says. "It's going to hurt."

She's not wrong. Every movement ignites fresh agony, sharp and relentless. When they lift me, the world blurs at the edges, my ribs protesting with every shift. Blood coats my tongue. A scream escapes as they settle me onto the stretcher.

"Breathing's getting worse," Elizabeth announces, her stethoscope pressed against my chest. The cold metal makes me flinch. "We need to get her across now."

"Careful, Leo," I murmur.

"We're being as gentle as we can," he promises.

"No . . . your arm. Be careful." He's taken his arm out of the sling. The brace is visible as the fabric hangs loose while he maneuvers the stretcher.

"Don't worry about me, honey. My arm is fine. You're the priority right now. We're going to get you out of here."

The journey seems endless. Each step they take jostles my injuries. The smoke thins as we move away from the blast site, but my chest still burns with every breath. Through half-closed eyes, I catch glimpses of frantic movement—people running, carrying supplies, helping other victims.

And the sounds. The sounds of pain and agony blend with shouted orders and the distant crackle of fire. A child's wail pierces through the chaos, tugging at something deep inside me, but I'm too weak to react.

"Where's the captain?" I ask between painful breaths, each word a struggle against my protesting ribs.

"We got him out," Jesse responds. "Chambers found him first. He was trying to help others, stubborn as always. Broke his ankle, the one on his partially amputated foot. Sprained wrist. Some other minor injuries. He'll live. He's already in the med school."

The bright sunlight momentarily blinds me as we exit the building. The parking lot between the buildings has become a triage area, with shell-shocked survivors huddled in groups while medical staff weave between them. The med school's familiar halls look different from this angle. They've converted the main classroom into an emergency treatment area. There're people I recognize as the hospital's patients and staff. Some faces are missing. I don't want to think about why.

They transfer me to an exam table. The movement sends black spots dancing across my vision. Doc Nettie appears, her face grim as she checks my pupils.

"You're okay?" Elizabeth's gaze meets Nettie's. At Nettie's confident nod, Elizabeth tells Leo to stay with me while she and Jesse go back to the hospital to find more survivors.

"Stay with us, Katie," Nettie orders. "No passing out just yet."

"David? And Jacquie?"

"I haven't seen either of them yet." Her hands falter for just a moment as she checks me over. There's a catch in her voice that tells me she's working hard to control her emotions. "Let's just get you taken care of."

"The box," I say. The image of it flashes in my mind—ordinary brown cardboard, deceptively innocent. "It was a box for the captain."

"We know," Leo says, his voice hard. His jaw clenches, the muscle twitching beneath the dirt and blood on his face. "Shaw's already on his way. But right now, you need to let us treat you."

"Were you injured?" I ask. "You have blood on your face."

"It's not mine," he assures me.

The next few minutes blur into a kaleidoscope of pain and voices. Scissors cold against my skin as they cut away my clothes. Nettie's quiet exclamation when she sees the full extent of the burns. Leo's sharp intake of breath at the sight of my injuries. Two broken ribs. Second-degree burns on my left arm above the elbow and up to my shoulder. Multiple cuts from flying debris, including a deep gash on my scalp that explains the blood on my face. Possible concussion. Smoke inhalation.

"No sign of internal bleeding," Nettie announces after a thorough examination. "That's something at least."

"Are you sure?" Leo asks. "The broken ribs . . ."

"We'll watch her. Let's give her something for the pain."

"The captain," I say as they work. "I want to see him."

"Soon," Leo promises. "He's two tables over. Conscious and already trying to give orders."

That sounds like him. I try to smile but it pulls at the cuts on my face.

A commotion near the door draws everyone's attention. They're bringing in another victim. Even from here, I can see how bad it is. Bollinger's hands are covered in blood as he works.

"We need more light!" he shouts. "And someone find me more clean bandages!"

I try to sit up, but multiple hands hold me down.

"Don't even think about it," Nettie warns, a tremor in her voice. "You're not in any condition to help."

She's right, but it goes against every instinct to lie here while others need care. A wave of dizziness reminds me why I need to stay put.

"Leo." I grab his hand. "Our children . . ."

"Are safe," he assures me quickly. "This was targeted. The captain already sent word to the ranch. They'll be on alert."

My heart rate slows slightly at that news. I haven't even had time to worry about whether this attack might extend to Opal's ranch. I'm glad to know they're safe.

The next few hours pass in a blur of pain and brief moments of clarity. I drift in and out, waking to different faces beside my bed. Leo is there as often as he's able, doing what he can to help the other survivors too. At some point, they move me to a proper room, away from the initial triage area.

I wake fully to find evening shadows stretching across the floor. The pain has settled into a constant throbbing, marginally more manageable than before.

"Hey there." The captain's voice surprises me. He's in a wheelchair beside my bed, his leg in a splint. His face is a mass of cuts and bruises.

"Sir," I croak. My throat feels like I've swallowed sand.

"At ease, soldier." He attempts a smile that turns into a grimace. "We need to talk about what happened."

"David," I say immediately. "Is he . . ."

"Still fighting. The next twenty-four hours are critical." He shifts uncomfortably in the wheelchair, the movement causing him to wince. "Shaw found parts of the device. No doubt it was meant for me. David had just set it on the table when . . . I don't even know how he knew, but he did."

"Jacquie? I heard— "

"She didn't make it."

My fingers clench the rough hospital blanket. Jacquie died because she happened to be in the break room. The unfairness of it makes my throat tight.

"We'll find who did this," the captain continues, his voice carrying the edge of steel I've heard only in our worst moments. "Shaw already has leads. This connects to Hugo somehow, we're sure of it."

"The mystery man?"

His jaw tightens, the bruises on his face darkening with the movement. "We might be getting closer to finding out who that is."

I want to ask more questions, but exhaustion pulls at me. The captain seems to notice.

"Rest," he orders, his tone gentler now but still firm with authority. "That's a direct command. We'll talk more when you're stronger."

The wheelchair's wheels whisper against the floor as he leaves the room. I hear Leo's voice in the hallway. Footsteps approach, and a moment later he's by my side.

"Sleep," he says softly. "I'll be here."

I want to protest that I'm fine, that others need help more than I do. But my body has other ideas. As consciousness fades, I hear distant voices discussing supplies, treatment plans, and security measures.

Leo's hand is in mine—rough and steady. It's there, and then it's gone as everything blurs and fades.

Chapter 31

Merissa

Morning sunlight streams through the plastic-patched window, lighting up the mess left from yesterday's attack. Even after airing out the house for hours, the sharp smell of tear gas still hangs in the air. Blood stains the floorboards near where Walt fell, washed but not gone.

Three dead. Three lives gone because I came here. If I'd insisted we stay at the safe house in Rapid City, they'd still be alive.

"Stop it." Pearl's voice snaps me out of my thoughts. She's sitting in the chair by my bed, sewing something in her lap. Even after yesterday, she won't stop working. Her hands shake, the needle catching as she pushes it through the fabric. Her red, swollen eyes glance at me, then look away.

She's so tired; I can see it in the way her fingers tremble. But she doesn't say anything. She just keeps sewing, each stitch a quiet defiance against the exhaustion threatening to swallow her whole. "I can see you counting guilt that isn't yours to carry."

"If I hadn't come here— "

"If you hadn't come here, those men would still be evil. Would still hurt people." She sets down her sewing and fixes me with that steady gaze I've come to rely on. "The sin is theirs, not yours."

The baby shifts, pressing uncomfortably against my ribs. Word was sent back to town along with the injured attackers, and I'm expecting Poppy to show up for our appointment. As far as the baby goes, I think I'm fine—no contractions, no signs of trouble even after being dragged out of the house and tossed in a pickup truck.

Still, I'm remaining on bed rest to make sure my baby is given the best possible chance. I check the top of my journal page showing the tic marks. Today is March 9. The end of my confinement period is March 17. Only a week and a day. Then I'll be able to get up and move around freely. Hopefully by then, whoever is after me will have been apprehended and Pearl and I will be able to return to our little house.

I glance at Pearl. Each day that brings me closer to the end of bed rest and the birth of my baby is another day we're losing her. It's hard to celebrate a new life when I know hers is slipping away. The joy and sadness feel tangled together, and I don't know how to hold one without the other.

"Walt's doing better," Pearl continues, picking up her mending again. "The bullet just grazed him. He's more annoyed about being kept from his duties than anything else, forced to stay in the infirmary with the other injured. He's concerned those rascals are going to try it again and he won't be there to try and stop them."

She pauses mid-stitch and pierces me with a look. "He feels awful that they took you."

Tears well as I think about Walt. "He shouldn't. He got shot trying to protect me."

"He did, but you know Walt. I'm half surprised he didn't convince Opal to bring a bed in here and plop it right next to ours so he could keep an eye on you."

I smile while swallowing the emotions threatening to well over. "Speaking of Opal, they've been outside awhile."

"It's a beautiful day. And after all that happened yesterday, she figured it'd do Nico and the babies some good to get fresh air. This house still stinks."

"Probably true." Over an hour ago, she and Alice had bundled Caleb and Zach into slings, securing them against their bodies, and announced they were heading out to gather eggs, with Nico bouncing along beside them. She even coaxed Gerry into joining the group— poor pup. His eyes watered from the lingering tear gas, and he couldn't stop sneezing.

Jason and Robert, who had been in the garage's safe room during the attack, tagged along too. Both seemed wary, sticking close to Opal as if afraid to stray too far after everything that happened.

Even with Opal, Alice, and the children gone, the house buzzes with activity. Abby and several members of the new team from Rapid City remain on high alert, stationed as guards, while Shawn directs others to tackle the necessary repairs.

Kevin, who took a blow to the head with the butt of a rifle, insists on helping despite complaining of a headache. Opal says it's a miracle that's the worst of his injuries—he could have been unconscious for weeks, or worse.

Yesterday, Abby sent part of her group into town to escort the patched-up prisoners to Deputy Shaw for interrogation. During the rescue, Kevin and the others made sure no one slipped through their grasp. Their dead far outnumber ours, and two more of theirs succumbed overnight, despite Opal's best efforts.

Mother Pearl clears her throat. "Robert's taken it hard, though. Losing his mother so recently, then this . . ."

"I wondered. Jason seems to understand that too."

She nods. "Those two have become quite close. It's been good for both of them, I think."

Boots on the porch interrupt us. Abby appears in the doorway, rifle ready though her posture is relaxed. "Just checking in. One of the teams reported movement near the creek, but it was just deer."

The increased security should make me feel safer, but instead, it just reminds me that everyone is at risk because of me. Abby expects Deputy Shaw to send out more patrollers when he learns about the attack. But how long can they maintain the level of protection we may need?

Maybe it would be best for me to move back into town. Maybe move to the medical school where Katie is staying? But how could that even work? Somehow, we'd have to get word to the bad guys that I'm no longer at the ranch. Otherwise, they may attack again and more people could die.

"Did the team make it to town?"

Abby shrugs. "Far as I know. We've yet to hear anything."

"It's still early, though, right? You're not worried yet?"

A commotion outside draws her attention. She steps onto the porch, rifle ready. "Stay here," she orders, though where else would I go?

Pearl sets down her mending again and moves to peek out the window. "Vehicle at the gate. Looks like the coroner's truck. Probably here for the bodies. Which means, yes, the team made it to town." She meets my gaze. "Probably Ritchie, right?"

Something in my chest flutters as Pearl stubbornly insists on calling Bowski by his given name—typical of her. In our letters, Bowski mentioned that he's taken over all the coroner duties Hugo used to handle, a task that weighs heavily on him. The dead from the ranch will be buried here when the ground thaws enough to dig proper graves.

As I smooth a hand along my hairline, checking how much of it has slipped free from the braid trailing down my back, questions churn in my mind. Does he know I'm here? Will he come into the house? Will Abby let him? Does she know about us? We talked briefly about her budding relationship with Shawn, but I didn't mention my feelings for Bowski.

Abby reappears. "They've arrived to retrieve the dead assailants. Deputy Shaw's going to send additional people . . . as soon as he can."

There's something in the way Abby's talking that concerns me. "What's wrong?"

She shakes her head. "The hospital. There was an attack on it yesterday too."

Pearl gasps. "The hospital?"

Abby nods. "I don't know the full extent of the damage. Captain Williams is alive. He sent a note with Bowski for his wife."

"Katie? Leo?" I ask, my chest tightening like a vice.

She shakes her head. "I don't have any details. Can Bowski come in? He asked to speak with you."

He appears in the doorway moments later, familiar and solid and real. His eyes find mine immediately, and everything else seems to fade away. He looks tired and worried, but alive. So wonderfully alive.

"Hey," he says softly.

"Hey yourself." My voice catches.

Pearl rises smoothly from her chair. "I should check on Walt," she announces to no one in particular. "Make sure he's not overdoing things." She pats Bowski's arm as she passes. "Good to see you, young man."

Abby offers Pearl her arm. "Let me help you. I need to take Mrs. Williams her letter."

For a moment, we just look at each other. All the words I've written in my journal, all the things I've wanted to tell him, are stuck in my throat.

"When I heard . . ." he starts, then stops and moves closer. "Shaw told me you were here. That they tried to take you. I would have come sooner, but— "

"Abby just told me about the hospital. Is Katie— "

"Alive. She's alive."

Something about the way he says it doesn't give me much comfort. "She's injured?"

"I don't know how badly. I'm going to go see her later. There's . . . there were several deaths."

"Who?"

Bowski quietly lists a few names. One is a woman who brings food to the patients—always kind. Then he mentions several patients, none of whom I recognize. "And Jacquie Haley," he adds.

"Jacquie? Why— "

"She just happened to be in the wrong place at the wrong time. From the information Shaw's put together, David Paul brought a package to the captain."

"A package? What kind of package?"

"You probably haven't heard, with everything that's happened, but we got mail. Several bags arrived with one of the drayers. Paul had made mail delivery the day before, but there was still some stuff being sorted. I heard it was a big box addressed to the captain, and David brought it to the hospital."

"Was David there when it exploded? Was he injured?"

Bowski nods. "Badly. He may . . ." His voice fades off as he shakes his head.

"He's not going to make it?"

"He's among the critically injured." He levels his gaze. "It was bad."

"And Katie? Will she survive?"

"She was pretty close to the blast. They're doing everything they can for both of them. Leo was at the med school when it happened, so he wasn't injured."

The baby kicks hard, sensing my distress maybe. I rest my hand on my belly, trying to stay calm. "What about the men that were captured? The ones who took me?"

"Shaw's people are questioning them. They're talking, apparently." He moves to the window and scans the yard. "He only told me a short while ago that you were here. That you have been here and what happened yesterday. I came as soon as I could.”

“You had responsibilities. The dead.”

He nods, moving to the chair by my bed and reaching for my hand. His fingers are warm, calloused, and real. “I brought some people I trust. Good men. They’ll help guard the ranch until Shaw can send more people.”

“You can’t stay?”

“Not yet. Things are happening fast now. The men they captured, they’re talking. And Hugo . . .” He sits carefully on the edge of my bed. “Hugo’s ready to talk too. He knows about the attack on the hospital. How they kidnapped you. They’ve already tried to get to him. I think he finally realized he’s not safe.”

“Abby said the captain sent a note to Alice. He’s okay?”

“He’s injured. Broke his ankle. Some smoke inhalation. I’m not sure what all. I’ll visit him later too. I only know what Shaw told me. He said the captain will be fine. He’s tough and will heal.”

“That sounds like him.” I try to smile but tears spill instead. “I heard things, during the kidnapping. Things I wasn’t sure I should tell anyone.”

“About Stone?”

I look up sharply. “How did you know?”

“The men they captured were soldiers on detail with Stone. When Hugo found out, he gave the name of Rangler, a captain on Stone’s personal detail. The whole thing, the biodiesel operation, it all leads back to Stone.” His voice drops lower. “Shaw’s people are closing in. He won’t get away with this.”

“The general?”

“Knows now. He’s not involved—just another thing Stone kept from his superiors.” Bowski’s free hand comes up to brush tears from my cheek. “It’s almost over. You’ll be safe soon. You and this little one.”

The baby kicks, as if recognizing his voice. Bowski’s eyes widen slightly as he feels the movement through our joined hands.

“Strong,” he says softly.

“Like his daddy.” The words slip out before I can stop them.

“Yes.” No hesitation, no jealousy. Just acceptance. “Braedon would be proud. Of both of you.”

Fresh tears spill, but these feel different. Cleansing somehow. "I've missed you," I whisper.

"I've missed you too." He leans forward and presses his forehead to mine. "When Shaw told me what happened . . . I've never been so scared."

"I was afraid too. Not just for me." I pull back slightly and meet his eyes. "For everyone here. For Katie. For you."

"For me?"

"If they knew about me, about the ranch . . . what if they knew about us? About the letters?"

Understanding floods his face. "You were worried about me?"

"Of course I was, you idiot." The words come out somewhere between a laugh and a sob. "I think I love you."

His breath catches. For a moment he's absolutely still. Then his hand comes up to cup my cheek, so gentle, so careful. "I've been in love with you for months," he confesses. "But I didn't want to push. Didn't want to rush you."

"I know." I lean into his touch. "Thank you for that. For giving me time. For the letters. For everything."

He brushes his thumb across my cheekbone and wipes away my tears. "Thank you for trusting me with your heart. I know it's not easy."

The baby kicks again, harder this time, making me laugh softly. "I think someone's feeling left out."

Bowski grins and moves his hand to my belly. "Don't worry, little one. There's plenty of room in my heart for both of you."

A knock at the door breaks the moment. Abby stands there, apologetic but professional. "Sorry to interrupt, but your assistant asked me to tell you he's finished loading up."

Bowski straightens, though his hand stays linked with mine. "I have to go."

"I know."

"You'll be safe. And I'll be back as soon as I can."

"Promise?"

He presses a kiss on my forehead. "Promise. Try to stay out of trouble until then?"

"I'll do my best." I manage a small smile. "But you know how things are around here."

"I do." He releases my hand. "Which is why I'm leaving the extra guards. They'll keep you safe until we end this."

"Please send Katie my love. Tell her . . . tell her I'm praying. For the captain and David too. And Leo, I'm sure he's exhausted. Make sure they know their children are doing well."

I watch him go, my heart both fuller and emptier somehow. He stops to speak with Walt, who's sitting on the porch despite orders to remain in bed. Their conversation is brief but intense.

"He's a good man," Pearl says from the doorway. I hadn't heard her return.

"Yes," I agree softly. "He is."

She comes to sit beside me again, picking up her mending. "God has a way of bringing the right people into our lives at the right time."

I rest my hand where I can still feel the warmth of Bowski's touch, where my child moves strong and sure. "Do you really think it's almost over?"

"The immediate danger? Perhaps." She threads her needle with practiced ease. "But life will always bring new challenges. What matters is facing them. With faith. With love."

The baby shifts again and settles into a new position. Outside, children's laughter floats through the air—Nico maybe, or Robert. Life carries on despite everything, a fragile thread of hope enduring even in the darkness.

"Together," I repeat softly. Looking toward the window where Bowski's truck disappears through the gate. "Yes. Together."

Chapter 32

Katie

Pain pulls me from sleep before dawn. The analgesic, a potent tincture of wild lettuce, has worn off, and every breath is a sharp reminder of my broken ribs and battered body.

Through the window, I can just make out the silhouettes of armed guards moving between buildings. Their presence offers both reassurance and unease, a shield against further attacks and a stark reminder of why they are necessary.

Voices drift in from the hallway, urgent but hushed. Shaw's distinctive growl catches my attention. ". . . said there were at least two more involved. Higher-ups. Things are starting to match with what we found in Hugo's records."

The voices move past the door before I can hear more. I shift carefully, trying to find a position that doesn't send daggers through my chest. The movement pulls at the burns on my arm, drawing a hiss of pain.

"Easy there." Leo materializes from the shadows of the predawn room. His chair scrapes quietly as he leans forward. "Been watching you toss and turn for hours."

"How long have you been sitting there?" My voice is hoarse.

"All night." He runs a hand through his disheveled hair. "Someone had to make sure you didn't try to sneak off to check on patients."

Despite the pain, I manage a weak smile. "You know me too well."

"Need something for pain?"

"Please." The word scrapes against my raw throat. "How's David?"

Leo's hesitation tells me everything. "He made it through the night. Nettie's with him now. There're several others in the critical ward."

"The critical ward? How many?"

"Five, I think. I haven't been working there. Just here and the other ward. Those who are less injured."

I nod, wanting to ask questions, but from what I can gather, I'm in the step-down unit. Not critical but not completely out of the woods yet.

More voices in the hallway interrupt us. Running footsteps, then Nettie's sharp commands. "Get Bollinger in here now! His pressure's dropping!"

Leo squeezes my hand. "I'll check."

He returns minutes later, his face grim. "David's having complications. They're doing what they can."

I close my eyes, feeling utterly useless. In my mind, I can picture exactly what they're doing, what supplies they're using, what alternatives they might try with our limited resources. But I can't help. I can't even sit up without the room spinning.

Leo doses me with two different tinctures designed to work together to help with the pain. "Feel like a cup of tea?" he asks. "Stella said you can have lavender tea along with the tinctures."

"Okay," I agree as my stomach growls. "Maybe some food too?"

"Probably a good idea. I'll be back shortly."

The faint squeak of wheels on tile announces the captain's arrival. He maneuvers his wheelchair through the doorway with careful effort, favoring his sprained wrist.

"You're up early," he says, settling himself between my bed and the window. His wheelchair catches on an uneven tile, prompting a muttered curse under his breath as he adjusts, using his good arm to spin the opposite wheel into place.

"Let me help— " I start to move, but the pain is immediate.

"Stay put," he orders, then softens his tone. "Sorry. We need to talk. Where's Leo?"

"Getting tea. What's wrong?"

"Keep your voice down," he glances at the other patients. "Everything's under control now, but there was a situation." He rolls closer. In a low voice, he adds, "There was a problem at the ranch."

"Are my children okay?" A strained whisper escapes me, each word scraping against the ache in my throat.

"They're fine. Merissa's fine." He hesitates as footsteps approach the door. Leo enters, balancing a tray with his good arm. Leo sets the tray carefully on a TV table beside my cot.

"Captain, you're looking better," he greets him with a smile.

"Feeling better. Thank you."

Leo's gaze shifts to me, his expression faltering. "What's wrong?"

"Something happened at the ranch," I whisper.

"What?"

"There was an attack. Merissa was kidnapped— " I gasp as the captain raises his hand. "They got her back. She's okay. It happened yesterday, but Shaw didn't tell me about it until this morning. There were some deaths, but I don't believe it was anyone we know. Bowski is sending some extra men out there until Deputy Shaw can get things under control here. Then . . . then I don't know."

"I overheard him earlier," I say. "Shaw, I mean. I think they are figuring out who's behind this mess."

The captain's mouth goes tight. "I think you're right about that."

"You know who it is?"

He shakes his head. "I can't say anything right now. Only . . . be patient. This may be almost over."

Before I can respond, commotion erupts in the hallway again. "Blood pressure's still falling!" someone shouts. "We need . . ."

The voices fade as they rush past. The captain's knuckles whiten on his wheelchair's armrest.

"David?" I ask.

He nods. "Internal bleeding they missed initially. The blast . . ." He doesn't finish the sentence.

The morning passes in a haze of pain and worry. Various people drift in and out—nurses checking vitals, Nettie examining my burns, Murphy stopping by briefly between helping with other patients. Each brings fragments of news about David's condition, none of it encouraging.

Around midday, an unexpected visitor arrives. Kerry Hendricks pauses by my cot, her eyes red-rimmed.

"Feel like talking?" she asks softly. "Jacquie . . ." She shakes her head.

"Please sit," I manage, though talking still hurts. Kerry has worked with Jacquie since the hospital was opened. She'd even known her in passing prior to the EMP.

Kerry perches on the edge of the chair, twisting her hands in her lap. "I keep expecting to see her, you know? It's a lot. Finding Rand's remains. Now Jacquie is dead. It's just . . . a lot."

"Too much," I agree.

We sit in silence for a few minutes before I ask, "Do you know how my amputee patient is? His son?"

She nods. "His son is in the other unit. He'll be fine. But your amputee . . . he's one of the ones in the critical ward. I'm not sure of his prognosis."

More commotion outside interrupts us. This time, the voices are triumphant. "He's stabilizing!"

Kerry squeezes my hand. Through the propped-open door, I've been catching glimpses of the organized chaos that follows any near-loss in our makeshift hospital. David is still critical, but he's fighting.

"That's good news," Kerry says. "I'd better get going. I'm on a break. It's crazy right now. With the hospital gone and so many of our supplies . . . we're just doing the best we can."

Late afternoon brings another visitor. Bowski fills the doorway, his massive frame barely fitting through. Despite his intimidating size, his expression is gentle.

"Thought you'd want news from the ranch," he says, settling carefully into the chair Leo usually occupies. "Saw your kids this morning. They're doing great. Nico's appointed himself the official protector of his baby brothers, with Gerry's assistance. It's quite something to see."

The mental image brings tears to my eyes. "And Merissa?"

"Tough woman." He runs a hand through his beard. "Some cuts and bruises, but she's more angry than scared. What she overheard while they had her, it matches what we're getting from the prisoners. Everything ties back to Hugo's operation, but bigger than we thought. More organized."

"I overheard Shaw this morning. It sounds like they're getting close. Do you know . . ." My voice fades as I glance at the cot next to me. The patient is sleeping, but it's still not smart to discuss this here.

Bowski follows my gaze and then gives a nod. "Close. Won't be long now and we'll have our answers." He stands, careful not to bump my cot. "Get some rest. Leo said he'd be back soon."

As if summoned by his name, Leo appears with a dose of medicine and more tea. The pain has been building again, making it hard to think clearly about everything I've learned.

But as the tea and tinctures begin to work, as evening shadows creep across my room, pieces start shifting in my mind. Shaw's closing in on the unnamed person from Hugo's records. The one behind it all. I think Bowski would have given me a name if we were someplace private. Does Leo know? He stepped out again, off to help where he could.

A sudden commotion outside pulls me from my thoughts—urgent voices and running feet suggest David or another critical patient has taken a turn for the worse.

I close my eyes and send up a silent prayer for David, my amputee patient, and whoever is in distress. Also for Jacquie's family and Merissa's recovery. Tomorrow, maybe there will be answers. Tomorrow, we might finally understand the full scope of what we're facing.

But tonight, all I can do is lie here, listening to the sounds of others fighting to save lives. And pray that when dawn comes, we'll all still be here to face whatever truth emerges.

Chapter 33

Merissa

Through the window, I watch Opal leading the children to the chicken coop. Nico bounces ahead, while Alice follows with Caleb and Zach bundled against her. After the kidnapping, even this simple morning routine feels precious. Dangerous too.

"Your letter won't write itself," Pearl says from her chair, noticing how I keep glancing toward the window. Her hands work steadily at her mending, though I notice she has to pause more often now to rest. "Bowski will want to know you're okay."

"Bowski just saw me yesterday. Besides, I wasn't writing to him. I'm writing a note to Katie to send back with Poppy."

Poppy was supposed to come to the ranch yesterday, but she didn't show. Abby said it was because of the explosion at the hospital. They're all still overwhelmed, trying to keep the injured alive.

Part of me wishes I were there, too, using the skills Captain Williams taught me. I know bed rest is the best thing I can do for my baby's health, but I hate feeling like I'm letting the team down, especially with both Katie and the captain injured. At least Elizabeth Powell and Dr. Bollinger are still there to help.

The baby shifts, pressing against my ribs. The end of my bed rest confinement is in sight—March 17th. One more week. It feels both too far and too close.

I glance at Pearl. She's doing so much better, only the one seizure, though terrifying. The new medication seems to have eased her pain and boosted her energy. Even the headaches seem to have subsided.

I won't lie, I'm hoping for a miracle—that one of the herbs will be exactly what she needs to cure her. Realistically, though, I know it's just a matter of time until the symptoms return. It'll likely start with headaches, maybe a seizure. If the cancer has spread to her brain, she could face vision or speech problems, fatigue, nausea, and pain. So much pain.

Boots crunch on the gravel outside. Abby's doing another perimeter check. She's barely left my side since yesterday, even sleeping on a cot near my bed. The front room is getting awfully full with Pearl, me, and Abby making it into our bedroom. Gerry also insists on sleeping in here with us.

The men Bowski brought patrol the property in careful rotations, their presence both reassuring and a reminder of why we need them. Walt is doing better. He's still under orders to take it easy—and for him, he is. That doesn't stop him from making regular visits to the house to check on me or Pearl.

I know he feels guilty for not preventing the kidnapping, but his concern isn't just for me. He's worried about Pearl and her health too. We both know the tear gas didn't do her any favors. She had a headache most of the night, possibly caused by the fumes. Possibly by the disease.

"Any word about Katie?" Pearl asks, picking up her mending again.

"Not since Bowski left yesterday." I try to sound more confident than I feel. "The captain's note said she was stable."

"Stable." Pearl shakes her head. "Such a careful word." Her voice catches. She clears her throat and continues sewing, but her hands tremble slightly. "Maybe Poppy will bring more information with her."

Through the window, I can see Jason and Robert move through the morning chores with quiet efficiency, their eyes darting to Opal as if tethered to her every step. Even the clink of buckets and scrape of boots on the ground carries a heightened tension, the unspoken need to stay close lingering after the recent events.

Abby appears in the doorway, rifle ready but relaxed. "All clear on the perimeter." Her gaze sweeps out the window to the west before returning to the room. "Shawn's team spotted some tracks near the creek, but they're old. From the day of the kidnapping, probably."

The baby kicks hard, as if understanding the word. Kidnapping. I rest my hand on my belly, feeling the strong movements beneath. I give a rub, trying to assure him we're safe now. I wish I believed it myself.

I pick up my pencil again, trying to focus on the letter to Katie. Poppy's going to be here shortly, and I've barely written anything.

The trouble is, I'm not sure what to say. *I'm glad you're not dead* is a little too blunt, but it's exactly what I'm feeling.

The distant ring of a bell cuts through our quiet morning.

"That's not our emergency bell," Pearl says, setting aside her mending.

"No." Abby moves to the front window, her rifle ready. "The neighbors." She pushes the curtain aside and draws in a sharp breath. "Smoke. A lot of it."

Through the window, people are already moving, grabbing buckets and tools. Shouts carry across the yard as ranch hands gather to help.

"What's burning there now?" Pearl asks, standing up and moving toward the front window. "The barn burned down not long ago. Killed the man, though I still say there was something odd about that."

"Looks like it might be their haystack."

"Humph," Pearl snorts.

The front door opens and Opal hurries in with Caleb, Alice right behind her with Zach. Nico and Robert slip in behind them, their eyes wide with concern. Gerry's there, too, alert but nervous looking.

"We'll need everyone who can be spared," Opal says, already moving to hand Caleb to Pearl. "The men who are injured, they'll be staying here . . . much to Walt's dismay."

I nod, imagining Walt's frustration with those orders.

"Jason's gathering buckets," Opal adds. "He knows where everything is—he can direct the men."

"I can help too," Robert says quietly.

"No, you stay here with Alice and the little ones." Opal's voice is firm but kind. "We need strong hands here, too, keeping everyone safe. Pearl? Please have Robert help you as needed."

Jason appears in the doorway, breathless but focused. "The men are ready, Mrs. Maher. I showed them where the extra buckets are stored."

"Good boy." Opal nods approvingly. "Let's go, then. The sooner we contain it, the better." She glances toward Abby. "Are you coming?"

"Most of our security will need to respond," Abby says, her voice tight with concern. "If that fire spreads . . ."

"We can't ignore it." Opal nods. "If it spreads, the next ranch over could be in trouble too."

"It won't come this way?"

"Wind's blowing wrong."

Abby nods. "I need to stay here. Stay with Merissa."

Opal glances my way, and I shrug. "I'm sure we're fine, but she has her orders. Be careful," I say.

"Always." Opal pauses at the door, exchanging a quick look with Alice before she and Jason slip outside to join the others in the yard.

"Seems awfully convenient," Abby mutters, moving from window to window. "A fire drawing everyone away."

"You think it's deliberate?" Pearl asks, pulling Caleb close to her chest with one arm, the other hand traveling to her temple.

"Mother Pearl?" I ask, leaning forward in my bed.

"I'm fine. Just a twinge of . . . of something."

"Do you need something?" I look toward Alice. "Can you get her some willow bark tincture?"

A flicker crosses the window, quick and deliberate, vanishing before Abby can fully react. Gerry growls low, and Abby whirls, but the door crashes inward before she completes the motion. A metallic clang rings out as a canister skids across the floor, bouncing once before erupting with thick white smoke that coils through the air like a living thing.

"Down!" Abby yells, her voice muffled by the growing haze, but the gas claws at my throat before I can duck. I choke, lungs searing, the bitter taste triggering memories of the last attack. "Gas," I rasp, coughing hard. "Just like before— "

Through a sting of tears, I make out Abby lunging toward Pearl and Caleb, her arms outstretched, desperate to pull them clear of the suffocating fog. A high-pitched cry pierces the room—Zach. Caleb's wails join in, tangling with Nico's sobs and growls from Gerry. Alice's scream cuts through it all, ragged and panicked. She stumbles blindly, cradling Zach, her silhouette swaying as she struggles to navigate the dense, shifting smoke.

Footsteps scrape against the floorboards, quick and light. Through gaps in the thinning smoke, I catch glimpses of movement—darting shadows that set my nerves on edge. A sharp, familiar laugh cuts through the chaos of coughs and cries. The smoke parts, revealing Major Stone's narrow face with his pointed features and beady eyes, reminding me of a weasel sizing up its next meal.

"Now this is disappointing." Stone strolls into the room, his voice casual. Several men follow close behind, weapons at the ready. Unlike the first group of kidnappers, who hid behind masks, these men make no effort to conceal their faces. "I had hoped to avoid such dramatics."

Recovering from the gas, Abby's rifle comes up, but one of Stone's men is faster. The shot catches her in the leg, and she goes down with a cry of pain. Her weapon skitters across the floor.

Gerry barks. The gun spins toward him, but Robert pulls him behind the breakfast bar.

"Keep that dog under control," Stone says. "I'd hate to have to shoot him, but Rangler wouldn't mind."

"Not at all," the man who shot Abby says with a sneer. "I'm not a fan of dogs. Especially mangy mutts like that one."

"Please," I manage between coughs. "Pearl needs her medicine."

"Shut up." Stone moves closer, his own pistol trained on me. "Your interference has cost me quite enough already. Though I must admit, I'm impressed. You've proved more resourceful than expected. Imagine my surprise to learn you were hiding here. Fortune certainly smiled on me, though it would've been helpful had you been at the hospital for the big boom."

He wiggles his eyebrows as if mocking his own words. A twisted grin spreads across his face. "But no matter. I'll make do with what I've got."

Abby's pressing her hand against her leg wound, her face tight with pain but her eyes alert, tracking Stone's every move. Alice has backed into the corner, clutching Zach while Nico presses against her, his face buried in her skirt. Her arms tremble, but she holds the baby tight, trying to shield him from the worst of the smoke.

Robert has his fingers laced in Gerry's collar and now stands in front of them, his posture rigid, defiant even as his eyes water and his breath comes in labored coughs. He doesn't flinch, doesn't hesitate. His small frame becomes a barrier between them and whatever comes next. Gerry has adopted the same stance, looking ready to pounce but seeming to understand the timing isn't right.

Pearl's breathing grows more labored. The smoke from the gas canister is thinning, but she's already pale, her hands pressed against her chest. Even a couple of Stone's men look uncomfortable.

"Sir," one starts. "The old woman— "

"Is none of your concern." Stone's voice carries the crack of command. "Secure the female." He motions toward Abby. "We're taking Mrs. Weaver with us."

"Everything has changed," I say, trying to keep my voice steady. Keep him talking. Give help time to arrive. "Hugo's talking. It's over."

"Over?" He laughs, but there's an edge to it. "You think a few dead bodies and some terrified witnesses can stop what we've built? This goes beyond one mortician, beyond this backward little community. Beyond what you think Hugo knows. That operation is just the tip of the iceberg. This is bigger than Rapid City. Bigger than the Black Hills." His eyes narrow. "Though I must admit, you've complicated things considerably."

I shake my head. "What do you mean?" The words are barely out of my mouth when things begin to make sense. "The Christmas Day explosion at Camp Rapid. Were you behind that?"

Rangler laughs. "You're right. She's too smart for her own good."

Stone raises his hand. "That was a stupid move on your part, Mrs. Weaver." He points around the room. "I can't let that information get out, now can I?"

Lifting my chin, I narrow my eyes. "I doubt you planned on any of this information getting out."

He shrugs. "True. But I did plan to make it painless for everyone."

The truth hits me with sickening clarity—he plans to silence everyone in this room who understands what's happening. Including me. Especially me. Tears blur my vision as my baby kicks, strong and innocent within me. The thought steals my breath. If I die, my child dies with me, never drawing a single breath of his own.

"So, it was you?" I persist. Nothing to lose now.

"Patriots, like Rangler here, did what was needed. And they will again and again and again. Not just here but around what is left of the United States. You don't think this was all by accident, do you?"

He shakes his head, a cold, twisted grin curling on his lips. "No . . . it was by design. I will admit, the Preacher made a nice patsy for a while. When he started his own deranged mission, we saw an opportunity—a way to push our plans forward."

"Cabal? Geoff Landers?"

"Another couple of chumps. Landers believed in our cause, to a point. But Melvin Cabal was only in it for himself. They are no longer a problem. Soon, word will drift back to Rapid City about their untimely demise."

Movement catches my eye—Pearl, leaning against the wall. She pales as Caleb whimpers in her arms. The sight sends fear through me stronger than anything Stone can do.

"She needs help," I plead. "Please. The smoke— "

"Major." The soldier securing Abby looks up. "She's right. The woman doesn't look good."

The major shrugs.

"Please," I say again. "At least let the children leave. Robert and Nico can take the babies." Determination hardens Robert's young features, a quiet resolve where fear should have been.

I want to be proud of Robert, standing his ground with such courage, but the tear gas burns my throat and stings my eyes, making it hard to focus on anything beyond the panic tightening in my chest. I know what Stone is capable of, what he's planning to do. I've seen what happens when people defy him, threaten him, and Robert doesn't understand the danger he's in. The danger we are all in.

The window explodes inward as a shot shatters the glass. Stone spins toward the sound, his pistol shifting away from me.

"Drop your weapons!" Walt's voice carries from outside, strong and steady. More shouts join his—the ranch's defenders have returned.

One of Stone's men goes down as a shot finds its mark. The other stumbles back, returning fire, but the smoke throws off his aim.

"Get down!" Abby shouts. Despite her injured leg, she lunges for her fallen weapon.

Stone pivots back toward me, but Robert's shout draws his attention. The boy has used the chaos to pull Pearl and Caleb behind the wall, Gerry positioning himself next to Robert. Alice drops to the floor, curling around Zach while Nico huddles close to her.

Walt stands in the doorway, his rifle trained on Stone despite his injuries. His voice carries the weight of barely contained fury. "Drop your weapons. We've got you surrounded."

"Hardly," Stone spits. But two of his men have already dropped their weapons, hands raised in surrender. Captain Rangler, so confident earlier, seems torn on how he should respond. Save himself or go down fighting.

Stone shows no hesitation. He lunges toward me, gripping my arm and yanking me from the bed. Cold metal presses against my temple.

"Back off," Stone orders, "or she dies."

The smoke has thinned enough for me to see everyone clearly now. Walt holds his position in the doorway, his rifle steady despite his injury. Abby has retrieved her weapon, though she remains on the floor, her injured leg stretched out.

"It's over, Stone," Abby says quietly. "They're on to you. They know everything."

"They know nothing," Stone spits. "And neither do you."

The baby kicks hard—too hard. Stone feels my body shudder as his gaze travels to my stomach. His grip loosens just slightly. Just enough.

I drive my elbow back hard, just like we've taught the women in our self-defense classes. It connects with Stone, sending him stumbling. His gun fires, but the shot goes wide.

Before he can recover, the door bursts open, and Walt's group pours in. My chest tightens when I realize these aren't the defenders—they're the men recovering in the infirmary, still injured from the last attack. One leans heavily against the wall, his face pale, eyes rimmed with red. Another clutches his side, wincing with every step.

They move as one, slow but resolute, every step clearly costing them. Yet their sheer determination shifts the atmosphere in the room, thickening the tension more than any weapon could.

"Drop it," Walt says, his voice filled with steel. "Drop it now."

Rangler drops his weapon first, shoulders slumping in defeat. The rest of Stone's men follow the captain's lead, their guns clattering to the floor one by one. But Stone remains defiant, his beady eyes darting around the room, searching for any advantage.

Even with all hope lost, he keeps his grip on his pistol until Walt takes a deliberate step forward. Only then does Stone finally let his weapon fall, his thin face contorted with hatred.

"Merissa?" Pearl's voice carries from behind the cabinet. "The children?"

"We're okay," Alice answers shakily. "We're all okay."

"I'm okay," I answer, untangling my legs from the bedding and finding my footing on the floor. "Alice, help Pearl. I'm going to tend to Abby. Walt, get us some help here."

Walt motions to one of the more mobile of his injured conquerors, who goes to the front door and begins rapidly ringing the dinner bell.

"Quite a mess you've made," Walt says to Stone, his voice rough but steady as he leans against the doorframe. "Kinda surprised a little weasel like you could pull somethin' like this together."

"You don't understand," Stone starts, but Walt cuts him off with a low chuckle.

"Oh, I think we understand just fine, son. Ain't too much to figure out when folks like you come struttin' in, thinking you're the only one who knows how to play dirty. But when you mess with my family, you're the one who's made the mistake." His tone hardens. "You won't find us as easy pickin's as you thought."

Stone gives him a hard look but stays quiet.

"Nothin' to say?" Walt adds. "Probably better that way." He raises his voice slightly, and it takes on a completely different tone. "Miss Pearl, you doing okay?"

"Fine, Walt. Just peachy," she replies, her voice hoarse and phlegmy. She releases a sharp, chest-rattling cough.

Alice is on her feet, ushering Nico to the door leading to the laundry room. "Robert?" She calls. "Take Caleb and go with Nico. Nico, you can carry baby Zach, right? Get out of this house and find someplace to sit with him. Get some fresh air. We'll be out for you shortly. Robert, take care of them all."

"Yes, ma'am," Robert says. "What about Miss Pearl?"

"I'll take care of her. Grab some of those coats hanging on the pegs. Keep everyone warm."

"You did good, boy," Walt calls out to Robert. "Real good."

Robert nods as he and Nico leave the room.

I press harder on Abby's leg, trying to stop the bleeding. "We need to get this treated properly. Get you to the hospital."

"I'm fine," she insists, though her face is pale. "Check on Pearl."

"Alice is with her." Through the settling smoke, Alice helps Pearl into a chair, speaking to her softly, assuring her the children are safe. As always, Gerry is at her side.

Walt and his injured men maintain their guard positions, their exhaustion evident but their determination unwavering. The dinner bell at Hayward's has finally stopped ringing.

A sudden movement. Stone twists. Something metallic glints in his hand.

Before anyone can react, a sharp crack splits the air. Stone goes still, a surprised look on his face as blood blossoms on his shirt.

Alice stands steady, her pistol unwavering. "That's enough of that," she says quietly.

And it is.

Chapter 34

Katie

"My Henry should be here soon," Miss Martha speaks from the next cot. The beds have been rearranged, and she's now close to the window. The new spot gives her a clear view of the walkway between buildings. She had been admitted to the hospital after a fall, and her son, Henry, was visiting when the explosion occurred. "They're moving him to our ward, you know."

"I've heard. That's wonderful. His leg must be doing better," I reply, my voice still sounding wrong to my ears. At least it doesn't hurt as much when I talk, thanks to the honey syrup I've been getting.

Henry took a face full of glass in the explosion, but it was his leg, crushed under a fallen beam, that had everyone concerned and kept him in the critical unit.

"Much better," she agrees with a smile. "He's a strong boy."

I smile in response. He's probably close to fifty, but to his mom, he'll always be her boy. Miss Martha is one of our neighborhood outliers—one of the few elderly survivors from the early days of the EMP and the brutal winter that followed. She attributes her survival to Henry's care and her lifelong commitment to vitamins and a nightly glass of red wine. Rumor is, Henry's still managed to keep her in wine thanks to the black market. Her recent slip on the ice, followed by the explosion, hasn't done her any good.

While her hip didn't show a fracture clinically, we can't rule it out without an X-ray. Out of Miss Martha's hearing, the captain reminded us that 18 to 33 percent of older adults with hip fractures die within a year. And that statistic was before the EMP. Now, with the explosion, I don't like her chances—especially if Henry is hurt and can't care for her. Most likely, they'll both end up in one of Poppy's care centers.

On the other side of the dorm, Steven is visiting his dad, who was moved from critical to this unit earlier today. In a few days, he'll likely go to a care center too. Then, perhaps, he'll be able to be fitted for an artificial limb.

Bollinger has said more than once that he should have been the one to handle the amputation, then maybe the man might have a better stump. Williams reminded the doctor that they were all a little busy the day of the building collapse and everyone did the best they could.

"You look tired, dear," she says, "Why don't you take a little nap? That handsome husband of yours should be here soon, right?"

"Soon," I reply, stifling a yawn. Dr. Bollinger planned to check his arm this morning. I noticed yesterday it was bothering him. He had it in the sling and brace but seemed to be rubbing it. The day of the explosion, he moved me—and several others, I'm sure—without regard to his own injury. I'm trying not to worry, but fear he's reinjured it. Possibly refractured the weakened bone.

"Well, get some rest so you'll be fresh when he arrives."

I give a nod and close my eyes. Soon, the sound of quiet voices draws me back. Leo stands by my bedside.

"Leo, hey," I say, trying to read his expression.

He settles into the chair beside my cot. "You look better. How're you feeling?"

"Mmm. Tired. Achey, but not quite so much. Have you heard anything about David?"

"Nothing new. He's stable . . . for now."

I know that's something, and part of me wishes to rejoice, but most of me knows that could change at any moment. I reach for Leo's hand. "And you?"

He gives a slight smile. "Bollinger doesn't think I hurt it. No new breaks, anyway. Nothing else has changed. The sling and brace remain in place except when I'm doing the specific exercises. No lifting— even in the event of an explosion." He pauses and flares his eyebrows.

I snicker. "No kidding. I could have told you that."

"I just wanted to get you out of there. Get you safe. Get you taken care of."

"I know." I squeeze his hand.

He returns the pressure. "Some function might return with time, but . . ."

"I'm sorry." The words feel inadequate. We both know what this means—no National Guard commission, no official position with their medical corps.

"Hey." He manages a smile. "I'm beginning to accept it. I've had a few months to get used to the idea. I can see now that Bollinger was introducing it to me slowly—Captain Williams too—understanding that I'd probably never be back to full ability with this arm. Being put in the official doctor training, instead of just assisting, was Williams's way of helping me. Helping us."

"Yes . . ." I let out a sigh.

He leans closer to me. "But it's not what you want."

"I want you to be a doctor," I say quickly. "That's what you want."

"But you don't want to be one. To continue with the studies."

My eyes fill with tears. I slowly shake my head. "I love helping people. But . . . but when the children come home, I just want to be with them. I'll continue as a nurse, of course, but the classes, the rounds, the multiday shifts . . . it's too much."

The silence stretches between us, filled with all the dreams we're having to reshape. Finally, he squeezes my hand. "Get some rest. I need to help Murphy with rounds." He pauses. "I don't think I told you. His name really is Murphy."

"What? How— "

"That's his first name. I guess when he found the real Dr. Murphy's identification, he kind of thought it was meant to be. Murphy Sumner. Captain suggested we just keep calling him Dr. Murphy."

I shake my head. "I guess that'll keep things simple."

"I'll be back later." He drops a kiss on my forehead. "I love you."

"Love you too."

The afternoon sun wakes me from an uneasy sleep. My room has that hushed quality that comes with late day, when even the constant motion of the hospital seems to slow. Through half-closed eyes, I notice Nettie in the chair beside my bed, dabbing at her eyes with a handkerchief.

My heart clenches. "Oh no, Nettie. Is it David?"

She looks up, and to my surprise, she's smiling through her tears. "These are happy tears. He's better. Not out of the woods, but . . ." She takes a breath to steady herself. "We think he's going to live."

Relief floods through me, momentarily drowning out the constant pain from my ribs and burns. "Really?"

"Really." She dabs at her eyes again. "There's still infection to worry about, and he probably won't regain full use of his arm. He lost an eye, but . . ." Her smile brightens slightly. "He may walk again."

"His right arm?" I ask, thinking of Leo's struggles with his left. "Maybe they can work something out—you know, between them they'd have a complete set of working arms." I give her a wide smile. I choose not to mention my own right arm that has burns from the shoulder to the elbow. They aren't as bad as they could be, and I'll heal.

Nettie gives a polite laugh at my weak attempt at humor. The joke falls flat, but I'm too relieved about David to care.

"Where's Leo?" I scan the room, realizing I haven't seen him for several hours.

"Not sure exactly." Nettie scoots her chair closer, glancing at the other patients in the room. "Deputy Shaw showed up just as he was finishing rounds with Murphy. He whisked both Leo and the captain away."

"Whisked?"

"Took them in his truck. Leo suggested the captain not go, since he's using the wheelchair, but he wouldn't hear of it, of course. Deputy Shaw folded it up and stuffed it in the bed of the truck and away they went."

"Away?" I try to sit up straighter, ignoring the protest from my ribs. "Away to where?"

"No idea." She lowers her voice further. "I'm sure they'll be back shortly."

We talk for a few more minutes about David's condition and the other patients until someone calls for her help. As she leaves, I watch the sun sinking toward the horizon through my window, thinking about dinner time approaching, when a familiar throat-clearing sound comes from my doorway.

I turn to see Leo's head poking in, and my heart nearly stops at what I see in his arms—Caleb. Nico peers around his legs, and tears blur my vision.

"My boys?" My voice breaks on the word.

Alice follows, carrying Zach. All three children are here, safe and whole.

"Why are they here?" I ask, carefully hugging Nico with my uninjured arm as he climbs onto the edge of my cot. "What happened?"

"It's over," Alice says, her voice oddly flat.

"Over?" My gaze darts between her and Leo. "They caught— "

"He won't be a problem anymore." Alice's tone leaves no room for questions.

Leo shakes his head slightly. "I'll tell you later. If you look toward the window, you'll see Gerry. Shaw has him."

My half-grown puppy is in Shaw's arms, peering through the window. His tail wags, and his movements are so frisky that I'm surprised Deputy Shaw can keep a hold of him.

"He's grown," I say. "Everyone has."

Shaw signals that he'll keep Gerry with him.

For the next half hour, Nico chatters away about life at the ranch—feeding the chickens, working with the horses, and everything in between.

Zach and Caleb have changed so much in the short time we've been apart. Almost five months old, Zach bursts into giggles when I pretend to tickle him, while two-month-old Caleb rewards me with a tiny, heart-melting smile.

When dinner arrives, Alice gathers the children to leave. "Merissa's still at the ranch," she tells me as she settles Zach on her hip. "She's decided to stay there until her bed rest is over. Maybe even until the baby comes. Pearl needs the care, and Opal will dote over them both."

"How is Pearl?"

"She has good days and not so good days."

"Where will you all go?"

"Back to the house Shaw originally set up. I'm happy to keep the children until you're well enough to come home. Chris is doing better too. He'll be coming home with me."

"I'll be right back," Leo says. "Shaw's going to drive them, but I want to help Alice get the kids and Gerry to the truck."

I can't stop smiling as my tray is put on the table by my bed. Miss Martha tells me how cute my children are and what a lucky woman I am. Her son, Henry, in the cot next to her, nods his agreement.

I work on my stew. A few minutes later, Leo returns and sinks into the chair beside my bed. His smile matches mine.

"They're so adorable. They look good," I say.

"They look great. Healthy and happy."

"It feels like forever since we saw them. Caleb has grown so much. Zach too. I barely recognize them."

"Three weeks. That's a long time for a newborn."

"Tell me," I say softly.

He runs a hand through his hair before leaning forward. "Stone attacked again. Went himself this time with a small group. Set fire to Hayward's hay to draw everyone away. Walt and some others stayed behind—the ones still injured from the kidnapping attempt. They helped with Merissa's rescue, but . . ." He gives a grim smile. "It was Alice who stopped Stone. Permanently."

My breath catches. "The others?"

"In custody, including Captain Rangler. He's talking fast, saying it was all Stone, that he thought it was legitimate orders." Leo's expression darkens. "Merissa says she's not so sure. Says Rangler seemed just as ruthless as Stone."

"But it's over?" I need to hear it again. "We're safe now?"

"Shaw talked to Hugo. Told him what happened. Hugo says it's over, that's everyone, so . . ." He reaches for my hand. "We think so. Yeah."

I close my eyes and let that sink in. After everything—the biodiesel operation, the threats, the explosion, Jacquie's death, David's injuries—it's finally over. We can stop hiding out and be with our children again.

"I'm ready to get out of here," I say. "Tell Nettie— "

"Not yet." Leo's tone is gentle but firm. "You need a few more days to heal."

I want to argue, but I know he's right. Instead, I look out at the last rays of sunlight painting the sky in shades of pink and gold. Spring is coming. Soon, the snow will completely melt, revealing the first green shoots of new life. Merissa will have her baby. David will heal. Our family will be together again. We'll mourn those we've lost, but we'll also celebrate how far we've come.

Chapter 35

Katie

Two months later . . .

Rapid Creek flows over smooth rocks, its sound steady and lively. Spring has turned the park green, from the grass to the pine needles overhead. Deciduous trees stand with fresh, pale leaves. Red-winged blackbirds call from the cattails, while robins search for worms on the thawed ground.

Voices drift across the park, children laughing in the distance and people talking on nearby benches. The sight of a frisbee flying through the air, a couple walking along a path, and leaves rustling in the breeze fill the space. The warmth of spring surrounds it all, bringing the park back to life after a deadly winter.

Pearl's wheelchair sits in a patch of sunshine, positioned so she can watch all the goings on. Her thin fingers trace patterns on the blanket covering her legs. Even from here, I can see how much her condition has deteriorated. The cancer moves quickly now, but she rallied enough to be here today.

Walt hovers nearby, adjusting her shawl against the spring breeze, his weathered hands gentle. When she declined his marriage proposal last month, he simply nodded, understanding as always. "Either way," he told her, "I'll be here." Now, watching his tenderness, I see the truth of those words. Their love doesn't need a ceremony to be real.

Merissa sways gently, her five-week-old son sleeping against her chest in a fabric carrier. Brody Thomas surprised everyone by arriving a week late on April 7. "Proof babies do what they want," Pearl said with a knowing smile.

"She looks good today," I say to Merissa. Even though she can no longer walk and had to be brought by wagon from their house, Pearl's determination to be present for these moments remains strong.

"It's a good day. Stella's trying something new. It seems to help with the pain and the grogginess. Still, I'll be surprised if she doesn't fall asleep in her chair. She spends most of her day napping."

I don't say anything, because Merissa already knows it won't be much longer until Pearl succumbs to the illness. I blink back tears as I remember how my mom was in her final days. With all that can kill a person now, in our apocalyptic world, it doesn't seem right that cancer is still a problem.

After the baby was born, Merissa and Pearl moved back to their little house. Walt found a room nearby so he could be there to help. I visit as often as I can to give Merissa and Walt a break. I always bring Gerry with me, who still has a fondness for Pearl after their time on the ranch.

Opal comes into town regularly, often bringing Jason and Robert, both of whom seem to be thriving on the ranch. Both young men had a few sessions with Elizabeth while she was here and continued talking with Nettie after Elizabeth left.

Kerry has also received extra training to help with their troubles. Robert has adapted well to life on the ranch but still asks about his sister, who remains in the main hospital facility under Elizabeth's and her colleagues' care.

There have been many changes in the weeks since the news about Major Stone broke. Once he was neutralized and the rest of his organization was apprehended, or in the case of Cabal and Landers, dead, the truth about what had been done to the bodies was made public. As expected, it sparked an uproar. When the ground was finally workable, the burials took place, providing at least some closure.

Stone's confession that he was behind the Christmas Day bombing of Camp Rapid brought some resolution, but it also raised many new questions. His claim that the operation was bigger than Rapid City left us wondering what he truly meant.

Captain Williams says it's unlikely we'll ever have the full answer, but he's not sure that's a bad thing. In today's world, it doesn't really matter. We do what we need to survive each day, and we trust that God's will is unfolding as it should.

"Is she ready?" Merissa asks, nodding toward the park building where Nettie is getting ready.

"I'll check," I offer, smoothing my dress.

"Well, David's starting to look nervous. Bowski said he's worried she'll change her mind."

"She's not going to change her mind," I say with certainty, watching as Bowski meets Merissa's gaze and sends her a smile full of love.

I'm surprised the two haven't married yet. While we were setting up for the ceremony, Merissa told me Pearl had said she was wasting time—time Pearl didn't have. "I think we'll just go ahead and do it," Merissa said. "It'll be at the house, something simple like Shawn and Abby did. Easier for Pearl that way. Maybe in a few days. I'm going to ask the captain to officiate, like he's doing for Nettie and David."

I glance toward the park building where Nettie is getting ready. Kerry appears, the flowers from Stella's greenhouse complementing her lilac dress beautifully. I'm also part of the bridal party but in a pale mint. Finding matching dresses wasn't possible, but no one cares, especially not Nettie.

"Looks like it's time," I say, catching Leo's eye. He nods, removes the front carrier, and hands Caleb to Alice before slipping on his suit jacket. Alice, already carrying Zach in his own carrier, adjusts to hold both infants during the ceremony. At Leo's urging, Nico rushes back toward me. He's acting as the ring bearer.

Leo takes his place next to David as best man. Jesse Talbot also stands up with them. David leans heavily on his cane, the patch over his destroyed eye and his arm in its permanent sling stark reminders of that day in March.

But his smile outshines everything else.

Those weeks after the explosion were touch and go—the loss of his right eye, the useless right arm, the shattered leg. Even now, two months later, his injuries are a stark reminder of how close we came to losing him.

Through it all, Nettie has stayed by his side, reading to him during the fever dreams—from the Bible, even. As he healed, so did Nettie. Her own heart listened to the words she was reading and finally understood God's love was meant for her too.

When General Truss offered David a position that would let him stay in the Guard despite his injuries, David declined. "I've given enough," he said. "I'm going to start fresh. Start a new life with the woman I love."

Captain Williams stands at the front as well. He's wearing a walking boot again and using crutches, but he left them with Alice, insisting that for the ceremony he'd look more dignified in his uniform without them. He's right—he does. Leo also looks amazing, the handsewn stripes on his suit jacket are the closest thing to a uniform the United Volunteers offers. He teased me about my bridesmaid dress, asking where I planned to put my stripes. I'm more than happy to be without them today.

Nettie emerges from the building in her blush-colored wedding dress. "That's what they called it at the clothing ration center," she had told us excitedly.

Stella fusses with the sweep train until it falls just right, then signals me forward. I wait as Merissa makes her way to her seat beside Bowski before starting my walk to the beginning of the aisle.

Kerry meets me there, grinning before she starts down the aisle between the chairs. One of David's friends plays guitar, the simple melody carrying clearly over the sound of the creek. It's not traditional wedding music, but it fits this moment, this new world we're building.

The ceremony is brief, yet beautiful. Nico excels in his role as ring bearer, making me smile more than once. They exchange rings provided by Bowski, thanks to his vast network of contacts. Their vows honor the hardships they've endured and the hope they carry forward. When David kisses his bride, Pearl dabs her eyes with a handkerchief, while Walt pretends not to notice his own tears.

The reception that follows is simple by pre-EMP standards but extravagant for now. Bowski's connections produced not only a small wedding cake but other desserts as well. Merissa whispers to me that they came from the underground dessert house they visited months ago.

This isn't just a wedding—it's a goodbye party too. Tomorrow, Nettie and David head to Kansas to be with her parents and daughter. Nettie is taking her medical skills with her, knowing her hometown could use the help. The most recent letter from home described a tough winter and the passing of their doctor. They have a few nurses, but Nettie knows she'll be needed.

They're leaving early in the morning, heading south with a contingent of National Guard and then meeting up with another group in Nebraska. General Truss helped with the arrangements, his wedding gift to the former lieutenant.

"Mama?" Nico tugs on my sleeve, his expression urgent, but hearing him call me mama still causes my heart to flutter. He started it shortly after we were reunited. "I need to go." His eyes dart to a pair of portable toilets stationed at the edge of a parking lot west of the ceremony and reception site. Brought in by Bowski for the occasion, his endless contacts and resources never fail to impress me.

"Okay." I hand Caleb to Leo, helping him secure the carrier to his chest to make things easier for the reception. "Should have taken the jacket off," I say, working it around the bulk of it.

"It's fine," he says, pulling on the bottom hem.

Leo's no longer wearing the brace, but we know Bollinger is right. His arm will never be what it was. Leo has come to accept it and has even let the new liaison to the Guard, the man replacing Paul, know that he won't be able to serve. I know he's disappointed, but he also believes it's the best choice. I'm not joining the Guard either. We'll both finish our year commitment to the United Volunteers, but that will be the end of our military obligation.

Leo will continue his med school training, but I've already stepped back from that. My recovery after the explosion put me behind, and all I really want is to be with the boys, not trying to do multiday shifts at the hospital.

I'm nursing still, finally working part time after recovering enough that I have the energy. The burn on my arm has healed, at least to the point where there's not much of a fear of infection. That was another thing we needed to wait on before I could return to work. The germs in the hospital could've been a bad combo with my burn.

The new skin is still delicate, but I'm healing well. Each day reminds me of the fragile balance we all live with now—one step forward, but always mindful of the risks.

"Did you want some dessert?" Alice motions to the table where the service has started.

"I'm going to take Nico to the restroom first," I reply, tickling Zach under the chin.

Alice looks stylish, as always. She's wearing slacks and a camisole top with a long sweater over the top. Even the fabric wrap holding Zach, something she made herself, complements the outfit. She commented on how exciting it was to have a wedding, a reason to get dressed up. The captain also looks amazing in his dress uniform. The two create a striking couple.

As I'm walking with Nico to the bathroom, there's a rumble of far-off thunder. We both glance up toward the mountains to the west. There are no clouds. "Is it going to rain?" Nico asks.

"Maybe. Probably not here, though. That sounded like it's in the mountains . . . in the Black Hills National Forest."

"I hope it doesn't rain. That would ruin the wedding cake."

"We'd better hurry if we want to make sure there's cake left for us," I say as we reach the restroom. "I'll wait right here," I add, watching him close the door behind him.

I stand there, waiting for Nico while I watch the wedding festivities. Everyone is having a great time. Nettie and David look so happy. I'm glad. They've both been through so much, and now, to be able to admit their love for each other, it's amazing.

"You almost done, Nico?" I ask, glancing at my watch. He's been in there forever. I look toward the mountains again, searching for signs of rain. The creek seems to be swelling, its current faster than usual, the sound of the water louder. Maybe they have been getting rain upstream.

A noise from behind the toilet makes me tense. "Katie." The female voice is barely more than a breath. "Don't move, just stay where you are. Listen to me and listen good. You need to get everyone out of here. You don't have much time. The Preacher's final plans . . . it's happening today. Happening now. It's his birthday—a tribute to him."

My mouth goes dry, muscles tensing at the urgency in her tone.

"Addison?" I hiss into the shadows. "What is this— "

"Don't ask questions, just go. Did you hear that little rumble about twenty minutes ago? They said it'd take about that long before the water reached town. You don't have much time. The creek's already rising. Shawna is here. I can't . . . I can't keep this up, but she deserves a chance. You can give her that chance if you hurry. Go now. Get away from the creek. Get to high ground. They've . . . they've blown the dam. Pactola Dam."

"They're blowing the dam?" I ask, not quite understanding what exactly is happening.

"No," Addison snaps. "They've already done it. The explosion already happened. That's what I'm telling you. The water will be here soon. You have to hurry."

A young girl—Kemeera's daughter, Shawna—steps into view, her eyes wide with fear. "Addison?" I call out while I motion for Shawna to come to me.

"She's gone," the little girl says with a shrug. "Said hurry. To run."

The creek's roar seems to deepen, as if the water knows what's coming. My mind races—the wedding party, all our children, Pearl in her wheelchair. If I scream a warning, panic could slow us down. I need to get to Leo—to my babies—then make sure someone helps Pearl. But we have to move now.

"Nico! Hurry!" My heart pounds as my son emerges, still buttoning his pants. "Hi, Nico," Shawna says shyly. Before he can respond, I scoop him up with one arm and tell Shawna we have to run. She nods and takes off.

His final plans? The Preacher died months ago, but we had heard there was still something in the works. Today. Today is his birthday? A tribute? They blew the dam! That could wipe out most of the town. It's happened before, when heavy rain caused a dam breach. Hundreds died. "Hurry." I urge the children forward.

We're just over halfway back to the gathering when I hear it—a deep rumble, but wrong somehow. The birds go silent. Then comes a roar that shakes the ground, growing louder by the second.

Chapter 36

Merissa

My son snuffles against my chest, his tiny fingers curled into my blouse, when the birds stop singing. The silence hits me in the gut—wrong, so wrong. My arms tighten around him before I even know why.

Katie's voice cuts through the air, sharp and panicked. "Run!" I turn, seeing her sprinting toward us, Nico in one arm, the other grasping a little girl's hand. "They've blown the dam. Run!"

For one heartbeat, I'm frozen. Then the sound comes—a low rumble, deep and growing, like something heavy shifting in the earth. The air thickens, charged with the unmistakable sound of rushing water, a relentless roar. It's getting closer, fast.

My world narrows to the warm weight of my baby and Pearl in her wheelchair, too far away. My feet move before my mind catches up, but Bowski's already there, his hand under my elbow, urgent but steady. "Let's go." He gestures toward the creek. "It's already rising."

"Pearl— " Her name tears from my throat.

"Walt's got her. We need to move. Now."

We've barely covered twenty feet when the creek's gentle murmur twists into a monstrous roar. I glance back and immediately regret it. Katie and the children are still running, but behind them, a towering wall of brown water barrels around the bend, dragging trees and debris as if they weigh nothing.

My son jerks awake, his cry swallowed by the deafening surge. I clutch him tighter, pressing his face into my shoulder, as if I can somehow shield him from the unstoppable force closing in.

"Move!" Bowski's voice cuts through the chaos. "Get away from the creek. Find higher ground!"

The first surge slams into the bridge to the west, shaking the ground beneath me. Water crashes against it, dragging trees and debris into its grip. Thick trunks snap like twigs, roots ripped from the earth. The bridge groans, steel bending and wood splintering, before parts of it vanish into the raging flood.

Katie is still running. One child in each arm now as the surge bears down on her. She's not going to make it. I want to scream for her to hurry. But she knows.

She already knows.

My skirt tangles around my legs as we scramble up the muddy slope. The baby screams, his cries lost in the growing roar.

David stumbles beside us, his injured leg giving out as he tries to help Nettie up the slope. Her wedding dress—pristine and lovely moments ago—drags in the mud. She reaches for him, but Kerry gets there first and supports his weak side.

Walt lifts Pearl from her wheelchair. Pain flickers across her face, but she stays silent. The empty chair tips over, its top wheel spinning lazily. Pearl's eyes lock with mine, heavy with a terrible understanding. "I love you," she mouths and gives me a smile while lifting her chin slightly.

"Pearl!" I call out. "Walt!"

"I've got her," he replies, cradling her close.

A crash like thunder—the porta-potties vanish, shattered by an old car tumbling in the current. How long since Katie's warning? One minute? Two? Not enough.

"Keep moving!" the captain shouts from somewhere behind us. "We need to reach— "

His words are cut off in a strangled cry. I turn in time to see the ground dissolve beneath him. Alice screams his name, clutching Zach tighter as he loses his footing. The captain reaches for them, managing to push them toward higher ground before the water takes him.

"Chris!" Alice's voice breaks on his name. Leo grabs her arm, dragging her up with one arm while he clings to Caleb with the other, the infant carrier already covered in mud and muck. My vision blurs with tears.

I hazard a glance behind me. Where's Katie? Nico? The little girl who was with them? The captain?

"Keep going," Bowski urges, dragging me forward.

The water chews at the hill's base, hungry for more. Walt still carries Pearl, but I see him faltering, the strain clear on his weathered face.

"Put me down," Pearl's voice carries over the roar. "Save yourself."

"Never." The fierce love in his voice shatters something inside me. They make it three more steps before Walt's legs give out. They fall together as the flood reaches for them with greedy fingers.

"No!" I try to turn back, but Bowski's grip locks me in place. Walt pulls Pearl close, their bodies entwined as the water crashes over them, sweeping them away in an instant.

"Go, Merissa! We've got to keep going." Bowski's voice is firm but compassionate. "You can't help them."

My dress shoes slip in the mud as we climb. The roar grows louder, and I can't help it—I look back. The wall of water hits like God's fist, brown and furious and hungry. A house floats past, looking fully intact. Cars tumble in the current, crashing into each other with metallic screams. A propane tank shoots past like a missile.

Through gaps in the debris, I catch glimpses of other things—a child's swing set, someone's front door, a dog desperately swimming, a body drifting motionless. The water carries it all away with indifferent fury, adding each piece to its arsenal of destruction.

My son's cries anchor me in the present—in survival. Bowski half-drags me as we push farther from the creek. We've gained some elevation, but it's not nearly enough. The water is too deep to move with ease. Every step is leaden, pushing against the water.

"The trees!" Leo shouts, one arm around Alice as she clutches Zach against her chest. Caleb screams from his carrier. "Get to the trees!"

A line of trees surrounds a battered sports court. The court's fencing has been torn free, snagged among the trunks.

"Go! Go!" Bowski urges, his voice tight as Leo and Alice struggle through the tangle of fencing and branches, embedding themselves into the fence.

"Will it hold?"

"I don't know! We've got to try," Bowski snaps. "Keep the baby close!"

The water surges around the trees, testing our hold on life. I climb the fencing, using it as a ladder to get into the tree. Brody's cries have quieted to whimpers that pierce my heart.

Next to us, Alice clings to Zach, her knuckles white against the cyclone fencing. Leo shields them both with his body, Caleb secured against his chest.

Another surge lifts us, the fence groaning as debris slams against the trees. My arms burn from holding this position. The baby squirms and screams, hungry or frightened, or both, but I dare not adjust my grip.

"Hold on!" Bowski's voice barely carries over the roar. He's wedged himself in next to us, trying to block some of the debris from hitting us. Blood runs down his face from where something struck him, but his eyes stay fixed on me. On us. On survival.

The flood seems endless, each surge bringing new horrors. A car hits the trees with enough force to shake our refuge. Through the spray, I glimpse other survivors clinging to high points across the flood plain. Some wave frantically, trying to signal for help that can't come. Others just hold on and pray.

My thoughts keep circling back to Pearl and Walt, to the captain's final act of sacrifice. To Katie, who I haven't seen since she was running for her life. She called out there was a dam break. That we needed to run. How did she know? I turn my head, trying to catch sight of Katie or anyone else from the wedding party. The water took so much, so fast. When it finally recedes, nothing will be the same.

But my son's heart beats against mine, strong and steady. We're alive.

Chapter 37

Katie

The world becomes water and noise and terror. My arms lock around Nico and Shawna as the flood takes us, their small bodies pressed against mine. The roar drowns their screams, drowns everything except the thundering of my own heart.

We go under. Water fills my nose and my mouth. Debris slams against my legs. I kick hard, fighting to the surface, lungs burning. Nico's fingers dig into my neck; he's attached himself to my back. Shawna's grip loosens—no, no, no—I clutch her tighter, and we break through into the air.

"Mama!" Nico's voice is thin with fear.

"Hold on!" I gasp, spitting muddy water. "Both of you, hold on!"

The flood is ice-cold, heavy with debris and mud. Something hard—a branch, maybe—scrapes across my back. My dress wraps around my legs like a shroud. Nico's fingers continue to dig into me with desperate strength, his arms around my neck, cutting off my air. Shawna is screaming but holding on to me, tight, her body scraping against the still-healing skin on my shoulder.

Something large and flat spins past—a broken sheet of plywood. I grab it with one hand. My shoulders scream as I heave Shawna onto the makeshift raft. "Go, Nico." I gasp, my air still limited from his tight grip. "Get on the board."

"No. I don't want to leave you."

"You won't. Get on it. Hurry." He shifts his body just enough that I can pull myself across the board. With my torso on it, he slides over next to Shawna. The current yanks us forward, past landmarks I barely recognize through the spray. How long will this hold?

"Stay flat!" I shout, though I can barely hear myself. "Like a pancake! Grab the edges."

Nico flattens himself, fingers white-knuckled on the board's edges. Shawna copies him, her braids heavy with water. I kick my now-bare feet, my dress shoes having come off at some point. I try to steer us away from the worst of the debris, but we're moving too fast. A propane tank rockets past, missing us by inches.

Then I see it—a silver sedan, bobbing like some bizarre boat, its roof still above water. "We need to move!" I yell at the children. "When I say now, we're going to jump to that car!"

The current carries us alongside, and we bump into the car, momentarily suspended in time and place. "Now!" I surge upward, pushing them toward the car's roof. The plywood hits the metal hard. Nico scrambles up first, then helps pull Shawna, while I brace her from behind. I haul myself after them, my hands slipping on the slick metal. The plywood disappears into the churning water.

"Look!" Nico points ahead. A two-story building looms, an old fast-food restaurant, its brick face somehow holding against the surge. If we can reach it . . .

The car slams into the building's corner with bone-jarring force. "Up!" I scream, boosting Shawna toward a first-floor window ledge. Nico follows. I jump last, fingers scraping brick as the car shifts beneath my feet.

"Keep climbing!" My voice breaks as I push them higher. "The drainpipe—use it like a ladder!"

We inch upward, the metal pipe groaning under our weight. Below, the flood carries away our car-turned-boat. The water keeps rising, chasing us toward the roof's peak. My arms shake from the strain of helping the children, but fear gives me strength I didn't know I had. "Please, Lord. Please help us," I murmur as we climb.

Finally, we reach the roof and haul ourselves to the peak. "Over there," I say. "Scoot to the gable." A decorative gable with the logo of the restaurant on each side sits in the middle of the building. The water keeps rising. I can only hope the brick building withstands the current, but if it climbs any higher . . .

"Let's go. We're going to the top." I point up.

Nico shakes his head. "How?"

"I'll help you." I lift him under the arms. "Now reach up. Grab on."

When he says he's got a grip, I slide my hands down his ribcage to his hips and push him higher and higher. "Pull yourself up," I urge.

When he's up, he lies on his belly and holds his hands toward me. "Okay. Shawna now?"

She weighs next to nothing, and between Nico and me, we manage to get her up. Now they're both on the highest section of the roof. I need to join them.

I stretch as far as I can, my feet gripping the slick metal roof. With my fingers wrapped around the gutter, I pull myself up.

I barely gain a few inches before my strength falters. My upper body strength has never been great, and the burns on my shoulder throb in protest. The raw, healing skin feels like it could tear open at any moment, each movement a test of how much I can endure.

I reposition, ready to try again. This time, I use the weathered logo bolted to the flat side of the gable, finding just enough purchase to press my feet against it and push.

"C'mon, Mama," Nico urges, his voice strained but determined. "You can do it."

My shoulder burns, the new skin tight and tender, stretched like it doesn't quite belong. Pain blurs my vision, but I grit my teeth and shove upward, the gutter creaking under my weight. *One more push*, I tell myself, *one more*.

With a final, desperate heave, I swing my leg over the edge and collapse onto the roof beside the children. My chest tightens as I struggle to catch my breath, the burn in my shoulder flaring with every beat of my heart.

Nico reaches for me, his small hands gripping my arm. "You did it, Mama," he says softly, but there's no relief in his voice—only fear.

The roof groans beneath us, the sound a grim reminder that we're far from safe. I glance at the rising water, only about a foot below the lower section of the building. Will we be safe here? Or did I make a fatal choice by bringing us to this peak? There's nowhere to go from here. The building is surrounded by a parking lot. All we can do is wait and pray that the water will soon subside.

From our vantage point, the scale of destruction stretches before us. The flood has turned streets into churning rapids. A playground slide twists past like a corkscrew. Someone's porch, rocking chair still intact, bobs along in the torrent. Cars spin and tumble as if weightless.

I catch fleeting glimpses of other survivors—people clinging to trees, rooftops, anything that might hold them above the water. A dog paddles by, struggling to keep its head above the current.

My thoughts drift to Gerry back home. Is our house far enough from the creek to be spared? I can't be sure. For now, we're still staying with the Williamses in the safe house Shaw arranged when Merissa went into hiding. We're not far from Rapid Creek, but hopefully far enough for Gerry to be safe.

My eyes scan desperately for signs of Leo, of our babies. The mint dress, now torn and filthy, reminds me of the wedding. Of Pearl in her wheelchair. Of all our friends. The grief tries to choke me, but I swallow it back. There's no time for tears.

"Mama?" Nico's voice quavers. "Where's Daddy? Where's Caleb and Zach?"

"They got to high ground, baby." The lie tastes like river mud. "They're safe." I have to believe that. Have to hold on to hope, if only for these children who trust me to keep them alive.

Chapter 38

Merissa

Time drags as the water swirls endlessly around our refuge. My skirt and blouse, soaked through, offer no protection against the growing cold. Brody shivers against my chest, his wet clothes clinging to him, his whimpers growing weaker.

"Here." Bowski shrugs out of his wool jacket, draping it around us. Even wet, the heavy fabric helps. Next to us, Alice clutches Zach close, her stylish sweater doing little to ward off the chill. Leo cradles Caleb, still secured in the mud-coated carrier, his suit jacket wrapped tightly around the baby.

"The babies are too cold," Alice says, her teeth chattering.

"Water's going down." Bowski studies the current. "We'll give it a little bit longer and it'll be safe to move. We need to get the children somewhere warm."

My mind keeps circling back to Pearl's final moments. Her face as she mouthed those last words—I love you. The sad smile told me she'd accepted what was coming. The image of her and Walt being swept away haunts me, his arms tight around her even as the water took them.

In a way, it was a blessing. The cancer had been winning, the pain growing worse each day despite Stella's best efforts. And Walt. Dear, faithful Walt, who'd loved her so completely—of course, he wouldn't leave her. Even knowing he could save himself, he chose to hold her close, to face the end together.

Like everything about their friendship—their love—it was beautiful and heartbreaking all at once.

A sob catches in my throat, but I force it back. There will be time for grief later. Right now, I have to focus on keeping Brody warm, on surviving. For Pearl.

She fought hard to see Brody born. To enjoy the previous five weeks with him. I hate that she won't have more, that he won't grow up knowing his grandmother, but she gave him everything she could in the short time she had.

I press my lips to Brody's damp forehead and whisper promises he can't understand. "We'll make it, little one. For her. For all of them."

For what seems like the hundredth time, Leo scans the area, no doubt searching for Katie and Nico. I've already told him what I know—that she was running toward us with Nico and a little girl, screaming that they'd blown the dam.

"Who was the little girl?" Leo asks, confusion lacing his voice. "I can't think of anyone from the wedding."

"There weren't any children we didn't know," Alice says, her voice ragged from the cold and grief. "Doc Nettie didn't have a flower girl. Just Nico as the ring bearer. Maybe . . . maybe it was one of the others at the park? A child who happened to be using the toilet at the same time as Nico?"

I close my eyes, trying to pull the image of Katie, Nico, and the little girl into focus. Katie said the dam was blown . . . how did she know? She'd taken Nico to the bathroom. Then came rushing back, Nico in her arms, dragging the little girl with her, yelling about the dam being blown.

I inhale sharply. "Shawna. I think it was Shawna."

"Kemeera's girl?" Leo asks, his head shaking in disbelief.

They'd found Kemeera in the secret warehouse, one of the dead in the body bags, but three-year-old Shawna's remains were not there. The assumption had always been she was with Addison.

"Addison!" I gasp. "What if she was there? Told Katie about the dam and gave her Shawna?"

"Addison? Why would she give Katie the little girl?" Leo asks, brow furrowed. "If she knew about the dam breach, why wouldn't she be elsewhere? Out of harm's way?"

"Why does Addison do any of the things she does?" Bowski mutters. "The woman has a screw loose."

More than one, I think to myself.

"Has the water gone down enough?" Alice asks. "We need to get the children out of these wet clothes."

Leo and Bowski survey the area. Bowski shrugs. "I think if we're careful. It's not rushing like it was."

"Let's do it," Leo agrees. "I need to find Katie and Nico. Shawna, too, if that's who it really was."

Untangling from the fence proves harder than expected, our limbs stiff from hanging on tight, along with the cold and fear. Leo helps Alice down first. "We'll go to our house," he says. "It's closest."

"It may have flooded," he adds, "but at least we have the upstairs and can get everyone in dry clothes." His voice catches. "As soon as I know you're safe, I'll head out."

"You'll need to change too," Alice says. "Get something warm and woolen on. Chris has— " Her voice cracks, the sentence left unfinished.

We pick our way through mud and debris. The water still runs knee-deep in places, hiding hazards beneath its murky surface. A sound draws us toward a cluster of brush—Nettie, David, and Kerry huddled together, alive. They see us and lift their hands in greeting.

"Safe?" David asks.

"Enough," Leo replies. "We're taking the children to our house. Then I'm going to find Katie."

"I saw her," Nettie replies, her face filled with grief.

"You know where she is?"

Nettie shakes her head. "The water . . . I don't think she made it away in time. The little girl that was with her— "

"Shawna," I interrupt. "I think it was Kemeera's daughter, Shawna."

"She fell," Nettie continues. "Katie stopped to help her up and had both of them in her arms. That was the last time I saw them. Things . . . things went crazy fast."

"You know that little rumble we heard earlier? Thought it was thunder? That was probably the dam going. We'll start looking for her," David says as he helps his new wife from the heavy brush.

"I'll need to go to the hospital," Nettie says. "There will be injured." She looks toward Alice. "Captain Williams?"

Alice shakes her head as tears fill her eyes.

"I'm going to look for him while I'm looking for Katie," Leo adds. "Pearl and Walt too. I'll do my best to find them all."

Jesse Talbot appears with another group of wedding guests. Leo invites them all to the house, but most decline. They work at the hospital and live nearby. They'll check their own homes first, change into better clothes for the task, and then return to help search or help at the hospital.

As we approach the neighborhood, my heart rate increases. There's a lot of damage, especially to the first floors. Windows missing, doors off the hinges. Leo's house is on this same street. People are moving around. Venturing out. We meet Deputy Shaw and his wife, along with their dog, Tank—littermate to Katie's dog Gerry—and Gerry himself.

"Gerry! Come here, boy!" Leo's voice breaks with emotion as the dog bounds toward him, tail wagging frantically. Despite holding Caleb, Leo drops to one knee and buries his face in Gerry's fur while the dog whines and licks his face, pawing at him in desperate joy. The reunion brings fresh tears to my eyes—one small piece of their family found safe.

"Your house is still standing," Shaw says. "Damaged, like the rest of them. We grabbed Gerry so he wouldn't be alone."

"Katie's missing," Leo says as he rubs Gerry's ears. The dog whimpers softly and presses closer to Leo's leg, his usually happy demeanor subdued, as if sensing something is wrong. His head swivels toward the flood waters, nose twitching, searching for Katie's scent.

"Where'd you see her last?"

"The park. Where the wedding was happening."

Shaw was supposed to attend the wedding as well, but something had come up that kept him away. He'd said he'd try to make it when he could, hopefully before it was over, but the flash flood cut the reception short.

The Burnetts' house stands waterlogged but whole. Several ground-floor windows are broken out, the rooms beyond dark with flood water.

Upstairs proves dry, though the journey up feels endless with cold-numbed legs. Brody nursed while we clung to the trees, but Caleb and Zach only had the bottles from Leo's rescued diaper bag. All three babies need warmth, food, and dry clothes.

Leo and Bowski change quickly, eager to join the search. "He's gone," Alice says when Leo mentions looking for the captain. Her voice breaks. "He's gone to be with the Lord."

The words pierce my heart. Pearl and Walt were also taken by the water. But Katie and Nico might still be alive. Shawna too.

"I need to feed Brody and make sure he's okay," I say. "I want to get all the baby's temps, get them warm and hydrated. Once they're asleep, maybe Alice can watch over them and I'll help look."

"Take care of the babies." Bowski's hand brushes my cheek. "I'll come back and check on you in a little while."

Brody latches on hungrily as soon as I settle in a chair. His tiny fingers are still cold, but his heart beats strong and steady against mine. Outside, others have begun searching, calling names as evening approaches. I close my eyes, remembering Pearl's final mouthed words. *I love you.*

Bowski, Brody, and I survived. But at such a cost.

Chapter 39

Katie

The water recedes slowly, leaving destruction in its wake. We've huddled on this roof peak for hours, the children pressed against me for warmth, all of us shivering despite the May afternoon. My dress, still dripping, offers no protection against the wind that's picked up.

Sunset won't be until around eight. It's five, maybe six o'clock now. We need to get off this roof before dark. Staying up here all night is not an option—the temperature drops quickly in the Black Hills, even in May. Shawna's teeth chatter constantly now, and Nico's lips have taken on a bluish tinge.

Where's my family? Alice had Zach in a cloth carrier. Leo had Caleb. Did they escape the rushing water?

I let out a sigh. The decision isn't really a decision at all. We have to get down. Then we can find some place warm and maybe even look for Leo and the babies.

"Listen carefully," I tell the children, forcing steadiness into my voice. "We need to get off this roof. We'll do the opposite of what we did to get up here. I'll go first, then help you both down."

Nico nods, but Shawna just stares with wide, frightened eyes. I survey the area, formulating my plan. There's a car slammed up against the building. Not the same sedan we rode earlier, I don't think, though it's hard to tell with mud coating everything. The water's dropped enough that it looks stable. Secure, even.

"Okay. Stay absolutely still until I tell you to move." I ease myself toward the edge, my wet dress hampering my every movement. The burned skin on my shoulder protests as I lower myself down, my bare feet searching for purchase on the slick roof.

I find the lower section with my feet. "Nico first." He's always been brave, following instructions perfectly as I guide him down. Then Shawna, trembling but trusting as I help her make the short descent.

We move carefully along the roof until we reach the spot where the car is wedged. The top of the car sits about four feet below. Close enough—if we're careful. I lower Nico first, then Shawna, before making the jump myself. My feet slip on the mud-slicked metal, but I catch myself.

Getting to the ground may prove harder. The water's receded to knee-depth, but the current still tugs treacherously. Worse is what floats in it—branches, trash, things I won't name in front of the children. The stench hits hard—mud and sewage and decay all mixed together.

"Hold my hands tight," I tell them. "We're going to wade through this carefully. It's still deep here, but we'll get out of it as soon as we can."

"I get wet again." Shawna shakes her head, her teeth chattering. "Too wet. Too cold."

"I know, sweetie. I know. But we don't have a choice. We need to go through the water so we can get to my house. Once we're there, we'll get you in dry clothes. Wrap you in a blanket too."

"And eat?"

"Yes. Eat too."

I step off the car, but my foot slips, and something sharp grazes my calf. Pain flares up, but it's quickly swallowed by the churned-up water. I bite down on the discomfort and keep my focus. "Just a scratch," I mutter, pushing forward as the murky water swirls around me.

"Okay. Nico, you're first. I'm going to put you on the ground. Hold on to my dress with both hands, okay?"

"I will, Mama," he assures me with a serious nod. Once he's on the ground and steady, holding tightly to my sodden dress, I let out a sigh of relief.

"Okay, Shawna. Ready?"

"You carry me?"

I look at Nico standing next to me. The water reaches my knees but is almost to his waist. Shawna is shorter than he is. "Yes. I'll carry you."

The muck sucks at my bare feet as we move. Every step brings fresh horrors—something soft brushing past my leg that I pray is a fish, glimpses of shapes in the water that I force myself not to focus on.

Nico's lace-up shoes offer some protection, but my feet, once in delicate ballerina flats, find every sharp edge and jagged piece of debris.

We finally reach slightly higher ground where the water only reaches my calves. I pause, trying to get my bearings. The flood has transformed familiar landmarks into alien shapes, but the setting sun guides me. West. Home is west.

"We're going to walk that way," I tell them, pointing. "Careful steps. Stay close."

My dress wraps around my legs as we resume our journey. Each step brings fresh pain to my bare feet, but I force myself forward. Somewhere ahead, Leo and our babies are waiting. Please, Lord, let them be waiting.

A sharp ache shoots through my shoulder, and I have to stop. "Shawna, sweetie, I need to put you down for a minute." The little girl clings tighter, but I manage to set her on a relatively dry section of pavement. My healing skin throbs where her weight pressed against it.

Nico keeps hold of my dress, his other hand reaching for Shawna's. In the distance, voices carry—people calling out, though I can't make out the names.

"Hello!" I shout. "We need help!"

Two men in Citizen Patrol armbands appear around a corner. I recognize them but can't place their names. They hurry toward us, taking in our bedraggled state.

"Can we help?" One steps forward.

"These children need to get somewhere warm and dry," I say. "We were at the wedding when— "

"Here, let me take her." The taller patroller lifts Shawna. "You're one of the doctors, right?"

"I'm a nurse. Katie Burnett. My husband, Leo, have you seen him?"

"Not yet," the man holding Shawna responds.

"You live next to Deputy Shaw, right?" the other one asks. "That neighborhood got hit pretty hard."

My heart clenches. "Gerry . . . our dog. Is he— "

"The houses are still standing, but there's lots of damage. Water and mud are everywhere. Can't imagine they're going to be livable."

"Can you help me get there? Help us get home?"

"Of course." The second patroller turns to Nico. "Want me to carry you, buddy?"

Nico shakes his head. "I'll walk with my Mama."

We've only gone a couple blocks when I hear it—Leo's voice calling my name. My heart leaps.

"Leo!" I try to run but my feet are too torn up. It doesn't matter. He's there, gathering me into his arms, Nico pressed between us.

"Thank God," he breathes into my hair. "The babies are safe. Gerry too. They're with Alice. But, Katie—the captain . . ."

"What? No. He's . . . maybe he did what we did."

"We got on a roof," Nico says proudly. "I helped."

"I'm sure you did." Leo hugs him close. "I'm sure you did."

"Who else?" I ask, my voice cracking.

"Pearl and Walt too. They're missing." He pulls back, noticing Shawna. "Is that— "

"I'll explain later. But it was the Preacher's people. Their final vengeance. The job they planned to finish. Today's his birthday. At least that's what Addison said."

Understanding dawns in his eyes. He takes Shawna from the patroller while Nico again takes hold of my hand. The two men head off to continue their search as we make our way home through the destruction.

"You're hurt," Leo says softly, noticing my limp.

"Just cuts. Nothing that won't heal." I squeeze Nico's hand. "We made it. That's what matters."

The sun sinks low as we head west. Rapid City, our home for nearly a year, is barely recognizable. Up ahead, our babies and dog await. We've lost so much today—people, security, any sense of control.

Leo takes my hand. "We're going to be okay, Katie. With God's help, we'll make it through."

I squeeze his hand, knowing he's right. God will carry us through.

Chapter 40

Katie

Six weeks later . . .

"Mama?" Nico calls from the bedroom. "I have all my stuff ready to go. Do you want to see?"

"I'll be right there," I reply, finishing Zach's diaper change. "Yes, I will," I coo to the baby, who rewards me with one of his bright smiles. "We'll get you all dry and then we'll go check your brother's packing." Zach laughs, kicking his feet in delight.

"Alice?" I call out. "How's it going?"

"Almost finished." Her voice carries a mixture of determination and grief that's become familiar these past weeks.

After the flood destroyed so much of Rapid City, we moved back into the guest house behind the Williamses' fire-damaged home. The captain's body was never recovered from the rushing waters—just one more loss in a string of losses that changed everything. His absence leaves a hole not just in Alice's heart, but in the entire community he helped build.

The changes ripple outward. Dr. Bollinger now runs the Guard District Hospital and med school, the students adapting to new leadership. The National Guard maintains official oversight of South Dakota's hospitals, but General Truss finally recognized what the captain always knew—doctors need to lead healing. Physicians have been shifted to allow better coverage at all the district hospitals. Poppy Gardner's nursing students will also graduate soon, carrying on the work of rebuilding.

Nettie and David postponed their Kansas plans, staying to help recover bodies and tend to survivors. Some, like Pearl and Walt, were found still holding each other. Addison was among those whose bodies were recovered. I still wonder why she showed up at the park when she did. Why didn't she get herself to safety? Why warn us? And why bring Shawna to me?

Alice appears in the doorway, Caleb on her hip and Shawna holding her other hand, with Gerry on their heels. "I think we've got everything ready. What time did they say we're leaving?"

"Daylight. Maybe a few minutes before. We want to make as many miles as possible."

"It'll be difficult," she says softly, staring at the burned shell of her old house. "Chris and I lived in Rapid City most of our lives. And to leave him . . ." Her voice catches.

We've had this conversation many times since the flood. While helping at the med-school-turned-hospital, Leo and I first whispered about returning to Wyoming, to my family. But Alice's grief was too raw to broach the subject. She came to us instead, somehow knowing our plans.

"I can't imagine not being with the children," she said. "Caleb, Nico, Zach, and now little Shawna—they're family. So are you two and Gerry, of course."

The plan evolved quickly from there. Leo approached Bowski about wagons and teams, and the next day, he and Merissa requested to join us. They're also bringing the Ebright sisters, whom Leo has taken to looking after. They'll travel with us to Wyoming, staying as long as they wish before possibly moving west to search for Bowski's daughter, who was in California when the collapse began.

"We need a fresh start," Merissa said, Brody sleeping against her chest, her new wedding band catching the light. They married days after the flood in a quick ceremony, right after finding Pearl and Walt's bodies. No more waiting—the flood taught us all how precious time is.

With Opal Maher's help and blessing, Bowski secured three wagons and teams. She also offered a pair of horses as a wedding gift for Merissa. Merissa's own horse, Blaze, will remain at the ranch along with the others they brought from Montana.

The horses, specially trained for horseback archery, were a perfect match for the ranch's needs. As soon as the winter weather had cleared, Walt had begun teaching the ranch workers—especially Jason and Robert—archery and riding. Merissa knew the boys thought of the horses as their own.

Nettie and David Paul will be in the third wagon, also leaving tomorrow. We tried to work out a way for us all to travel together, at least part of the way, but they're heading south to Kansas while we turn west toward Wyoming.

They found a few other people who wish to travel south, so they'll be forming a small wagon train for safety's sake. We'll follow the heavily patrolled Interstate 90. Both Leo and Bowski agree it should be safe for us, given the strong security presence.

I draw a deep breath and join Alice by the window. So much has happened since Leo and I arrived in the Black Hills almost a year ago. Those first days were tough. I was still grieving my mom and questioning whether I had rushed into joining the United Volunteers. I knew I needed a change, and I got that along with more than I ever expected. The challenges have been many, but they have been good too. My friendship with Merissa has been a blessing, and Alice is a gift from God.

The loss of Captain Williams still stings, as if I have lost a piece of my family. A part of me wonders if I am running away again, trying to escape the grief, but deep down, I know going home is the right thing to do.

Leo and I will take the medical skills we learned under Captain Williams back to Bakerville. We have sent letters ahead to let our family know our plans and to prepare Belinda Bosco, who runs the clinic there. With the way mail travels, though, we might arrive before the letters do.

The front door opens and Leo enters, bringing the scent of horses and hay. "We're just about loaded," he says, smiling. "Got the essentials packed. Ready for personal bags in the morning."

"We're ready," Alice says, her voice strong despite the tears in her eyes.

My own vision blurs. We're going home—not just to Wyoming, but to a new version of family we've built from loss and love and survival. Behind us lie graves and memories, a city forever changed by the Preacher's final act of vengeance. Ahead lies hope, and family, and whatever tomorrow brings.

We're ready.

Thank you for spending your time with Katie, Leo, Merissa, Bowski, and everyone else in the Black Hills! If you have a few minutes, leaving a short review on Amazon, Goodreads, Bookbub, or your favorite review site would mean the world to me.

The *Dakota Destruction* series first took shape when I visited Deadwood for the Wild Deadwood Reads event. I'd been to Deadwood several times before and always loved the area. Sending Katie and Leo to Rapid City, which is less than an hour from Deadwood in today's world, seemed like a great adventure. Of course, I had no idea just how much trouble they would run into, how many friends they would lose, or that they would end up as parents to four young children.

What's next in the Havoc World? Right now, I'm not sure. But I have a feeling we will one day catch up with Jake and the others in Bakerville as they continue rebuilding their little corner of Wyoming.

Until then, I hope you'll join me for a brand-new series set in a brand-new world. *Stars Invade Earth* may sound a little like science fiction, but I promise it is a survival story at its core. The short story prequel, *Starborn*, is free to download. Grab your copy at MillieCopper.com/freebie.

Join my reader's club!
As part of my reader's club, you'll be the first to know about new releases and specials. I also share info on books I'm reading, preparedness tips, and more.

Please sign up on my website:
MillieCopper.com/Join

Also by Millie Copper

The Havoc in Wyoming Series

When a series of coordinated attacks devastate the United States, the people of Bakerville, Wyoming, must come together to survive. Unfortunately, not everyone has the town's best interest at heart. Some are striving for personal gain during the apocalypse.

The Montana Mayhem Series

A group from Bakerville, Wyoming strikes out on their own while searching for the desires of their heart. Unfortunately, the road will not be easy, and sometimes the heart is hardened and deceitful.

The Dakota Destruction Series

After a series of coordinated attacks devastate the United States, Katie and Leo sacrifice everything to help their country. But some things aren't as they seem. Is it time to go home and start fresh, or can something good come out of this terrible situation?

Wyoming Fall Series (In The October Fall World)

In the blink of an eye, an EMP changed everything for Lauren and her family. Now they are in a fight for survival, trying to keep their loved ones alive as society collapses around them.

Nonfiction Books

Millie has penned seven nonfiction, traditional food focused books, sharing how, with a little creativity, anyone can transition to a real foods diet without overwhelming their food budget. Many of her books also include preparedness and food storage tips.

Find these titles at: MillieCopper.com

Acknowledgments

Thanks to:

Ameryn Tucker, my editor, beta reader, and daughter wrapped in one. I had a story I wanted to tell, and Ameryn encouraged me and helped me bring it to life.

Dee from Dauntless Cover Design.

My husband, who gave me the time and space I needed to complete this dream and was very patient as I'd tell him the same plot ideas over and over and over.

Three more adult daughters and a young son, who willingly listen to me drone on and on about storylines and ideas while encouraging me to "keep going."

My amazing Beta Readers! Thanks to Barbara, Christy, Christine, Glen, Jim, Linda, Tammy, and Tracy for your help in creating the final story. Your insights and abilities to see the things I miss are very much appreciated!

A special thank you to Kristy who gave me a peek inside the world of the Coast Guard and Forest Service. And also a special thank you to Tim, a specialist in all things that go boom, for always answering my questions and pointing out things I wouldn't even think about.

And to you, my readers, for spending your time on our new South Dakota adventure. If you have five minutes, you'd make this writer very happy if you could leave a review. I appreciate you!

About the Author

Millie Copper, writer of Cozy Apocalyptic Fiction and preparedness mentor, was born in Nebraska but never lived there. Her parents fully embraced wanderlust and moved regularly, giving her an advantage of being from nowhere and everywhere.

Millie Copper lives in the wilds of Wyoming with her husband and young son, tending chickens and attempting a food forest on their small homestead. After living off the grid for several years, they've recently gone back on the grid. Four adult daughters, three sons-in-law, and five grandchildren round out the family.

Since 2009, Millie has authored articles on traditional foods, alternative health, homesteading, and preparedness-many times all within the same piece. Millie has penned seven nonfiction, traditional food focused books, sharing how, with a little creativity, anyone can transition to a real foods diet without overwhelming their food budget.

The twelve-installment *Havoc in Wyoming* and six-installment *Montana Mayhem* Christian Post-Apocalyptic fiction series use her homesteading, off-the-grid, and preparedness lifestyle as a guide. The adventures continue with the *Dakota Destruction* series.

Find Millie at www.MillieCopper.com
Facebook: www.facebook.com/MillieCopperAuthor/
Amazon: www.amazon.com/author/milliecopper
BookBub: https://www.bookbub.com/authors/millie-copper